Skyscraper Legend

SKYSCRAPER LEGEND

A FANTASY NOVEL

ROBERT A. TUFANO

Mill City Press

Copyright © 2011 by Robert A. Tufano

Mill City Press, Inc.
212 3rd Avenue North, Suite 290
Minneapolis, MN 55401
612.455.2294
www.millcitypublishing.com

All rights reserved. No part of this publication may be reproduced, stored in a retrieval system, or transmitted, in any form or by any means, electronic, mechanical, photocopying, recording, or otherwise, without the prior written permission of the author.

ISBN-13: 978-1-936400-84-3
LCCN: 2010942150

Book Design by Robert A. Tufano

Printed in the United States of America

DEDICATED TO:

- …the memory of **Anne Cheshire DeLaVergne**, artist and friend, whose editing talents and suggestions attempted to transform me from a writer of limited skills to one of more pronounced abilities. Unfortunately her premature death prevented her from seeing this book to completion, and from nurturing me on the path to a more noteworthy product.

- …**Josephine**, my mother, for just being "mom", a person full of love and understanding, and who is always there when I need her – no matter what.

ACKNOWLEDGEMENTS

This book could not have been possible without the generous contributions of talent and time of the people listed below:

- **Linda Brooks**, her tireless editing, and helpful remarks kept my writing on track.

- **Peggy Thomas**, formerly a special agent with the Internal Revenue Service (IRS), for providing information about IRS field investigations.

- **Charles G. Kick III, PhD.**, Professor Kick was a strict but fair reviewer and critic of my book. Never satisfied, the professor suggested adding another two hundred additional pages of narrative to improve the overall quality and depth of the story. The additional pages were not provided, but in hindsight, his suggestions had merit.

- **Jim Wertman**, Marketing Partner, CTA, Architects - Engineers; Billings, Montana: his experience with the implementation of reservation specific architectural projects was a critical and essential element to the story's credibility.

- **Hubert B. Two Leggins,** Crow Historian, Little Bighorn College – Mr. Two Leggins, was invaluable in providing me with information crucial to understanding the historical perspective, and present day social environment and lifestyle, of the Crow people. His fascinating insights are found distributed throughout my book.

PROLOGUE

SUNRISE – A DAY'S JOURNEY –
BY JOHNNY THUNDER EAGLE

Imagine waking up in the forest at dawn – no -- just before dawn, as the sun starts to peek over the horizon, through the trees and the morning dew is like a wet blanket over every one of the Great Spirit's creations. The first rays of the day's new light glisten on every dew drop.

You listen for the sounds of life in the forest as they begin to awaken – birds searching for an early breakfast, squirrels scurrying secretly from dew covered branch to dew covered branch collecting their day's food.

You feel the air. The air is fresh and cold and light. You breathe deeply and feel the intoxication of Mother Nature's simple smells. It's free. It's alive. It's honest.

You look and wonder and watch as the sun rises higher in the sky and molds this magic moment of time into an extraordinary day, a day that will have no equal in its beauty or purpose.

It makes you happy and sad knowing that this moment, this special place in the time journey of your life goes unnoticed, unappreciated, wasted by those people who welcome the new day with morning radio, coffee cups, traffic jams, and anger.

The experience of an early morning sunrise in the forest is one of those simple pleasures that begs to be shared with someone you love and with whom you can truly share your feelings and perceptions with, fully, honestly, and completely.

This is what we truly strive for in our life – to share happiness and beauty. We want to appreciate those things in life that are life and share those precious moments with someone who loves us and who we can love completely. It can be the ultimate fulfillment of living.

But most times we are not afforded the opportunity to completely share these precious moments with someone we truly love. So we must learn to share within ourselves the love of life and nature's beautiful experiences that are here for the taking – free, alive, and honest.

As the sun slowly sets in the forest of your life, begin to understand that the mystery of life is to be true to yourself, awaken your inner spirit, know who you are and what you mean to the life that is nature's gift to you. Guide your journey through life with one thought – love, love honestly and without reservation. And if you never find someone to love honestly and completely – love life and take comfort in knowing that the spirit of the one you truly are destined to love is with you always.

PART 1: BIRTH

CHAPTER 1

THE JOURNEY BEGINS

The Native American Crow gave a name to their divine creator. They simply called IT - *Ab-badt-dadt-deah* or "the one who made all things." Over time, this name has more commonly evolved into *First Maker* or *Great Spirit*. It is through the *Great Spirit* that Johnny Thunder Eagle, a Native American Crow, will tell this story.

— — —

The sun was setting as Johnny rode into the evolving darkness. He stopped his ride, dismounted near a stream bordering a light timber forest and set up his camp.

...This is a good place to sleep... he thought...*a good place to sleep...*

The stars high above his head began to fill the sky in all their infinite beauty.

...It is a good place to sleep...

He took his journal from his saddlebag and with his pen he began the story – the story of a skyscraper – a legend that would forever change the destiny of humanity and his people's future.

———

It was the beginning of an ordinary day on Earth.

For three men, a sun driven spiritual power, inherent but unknown to them on this ordinary day, was about to alter their lives in ways that none of them could ever imagine.

Take a journey with these men on a path filled with the promise of life, sharing, hope, and love.

Be prepared to be detoured from this path to one ruled by the Earthly human realities of death, greed, despair, and hate.

Millions of miles from the Earth's living surface, the Great Spirit, the creator and caretaker of all life, allows its being to become visible as a large expanding solar flare of energy directly emanating from the flaming surface of *Helios* - the Sun. As this fireball travels on an ever-expanding solar wind the ninety three million miles to the Earth's surface, it transforms its energy into a perfectly defined white eagle of giant size having unlimited supernatural powers. It is the Great Spirit's avatar and messenger.

Its mission - deliver a single unifying message to three chosen men.

The message – devote their lives to seeking the truth.

———

Transported at a timeless speed, the eagle reaches Earth. Following the northeastern coast of North America it stops above the island of Manhattan.

It is early morning on Friday, July 15th, in the year, 1973. A man standing alone among the masses in New York City's Central Park, looks towards the sun, adjusts his sunglasses against the glare, and feels a soft gentle breeze blow across his brow. It fails to cool him from the intense summer heat. He wipes the sweat from his face with a white linen handkerchief, monogrammed with the initials "JJB". He walks toward his chauffeured car and directs his driver to take him to his uptown penthouse office. The passenger door is opened for him. He folds his tall forty-year-old frame draped in a gray Armani suit into the passenger area of his air-conditioned Lincoln Town Car. He sits down on the cool black leather seats and begins to think about the possibilities surrounding his future.

"The sun's not hardly up yet, but it's still hot as hell out there Joseph," he said to his chauffer.

"Yes it is sir. Is the AC okay? Are you comfortable?"

"Yes it is. I'm fine."

"Busy day today?"

"Very. Today I'm searching for my destiny."

The chauffeur laughed. "Very good sir. Good luck with that. Let me know how you do," he said.

"Oh I will Joseph. I will."

High above Manhattan the eagle circles the Central Park area of this tiny island and gazes upon the Lincoln Town Car, following it as it travels north on Central Park Drive toward the Park Avenue office of the man in the Armani suit. This messenger from beyond time and dimension prepares to alter the life path of that man in the Town Car, influencing him to initiate a powerful concept in the world's ability to harness, control, and distribute the sun's energy for the ultimate benefit of all life on Earth.

The eagle hovers at two thousand feet. It remains motionless for a moment, floating on the thick summer air before beginning its descent toward the Town Car. Accelerating to an immeasurable speed, it passes through it, releasing the spiritual energy of its message upon the Armani man. This energy transforms within the man - becoming an eternal flame fueling his quest to fulfill his destiny. The Armani man's body shakes uncontrollably for a moment, stops, and then evolves into a calm uniting both body and spirit.

"Joseph?"

"Yes sir?"

"Did you feel that?"

"Feel what sir?"

"I felt a chill – a sudden chill. I shivered. You didn't feel that?

"No I didn't. Should I turn down the AC? Maybe it was a sudden blast of cold—"

"Pull over Joseph! Stop the car! Stop the car…"

The startled chauffeur pulls over to the curb, stops the car, and opens the door for his boss.

The Armani man departs his steel chariot and stands on the crowded New York City sidewalk admiring the City's skyline with its magnificent skyscrapers. He feels the adrenaline rush through his body as he realizes now what he must do. The sun will be the power behind it. His money, resources, and the integrity of nature will make it happen. He knows where it will be. He knows that to transform it into something real he needs to immediately begin to secure its location, assemble hundreds of talented visionaries like himself and organize them into a unified working team dedicated to a single purpose.

After a few minutes of contemplating his vision, the man reenters his car and continues to travel to his intended destination. Arriving in front of his fifty-story office building, the Armani man removes himself from the Town Car. He looks into the sky searching for something every instinct in his body feels is there. He sees nothing, but he knows something is there. Unsatisfied and convinced that his senses have deceived him; he proceeds to walk up the plaza stairs to the building's glass enclosed entrance.

Halfway up the stairs he stops and says to himself so no one could hear,

THE JOURNEY BEGINS

"Zeus, have you sent your bird to bestow upon me this destiny?"

The eagle, satisfied that its mission here was fulfilled, begins a new journey. It seeks the next chosen one, the one destined to transform the energy from the sun into a practical source of beneficial power.

— — —

It arrives at its new destination in an instant, immediately locating its second target. The unsuspecting victim is a young unemployed architect walking alone, without purpose, on the nearly deserted early morning downtown sidewalks of Baltimore.

The architect was walking toward Baltimore's Inner Harbor as the sun was gently rising over the Chesapeake Bay distributing its glow upon the dark still water. He looked east toward the horizon contemplating the enormous energy potential of this yellow fireball. If only he had the opportunity and resources to develop his solar visions into physical realities. He wanted so much to succeed in realizing these visions - to fulfill his undeniable goal in life in utilizing the energy of the sun to provide power to all the buildings on Earth. Now, instead of experiencing this creative journey, he was experiencing a journey filled with failure, unemployment, and doubt.

Finding another job as an architect was something he was not certain he wanted to pursue. In fact, he realized he didn't know what he wanted to do with his life beyond this pointless moment.

He reached the harbor and studied the greenish brine on the water's surface.

*...I wonder how deep the water is...*he thought...*What would it be like to submerge myself beneath its surface and drown...?*

He sat on the edge of a dock and reached down to test the temperature of the water with his outstretched hand. The water seemed too cold for such a hot July day. He sat on the edge of the dock and continued to stare into the sun. His eyes squinted and burned in an immediate protest to the prolonged unprotected glare. Stubbornly giving in to the need to protect his eyes, he put on his sunglasses and began to relax his thoughts as the heat of the sun washed him with a calming energy that melted his problems into a pool of uncertainty. He could find no immediate solution today to give him a reason to move forward on his life path, but it did not matter. He decided to keep his life on hold for today. His decision on what to do tomorrow however, was unknown and riddled with fear.

His excursion into his private world of self-pity was suddenly altered as he felt an undeniable feeling of optimism consume him. The young Architect instinctively looked up into the sky to find the source of this force and could see nothing. Without knowing why, he said the words, *"la aquila."* Confused, he continued to sit by the bay watching his distorted reflection on the water's surface stare back at him without revealing its newly captured secret. He took the letter from his pocket, the letter that documented his troubled existence. It was intended to reveal his deepest thoughts about his life before he left this world. He threw it into bay. He watched it float away. He didn't need it anymore – not today.

Absorbing the thoughts of this young architect, the eagle knew this man would survive to see his dreams become reality. The architect needed only to be patient and confident in his ability to fulfill all that he held true in his heart and soul. The eagle understood that this person's destiny was to follow a frustrated and less obvious path to fulfillment, but fulfillment was inevitable nonetheless. Their paths would cross again in the future for a purpose only they would fully understand.

The eagle's mission was successful. It had given its second target the fuel he would require for his spiritual growth and with it the reasons to move forward along a destined path. It was time to leave him and seek target number three.

This third target was unique. It was the only one that was fully capable of understanding and believing in the eagle's otherworld existence and purpose. It was a man chosen because of his historical bond to Mother Earth, purity, spiritual energy, and reason.

— — —

The eagle headed west to spread its word among the big empty sky of Montana's chosen people. Arriving at a location east of Billings, gliding along the path of the Little Bighorn River, it reaches its predetermined destination. Looking down upon the Earthly plains, it could see a lone man on horseback traveling slowly on an early morning soul-cleansing ride.

As Johnny Thunder Eagle was riding across the flattened prairie grass along the banks of Pryor Creek, just after the dawn of a new day, atop his bay paint, Swiftwind, his horse since his youth, he felt a subtle energy enter his body. His taunt muscles quivered in spasm. His head jerked backward from this unyielding force and his buckskinned covered legs kicked into Swiftwind. The horse did not respond in gallop, but instead looked at his rider with an inherent understanding.

Johnny Thunder Eagle looked up at the sun and knew the force that surrounded him came from the power of the sun. He knew that the awaited event, one of unrevealed powerful historical significance, was about to take place here at his feet, here on the reservation that was his home, and the home of seven thousand of his brethren, the Native American Crow. He turned Swiftwind and rode back home to share his revelation with the Tribal Council. The rays of the sun pushed at

Johnny's back with a force and intensity that was a precursor to the power that was soon to come.

"The Great Spirit has spoken to me today," he said to Swiftwind. "It is time for our man to return."

— — —

Its mission completed, the Great Spirit's avatar flew into the Montana sunrise, disappearing into a new world of hope. It was flying into the future. It would return in time, but for now could only watch and observe the powers of the Earth below collide from the influence of these three men, as they battled with the uncompromising ignorance of the conflicted human soul.

CHAPTER 2

THE VIGIL

DECEMBER 1974

The sun, a young thermonuclear yellow star, is an insignificant member of a vast universe filled with an incalculable number of larger more powerful mature white stars. However, to the inhabitants of Earth, it is the most significant phenomena imaginable. The sun's heat and light are what provide the Earth with the energy required to support life. Without it, the Earth would be lifeless, frozen, and dark, a rock floating in space.

The sun, though only an infinitesimal speck in the universe, is overwhelming in size compared with the Earth, having a diameter of over one hundred Earths. It is the supreme master and center of its solar system. Around it, orbit its nine planets, its children, in which an abundance of life is provided to only one, the third planet in orbit from its surface, our Earth.

The sun's core reaches an unimaginable temperature of twenty-seven million degrees Fahrenheit with nuclear explosions a frequent and daily occurrence. Its surface temperatures are much cooler, reaching only ten thousand degrees. The heat from this surface is transmitted as radiant solar energy through the vacuum of space and travels at a speed of one hundred eighty-six thousand miles per second, over an average distance of ninety-three million miles, to reach the Earth's surface in approximately eight and one half minutes.

It is estimated the Earth receives more energy from the sun in one hour than its inhabitants could potentially use in one year. Every beam of sunlight that touches the Earth's surface represents an opportunity for humanity to free itself from its self-imposed ignorance driven energy burdens through the efficient utilization of the sun's unlimited resources

— — —

Today, at dawn, beams of sunlight are traveling toward Earth, focusing on a Billings, Montana, hospital window in a room occupied by a seriously injured patient. Today, this sunlight will enter the room with the deliberate intent of waking someone from a coma. Today, its beams will concentrate on the patient's closed eyes and its brightness and subtle heat will breathe a new life and purpose into a broken and bruised body. The beams found its target and washed over his face. The target's eyes opened and saw the light.

He was conscious again; conscious that every breath taken was a gift; conscious that every bodily movement was accompanied with pain; conscious of the loneliness and fear he felt when he awoke in this hospital room with no memory of how or what caused him to be here.

Tony's only certainty was the truth in feeling his body's pain. He could only imagine the circumstances that produced this damage to his body. Somehow, someway, he would put the pieces together as to the "why", but right now, all he wanted was relief from the pain. He lay still, his eyes heavy with sleep. A warm numbing sensation was felt, as the morphine drip was flowing into his body with the welcomed relief. Falling asleep, the whispers of reality disappeared into the valleys of his dreams. He never saw the nurse enter his room. He never heard her leave, as she passed two men sitting in vigilance at his bedside, a short-haired white man in an Armani suit and a long-haired red man dressed in blue jeans and a white cotton t-shirt adorned with a necklace of eagle feathers and bear claws.

The sunlight continued to smile on Tony and washed the room with a glow that defined the beginning of a hopeful future.

CHAPTER 3

THE ARCHITECT

In dreams that were illusions of reality, Tony's mind slipped in and out of consciousness. His memories drifted back to the time when his life was beginning a new era, embarking on a new path. It was a time that had its beginnings on the day of his graduation from college.

It was a year when the giant cloud of protests and dissent covering the United States was lifting, as its involvement in the Vietnam War was slowly and painfully coming to a welcomed end.

It was 1972. On this 17th day of May at a small insignificant Midwestern university known more for its fraternity houses and football games than for its academic excellence, Anthony "Tony" Rullo, a twenty-four year old rebellious disillusioned third generation Italian from New Jersey, the only child of parents Louis and Maria, was graduating with a degree in the profession of Architecture.

Earning this degree did not come easily for Tony.

— — —

During his senior year of high school, Tony applied to eleven universities offering an accredited architectural curriculum. All eleven rejected him. Convinced that these rejections meant that a career in architecture was not to be in his future, he was prepared to abandon his dream and pursue another vocation at Hoboken Community College. His dream was renewed one day serendipitously through one of his mother's weekly long-distance telephone calls from her brother Dominic who lived in Springfield, Illinois.

While Tony was casually mentioning to his Uncle Dominic about his eleven college rejections, Dominic remembered reading about an Illinois school, *Franklin State University*, which was establishing a new five-year architectural program. In the article, he told Tony, it stated that since the program was still in its infancy, not fully accredited, its acceptance criteria was less stringent than colleges with an established accredited architectural curriculum. In addition, the article noted that Illinois state law required ten percent of the students accepted into *Franklin State's, School of Architecture* be non-residents, and at the time the article was written, the out-of-state applications submitted for enrollment were well below this requirement. Time was running out. The school desperately needed to reach its mandated quota by the August 31, deadline or face a severe financial penalty. It was essentially advertising for out of state applications.

"Give it a try Tony," Dominic said.

"Okay Uncle Dom. It's worth a shot. Thanks for the info," Tony said.

Tony applied. The response from Franklin was encouraging. Based on the originality of his freelance work and impressive theories on solar design that were enclosed with his application, this University conditionally accepted Tony and his mediocre high school grades, pending the results of a personal interview.

Early in the summer of '66, he boarded a Greyhound bus to Franklin, Illinois, where his mandatory personal interview before five strangers awaited him. Despite being exhausted from his ride, he performed well. His determined belief in solar design and its potential in the future of architecture was a novel and refreshing concept. The review panel was impressed. He was accepted. His strong convictions sold his personal worth to these strangers. Tony was pleased that his unique talent would not go unrewarded. He was going to like it here.

— — —

Unfortunately for Tony, his experience at Franklin was not as he imagined. His five years there were laced with frustration and disappointment.

Tony's idealistic convictions in what present day Architects should offer to society were the underlying reasons for his rocky road through college. He was greatly influenced by the contributions of architectural visionaries; Antonio Sant Elia, Le Corbusier, Frank Lloyd Wright, and Paolo Soleri. These twentieth century contemporary architects promoted the development of an architecture that harmonized with nature similar to villages of North America's Native Americans, before they were destroyed by the onslaught of the white man's environmentally insensitive industrialized and environmentally exploitive America.

Soleri, a fellow Italian, promoted his concept of "Arcology", in which both architecture and ecology were united in a complex eco-system of environmental design. Elia's designs of environmentally responsive futuristic cities and buildings were conceived in the early twentieth century but largely ignored and consequently never developed to any appreciable extent throughout the century.

It was the embracing of these concepts that caused Tony many inadvisable arguments with his design studio professors. Tony's perceived unrealistic approaches to architectural design were not conducive to his success in adapting to the reality of classical architecture as it was being taught at Franklin. Most of the teaching staff were not comfortable with the progressive concepts of this arrogant outsider.

Tony always wondered what became of those five liberal thinking professors from his initial pre-acceptance interview. After that interview, he never saw them again. Most of the professors who were permanently assigned to the program were anything but favorable to Tony's visions of urban buildings in suburban environments, self-sufficiency and all those eco-friendly design theories that he wished the world would embrace, but couldn't or worse, wouldn't.

― ― ―

During Tony's fourth year, at the beginning of the second semester, his design studio professor, Professor Grimes, took particular exception to Tony's unconventional design solutions. He lost patience with Tony's rebellious attitude and counter productive "C-" work. He placed Tony on academic probation and aggressively promoted the idea to the Dean that Tony did not possess the talent or ambition to be a successful practicing architect. He then tried to persuade Tony to transfer from Franklin's architectural program to a less challenging Liberal Arts undergraduate curriculum. When Tony refused, Grimes petitioned to remove him from the program. This action was detoured when Tony received word that his father had died from a heart attack. A sympathetic Professor Grimes decided to withhold any disciplinary action until after Tony completed his fourth year. However, when Tony returned from his father's funeral and the reality of his mother dying from cancer, his attitude changed. Out of respect to his parents, he was determined to adapt and make it through this academic architectural hell despite the efforts of this narrow-minded professor and his uncompromising agenda. Tony successfully completed his fourth year and managed to raise his grade to a solid C. He was approved to enter his fifth and final year at Franklin.

In many ways, Professor Grimes was correct in his assumptions about Tony. Tony's erratic performance was directly related to the reality that he honestly did not know why he wanted to continually torture himself and enter the stilted world of 1970's architecture. It did not offer him the opportunities he required to pursue his dreams. Nevertheless, he sincerely believed in his heart that somehow, in some way, despite its implied limitations, he was destined to do something with it that was liberating and meaningful, although he did not know what that something was.

Relieved he had survived his troubled fourth year, Tony's brief period of satisfaction ended on June 15, exactly six months following his father's death, when his mother passed away after her courageous two-year battle with breast cancer. Tony was convinced his father's earlier death was the result of a broken heart knowing that his beloved wife would soon pass. Tony was well aware that the intensity of his parent's love for each other never diminished in their thirty-two years of marriage. It went beyond the restrictive measurements of time. Tony always knew that neither one could live very long without the other's love. They died too soon, both only fifty-two years old.

The emotional trauma from his mother and father's deaths devastated Tony to such an extent that he took a one-year, soul-searching sabbatical away from life and college. He used the year traveling aimlessly around the country hitchhiking, backpacking, taking odd jobs, and sleeping anywhere he could lay his head. At the end of his lonely journey, he finally arrived in Springfield, at the doorstep of his Aunt Carmen and Uncle Dominic, penniless, exhausted, and ready to continue, to him, his pointless final year of college. They welcomed him back without question, thankful that he was alive and unharmed. He filled the summer of 71's final days entertaining them with his endless adventures during his year on the road.

When Tony returned to school for his fifth and final year, he had the good fortune of being assigned a progressive design studio professor, Professor Clark. Clark was aware of Tony's reputation during his tenure at the school. Nevertheless, he always liked Tony and believed he was simply misunderstood and ahead of his time. He did not approve of Professor Grimes heavy-handed tactics and narrow-minded approach to Tony's unique personality and talent. He understood and encouraged Tony's beliefs. He became his mentor and more importantly a friend. It was exactly what Tony needed, someone to nurture him and convince him to perform up to his potential on his final year's critical design projects. Thanks to Professor Clark, Tony maintained a solid "B" in design studio and raised his overall grade point average considerably. Even with this fifth year boost, his GPA at graduation placed him in the uninspired bottom third of his graduating class.

— — —

After five years of intensive academic gymnastics, and one year of mourning, graduation day had arrived, forcing itself through Tony's self-imposed turmoil. It was a day that would be dominated by thoughts of his bittersweet past and its relationship to his awaiting journey into the unknown future. The graduation ceremony was held outside in the university's football stadium with an intimate graduating class of over three thousand students and guests. Tony's only guests were his Aunt Carmen and Uncle Dominic.

When Tony's name was announced, he walked the long walk from his seat, mounted the stage, and was handed his diploma by a faceless dignitary with a handshake and a smile. He felt an immediate sense of satisfaction and relief, and suddenly had visions of throwing this glorified piece of paper into the trash, and with it, the profession of architecture. It was unsettling to him that this ceremonial step through the portal to his unknown future would be represented in the form of an official document known as a diploma. He could not imagine the path to his future was meant to be defined within the boundaries of a paper rectangle.

On his walk back from the stage he found the nearest trash receptacle and enthusiastically heaved the official document into the void. He looked around and felt the attention of three thousand pairs of eyes monitoring his action. He slowly walked forward a few more steps, thought about what he had just done, stopped, turned around and retrieved his degree from the trash.

...Maybe I'll just shove it in a drawer and forget about it for now...

Making his way back to his seat, he waited patiently for the remaining students to receive their diplomas. While waiting, his mind wandered in a direction desperately searching for the ultimate path toward something meaningful in his life. He sat there and waited for this path to be revealed. The future sat there too with him, and offered nothing.

CHAPTER 4

THE CELEBRATION

After the graduation ceremony was over, Tony laboriously filed through the student crowd finding his way to the welcoming arms of Uncle Dominic and Aunt Carmen. Since they couldn't have any children of their own, they posthumously adopted Tony as their only son. He could not have made it through college or the past few years of his life without their love and support. Aunt Carmen met him first shrieking with pride.

"Tony! Tony! Congratulations! I am so proud of you! Your mother and father would have been so proud of you too."

Aunt Carmen embraced Tony with a hug and a kiss on the cheek that could only come from someone who truly knew how to love. Uncle Dominic stood beside them both and waited patiently for his turn. When Tony was released from his Aunt's embrace the little Italian uncle grabbed Tony in a hug with a greater enthusiasm than either expected.

"Tony! Congratulations! You made it, but why'd you throw your 'ploma in the garbage? Why you do that?"

"You saw that? It was only a, joke, Uncle Dom. I was just kidding. Didn't think anyone was watching, but forget about it. It's not important. What's important is thanking you and

Aunt Carmen for all you've done for me. I love you both. I can't tell you how much I appreciate your help through my years at Franklin. It means so much to me. I only hope I can live up to your expectations and make you proud of me in the coming years."

"You will Tony. You will," Dominic said. "We have faith in you. Your mother and father will help guide you through life. You'll do great things."

"Thanks, Uncle Dom. Thank you. Okay, I think it's time to celebrate my release from school. *Giuseppe's?...*"

"You bet. We have reservations. We'll drink and eat until we can't stand up. Let's go. After…we'll give you your graduation present," Dominic said.

"My what? No. No. Don't tell me that. You didn't have to do that. I don't expect any graduation gift from you guys. Both of you have done so much for me already. It's me who should be giving you something," Tony said.

"Nonsense. We were happy to see you through school… provide you with a loving home after Maria died – rest her soul…" Dominic said.

"Your Uncle's right – for once," Aunt Carmen said. "After five years of hard schoolwork plus that year – my God – that year we thought we lost you, you've earned it. I know you will love it. It is your uncle's favorite subject. He spent lots of time working on it and it was killing him keeping it a secret from you. He's very proud. It's from his heart. Mine too."

"All right. All right. I won't argue. Thank you. I know I'll love it, no matter what it is. But now, since you ruined the surprise, I won't be able to enjoy dinner unless I know what it is. You know how impatient I can be," Tony said.

"Okay Tony. You win," Dominic said. "I'm tired of trying to keep it a secret from you anyway. Let's go to the motel before we get somethin' to eat. Come on. Get in the car and I'll take you to your present."

— — —

They walked to Uncle Dom's car filtering through the crowds around the stadium parking lot. Tony entered the back seat of his uncle's brand new 1972, Fiat 124. His uncle would only buy Italian cars and the Fiat was his only practical choice since he could never afford a Ferrari, Maserati, or even an Alpha Romeo. Fiats were notorious for their fun ride and awful repair history. Uncle Dom always said that "FIAT" was an acronym for "Fix It Again Tony." Nevertheless, Dominic was determined to keep his Fiat running as efficiently as an Italian soccer game.

Dominic started the car and listened to the smooth running engine. "Doesn't she sound great, Tony? I love when she purrs." A few pushes on the accelerator gave emphasis to the engine's finely tuned sound.

"I wish he loved me as much as he loves this car," Aunt Carmen said.

"I do love you Carmie, baby. I do, but in a different way"

"We'll see how much the next time I ask you to take me to Novena on oil change or tune-up day."

"That only happened once. I told you, you need to give me a little notice before you ask for a ride on tune-up day. You know I wouldn't want you to miss Novena."

"Okay. Let's not bore Tony with discussions about your love child."

Tony loved to hear his Aunt and Uncle bicker. They never argued with any malice or hurtful intent. They always had a playful quality to their oral sparing. It was comforting.

Uncle Dom put the car in gear and began driving the Fiat like a frustrated Italian race car driver in a prestigious road race. He was weaving in and out of traffic as if he was driving for Enzo and first place at the *Italian Grand Prix*. He made his way quickly and safely to the *Campus Motel*, where they were staying for the night.

Before entering the motel parking lot, Dominic said, "Tony, look to your left as we enter the parking lot. Look for something red."

As they pulled into the parking lot, Tony saw it. It was red, small, and shiny. It was a 1968 Fiat 850 Spider convertible.

Now to understand the Fiat 850, you needed to know the history of this little car. It was a car catered to the specific European tastes of the Italian motorist. It was small, quick, stingy on gas, handled great, and parked in tight places, but it was not fast. It only had a sixty horsepower engine Tony knew all of this, but it was a car, his car, a convertible, and a gift from his Uncle and Aunt. To him it was as beautiful as a new red Ferrari GTO. Nothing could have made him any happier. He was speechless.

Dominic grabbed Tony's shoulders and shook them. "Hey Tony. You okay? You like?"

"What? Yeah. Love it. I love it. I don't know what else to say. Thank you. Thank you so much. You guys are just too great for words."

"Ah! It's nothing. Happy to do it," Dominic said. "Come on...start it up. See how she sounds. Give it a ride. She handles great! I know you're gonna like her a lot."

Tony started the car, put it in gear, drove it out of the parking lot and did a couple of warm up laps around the block. He finally had a fun car to call his own and it couldn't have come from a more satisfying source.

The car held only two, so he invited his Aunt Carmen in for a ride to *Giuseppe's Ristorante*, their favorite Italian restaurant in Franklin. Uncle Dom followed the taillights of the 850 in his 124, grinning from ear to ear like a proud papa.

However, his prideful euphoria soon ended, as they arrived at *Giuseppe's* in only a few minutes.

— — —

Uncle Dom and Aunt Carmen were weekend regulars at *Giuseppe's* and the staff knew them all well. Tony occasionally would find time away from his studies to join them. The restaurant's atmosphere was one of intimacy and warmth. Eating here was like being part of an Italian family dinner in a large dining room. Seated at their usual table, reserved for this special celebration, the owner, Enrico, personally greeted them with a bottle of wine.

Enrico Rizzo was a first generation Italian-American, whose late father opened this restaurant over twenty years ago. It was fully staffed with relatives, with Enrico's mother, Connie, as its master chef. The pasta sauce and meatballs were prepared from scratch every morning by Connie and every evening there was always a line of eager people waiting to sample the great tastes of everything Italian on the menu.

Enrico enthusiastically spoke, "Welcome, Dominic, Carmen, and Tony, the college boy! Congratulations on your graduation, Tony! Tonight for you, everything is on the house. It is *Giuseppe's* gift to all of you. Before you eat yourselves silly, we will drink. I have in my hands a bottle of my favorite red wine. I hope you like *Chianti Classico*. It's been in my family for years. Let me pour all of you a glass and propose a toast." He filled four glasses with wine, held his up toward heaven and said:

"Here's a toast to three of the best people in the world, good people, great customers, and forever my friends. May the future hold nothing but the best for all of you. God bless… *Salute*…!"

In a traditional reflex response, all four glasses met with a composite gentle "clink" and a chorus of *salutes*. It was a happy simple celebration that Tony would remember for a lifetime. It was these simple pleasures in life that Tony enjoyed the most.

Tony, Carmen, and Dominic ordered their favorite main courses and added plenty of appetizers and desserts. They ate and ate until, as Uncle Dominic had suggested, they could hardly stand up. They waddled to the parking lot and their respective cars. There they stood, talking for it seemed like forever, exchanging family stories, laughing, crying, and sharing warm and loving moments together.

Eventually, it was time for this good time to end. Tony sadly said his goodbyes. A few more laughs were generated and tears shed. He thanked his Aunt and Uncle again for dinner, the car, and their support throughout his troubled college years. He opened the car door for his Aunt, and after she was safely seated, he closed it gently. He watched his two favorite people in the world drive back to the motel in their little green Fiat. He wanted them to stay with him a little longer, but he knew it was late. They needed to get their rest. He would see them again soon.

CHAPTER 5

THE FINAL PARTY

The time had arrived for Tony to put all his troubles behind him and party, time to celebrate his release from five years of academic bondage with some friends and, if he was lucky, time to take advantage of a few drunk and horny coeds.

He left his Fiat in *Giuseppe's* parking lot safely under the watchful eye of the Rizzo family and began his walk toward the bright lights that were the beacons guiding him to a fun and crazy evening. He found his favorite bar, *The Crease*. The two regular greeters were standing guard at its entrance, checking identification for those under twenty-one and ready to keep the peace if any guests developed "disruptive" tendencies. After many years of frequenting this bar, Tony knew them both well. Their names were Tiny and George, both former football players from Franklin. Tiny was anything but what his name implied. He stood six-foot five and two hundred seventy-five pounds, an impressive physical specimen who had a promising pro football career as a defensive tackle until he blew out a knee. George was a little smaller at six-two and two forty. He played linebacker, but his talent was less than ordinary so his football career ended at Franklin.

Tiny approached Tony, pulled him over with one arm, and gave him a giant bear hug. At barely five-eight in shoes, Tony always felt like a child standing next to these two giants. Tiny's hug only magnified this reality. It had him surrounded making him feel helpless and vulnerable.

While maintaining his forceful embrace, Tiny yelled, "Hey Tony! Congratulations! I heard they actually let you graduate today. Boy, they're really lowering their academic standards here by a lot. How much did you have to pay them or did you make them an *offer they couldn't refuse* - you crazy guinea bastard!"

Tony answered, "Let go of me you black mafia reject. I think ya broke a couple of my ribs. I'm not your personal tackling dummy. Let me go or I'll have to put a major hurt on you."

"Okay. Don't go getting all *Dirty Harry* on me. I know you little Italian dudes are dangerous. You ain't packin' are you?" Tiny thankfully released Tony from his embrace.

A relieved Tony answered. "No I ain't packin', and everybody's a little dude around you, Tiny. But why am I wasting my time talking to you two losers? Point me to the women and the booze…it's time for me to party!"

It was George's turn to acknowledge Tony's special day. George was not as physical and cordially extended his hand for a handshake that spared Tony any further physical embarrassment.

Tony talked with Tiny and George for a few more minutes, knowing it was most likely the last time he would ever speak to or see them again. He would miss them. To postpone the inevitable for just a little while longer, Tony invited them to join him for a few drinks later at the end of their shift. .

Tony entered *The Crease*. He found a large table with dozens of his fellow graduates. He wedged himself into an open seat and began his intensive search of the bar looking for any delicious coed who could help make this, for him, a very memorable evening.

He started ordering pitchers of beer and drinking plenty of full glasses between dancing with any woman who would say *yes*. The evening soon started to disappear into a blur of action filled fun and illusion. A major drunk was starting to develop in Tony, an event that would be remembered by almost everyone else, except Tony.

— — —

The next morning, Tony woke up with a tremendous headache, naked, in a strange bed, with a strange woman, whom he assumed he had spent the night, doing what and how was something he could not remember. She too was naked, and asleep. He noticed a couple of consumed marijuana joints in an ashtray on the end table beside the bed.

…God…I even smoked some dope last night…I must have had a really good time…too bad I can't remember any of it…

He cautiously left the bed so as not to wake her, put on his clothes, visited the bathroom to clean up, and took a piss that seemed to last forever. He vaguely remembered his partner's name as *Kathy* and that he knew her from one of his non-architecture classes, maybe Philosophy, but that was as far as his memory could take him.

He left her his telephone number, address, and a thank you note with an invitation to call him sometime. He knew she never would. It happened to Tony dozens of times while attending Franklin and it seemed like hundreds of times before, during his post puberty years, but right now at this point in his life, he just didn't care anymore. He left the apartment and his mystery woman without a good-bye.

…If records were kept for being the victim of one-night stands… Tony thought…*I would be somewhere near the top*

of the list...when I'm interested in them, they're not interested in me...

It was Tony's contribution to the newly evolving energy of women's liberation. He was a classic gender reversal victim, the exception to the rule. The guys ditched the girls, not the other way around. With Tony it was different. He had learned to accept it.

It was that simple and no matter how hard he tried to change the inevitable outcome, he couldn't. He never understood - why him? Why wasn't he ever allowed a fair chance for a serious relationship?

For Tony, finding love was as elusive as the reasons he decided to become an architect. Abandoning Kathy, without any explanation or expectations was the best thing he could do to keep himself insulated from any eventual disappointment. It was a lonely but safe decision.

— — —

It was six o'clock on a Thursday morning. Tony was walking the just awakening streets of Franklin, Illinois, not only to his new car and the short drive to his campus apartment, but to a new life out of college and his unknown future - one that would hold him in its grasp until it forced him to fulfill his destined purpose on Earth. Falling in love and having a sustained relationship with anyone, was not to be part of this future. Tony's emotional destiny was headed in another direction. It was a destiny that he would require a lifetime to understand and an eternity to fulfill.

CHAPTER 6

THE MESSAGE

JULY 15, 1973

The morning was still in its infancy as Johnny rode Swiftwind in a gallop back to his home in Crow Agency, the largest city on the Crow Reservation, but not anything like a typical small American town. It had a lot of nothing and a lot of something called poverty. The people living here were dissolute and wanting; their existence dependent on welfare handouts and Government funded programs. It was a life spawned from the injustices and deceit handed to the red man disguised as truth by the United States Government. There were few real jobs and unemployment and alcoholism were the normal life expectations found on this reservation.

A few years back from college, Johnny, at twenty-five, was still readjusting to his post college decision to remain here and make a difference in improving the quality of life of his fellow Crow. He was working in Crow Agency, as an administrator of reservation policy through the Tribal Council Government. He would write proposals to the Bureau of Indian Affairs, the BIA, for funding and job programs to help reduce the reservations eighty-five percent unemployment rate. Most of these proposals never were approved. The few that were, gave him a great sense of accomplishment, and hopeful opportunity for his people.

———

Today, all that was not relevant. Today, Johnny had received an important message from the Great Spirit. It was his ancestral obligation before the early morning hours disappeared into their journey into tomorrow, to summon the elders and others that comprised the Tribal Council to an emergency meeting, sharing with them this message.

Without hesitation, he began riding Swiftwind miles through the emptiness that surrounded Crow Agency. He rode from isolated house to isolated house, waking many Council members from their sleep, informing them of the urgency and importance of this meeting. Word spread rapidly throughout the reservation's people like a wild prairie fire. Within hours, the majority of the Council members were contacted.

They arrived and assembled at the modest Crow Agency Town Hall building, one of the few buildings on the reservation built with government funds that served a honorable purpose. Tribal Council meetings were held here among other social and tribal events. It was the newest and largest building in this small town. It was built in 1960 with Federal Funding channeled through the BIA and came with an abundance of strings attached. Political harassment and Tribal Government manipulation were part of the BIA's standard operating procedure on the "rez."

A crowd of people, mostly idle Crow, had become aware of this meeting, and gathered outside the building to hear the given word first hand. The Council members filed silently past the curious crowd and entered the Council Room. They entered the room in single file and sat on the bare wood floor one by one forming a circle. When the circle was complete, they were ready to begin.

Each member opened the meeting with a personal silent prayer to the Great Spirit. A ceremonial pipe was passed to each, and the sacred tobacco of the Crow smoked. Johnny was the last to receive the pipe. After his smoke, he was invited to speak. He was asked by the Council to address them in his native language. Johnny was not proficient in the language from too many years away from the reservation in the white man's world. He asked the Council for permission to speak in English. The Council reluctantly agreed, but assigned an interpreter to record the proceedings in Crow.

Johnny entered the sacred circle and while standing, facing the head elder; he delivered his message to the Council.

"Honored members of the Tribal Council, I want to thank all of you for honoring my request to meet with me this morning," Johnny said. "I am hopeful your time here will be rewarded well. I will begin my story. Today I was blessed. This morning, at sunrise, the Great Spirit spoke to me. He spoke to me through a messenger, his messenger, a messenger sent with the spirit, body, and soul of a great white eagle. My horse Swiftwind, understood what was there. We both sensed its presence and felt its power." Johnny stopped and opened a leather pouch and from it gathered his gift from the Great Spirit. He opened his hand and allowed fragments of white eagle feathers to float to the ground. He awaited his invitation to continue.

The head elder, Grey Wolf, said, "Tell us Thunder Eagle of your vision. What did the Great Spirit say to you?"

"The Great Spirit told me that our 'saved man' would finally return to our reservation to bestow upon our Nation a powerful gift, a gift not yet known to us, a gift that will use the sun's power for its life, a gift that will give our people a new life – a prosperous future," Johnny said. "This great man will create this gift here on the reservation. All of us now must prepare for his arrival. We must prepare for our rebirth. That is all I was told. I do not know what this gift will be. What I have told you is all I know. Gray Wolf, my message is finished."

The entire Tribal Council nodded their approval and understood. No more words needed to be spoken. The pipe was passed around once more, the meeting closed, and a mission began, a mission to immediately spread Johnny's message from the Great Spirit to all the reservation's people. This Tribal Council meeting was over, but a new life for the Crow Nation was just beginning. This reservation would soon become one Nation in harmony with their arriving hopeful future

Johnny personally thanked all Tribal Council members for blessing his message today. He abruptly left the Town Hall building to be alone to reflect, pray, and rest. He walked alone to a secluded spot near his home, sat on the earth and thought of what this message could mean to the lives of his people.

— — —

Johnny contemplated his people's history. It was this history, a history that followed many distorted paths through time that Johnny wanted to make true today before his life on Earth would end. He knew there was little that he could do to correct these historical distortions now. That, he hoped, would soon change. He was assured the arriving "gift" would pave the way to the truth and reestablish the traditions, nobility, and honor not only to his Crow people, but also to all Native American Nations throughout this country.

His thoughts continued to the many memories from his youth; the Little Bighorn River, where he fished, the Pryor Mountains where he hunted and had his first Vision Quest, the run down school house where he learned to read and write the white man's and Crow words. All of these represented his history, but not his soul, for his soul was defined by the day of his birth.

The day of his birth was his special connection to the Crow Nation. The date was June 24, 1948. It was on this day when the first Tribal Constitution was chartered, officially governing the Crow Nation. It was a rebirth for the Crow Nation and the birth of Johnny Thunder Eagle in a Crow Medicine Tipi. From that day forward he began his life's journey among the poverty and squalor that was the Crow reservation.

— — —

When he was old enough to understand, his mother told him of the vision she experienced at the moment of his birth,

"...when you were born, a great white eagle surrounded by a fiery glow appeared to me, and while having this vision I heard a great clap of thunder, an ovation, resounding throughout the plains...the eagle said to me, this is your son, your 'Thunder Eagle' given to you from the Great Spirit...this is who you are Johnny...you are destined for great things here on Earth...you flew to Earth on the back of a giant eagle, a messenger from the Great Spirit..."

Despite his mother's bold statement Johnny believed himself, not a special messenger from the Great Spirit, but only another Native American trying to understand and adapt to his place in the w*hite man's* world. Johnny's world was not a spiritual heroic one with allegiance to a higher power but one confined to a reservation, a place surrounded by a vast country known simply as "America"; a country that restricted his freedom within its government mandated physical and racially imposed boundaries. He was not special. He was only one of the many subjugated repressed reservation bound Crow people.

Johnny always doubted his mother's story...*just another loving mother, trying to make her child feel special...*he thought. Today he concluded, maybe she was right. Perhaps his mother's vision was true – *perhaps.*

CHAPTER 7

THE JOB

In the year following graduation, Tony's time would speed by in a blur of unfulfilling days. His life was defined by his job - that everyday mundane routine called work. This reality began immediately with his decision to put his reservations behind him and pursue a career as an architect. The problem was – in his apathetic, *I don't give a shit,* state of mind he didn't care where he found employment, only that it was a paying job in an architectural office. He would adapt. He decided to let fate choose for him. So one evening after a six-pack beer primer, he taped the map of the United States on his apartment wall, secured three highly prized darts, attached a blindfold to his blurry eyes and threw the darts at the map. After many failed attempts of off target darts missing the map and puncturing the unprotected wall, all three finally found the map, sticking their pointy noses in three distinct locations – Alaska, Montana, and Maryland. The die was cast. His future was chosen. The decisions were easy - not Alaska - it was too remote and wild - not Montana - it offered little architecturally and harbored unpleasant memories. By default, it was off to the east coast and a job somewhere between Baltimore and Washington, D.C.

— — —

After two months of job-hunting up and down the Baltimore-Washington corridor, in his little red Fiat, he reluctantly found employment with a small uptown Baltimore architectural office within walking distance of an affordable unfurnished apartment. Initially, he wanted to live and work in the highly charged energy of Washington, DC, but when he discovered the salaries offered him couldn't compensate for the commuting nightmares or prohibitive cost of living realities of the DC environment, he was forced to set his goals a little lower, and settled for Baltimore.

The firm, *Martin & Associates*, was ordinary, but professionally competent. It lacked imagination. It had no character and played on every cliché that architecture had to offer. Tony knew this, but still, it was a job and money and a start in some direction. He found his co-workers friendly and the firm's principals tolerable. The pay was minimal, but it enabled him to live a comfortable lower middle-class life, as long as he didn't buy furniture and prepared all his own meals.

Each day that Tony labored at this job he had to constantly fight his impulse to quit, but he persevered and quietly and competently performed his work. He hated working at this place. His desires to succeed in something better constantly dominated his thoughts. At the end of the workday he walked out the door to search for a more meaningful purpose in his life, something that would be more fulfilling than what he was doing at work each day. He concluded his darts had deceived him. This place was definitely not where he was supposed to be.

In the evenings Tony would occasionally socialize with some of his coworkers to have a few laughs and a few beers. Most of his free time however, was used doing research at the Enoch Pratt or University of Maryland libraries. It was the only thing that made any sense to him. In the evenings when he didn't drive, his research sessions ended with an evening's jog home with his backpack in tow. He thought of his run as a much-needed stress relieving exercise. He loved running, a regiment acquired from his daily workouts training for the quarter mile on his high school track team. While running, he reflected on futuristic buildings and homes powered by solar energy. These visions had obsessed him his entire life. During his time at Franklin State he had written many articles on the subject. Several were published in the college's engineering newsletter. It was one of the reasons Professor Clark befriended him and helped him successfully complete his final year.

His solar design obsessions gave him the reasons to complete another day with some purpose, although he realized in today's world, transforming his visions into reality was not practical and next to impossible to achieve. He could only hope that sometime in his lifetime that would all change.

After arriving home, he would catalog his latest concepts and theories from his evening's research for possible future use. When he finished filling his solar energy journals, he began work on another. In this one, he wrote poems and stories about the unfulfilled promises of finding love, and finding meaning to this meaningless misadventure called life.

— — —

Before long, fifty-two weeks of employment had come and passed. Unfortunately for Tony, this one-year anniversary at *Martin and Associates*, was not honored with a celebratory toast but with the news that the need for his services had ended. It was a common practice with small architectural offices. When projects were completed and new contracts weren't in place to sustain a continuing workflow and income, architects lost their jobs. He was given two weeks notice.

At the end of this eventful day, he sat alone at his drafting table reflecting on the traumatic crossroad set before him. He had to make a decision. Did he want to continue in this profession? Were his professors right about him, that he did not possess the talent or practical ambition necessary to make it as an architect? He had given it his best shot for a year and it gave nothing back to him. It was a stifling and creativity choking experience. Should he try something else, something unrelated to architecture?

— — —

Tony spent the next few weeks of unemployment not knowing what he should do. There was one thing he did know. He was without purpose, a visionary talent with a bankrupt soul, wasting away under one of life's most basic problems, to continue in a chosen profession at any cost, only because the alternative - to give up - was to potentially waste away in obscurity and failure.

This question presented itself to Tony over and over again…*should I abandon architecture…could I abandon it… is this what being independently creative means…is this what frustrated creative people ponder millions of times a day as they waste away in factories, taxicabs, and executive offices… will I look back fifty years from now and discover my true purpose in life… only with no time left to pursue it?*

This time he could not use darts to make this decision for him. To leave his profession of expertise was not an easy decision. It had an ugly face of failure attached to it. It was clearly visible to him.

CHAPTER 8

THE THUNDER EAGLE

Johnny Thunder Eagle grew up proud and determined. He loved his heritage, his history, and his people. On the reservation, everyone was part of his extended family. As a youth he was very aware of and saddened by the injustices imposed by the United States Government, through the Bureau of Indian Affairs, on his Native American brothers and sisters living on the reservation. When he left its boundaries, he witnessed prejudice in every way, in every form from almost every "other". As a naïve young child new to the world surrounding him, he couldn't understand how these "others", people not of Crow blood, could despise his people with such passion, with such conviction and without just cause.

He was blessed to be born of strong parents, who valued the health and welfare of their children above anything else. He was from a family of two brothers and one sister. His mother and father were full-blooded Crow and attended high school off the reservation in Hardin, where they met and fell in love. They married quite young. Johnny estimated that they were between eighteen and nineteen years old.

His father was a productive farmer and routinely worked off the reservation on construction projects. He provided well for his family and was wise beyond his years and education. After his high school graduation, he continued to read anything and everything he could. He gathered books from the Hardin library and purchased many from used bookstores in Billings. He wanted to pass whatever useful knowledge he had on to his children. He read to Johnny whenever he could. His father's influence enabled him to understand the importance of an education. When Johnny reached school age, he enthusiastically began his formal education in one of the better staffed, but typically poorly maintained and furnished Crow Agency reservation elementary schools.

When his eight years were completed, in the normal order of things American, high school followed, not so with the typical elementary school Crow graduate. They decided that an eighth-grade education was all that was needed to carry them through reservation life. This was not an acceptable decision to Johnny or his parents. There was so much more Johnny wanted to learn. His academic performance and attitude in school reflected this. His efforts were rewarded. He was offered a special educational opportunity, with dozens of other Crow teenagers like him, to attend the prestigious *Paterson Barnes,* an off-reservation private high school just outside the city of Billings. Johnny did not understand the reasons for this opportunity, but it had something to do with recently passed Federal Government legislation that provided special educational opportunities for gifted and talented impoverished minorities.

Paterson Barnes, received a generous financial compensation from Uncle Sam for their efforts in educating small select groups of gifted "Reservation Indians." A Government furnished school bus provided the daily transportation. The ride to the school on the state highway took over an hour. It exhausted Johnny. It discouraged him from wanting to continue, but his family would not allow him to abandon this treasured opportunity.

During his four years at *Paterson,* despite the best intentions from the school's staff to encourage their Native American students to complete high school, Johnny witnessed many of his Crow Reservation classmates drop out from racial pressures and failure to adapt to life outside the 'rez.' Instead, they returned to the reservation only to be absorbed into its shamed world of alcoholism, crime, and perpetual unemployment. Johnny was determined not to allow this to be his fate. With his parents' unyielding love and support, he persevered and completed four tough years among the "others," graduating with honors.

After high school, what Johnny decided to pursue was rarely considered by a reservation Crow. He applied for admission to college, specifically Montana State University in Bozeman. Surprisingly, not only was he accepted, but was awarded a four-year academic scholarship. Unlike high school - he was treated as just another MSU student. With this newfound reality came unlimited opportunities to open up his future in a positive way. His four years of college were the best part of his young life. He completed his college education in 1970, with a major degree in Business Administration and a minor in Native American History.

— — —

During Johnny's college years, Native American history was of special interest to him for many reasons, the most important being his insatiable need to discover the true identity of the Native American peoples in this country before Columbus, before it became the land of the many "united states." It was an obsession with Johnny that written history should represent an accurate story of his people, documenting their heritage, traditions, religions, faults, contradictions, and contributions.

Johnny was initially introduced to Crow history orally, in the centuries old Native American tradition of "storytelling," by the honored reservation historian, Spotted Owl. This was years before he was formally introduced to it in written form in his Native American history studies at MSU by Professor Two Wolfs, a Crow historian.

Once a week, Spotted Owl would gather up hundreds of young Crow boys and girls from Johnny's clan and assemble them in a circle in front of his house. There he would pick a random story from his past and totally captivate his young crowd with his eloquent, detailed accounts of Crow history. He would tell all his stories in the languages of Crow and English, adding to their authenticity. Johnny looked forward to these weekly sessions well into his teens.

— — —

Throughout Johnny's years in elementary and high school, only a few examples of Native American authored literature were made available to him. His white teachers informed him, in their ignorance, the "reasons" for this deficiency were easily explained; his ancestors simply lacked the formal education needed to transform the spoken word into the written word.

Furthermore, they reasoned, few authentic documents written by North American - Native Americans, existed before the conclusion of the nineteenth century when many reservation Indians were "thankfully" taken from their native homes and forced to attend the white man's Christian schools. At that time, reservation schools were nonexistent. Johnny was led to believe that Native Americans were illiterate and partially to blame for their own lost past, since they rarely recorded their own history using the written word. Instead, the spoken word, through oral storytellers, such as Spotted Owl, or the painted image were substitutes for the written word. Finding any accurate chronological written accounts of Native American history before the twentieth century, he was told, would be nearly impossible. He was deliberately kept from knowing that any relevant historical facts as witnessed and written by fellow Native Americans before the twentieth century even existed.

It wasn't until he began his college studies in Native American History, that Johnny found in the MSU library, hundreds of volumes of published books written by Native Americans - books of notable historical significance and literary merit. Many were written by Crow authors. Dozens were written at the beginning of the nineteenth century with hundreds more authored after 1890; following the end of the Government induced Indian Wars, and the start of mandated formalized Indian education in eastern boarding schools. Most books were autobiographical, describing the author's life, family, and tribal traditions. There were also many publications of poetry, music and art, all capturing the life events and emotions from the perspective of insightful talented Native Americans.

His favorite literary work however, was a copy of the first known novel by a Native American. It was published in 1833, titled "Poor Sarah" and written by Elias Boudinot in his native language of Cherokee. Boudinot was also the editor of the Cherokee Phoenix, the first Native American newspaper. This book was instrumental in lifting the barriers of ignorance from Johnny's mind and at eighteen he began his unquenchable thirst for anything authored by Native Americans.

To supplement the library's existing inventory of Native American literature, Johnny decided it was his duty to record Crow history based on the stories of Spotted Owl. Throughout his four years of college, during his summer months, on the reservation between semesters, he would confer with Spotted Owl, listening to the master historian's carefully crafted stories, as he interpreted them from Crow to English. After every session, Johnny would preserve Spotted Owl's legacy, using the written word, ensuring that these stories would never be lost or forgotten.

He filled dozens of journals with his accounts of this one man's priceless link to Crow history. Two month's before Johnny's graduation from college, in 1970, Spotted Owl died. He was one hundred years old. With his death went the last of the great traditional Crow oral storytellers. There was no one on the reservation that could take his place.

Thanks to Johnny's dedicated work, Spotted Owl's stories were kept alive and his legacy preserved forever. His stories would now stand with their truth unaltered, waiting to be read by the generations of Crow that would follow.

— — —

Spotted Owl's honorable but tenuous documentation methods could be conceived by the white man as an impossible way to determine what body of it was truth or fable. This never was a concern to Johnny. He had no reason to question Spotted Owl's stories as not being true historical accounts. To Johnny, the stories were gospel. After all, was the written word any more accurate than the honest memory of events personally witnessed and told by the storyteller? Johnny believed it was not. Written words are no more a guarantee for truth than a spoken word. It is the source that holds the truth not the method.

Spotted Owl would say to Johnny, "It is impossible to see the truth in a man's eyes when his eyes are hidden by his words on paper. I wish to see the honesty of a man through his eyes and by the manner in which he speaks, only then, can I judge him as a man of truth."

These words were reinforced when Johnny's college research uncovered volumes of early accounts of Native

American history altered, enhanced, and exaggerated, mostly containing questionable "historical facts" as documented by white authors; prejudiced to the white man's benefit and the red man's demise.

It was an unpleasant and sad story, Johnny thought, but such was the plight of not only the Crow Nation, but of all the Native American Nations of North America. It was a history filled with centuries of needless deaths by European diseases, guns, whiskey and unwarranted aggression, the raping of their land with metal tools, superior technology and railroads, the starving of their people by the elimination of and restricted access to their traditional food sources, the destroying of their independence and the creation of their dependency on the US Government for survival. These events are all part of their true American history.

However, in America, a popularized sanitized history buried the accounts of the United States' premeditated Native American genocide policies and substituted a cleaner more acceptable story. This sanitized history altered the United States Government from its true identity as a predatory wolf indiscriminately devouring its prey without mercy or reason to one of a meek and mild misunderstood shepherd tending its flock, one with honorable Christian intentions. Native Americans were rendered helpless and forced to be at the mercy of their aggressor to record for them their accounts, their deeds, and their actions.

They were conveniently molded by the white man, from a noble race of people into one seen as savage, hostile and uncivilized - their identities tarnished, and destroyed. Their image would always be distorted, since the victors always recorded history to their advantage, in their own favor, in their own way, in their own image. The victims were conveniently given identities that covered their bewildered faces with inhuman masks of hopelessness and inferiority.

CHAPTER 9

THE INTERVIEW

SEPTEMBER 1973

It was a cool bright beautiful day, a crisp day with trees showcasing leaves of bright gold, crimson, and the deep browns of autumn. It was the kind of day Tony enjoyed most and the time of year he found to be his very favorite. It left him mysteriously happy, uplifted, spirited, and full of that something that only visited him once in a while and always at this time of year.

The exhaust fumes entering Tony's lungs through an open window on the Baltimore city bus were in stark contrast to his feelings about this time of year and the fresh autumn air. Sitting complacently on the bus searching his mind for anything that would make sense to him, Tony was becoming frustrated and totally without hope during the nearly two months he was seeking diligently, but not enthusiastically, a new job in his unrewarding chosen profession. Looking out the bus window he counted the streets and read their names until he found his landmark. He pulled the cord signaling the bus driver to stop. He got off the bus, captured a welcomed breath of fresh air, studied the directions on the small piece of paper he held in his hand and started to walk.

— — —

Tony walked uptown for blocks, through neighborhoods of office buildings, churches and schools, until he arrived in an intimate neighborhood of row homes and small privately owned storefront businesses. Reaching an alley just before "Jimmy's Barbershop," he cut through its garbage can bordered passage to a parallel street of newly renovated homes, pre World War II buildings that had been converted into modest professional offices. Tony searched the streetscape until he found his building. It was as described, a small solitary three story red brick and gray granite structure. The building was loitered with dozens of gray and white pigeons, standing sentry fifty feet above its ornate granite cornice ledge; their droppings adding an interesting texture to its chiseled grape leaf motif. He secured the portfolio of his life's work under his arm and approached the building's entrance apprehensively.

Whatever awaited him inside this unimposing structure would provide him with his third and final job interview of the day. The first two delivered less than promising results. This interview would most likely be no different. It did however, have a unique circumstance wrapped around it the others did not. Tony's previous interviews were set up in one of two ways, through a typical help wanted newspaper ad or from a specific professional reference obtained from the local chapter of the *American Institute of Architects*, the AIA. This one did not follow either path. It emerged from an unsolicited personal telephone call from the interested office. It was not usual to be contacted for an interview in this manner, unless you were a prominent or noteworthy architect. Tony was neither.

— — —

As he climbed the concrete stairs to the entrance, Tony surveyed the neighborhood's buildings and the dark muted tones that defined them. Their monotone palette contrasted starkly with the bright blue sky. Tony concluded that this neighborhood once was home for blue-collar breadwinners and their families, until recently, when it was transformed by economic necessity to forcefully accept the infiltration of professional offices - white-collar intruders. It was an unwanted marriage, one arranged between two families of conflicting social standing - a shotgun wedding.

Tony's eyes focused on two large wood and glass panel doors. Above the doors sunlight reflected off the beautiful red and gold stained glass transom. On the left door, painted large gold letters centered on its glass surface read 2625. On the other, neatly blocked, was printed *Neil Hagman and Associates; Architectural and Interior Design.* This was the place. This is where his interview awaited him.

...It had to be a small struggling architectural office... who else would want me...what could possibly be waiting for me here inside these brick walls other than a meager salary, small insignificant projects and more boring work...?

Staring at the doors' imposing barrier, Tony decided... *why bother...this office most likely is not worth my time...*

He turned to leave, but then had second thoughts for selfish reasons. He had to pee, was hungry, tired and desperately needed a cup of coffee. Besides, his curiosity about the call was obsessing him. These were good enough reasons to enter.

He reached out to open the doors to the building, but they were locked. He rang the doorbell. A loud vibrating buzz was heard indicating that someone from inside had approved his entry and released the building's outer electric door lock. He pushed the door forward. It opened quietly. He passed through an inner vestibule and entered the building through a second set of doors.

Once inside he stood alone in the building's empty lobby. This was not the interior of a typical architectural office, or any office for that matter. It was unfurnished and abandoned. It had a sense of conflict to it as if it were struggling between something it was forced to become and the something it was.

...Where is everyone...why was I asked to come here, to an empty building...maybe I have the wrong address, but who the hell let me in...this whole thing doesn't feel right... it feels like I just entered the Bates' Motel...

Tony walked forward a few steps on the bare oak hardwood floor. He looked around the empty space for any signs of life. There were none. The large room that he entered was framed on his left by an ornamental open wooden staircase gracefully flowing its way to a second floor that was partially open to the first floor below. Framing the other side was an expansive wall containing large glass panels and an open arched entrance to a parlor or living room. In this room, through the glass, Tony could see a stone fireplace that stood prominent in its elegance and seemed to still have the warmth of endless fires radiating from it, although it was obvious it had not been used in quite some time. There was no furniture. There were no indications of anyone living here.

He continued to look around at the building's remaining walls and became distracted by their thoughtful detailing. From the floor up to a continuous oak chair rail the walls were a painted plaster, peeling from age and neglect. Above the chair rail they were wallpapered in a faded earth-toned floral pattern up to an elaborate painted perimeter frieze of the wildlife inhabiting the woodlands of Maryland's northern hills and valleys. It was a beautiful but now deteriorating work of art.

The high ceilings were textured with plaster stucco and their intersection with the walls bordered with an oak cornice.

Just above Tony, along the entry wall, were a series of built-in wooden shelves - all empty save for one. Upon it sat a solitary bronze bust of an unidentifiable Confederate Civil War General, most likely left behind by the former owners of this house, too ambivalent about its historical worth to decide - heave it into the trash or take it with them. So there it sat, oblivious to its fate, not reacting to the hundreds of curious glances cast its way, but proud of the fact that it had commanded their attention by its mere presence.

—— —— ——

Tony's visual tour was interrupted by sounds coming from the floor above.

...At last, I am not alone..., Tony thought, as he heard a female voice shouting from the top of the stairs.

"Hello down there? Who's there, please?"

"Hello up there. It's Anthony Rullo. I'm here for the four o'clock interview with a Mr. Neil Hagman. I'm interviewing for the graduate Architect's position."

Tony could hear the muffled tones of two voices talking in a whisper.

"Of course, Mr. Rullo, please come on up. Neil is expecting you. You can hang your coat up down there. There's a closet down the hall on your left and a bathroom if you need to freshen up. I'm Lisa, Neil's secretary, interior designer, and wife."

"Thank you Mrs. Hagman. I'll hang up my jacket. Be up in a minute."

Tony thought, *...it seemed unusual to begin an interview by shouting up the stairs to someone you couldn't even see, or that you didn't even know...*, but this building, with its subtle charm, made it all seem like it was expected of him and that it was an accepted way of making yourself welcome here. He set his portfolio of work on the floor, hung his jacket in the closet, next to two others, a man's and a woman's, and used the welcomed convenience of the bathroom.

He walked down the hallway and climbed the stairs. Every footstep had a sound connected to it - memories of all who passed up these stairs in the years before him. The rest of the building heard and remembered each sound as they echoed throughout its history.

Arriving at the top of the stairs, he could see packed boxes piled high, forming a temporary corridor to an empty desk of the receptionist who earlier had voiced his arrival from the top of the stairs. Books and catalogs were neatly stacked along the wall, a little too high, he thought. It seemed like a mild tremor generated from walking would topple them over like dominoes. He walked a little further through the canyon of boxes searching for someone who would acknowledge his presence.

"Mr. Rullo we're in here." Lisa shouted. Her voice originated from a room to his right. He noticed its door was half open. He walked toward it, pushed it open slightly and peeked inside.

What happened next would forever impact Tony's life.

Tony saw sitting on the floor the two people who were the architectural firm of *Neil Hagman*. They were sorting through boxes of files and organizing their contents in neat stacks on the floor along the wall. There was Neil, bearded and tall. He was in his mid to late thirties and had a strong likeness to Burt Reynolds.

Sitting next to him was Lisa, the voice at the top of the stairs. Tony's eyes locked on her with some unknown predetermined purpose. In that brief moment he was awarded a lifetime of obsession. Her beauty captivated him, but it was more than just her beauty. It was her overwhelming presence. There was something about her, not only in a physical sense, but also in some spiritual way that made him feel connected to her. None of this made any sense to him. He didn't understand what these feelings could possibly mean. The only thing he did know was that, for him, attractions like this had a way of evolving into something bad. With his history of failed romances, it was undoubtedly a situation flawed and doomed to embarrassing failure.

Even though he desperately needed the job and the money, he could not work here, not with the possibility of such unbridled feelings toward the principal's wife constantly distracting him. What was it about this woman that was causing this reaction? It didn't matter. He was not about to allow himself the opportunity to find out.

...Complete this interview...be gracious, but by all means, respectively decline...there would be other jobs, other interviews...don't add this new trauma to your already uneventful troubled life...you're too tired to deal with this bullshit today... it's been a busy day...just go home and sleep this nightmare away...

Tony stood passively in the doorway, waiting for his invitation to enter. He wanted to disappear. Before he could make himself invisible, there was a response from within the room.

Standing up and facing Tony, Neil said, "Mr. Rullo! Hello! I'm sorry to keep you waiting. Please come in. I'm Neil Hagman. Please call me Neil. Excuse the informalities and the mess. I never seem to be able to keep up with organizing all my files and drawings. We just moved here from my old office downtown and my wife and I are working as fast as we can to get everything sorted out. Isn't this a beautiful building? Built in the 1930's, I believe. Some prominent southern family related to Robert E. Lee, lived here until just after the Second World War. Isn't that interesting? We were fortunate to find it available for my new adventure. It suits our needs perfectly and it's in a comfortable area to work – away from the downtown crowds and traffic. It will be a wonderful place to fix up. Lisa can't wait to impose her interior design skills on it. Isn't that right, Lisa?"

"Yes it is Neil, but I think we are ignoring the purpose of Mr. Rullo's visit," Lisa said.

"Of course. I'm sorry Mr. Rullo. Forgive me. We can talk about this building later. Welcome to my new office. I am in the process of staffing up for an exciting new project. That's why you are here. You are my first interview. I am pleased to finally meet you."

Neil held out his hand, which was slightly sweaty from his filing and sorting activities. Tony not wanting to offend, shook it without hesitation and then the extended hand of Lisa was offered.

"Hello Anthony. Pleasure to meet you. Please…call me *Lisa*." Tony nodded in agreement as he grasped her hand. Her hand was not sweaty, but soft and slightly cool. He shook it gently.

"Thanks. By the way, only my mother called me *Anthony*… please… use *Tony*."

"Okay, *Tony* it is. Now that everyone's on a first name basis, let's not waste any more of your valuable time. First, before we review your work, do you have any questions about me or the firm?" Neil said.

"Well…a couple I guess. How long have you been practicing and what type of work will I be involved in?" Tony said.

"Okay –fair enough. Let's see…I've been practicing for fifteen years. Started my own firm with Lisa after graduating from Princeton. Never wanted to work for anyone other than myself. I've been fortunate through the years. Had quite a few well paying clients in my beginning years, thanks to Lisa's talent and charm. Couldn't have made it without her. We work mostly on commercial office buildings and interiors. We're a small office with a staff of six. IBM and XEROX have been our most notable clients. Sorry…we aren't prepared to show you any examples of our previous work. It's mostly still in boxes downtown. We've just received a lucrative contract to design a large office building. Need to staff up. It's a big project – our biggest to date…that's about it in a nutshell. We can get into more detail later, if you want," Neil said.

"Yes. That's fine. Thanks. I've always wanted to work on an office building. Is it a high-rise?" Tony asked.

"Yes it is"

"Great! By the way how did you select me for this interview?" Tony said.

"You might say I picked your name out of a hat from a list of possibilities obtained from the AIA. Then, I did a background check on you."

"That's strange. Don't recall giving my resume to the AIA."

"Well, you were there. How else would I know? Anyway, if you're ready to show us your work - we're ready. Impress us," Neil said.

"Be happy to." Tony reached inside his shoulder slung brief case and produced the relevant documents. Tony handed them to Neil and Lisa. "Let's start with my resume and personal references," he said.

Tony waited a few moments as he watched their eyes casually survey the five pages of documents. There were no reactions. Then, Tony said, in his bored matter of fact *let's get this over with* voice, "Neil…Lisa - if neither of you have any questions about my resume or references, I can proceed to showing you examples of my previous work...if that's okay."

He couldn't wait to begin this part of the interview. The drawings and portfolio that Tony was carrying were beginning to get rather heavy. He couldn't wait to put them down somewhere, anywhere.

"Yes, that would be fine. Your resume appears complete – no surprises – nothing out of the ordinary. Your references are very complimentary. I don't have any questions about your experience just yet. I'll save any questions I may have until after I see your work. I know you'll want to spread those drawings out as soon as possible," Neil said.

Tony thought...*it's about time...okay phase one appears to be over...let's quickly move along to phase two so I can go home...*

"Yes sir. That would be most welcome," Tony said.

"As you can see we are without any furniture at the moment," Neil said. "The movers have promised it will all arrive sometime tomorrow along with the rest of my staff. In the meantime, I think we can find a chair for you and a table to place your drawings. Please relax. You seem a little nervous. There's no reason you should feel anxious. We're very friendly people - honest. This is an informal interview. No need to feel uncomfortable..."

...If he only knew...

Neil removed a card table and three folding chairs from a closet. They were set up quickly and placed in the middle of the room. Tony put his work on the table and sat down. He carefully unrolled his drawings. The Hagman's sat next to him. Neil was on Tony's right hand side and Lisa sat opposite him trying not to get in their way. Already there was a problem. Tony couldn't concentrate. He could barely keep from staring at her.

...she is so pretty...this is not good...

Lisa's blond hair and piercing blue eyes were complemented by an athletic petite body that was alarmingly sensuous and understated. She wore a simple plain dark blue dress that draped her body contours perfectly. As far as Tony was concerned, it existed only to be worn by her.

As the drawings were unrolled on the table, Tony noticed that it was hardly big enough to display them, but he did his best. To help keep the drawings from rolling back, he held the corners down keeping both hands awkwardly occupied. Neil seemed uninterested until, noticing Tony's dilemma; he too, helped hold down the recoiling drawings. Lisa just sat quietly, smiled and amusedly watched.

"Thanks for your help". Tony said, "I'll start with these construction drawings from a multi-family residential housing project I prepared while working at *Martin and Associates*. I completed the design and construction documents practically on my own in less than three months – ahead of schedule and under budget. *Martin* was very satisfied with the final product. I received a modest bonus for my efforts."

Neil looked over the drawings thoroughly, inspecting each sheet with a very critical eye. The work was well organized and impeccably detailed. Neil was impressed. He said to Tony in a very casual manner. "Very good...Nice work... Very nice...Very professional..."

Tony heard the compliments and felt he was well on his way to a potential job offer. It was a good feeling even though he knew, because of the *Lisa* problem, he may have to refuse. He would wait to see what was offered before he would decide.

After displaying the remainder of his *Martin and Associate's* presentation and production work, it was time for

Phase 3 - his favorite subject. He deliberately saved his most impressive work for last.

"That's about all I have to show you regarding my practical experience. It's not much, but I hope it's enough to meet the requirements for the position you're trying to fill. Now… if you don't mind and if you've finished looking through these drawings, I'd like to present some additional work showcasing my college and freelance work in solar design. Allow me to show you -" Tony began to reach inside his portfolio.

"Tony, wait a moment. That won't be necessary..." Neil said.

The response was abrupt, startling Tony.

Contrary to what Tony thought, Neil obviously was not impressed with him or his work. Neil's favorable comments now seemed as if they were only setting him up for a polite dismissal.

…I don't get it…why so quick to judge…he didn't give me much of a chance…

"Okay. I get it…", Tony said.

"Get what?" Neil said.

"Come on Neil. I know what's going on. It's obvious. You've made your decision. I was hoping I could at least show you the rest of my work..." Tony said.

"Tony, you don't understand. Let me -"

A tired and impatient Tony abruptly stood up and disappointedly addressed his audience. "Don't bother. I understand…Mr. and Mrs. Hagman, I am very sorry I didn't qualify for this position. There is no point in me wasting any more of your time. Thank you for this opportunity. It's been a pleasure meeting you both. If you change your mind, please… give me a call. I'll just take my stuff and go now. I know my way out."

Neil reached over and gently secured Tony's arm, keeping him from leaving. Releasing his hold he said, "Tony… please…sit down. You've misinterpreted my intentions. Give me a chance to explain. After you've heard what I'm about to say, then decide if you want to leave. For now though, stay, sit, relax and listen. I insist…please."

A visibly shaken Tony sat down.

"Okay, but I must admit I'm confused. Why didn't you want to review the work in my portfolio? I am very proud of that work. It appears you weren't very impressed with my work from *Martin and Associates*," he said.

"No, it's not that at all. I wasn't dismissing you. I apologize if my reaction gave you that impression. It most certainly was not the best way to convey my intentions."

"What's going on then? What *are* your intentions?"

"I'll explain. First let me ask you, from our telephone conversation, what do you remember about the position I'm interviewing you for?"

"Is this a test?"

"No, just tell me what you remember. It's not a test…trust me."

"Okay. If I remember correctly, you said on the phone you were looking for a graduate architect, someone having a limited amount of practical experience in design, unlicensed, with a satisfactory command of production fundamentals. That's pretty much how I remember it and that pretty much describes me. How'd I do? Was that close?"

"Yes, that's about it, but I wasn't being entirely honest with you. The circumstances surrounding this position are not exactly as I described them to you. You're not being interviewed today for your practical design or production experience. I can get that from almost any experienced graduate architect--"

"Then why am I here?" Tony asked.

Neil stood up and walked toward a window in the room. Looking out the window for a moment he turned around and faced Tony while sitting on the windowsill. He continued his comments in a more concerned manner.

"Why are you here? Good question. Before I get to that, here are the facts about you as I know them...been out of school for a little over a year...unlicensed...with limited production experience...your background is limited...not much to go on...so there must be something else about you that's of value to my new project. Correct?"

"I would hope so. What?"

"Your value to this new project is your extensive knowledge in solar design."

"Why? Why is my solar design experience *so* valuable? More importantly...how could you possibly know this without seeing or knowing of my work? No offense, but I know for sure, that I never submitted any solar related work to the AIA -"

"I know you didn't Tony. Let me explain. This is where it gets a little unusual-"

"I can't wait to hear this," Tony said.

"Okay. For starters, I didn't get your name from an AIA list of eligible architects. That was a lie. Sorry. I wasn't prepared earlier to tell you the truth," Neil said.

"I thought so. What's the truth?"

"The truth is you were *pre-selected* by the sponsor of this new venture. He gave me your name and college. This allowed me the opportunity to contact your professors and instructors at Franklin State. I had a long conversation with Professor Clark. It seems the two of you spent a lot of time together discussing the future of solar architecture. He was very impressed with your work. He told me you developed many concepts specifically related to self-sustained building architecture. He sent me copies and photos of your work, some of which are probably represented in that portfolio of yours. That is why I do not need to see it now. Although, I am very interested in seeing what you've added to it in the past year. He liked you. I liked him. He was very supportive. He had nothing but good things to say about you. Many of your instructors did. Although some said you were a little rebellious…unconventional. I liked that about you. A few professors I interviewed weren't as positive, but I didn't like their attitude, so I ignored them. That's how I knew about you and your work before I met you. It was a pretty sure thing you were going to be offered a job here if you passed the preliminary requirements."

A bewildered Tony was trying to filter through the unusual information thrown at him.

All he could say was, "Did I pass?"

"Yes you did. You did very well. I like you…we…like you"

"That's good to know. So I passed, huh? What happens now?"

A proposal was then offered with the subtlety of an avalanche.

"With that said, here is the bottom line with no hidden agenda – no bullshit - I have been ordered by the owner to offer you a job with my firm, based on what I know about you from this interview, your prior work experience, and what I have confirmed from many personal references about your character and solar design experience. Your salary will be fifteen thousand dollars per year to start, plus benefits, bonuses, and annual increases. However, you most likely will be working twelve-hour days and six-day workweeks. You'll be exhausted, overworked and underpaid, but the personal rewards will be beyond any that you can imagine. I'm in the process of assembling a talented team of highly skilled architects, engineers, physicists, and scientists. You are my first and most important interview. This office will be increasing to nearly ten times its present size. I have many people to interview before the end of the month. Save me the extra work of interviewing another architect to fill this position. I need your unique talent, more importantly I need your vision. I need you. You can start immediately with one week's salary in advance. All you need to do, is say *yes.*"

The offer was difficult to believe. With Neil's enthusiastic research into Tony's solar design background, there wasn't a good reason why he should doubt the validity of the offer, but, he still had reservations. It seemed too good to be true, which probably meant it was. Without more specific information, he felt the offer was just exaggerated lip service from an unknown desperate employer, whose previous work examples were conveniently "stored" away.

Tony responded cautiously, "That's a great offer Neil, but something doesn't feel right. It doesn't make sense. Why would you be offering me, an unproven commodity, just off the street, a position like this? I'm not comfortable making a decision without more information – more specific information. After all, wouldn't YOU think your offer was a little suspect?"

"Yes I would, but -" Before Neil could respond, Lisa provided the men a welcomed interruption.

"Excuse me gentlemen. Tony, you'll have to excuse Neil. Sometimes he can be too *matter of fact* about things that in reality are somewhat complex and very intimidating to others. He's working on improving his perception skills along these lines. In the meantime, I can assure you that he is very serious about what he's told you about this project and his reasons for hiring you. He has specific orders from the owner. Don't ask *why*. You won't get an answer. Now - may I offer either of you a coffee and bagel? ... And Neil - go easy on Tony. You're scaring him."

"Okay *Hon*. I'll try to ease up a bit. You know why this is difficult for me."

"I know *why*, but remember...Tony doesn't. Be aware of that. It's a lot of obscure information for this handsome young man to digest." Lisa said.

...oh please don't say that Lisa...I don't need you to put any inappropriate thoughts in my head...you're driving me crazy as it is...

"All right I get it. Now, I sure would like a cup of that coffee. How about you Tony?" Neil said.

"Yes, that would be great. Cream and sugar please," Tony answered.

Tony watched Lisa walk away thinking that by now this interview should have been over, allowing her to evolve into a distant memory. She returned shortly with a tray displaying three toasted bagels and three cups filled with coffee. Neil and Tony remained quiet awaiting her return. Tony reached for his cup as she offered him the contents of the tray.

"Don't forget to take a bagel. There's two with cream cheese and one plain," Lisa said.

"Thank you, Lisa," Tony said.

Lisa handed Neil his cup. Declining a bagel, Neil took a sip of his coffee. He looked directly at Tony. He continued his discussion in a more calming manner, but with the same intimidating tone. Some things never change.

"Okay Tony, I understand your concern. If I were you, I would be skeptical too. As per my wife's instructions, I will try to eliminate your doubts and calm your fears. First of all, you have to trust me. I have been completely honest with what I have told you so far. All of it my sound a little strange, but it is all true – very true. Now, allow me to provide you with the information that I hope, will help you with your decision."

"Here it is. While working for this office, your talents will be devoted exclusively to one major project – our 'high-rise' building. My entire firm, that is, the future firm, will be working on this one exclusive project continuously for three years. Presently, I am not at liberty to reveal to you much about it. There are many details about its purpose that I don't even know. There is also a very restrictive security protocol defined by the owner on all information. There are personal disclosure forms and a binding exclusive contract to sign. In addition, so you are fully prepared for an abrupt change in your life, a branch of *Hagman & Associates* will remain here in Baltimore while the majority of its staff, including you, will relocate to another state. Don't ask me where or why, because at this time, I don't know. That's the nuts and bolts of it, but it's not the best part. I saved the best part for last."

"…And what's the best part…?" Tony said.

"The building…Tony…the building. You never asked me about the building."

"…What about the building…!!?"

"Ah…the building, our building – our high-rise - our masterpiece - will be the tallest in the world, not only the tallest, but completely self-sufficient, harnessing its power by using solar, wind and geo-thermal energy. Think about it. You will be part of a project team whose sole purpose will be to design a totally self-sustained solar powered building, destined to be the tallest building in the world. It doesn't get any better than that - does it? It was purely by chance that I was given this opportunity to manage this fantastic project. I am very fortunate to be part of its creation. Now…today…you have the opportunity to be part of its creation too. That's it. No more information until you say *yes* and sign the contract. What do you think? Does that do it for you?"

"Holy shit!…Sorry."

"That's okay. I think that was my response upon hearing about this building. Tony… your answer?"

"You're serious aren't you...?"

"…As a heart attack…you're stalling…*yes*…or …*no*?"

— — —

That was the extent of it. The seductive beginnings of Tony's journey were mapped before him. He had no choice. He had to have faith and accept Neil's story as truth – but what a story! The intrigue and possibilities of such a project definitely outweighed any risks. This was what he had always wanted. This is what he had always envisioned. Now fate had given him this opportunity. His solar design obsessions were being rewarded. He didn't know why, but he didn't care why. It was time to turn his ideas into something real. The reason he studied to become an architect was finally realized. It was because of this opportunity. It was always because of this opportunity.

Tony said the only words capable of leaving his mouth.

"Are you kidding? Yes. Of course. *Yes*. Thank you. Thank you so much. You have no idea how much this means to me. I've always wanted a chance to do something like this since I was a kid. It's a dream come true. Can't wait to start. I won't disappoint you. I promise. If I do, I'll personally end me. I've worked too hard to get here. Look what you've done to me. I can't stop shaking. Too much caffeine, I guess."

"I think it's a little more than caffeine. You're excited. I can see that. Who wouldn't be? You'll be okay in a couple minutes. The same thing happened when the project was first introduced to me. It's normal. *It is* quite a proposal and a *once in a lifetime* project. You're only human...and you're quite welcome. See Lisa, I told you he couldn't say *no*."

"I don't think you would have allowed him to leave here if he said *no,"* Lisa said, as her engaging smile forced Tony to look away - again.

"You're *right on* Hon! You see Tony; you really didn't have a choice. By the way, thank you for helping to make my job a little easier today. Now I don't have to explain to the owner why I had to kidnap you and hold you captive until you would accept," Neil said.

"So...you were ordered to make me *an offer I couldn't refuse?* You sure the owner funding this project isn't named *Vito Corleone*?" Tony said.

"I can assure you he's not. That's funny. You made a joke. I was worrying you were some serious stiff who didn't know how to have fun. I like to have fun with life. You'll see that after working here awhile. Enough talk! Mr. Anthony Rullo, come here and let me welcome you to the new firm of *Neil Hagman and Associates!* Congratulations!"

Neil and Tony shook hands. It would represent the beginning of Tony's life renewal and an enduring friendship with Neil.

Lisa shook Tony's hand and simply said, "Welcome to the firm Tony. It's going to be an interesting adventure working on this project with you."

"Thank you Lisa," Tony said while thinking,...*I hope it's not that interesting with you Lisa...make it easy for me - stay here in Baltimore...*

Tony turned from Lisa to face Neil and said, "One more question, if you don't mind," Tony said.

"What's that?"

"I'm confused. How was I *pre-selected*? There must be thousands of talented solar design Architects out there. How did this mystery owner select me? How could he possibly have known about my solar design interests before he even knew who I was or what I was about?"

Neil smiled and shrugged. "I don't know Tony. No idea how he did it," he said. "In a private meeting over dinner here in Baltimore City, he presented to me your name and background. We talked about you for quite awhile. It was, I agree, a very unusual way to hire someone, as I'm sure you've experienced today. He gave you the *Good Housekeeping Seal of Approval*. So, that's all I needed to know. He wants to meet with you after the project's completion, but only then."

"Why? That's a long time to wait to meet and personally thank him…but hell, right now it doesn't matter. I'm just happy he picked me. How many others?"

"What's that?"

"How many others were chosen like I was?"

"You're the only one"

"Really - the only one?"

"Yup. You're special Tony …special. Accept it. Fate has smiled on you."

"This is so weird."

"Yeah, tell me about it. Quit trying to figure it out. It'll drive you crazy. The bottom line is - it's all good news. You're here. That's all that matters. Now – relax. Let's look at your solar work in that valuable portfolio of yours, and then we'll use the rest of our available time getting to know one another. Let me get that contract. Lisa, more coffee please," Neil said.

— — —

After a stimulating hour of talking with Neil and Lisa about the work, life and just about everything else, Tony left his new employer with an unfamiliar feeling. He was happy, genuinely happy, and what made it even more of an anomaly, it wasn't because of drugs, love, sex, or the beautiful autumn day. He was just happy. This feeling was something that wasn't experienced very often in Tony's short life. He was twenty-five years old, only one year out of college with just one major project behind him, and now for reasons he couldn't comprehend, he was to be part of a dream team working on a dream project.

Tony would go home and reflect on this extraordinary day. It was a day filled with everything he could ever hope for - a job he would love, a solar powered building, and Lisa. Unfortunately Lisa could never be part of the final equation. In time, that intense infatuation he felt for her, that would pass. She would be replaced with the euphoria he felt from accepting this exciting new job. His feelings for Lisa would be buried along with the others in his emotional graveyard of failed relationships. She was after all, the boss' wife. That should be enough reason to keep Tony's head on straight and his goals in focus. This project was all that he would allow to occupy his mind. In two days his journey would begin. He would be working on a building that would rise out of the ground like a living tree; its purpose and design a mystery.

CHAPTER 10

THE TRIP BACK HOME

JUNE 1970

The next morning, Tony lay awake in bed thinking about this incredible opportunity that had just fallen into his lap. He wished his parents could have been alive to share it with him. Somehow, he hoped, they were looking down from somewhere, knowing and guiding him safely along this uncharted path. His thoughts drifted to his mother and the last days before her death.

On the morning before the day she died, as he boarded his airplane in Chicago, Tony remembered the sunrise as brilliant and beautiful. It was a glorious beginning to a journey that would end in such a tragic way. The flight east was spent sleeping and remembering those fragmented memories of his childhood that awaited him in New Jersey as ghosts of his past. The miles were quickly devoured. It seemed he arrived at Newark Airport in a matter of moments - not hours. At the airport, he waited for the bus that would take him to the familiar streets of his hometown.

On the walk from the bus station, carrying his only piece of luggage, a large lightly packed duffel bag; he felt nothing could ever temper this moment, this heartbreak for him - to see his mother for perhaps the last time. He knew that the now, the present, was all she had left of her life to give him. That was enough, for today she would be seen not as a terminal cancer case, old beyond her years, without inspiration, but as the beautiful and loving person that she was. He had these memories of her safely stored in his heart.

When he was just a toddler, just old enough to remember, he would recall waking up and feeling her love around him. Feeling this and then seeing her was what made each day so enjoyable and his childhood so comforting. That's what greeted him on every awakening. She was always there.

As he grew older, he would have to leave this sheltered comfortable world, and enter one filled with cynicism, hypocrisy and deceit. This "other" world was thrust into his life during his early teenage years and became part of his daily existence ever since. He was determined to change this world for the better, no matter how small the change or insignificant the outcome, using whatever God given talents he had.

— — —

Tony looked across the Hudson River and saw the silhouette of two massive structures just completed on Manhattan's southern shore, the two World Trade Center Buildings, twins of modern greed. These two identical monoliths of modern technology though taller, lacked character and were no match for the artistry and elegance of New York's elder statesman of skyscrapers. Although they now dominated the New York skyline, they could not compete with his two favorites, the Empire State and Chrysler buildings. Anyone could build tall, but to build tall with a commitment to architectural excellence was the harder challenge. He knew he could do better.

How he did love those magnificent skyscrapers. The fascination of building something tall, something larger than life itself is what drove Tony into the world of Architecture.

— — —

Tony's attention was diverted from the New York skyline to the reason he was here, back in Hoboken, his mother - his mother who was dying of cancer.

Hoboken was not an inspired place to live, but it was part of Tony, part of who he would eventually become. He grew up surrounded by the hard life and busy streets of the city in a small two bedroom flat on the third floor of a forty-year-old rent-controlled railroad tenement, the type built just after the Great Depression. Most of the apartments in the building were one-bedroom units sharing two unisex bathrooms per floor. There were only two two-bedroom apartments with private bathrooms on each floor. Tony's parents managed to obtain a two-bedroom unit by winning a building lottery for a death related vacated apartment. They were lucky. Tony grew up having a private bathroom, and his own bedroom.

Tony's neighborhood was always peaceful, crime free, and racially segregated. His neighbors were like himself, predominantly Italian Catholic. Irish, German, Jewish, and Eastern Europeans were also scattered throughout the neighborhood, but they were definitely in the minority. The *colored* and *spics,* as Tony's dad would so eloquently put it, *had their own place*. It wasn't equality, but it was the reality of his life as a child of the fifties in this intimate inner-city neighborhood.

Neighbors were always looking out for one another, helping to keep the building clean, both inside and on the street. Block parties were frequent. And the Italian festival on "All Saints Day" brought out the best in food, music and dance that the neighborhood had to offer. But that all changed in the sixties, as drugs and crime started to infiltrate the area and the second generation immigrant families left in droves for a safer place to live. The people still living in this building were mostly like Tony's mother, people who couldn't afford anything else, living off their small pensions, Social Security or welfare checks. That small luxury was soon to change. The building was scheduled for demolition in less than six months as part of a federally funded Urban Renewal project. Every one living here would need to find a new home.

Tony entered his mother's building, walked through the dimly lit hallway with its graffiti adorned walls and climbed the stairs to the third floor. This is where he would find his mother, apartment 3-C - first door at the top of the stairs. He placed his hand on the doorknob letting it rest there for a few seconds before turning it and entering a place that for him was always one of comfort and love, but soon would be felt empty and lifeless. He was afraid to enter. He turned the knob and opened the door very slowly, postponing the inevitable for just a few moments more. He entered and saw his mother in a hospital bed that was placed in the small living room. Folding chairs surrounded it. All the chairs were occupied by her visitors. The doctors knew there wasn't any more they could do, so they sent her home from the hospital to spend her last days in the supportive comfort of her family and friends. His mother was alert, talking and resting peacefully.

In the apartment were many of Tony's closest relatives and a private nurse hired to tend to his mother's needs. All heads turned as they looked toward the door and saw Tony. Shouts of "Tony! Tony!" filled the room, followed by the overwhelming deluge of adoring hugs and kisses as only his Italian relatives could provide. His Aunt Lucy shouted out to his mother, unintentionally startling her in the process.

"Maria, Maria, look at who's a here. It's Tony. Tony comes all the way from Ohio to see you. He look good. No? So handsome. Come Tony. Come. Sit. Sit by your mother."

"Thanks Aunt Lucy. It's Illinois, not Ohio," Tony said. "I came all the way from Illinois, but that's okay. Ohio's close enough. Thanks for all your help in taking care of my mom. You're a jewel. It's great to see you." He gave his short well-rounded aunt another hug. A chair was offered and Tony sat next to his mom's bed.

"Mom? Mom, how you doin? You look well. How you feelin?"

"Antonio, is that you? Come here leta me hug you. You look soa good – soa handsome. Me – I just a little sick, but I be okay. Don't you worra bout me."

The hug and the kiss on the cheek was always something he looked forward to. What was missing was the smell of garlic; always an aromatic by-product of his mother's fabulous cooking.

Then in a strange twist, the reality of his mother's illness kicked in.

"Antonio. Antonio, where isa yo father? Why dona Louie come home with you?"

The cancer was making its presence known. Her mental capacity and eyesight were failing at a progressively alarming rate.

All eyes in the room looked at Maria, and then Tony, with a look of both sorrow and hopelessness. His father had been dead for six months. Tony knew the drill. He knew what to say.

"Dad's not here mom. Dad won't be coming around for a while. He's really busy down at the docks. He's working double shifts so he can buy you some pretty dresses to wear to church. He'll be home soon. He sends you his love."

"Tell him to forgeta 'bout the dresses. He beta hurry and come a home soon or I gonna have to divorce him. I don't care what a the Pope say. I'm tired of sleeping alone. Call him Antonio. Call him and tella him stop by *Rosseto's Bakery* and pick up some cannolis. Haven't had a good cannoli in a long time – no chocolate ones! I hate chocolate cannolis!"

"I'll tell him Mom. I'll tell him. Now, you get some rest. I'll be staying here tonight. I'll take care of you. I love you, Mom."

"You a good son. I love you too. Now, have Aunt Lucy feed you. You must be hungry from your trip from Ohio. Do you lose weight? You looka like you lose weight. You feel okay? You looka like you no feel good. You looka sad. Don be sad, Antonio. You need get some sleep. We fixa up your room like you like it – clean sheets too."

"Thanks Ma. I feel fine. I'll tell Aunt Lucy to feed me. Now you need to sleep. I'll be fine."

"Okay. I take a little nap now. Say your prayers."

"Okay Ma."

Seeing her lying there, he realized his prayers for her recovery were not to be answered. God clearly, had other plans for his mother. Tony left her side and entered his childhood bedroom knowing that this most likely would be the last time he would ever see her alive. His mother smiled at him and gestured for him to return, but he could not. The nurse would quiet her now and Tony would get the rest that he had taken from himself in order to see his mother and give her the attention and love she deserved.

— — —

Resting in his bed, the same bed he slept in as a child, staring at the ceiling, Tony's memories wandered to the times he would just lie here and listen to his 45's. The "do-wop" music of the late fifties and early sixties were so much a part of his teenage life.

He could still hear the falsetto delivery of *Frankie Valli and the Four Seasons*, the teenage lover's pain in the songs of *Dion and the Belmonts* and when the mood would be mellow and cool, he would listen to *Frank Sinatra*, Hoboken's national monument. *Those guineas could sing.* His mother loved *Frank*, his father too, but dad didn't have much time for music. He was too busy working his two jobs down on the docks.

God, Tony wished he had that music with him now. He needed the comfort of his music. Tony's teenage memories were interrupted by the invitation from the kitchen to eat. A pasta and meatball feast prepared by his Aunt Lucy awaited him. After dinner he spent hours at his mother's bedside, until he dragged his exhausted body to his bedroom and slept through the night. He slept "like a ton of bricks" as his mother would say. He didn't remember anything until he was awakened in the early morning by the sounds of many voices.

Aunt Lucy entered his room.

"Tony honey. It's time," she said.

— — —

The final morning of Maria's life, Father Gianelli from Saint John's, a close friend of the entire Rullo family, would arrive to give "Momma Rullo" Communion and to administer the *Last Rites*, the required Catholic sacrament for those close to death. Tony grew up a strict Catholic, an alter boy in his youth, with thoughts of becoming a priest. But when puberty arrived along with the Vietnam War, protests, hippies, and the Woodstock Nation, he abandoned Catholism and never looked back, until today, when he embraced it with all the strength and faith he could manage. He asked Father Gianelli to hear his confession and to give him Communion with his mom. It made him feel secure and safe, and part of his mother's life, at least for a little while.

At one o'clock in the afternoon, Tony's mother passed away. The sorrow and grief filled the small apartment with a flood of tears. Tony's family had lost a loving mother, sister, and friend. The world had lost a truly loving and caring person. The gap in Tony's heart widened. He never felt such pain. He felt it peak several days later at the funeral, as he began to withdraw from himself and from all those around him. It continued to deepen at the cemetery, as he saw his mother's casket enter the hole in the ground and disappear from his life forever. His father and now his mother lost to him in the same year. It was more than he could accept in his life. He needed to get away. He needed to deal with the grief and loss in his own way.

— — —

Tony arrived back at his parent's apartment alone. He had escaped the after funeral family gathering at his Aunt Lucy's home without anyone knowing. He walked aimlessly through the city. He walked for hours. He couldn't remember where he had walked or where he was going, only that his aimless path carried him to the only place he could ever call home – Apartment 3-C.

He entered his parents' bedroom and searched for his mother's jewelry box. Finding it in its usual place on his mother's dresser, he held it in his hands and cried from the strength of its loving memories. Handcrafted in Italy from rare hardwoods, it was a beautiful work of art. His mother loved it for as long as he could remember. It was a birthday present from his father to his mother on her twenty-first birthday. It was one of those small insignificant gifts that carried a lifetime of meaning. He found the key, opened the box and searched for the two items that would capture the memory of his parents for the rest of his life. He found his father's gold pocket watch and his mother's favorite gold heart-shaped pendant necklace and put them safely in his pocket. He packed his duffel bag with everything he could find that would aid him in his journey, emptied his mother's secret "emergency funds" coffee can of all its cash, and headed for any highway that would take him far away from his home and anyone that would remind him of his mother and father.

The next year was his personal adventure in self-pity, mourning and loneliness. How he survived the year to return to his aunt and uncle in Illinois was a testament to determination, luck and the accepting goodness of strangers.

CHAPTER 11

THE INTRODUCTION

It was over two months since the interview. From the moment he said "yes," Tony's experience at *Neil Hagman and Associates*, had been a non-stop barrage of activity with very little work in the areas of research, project development or architectural design. Instead, his workdays were filled with filing, sorting, and packing. Every hour was devoted to the organizational and administrative preparation required for the proposed project. Tony was slowly adjusting to its inevitable complexities.

Tony understood from that first day he was hired that this Baltimore office was only a temporary location, somewhere for him to "hang his hat" until it was time for the firm to relocate to its new home and begin work on the world's tallest building. He had no idea where this new building would be constructed. Not even Neil knew of its location. However, this morning, as Neil, Tony and twenty-three selected members of the *Hagman & Associates'* new project team eagerly boarded the 6:30 AM, Amtrak from Baltimore to New York City's *Pennsylvania Station*, the unknowns surrounding the project would be revealed at a noon meeting today in the *Empire Room* of the midtown New York *Verona Hotel*. The *Empire*

Room was generally reserved for high society weddings, but not today. Today, it would be filled with hundreds of talented people from a wide variety of professions waiting for answers to their many questions about this mysterious project.

Neil and Tony shared a taxi for the short uptown ride to the *Verona*. The rest of the *Hagman* team secured their transportation in rapid sequence. Arriving through the maze of traffic with an hour to spare, they gathered in the hotel's lobby opposite the entrance to the banquet room eagerly waiting for the doors to the room to be opened and their meeting to begin. They noticed the lobby slowly filling with strangers who appeared just as anxious to find out what awaited them on the other side of those doors.

The wait ended at precisely fifteen minutes before noon when a small group of men made their way through the lobby past the crowd and assembled in front of the *Empire Room's* doors. The men introduced themselves as representatives of the anonymous corporation that was responsible for the meeting. They wasted no time in asserting their authority as they immediately instructed everyone to form two lines according to the first letter of their last name, "A" through "J" in one line, the remaining alphabet in the other. They began the process of checking invitations and verifying identities. The approved were given a nametag, permitted to enter the room, and instructed to sit and wait at an assigned table. The room was brightly lit and comfortably warm. This did nothing to quell Tony's anxiety. Neil was nervous too. The others in the room shared the same common apprehension, an apprehension tempered with hopeful optimism.

Tony and Neil were sitting at a table with four people they did not know, two men and two women. The remaining members of Neil's project team were scattered randomly throughout the room. The strangers at Neil's table politely introduced themselves. After that, everyone remained silent and kept their personal information and thoughts to themselves. Tony hastily counted approximately two hundred people in the room.

The tables fronted a small portable stage. On the stage was a centrally located microphone equipped podium and eighteen chairs. All but two of the corporate group of twenty made their way from the room's entrance toward the stage. Once there, they stood and each counted the seated guests with a deliberate intensity. They compared numbers - and satisfied with the results - sat down. At precisely noon a man stood up and signaled the two men guarding the room's entrance to close and lock the doors. No invited guest from this moment on would be allowed to enter the room and would effectively be eliminated from any future participation in the project.

The standing man walked to the podium. He was tall, slender, well groomed and wore a tailored dark-blue silk suit. He checked the microphone's operation. It was working perfectly. The room was silent. He addressed the crowd.

"Ladies and Gentlemen - hello. My name is Charles Wilson and I represent one small part of an organization represented by a great man who will lead you all on an incredible journey. Thank you for accepting the opportunity to be with us today. I want to congratulate all of you for making the exclusive guest list. You are most deserving of this honor. So give yourself a well-deserved pat on the back."

"Now do me a small favor. Look around the room. Become familiar with the talented people who will be working with you as architects, engineers, scientists, physicists, and specialists in technical areas I am not sure how to define. Together you comprise a team of highly qualified professionals who will be asked to dedicate your valuable time and talents to the success of a once in a lifetime building project. Assembling this team of specialized talent was not easy. It required a careful and thorough process. That is why you were exhaustively interviewed, checked out, prodded, quantified, and qualified before being approved."

"Now for the purpose of this meeting. I know you are curious as to why you are here. The reason is simple. Today, you will finally hear from the man who is responsible for this great adventure, a man most of you will only know as, *Mr. Mogul*. I know the name is a little unusual, but that is what he prefers to be called and I think a billionaire has earned the right to be addressed by any name he so desires. Agreed?"

The assembled crowd nervously responded in agreement to a question that had only one answer. Charles smiled his approval and raised his tone of enthusiasm a few notches above the norm.

"In a few minutes, you will hear from him, not in person, but by telephone carried over the public address speakers in this room. However, I have been instructed, before he calls, to fill you in on some of the mysteries surrounding this project."

"All any of you know right now is that you will be involved in the design and construction of a building like no other on this planet. This building is planned to rise to a height of two thousand feet in honor of the United States' 1976 Bicentennial Anniversary times ten. It also is scheduled to be designed and constructed in a little over two years. Our benchmark is the Empire State Building. If that building can be built in 1931, in a little over a year, we will build this one in two."

"As some of you already know, the building will be completely self-sufficient, that means, ladies and gentlemen, that it will not be dependent on any public utility energy sources for its power. Its power will be provided with energy from the sun, wind, and water. Fuel cells and batteries will be used to supplement and store this energy. Water will be distributed from wells or transported via aqueducts from local rivers or lakes. Its hot water will be provided using the sun's energy. Human waste will be collected, stored and naturally decompose, creating methane gas to power emergency generators and fertilizer to feed the gardens of flowers and stands of trees that will surround this building."

"The building will be sited on over two hundred acres, again symbolic of the United States' Bicentennial, and ladies and gentlemen, the physical location of the building will not be revealed at this time. The only thing I can reveal is that its creation will be autonomous - free of any Federal, State and Local Government interference. It will rely on the people represented in this room to assure that this grand building is safe and devoid of any potentially harmful characteristics that will endanger its occupants or hinder its noble purpose."

"All of you will be held personally responsible for its success and its mission. As I have mentioned before, you were carefully selected not only for your individual expertise, but also for your personal integrity, strength of character, and quality life choices. For instance, none of you have a history of drug use or dependency. Incidentally, Mr. Mogul considers tobacco and alcoholic beverages as drugs and extremely addictive. If you think any differently, you have been duped by our hypocritical society and your personal rationalizations. This doesn't mean an occasional drink or smoke will have you removed from the job, it does mean however that Mr. Mogul's tolerance for any substance abuse is minimal, almost zero. No more. No less. This is his firm belief. So consider yourself warned. Please keep that in mind. By the way, with the long hours and lack of sleep necessary for this project to be completed by 1976, an occasional caffeine boost from coffee, tea or cola is allowable, free, and always in supply, but that's are far as it goes."

"Okay, I've said what I have been instructed to say. Within the hour, Mr. Mogul will call, but in the meantime while you are waiting, enjoy your lunch and take the opportunity to get to know one another."

— — —

Among a din of idle chatter, the hot lunch of salad, roast chicken, asparagus and glazed scalloped potatoes was served, although it appeared most of the people in the room were not interested in eating. Tony was among those with a muted appetite. He was eating in a tasteless daze caused by the anticipation of what was to follow lunch in less than an hour.

During the meal, casual conversations developed between Tony, Neil and the four others seated at the table. There were nervous pleasantries, jokes, and an occasional insightful comment. The initial tension at least had temporarily subsided until the after dinner desert and beverages were being served and Charles quietly made his way from his table to the podium.

"Excuse me ladies and gentlemen! Excuse me! May I have your attention please?"

The low din murmur in the room stopped. All eyes were directed toward Charles.

"Thank you. I hope everyone enjoyed their lunch. I certainly did. It was delicious. Now…back to the business at hand. Invited guests, I am pleased to announce the moment you have been waiting for is here. I have been informed that in approximately two minutes we will be receiving a telephone call from Mr. Mogul. All you have to do is sit back, relax, and enjoy his message."

Neil and Tony looked at each other and smiled. They knew that waiting for the next two minutes to pass would seem like an eternity. They only hoped that what was to follow was worth the nervous anticipation. Their waiting ended exactly two minutes later by a definitive voice radiating from the room's dedicated ceiling speakers.

"Ladies and Gentlemen, welcome to the New York *Verona*, and my skyscraper adventure. I hope all of you enjoyed your lunch. Now it is time for everyone to relax and have fun as we begin our marvelous journey. Let me begin my short speech by introducing myself."

"I am to be known as Mr. Mogul. However, as you all know by now, that is not my real name. I want to welcome all of you to my world. Charles has briefed you on my dream to create the world's greatest humanitarian building project. To me, it seems this concept is so simple and matter of fact that I've always wondered why no one has ever accomplished it before. Nevertheless, today we begin our quest to make history and I am very excited to finally begin."

"As you probably have deduced, I am a very wealthy man. I made my money in an unscrupulous but perfectly legal and socially acceptable manner, with the production, manufacturing, and selling of oil, tobacco and consumable alcohol products. Selling legalized drugs to the addicted masses and gasoline to people forced to drive gas-guzzling air polluting automobiles were the methods used to acquire my fortune. Greed, my friends, is very addictive and has no barriers. The more money I made, the more money I wanted to make and the more money I was able to make through exploitation. It was a bottomless pit of self-indulgence and I was suffocating on its pointless and meaningless reality."

"Then one day my greedy existence was derailed. I was diagnosed with lung cancer and assured that all the money in the world could not buy me a cure. It was clear to me at that time, how meaningless my life choices were. All my wealth and power were worthless. I could not buy back my life at any price. Well, by some miracle, which I will reveal later during this project, my body was cured of the cancer. The cure was free and carried out without any traditional medication. It was a simple process and the most uplifting spiritual experience any of you could ever imagine. I was given a second chance at life."

"After this miracle, I had a vision, an epiphany, that directed me to change my life. I decided to use my wealth and power for more positive humane purposes, such as developing that cure for cancer that was my salvation, providing opportunities to the less fortunate, and constructing a building that would help me achieve these two goals - a building that would be as alive as you and I. The first two items, of course, are very limited to my control, but the third was something I could accomplish and within its walls, find a way to contribute to solving the other two goals, hopefully paving the way to an endless parade of humane contributions."

"Throughout my life, I was an illusionist of sorts, mystifying the crowds with my tricks. I have always wondered and became upset about the uncontrollable circumstances that have altered my life for better and for worse. Now I am not upset. I am comfortable with my life. I am overwhelmed by my good fortune and I emphasize the word *fortune*. It is not without a many faceted interpretation. I always thought of it as that which defines monetary wealth. At this point in my life, at forty years of age, it is not in my personal definition of it as having anything to do with money. Good fortune is defined by the quality of life, and the quality of my life now is without question at a level that fills me with much optimism and happiness. I cannot wish for more except that others may share with me my wealth of life's good fortune. Infuse the people of this Earth with truth, with purpose, and their lives will be rewarded with an abundance of good fortune."

"That is my dream. That is your mission. That is our reality, and that is all I have to present to you at this time. More details will be presented at the appropriate time. So right now the fun begins for all of you as Charles hands out your assignments and coordinates your activities. Your work will begin on this project immediately when you arrive at your destination. I will talk with all of you again soon in the New Year. Enjoy your holiday season. Good luck and good fortune to all of you."

With that closing statement, the brief Mr. Mogul introduction was over.

--- --- ---

Spontaneously, as if on cue everyone in the room started discussing what they just heard. So many questions were left unanswered. So many answers were given without question.

Tony was hoping for more information. He assumed the meeting was just a test to weed out anyone not dedicated to or believing in this project. Is this why we were invited here, just to learn the man behind the mission had a life altering epiphany related to his cancer cure? There had to be more to it then this. Tony knew this was just the tip of the iceberg. Mr. Mogul, or whatever his name was, was an intelligent motivated man. He had given this information to this talented group of people to wet their appetite into wanting to know more. They knew this man was dedicated to a goal and that no one was going to alter his path toward this goal. It was a cloaked uplifting message from a rich and powerful man, who was promoting a rich and powerful cause.

The crowd continued their discussion as members of Mr. Mogul's entourage handed a 9" x 14" manila envelope to each guest. As the recipients began opening and reading the contents of their personal envelope, the confident atmosphere in the room changed to one of controlled panic. Inside each envelope was a brief description outlining their assignments and an airline ticket, dated January 6, 1974, to Billings, Montana. They had until the end of the year to gather everything they wanted to take with them for two and a half years, pack it up and have it shipped to their assigned residences in Montana. The location of the future home for all of these professionals was now known. Their specialized expertise would be focused in Billings, but the skyscraper's location still remained a mystery.

— — —

A troubled Tony sat, his stomach churning and grumbling from its unfilled state. Tony's reaction appeared to be no different from everyone else's, but it was different. It was linked to a very personal Montana experience. He looked over at Neil afraid to say anything. He wanted to tell his story to someone close to him, someone he could confide in, but there wasn't anyone that would understand - except Neil. He put his envelope on the table.

"Neil."

"What?"

"The location of this building is Billings, Montana. This may be a problem for me."

"Why? Is there something troubling about Billings? I know it's a little further west than New Jersey."

Tony was not amused by Neil's comment. He got up from his seat and motioned Neil to follow him to a private location in the room to continue their conversation. Neil followed Tony's lead.

"Tony, why all the cloak-and-dagger? What is it?" Neil asked.

"This is the deal. Of course it's not the distance. Well, not exactly. It's not that, but several years ago after my parents died—"

"What? What happened after your parents died?"

"Well after my mother died in '70, I couldn't deal with the grief so I went on an extended leave of absence from college and tried to drop out of my routine life for a year. I filled that year with hitchhiking across the country, sleeping wherever I would land for the day, and finding odd jobs to help pay my way. One of the stops in my journey was a *little* ten thousand acre ranch northwest of Billings. I stayed there for what seemed like forever, but it was only eight weeks. It was a cattle ranch. I got up at the crack of dawn, attended to the livestock, did my assigned chores, and became Montana's worse imitation of a cowboy. Despite my pathetic inexperience, everyone there treated me well and managed to teach me, with great patience and amusement, how to ride a horse and use a rope, among many other unmentionable ranch-hand things. I had a great time. It was a unique experience with the friendliest people I have ever known. What made it more unique, is that every day there, I felt more and more like this place was my home, and that I had been here before in some other life. I felt I was never going to leave. And if I were ever forced to leave this place, I knew I was going to return someday. I guess that someday is now…"

"A cattle ranch? You on a cattle ranch?" Neil said. "Wish I could've seen you in action. It sounds like hard work. I'd love to hear your cowboy stories. But apart from that, you know what? It doesn't matter why you ended up in Billings a few years ago. The important thing is that you're returning for a very good reason and that can't be bad - right? I'm sure Billings will welcome you back with open arms and without—"

"Wait. There's more to the story."

"More? Okay. Let's hear it."

"When I wasn't working the ranch on weekends, I would visit Billings with a few of the ranch hands, a cowboy's time on the town you might say. There were women, lots of them, booze, and awful Sunday morning hangovers. Well, one hangover free Sunday morning on one of these weekend adventures, I decided to take a tourist bus trip to visit the *Custer Battlefield National Monument* on the Crow Indian Reservation. It was a very troubling, informative and educational experience, but walking around the battlefields had a strange and surreal feel to it. When I returned to the ranch, I started having these recurring dreams of my parents as if they had never died. In the dream they would be walking ahead of me toward the battlefield's cemetery. They would turn and motion me to follow them. I happily complied. I would run as fast as I could into the sun, but could never catch up to them. The sun blinded me. I couldn't see. When my eyes cleared, I would be at the cemetery's boundary. My parents however, would be gone. They disappeared. Then, the sky would turn black and there I would be, alone in the dark. That's when I would wake up - every time. The dream troubled me. It was unsettling, so bad I couldn't sleep and wasn't able to work on the ranch during the day. After over a week of trying to fight through my insomnia and the effects of this dream, I left the ranch. I had to leave. I decided it was finally time to give up on my journey, return to Illinois and complete my final year of college. The dream stopped as soon as I left Montana. Now, after all these years, I am returning to Montana. So, I am a little worried that I'll start having this dream again, or worse, that something awful will eventually happen to me there. I'm sorry Neil. I know this all sounds so crazy, but I had to tell you for the sake of my sanity and the project. I don't want to flip out again. If I do that I'll be no use to anyone, especially me. I am afraid of what'll happen in Montana if I return."

Neil tried to think of something comforting to say. He moved closer, putting his arm around Tony.

"I don't know what it could mean Tony. Don't have a clue, but it doesn't have to mean anything does it? Don't worry about that dream – forget it. Know why? Because we're going to have an unforgettably great time in Montana working on this building. I've got your back. Start believing it. Everything's going to be okay."

"Hope you're right. I was going through a lot of emotional drama back then. Guess my little episode was my way of not accepting my parents' deaths."

"You're probably right, but that experience is all in your past and your work on this building is your future. Your parents would have been proud of you. They'd want you to move forward with your life - and your life right now is this building – and its home is in Billings. You need to concentrate on making Billings your new home for the next few years. You have to be one hundred percent sure about that or don't do it. So let me ask you – are you sure? 'Cause if you're not, then don't do it. You need to decide. Do you need some time to think about it?"

"No...No... I don't need any time to think about it. I'm going."

"Then it's settled?"

"I'm sure. It's settled."

"Good. I'm relieved."

"Me too. Thanks for listening. Can't tell you how much I needed to tell someone that story. Just telling it is a relief. You're the only person I've ever told it to. Thanks. I feel better now. I'll be fine."

"Well...I'm happy to hear it. Don't hesitate to talk to me anytime, about anything. You know in these past few weeks you have become more than just an employee to Lisa and me, you have become part of our family. We like you. We don't want to lose you."

"I'll keep that in mind."

"Good. Now we need to concentrate on getting our butts on that train to Baltimore and begin packing for our trip. We only have two months. That's not much time and there's so much to do. Everything's happening too fast to make much sense of it, so let's not try now."

"I agree, but what still doesn't make sense to me, is why I'm here in the first place. What the hell am I doing here, Neil? Seriously…look at these people. There are so many experienced, talented professionals here, for God's sake. I'm so far out of my league. I'm not sure I have the talent and experience to be working on a project like this. Can you help me out here? It's bugging me. Explain to me again so I can fully understand. Why did Mr. Mogul choose me? Why me?"

"Jesus Tony! If it isn't one thing with you, it's another. First the dream and then this again. As I've mentioned to you before, I honestly don't know how Mr. Mogul chose you. But from getting to know you these last few weeks, I know *why* he picked you."

"Why?"

"In choosing you, not only did Mr. Mogul know of your talent he must also have known something of your character."

"Such as? Sorry. I'm just feeling a little unsure of myself right now."

"That's okay. I understand. As for your character…let's see…there are many things. Most importantly, you have vision. You're always open to exploring new ideas, new technologies, and applying them to improve the way we design buildings today. Hell…the way we should live our lives. I call it a stubborn benevolent optimism."

"Really? You know some of my Prof's made it very clear to me that my *stubborn optimism,* as you've labeled it, made me too unconventional – too rebellious to be a successful architect. Told me I didn't have what it takes to be an architect in today's world. Said my head was lost in the clouds."

"Well, they were obviously mistaken. You're head will be lost in the clouds, except it'll be at the top of a two-thousand foot building. Send them a picture *from the clouds,* proving them wrong. But seriously - you have what it takes. Sometimes greatness has to be awakened by the right opportunity. You have been given the opportunity and will rise to the occasion. I sincerely believe that."

"Thank you, Neil. It means a lot to me hearing you say that, but I always feel like I am constantly the rebel – always swimming against the tide."

"Tony, you *are* rebellious, but not in a destructive way, in a positive creative way. You see things in this world - the hypocrisies, the lies, the deceit and you want to eliminate these negative elements from the world. That is exactly the type of person that we want on this project. Mr. Mogul knew that about you when he selected you. Most of the people he has recruited for this project are just like you. They are talented. They are anxious. They are frustrated. They want to contribute and they believe in this building's potential. I was greatly impressed after reviewing your solar design work before and during our interview. It wasn't so much the illustrated concepts or written theories, but the humane tone - the attitude. It related to someone who wanted to offer something of value to the world. It was unfortunate that some of your college professors couldn't recognize your special talents."

"Okay. I guess it's time for me to stop asking *why* and to start concentrating totally on the *how* of designing this building."

"That would be good place to start."

"Neil…one more question…"

"Oh God. Another one? This can't be good."

"It's a personal question. Nothing big."

"With you, it's never anything small. Okay - what is it now Tony?"

"I was just curious. Do you know Mr. Mogul's identity – his real name?"

"Nope."

"…but I thought you had met with him personally before my interview."

"I did. It's always been at my office in Baltimore under heavy security. He travels by private jet with two very large scary bodyguards. He has a limo waiting for him at the airport to take him anywhere he needs to go. I don't know his real name or his organization other than it's located in New York City. I don't ask too many questions. I just accept the arrangement. Besides being very wealthy, he's a helluva nice person…smart…confidant and dedicated. Couldn't ask for a better owner."

"What do you think of the unusual relationship? Is it working?"

"Yeah - it's working, although not in the traditional 'Owner-Architect,' sense. It's still way too early in the project to know for sure, there's so much to do yet, but yeah - it works for me. I like it. It's never dull, that's for sure. I talk to Charlie a lot. He's Mr. Mogul's right hand man. Pretty smart guy too. I think he's a civil engineer. Don't really know. He keeps his background to himself. What I do know, what I was promised by Mr. Mogul, is that sometime during the duration of this project, he will reveal his identity to me - just not now. Does that do it for you? Curiosity satisfied?"

"That'll do it for now. It's a strange story, but a good one. Thanks. Just had to ask. Well...looks like the room's clearing out. We better follow the crowd and start heading back to Baltimore."

"Yeah. Can't wait to get back home to tell Lisa of our new Montana home."

"Lisa? Lisa's coming to Montana? I didn't know that. Thought only those people invited here from our Baltimore office were relocating."

"Come on Tony. Did you honestly think that I would leave Lisa back in Baltimore? She's my Siamese twin – the love of my life. I could never survive this project without her. I have her ticket right here. She'll be excited."

"That's great. That's great. Happy to hear it. That's great," Tony said.

The two men with the *Hagman and Associates*, project team in tow, pushed their way toward the exits, through the crowd of their newly adopted brothers and sisters. This skyscraper project team, empowered with an enlightened sense of determination and purpose, was on its way. Their once in a lifetime adventure was about to begin.

CHAPTER 12

THE ARMANI MAN

The mysterious "Mr. Mogul" was born James "Jim" Jeffrey Bradshaw on March 23 in 1933. He grew up on a forty-acre estate a few miles west of downtown Houston. On the estate was a six-thousand square-foot, eight-bedroom house adorned with a swimming pool and tennis court. Jim had two bedrooms, one for him and one for his invited overnight guests. There was also a small house, a few hundred feet from the main, where the servants lived. The detached four-car garage housed three cars that were strangely un-American and all named Mercedes-Benz. The fourth car was always a more typical Texas made Lincoln Continental.

His parents were stereotypical high school sweethearts. His father was the senior varsity quarterback - his mother the junior homecoming queen. It was an inevitable romance. They attended the University of Houston together and married one year after graduation. Before he was thirty, Jim's father quickly ascended the corporate ladder to become a prominent *Vision Oil Company* – VOC – executive vice-president.

Entertaining guests with weekly gourmet dinners, cocktail parties and extravagant outdoor barbecues was the normal routine practiced by Jim's parents at the Bradshaw residence.

The predominance and free consumption of alcohol and tobacco by the guests at these affluent parties and his constant exposure to oil industry executives, continuously surrounded Jim throughout his formulative years. This seductive party atmosphere coupled with the city's cowboy and oil baron culture strongly influenced him as a child and was woven into the fabric of whom he was eventually to become.

As a child Jim did not fully comprehend how his father was able to amass such enormous amounts of money. He did know it had something to do with selling oil, lots of oil – specifically petroleum. As he grew older, Jim became more aware of his father's importance in the oil business and how it enabled him to experience a life that was for him, without financial limits. Knowing this, he took full advantage of every opportunity made available to him. He was provided an exclusive private elementary and secondary school education. He loved school, never missing a day, always placing at the top of his class in every academic subject.

He was born with an abundance of natural physical ability. Despite this athleticism, he avoided any meaningful participation in team sports of any kind. He thought of organized sports as a waste of his valuable time. He was not a team player. He felt true winning, could only be achieved by individual accomplishment.

Jim grew to be an exceptionally handsome, personable and confident young man. Women loved him, but he never allowed himself to be involved in a serious relationship. He discarded women in the same manner as his empty cigarette packs. His parents wanted him to marry one of the many high society debutants from Houston's elite social strata, but Jim rejected this cookie cutter approach to life. He had other more worthwhile plans for his future.

— — —

After his graduation from High School, he chose to break from family tradition and attend a public institution, accepting a full academic scholarship to the state supported University of Texas, in Austin. It was time, Jim decided, to leave home. Austin provided him the needed distance from Houston's social climate and his parent's influence. It allowed him the opportunity to achieve independence and a renewed perspective on his life.

To fuel this independence, between academic years, Jim wouldn't return home for the summer. Instead he visited Europe, traveling its many roads and countries, while freely spending his father's money, and experiencing the European life style.

On the day of his Phi-Beta-Kappa graduation from the University of Texas, his father offered him a generous graduation "gift." It was unsurprisingly, an upper management position with VOC. Jim was grateful and flattered by the offer, but to his parents' amazement, he refused the opportunity. He explained his reasoning to his father - *it just wasn't something he wanted to do with his life now. He wanted to give himself the chance to make it on his own, without his father's help.* It was a convenient lie. What he did not tell his father was what he *really* wanted. Jim wanted to achieve more power, influence, and wealth than his father ever did. With his postgraduate degree in Business Administration in hand he began to examine the reality of that goal.

CHAPTER 13

THE MONTANA TRIP

JANUARY 1974

The flight from Baltimore to Chicago for Tony, Neil, and the Hagman project team was uneventful. The connecting flight to Billings however, was anything but forgettable. There were more than seventy-five people on the privately chartered Boeing 707, all associated with the project. The passengers were apprehensive and unsure about what awaited them in Montana. What was expected of them there? The state appeared too remote and desolate to be seriously considered as the site for this state of the art building.

Since his unsettling experiences in Montana, except for his one infamous dart burying its pointy nose within the state's boundaries, Tony hadn't allowed himself to think much about this obscure state. Still, his feelings about returning and living there were so detached from reality, he felt like he was taking a trip not to Montana, but to the *Land of Oz*.

During the flight, Tony and Neil sat together. Tony occupied the aisle seat and Neil sat by the window. The middle seat was intentionally left empty. Thirty minutes into the flight, an exhausted Neil fell asleep. Tony soon followed. It was only two o'clock in the afternoon, by Central Standard Time standards, but it felt to them both like it was after midnight. They slept until the sounds of an early dinner being served a hour later, jolted them from their well-deserved naps.

Neil leaned over to Tony and gave him a friendly shove. "Tony. Hey Tony. Wake up. It's time to eat," he said.

Tony needed a few seconds to clear his head and realize he wasn't safely home in his bed, but in an uncomfortable passenger seat on a plane to Billings. As he slowly returned to a useful consciousness, he looked at Neil and smiled.

"Hey buddy. What'd you say? Dinner? Good. That's good. I'm really hungry. When do we get ours?" he said.

"Soon. Smell it? Smells good. What do you think they're serving?" Neil said. "Welcome back to the land of the living. Good nap? How you feelin?"

Before Tony could answer, he was interrupted by the pilot's amplified voice coming from the aircraft's speakers.

"Ladies and Gentleman, this is Captain Wainwright, your pilot speaking. I hope you all are comfortable and being provided with the best possible accommodations during this flight. Our flight conditions have been excellent and we should be arriving in Billings in about thirty minutes."

"Now, I have been instructed to pass on to you a previously recorded message by the man who is paying all the bills and my salary, Mr. Mogul. So sit back, relax, listen, and hopefully learn. After you hear this remember, *Dorothy*, you're not in Kansas anymore."

...I knew we were going to Oz... Tony thought.

The message began.

"Greetings my esteemed colleagues, scientists, engineers and architects. You'll notice I omitted any reference to my lawyers and accountants. They are on another flight and I will spare you too much contact with those people who will be involved with the unfortunate, but necessary, aspects of this project."

"Without further *adieu*...forgive me, I always wanted to say that...I will now reveal the project's location. This great building of ours will be constructed on the Native American Crow Reservation. The Reservation is located approximately sixty miles east of Billings, Montana. The building's design and construction personnel, except for a few select individuals, will be living off the reservation in and around the city of Billings."

"In addition to my personally selected staff of professionals, I will be employing the Crow people from the reservation to assist us in the construction of our skyscraper and will be providing employment opportunities for most of them within the building after its completion."

"As you know, the building will not require power from public utility companies, since its power will be self generated using solar panels, wind turbines and hydro-electric resources. What you did not know, is the primary function of this building, upon its completion, will be to house a corporation focused on utilizing the unlimited potential of our natural resources to develop our built environment in a less destructive manner. This corporation will concentrate on the extensive development of alternative energy sources that could be used to power everything from automobiles to the way we dispose of our garbage. It will also concentrate on acquiring funding for the construction of new roads, homes, businesses, and schools for the reservation. From within its skyscraper's walls, it will attempt to provide much more of what will fully benefit humanity."

"That's it. That is all I have to say to you today. Have a safe journey to Billings. Good luck and good fortune."

Tony began to reflect on the obvious impact that this message had on him and his future...*I knew it...I'm returning to the site of my dream...how bizarre is that... how am I supposed to react...will I end up a casualty like those buried in the battlefield's cemetery...?* These questions were served to Tony along with dinner, as the 707 cruised to the Promised Land.

CHAPTER 14

THE PARIS CONNECTION

SUMMER 1956

Jim Bradshaw used his post graduation time remaining in Houston filling his days with hours of serious leisure. After three months of this pointless routine, the defining moment in his life had arrived. He decided it was now time to get to work, time to embark on a financially rewarding career that would carry him through life with all the wealth he required to satisfy his unquenchable thirst for material desires, and most importantly to him - power.

He began his quest by returning to Europe, specifically France, to think through his future in the beckoning world of endless financial opportunity. It was here, in the summer of 1956, at an outdoor Paris café, where Jim was sorting through his many possible career choices, that fate offered him a subtle answer to his future, placing him in the presence of a prominent *Teamspring Tobacco Company* employee.

This person was placing his *derrière* in a chair at an unoccupied table, unaware at the time that a distracted Jim, was trying to achieve the same result. They became aware of one another as their rear-ends bumped while simultaneously selecting the chosen chair. Jim was the first to speak. Excusing himself, he politely offered the chair and desired table to the stranger. The stranger did the same to Jim. As each person tried graciously to decline the table's offered occupancy to the other, a conversation developed leading to the discovery that both men were born and raised in the "great lone-star state" of Texas.

Sharing this common bond, the two men, one, young brash and twenty-three, the other – Richard Runor - eighteen years older, and a worldly experienced corporation executive, had no trouble agreeing to share the table, striking up a conversation about everything Texas, Paris, and female. After a few hours of talking and consuming large quantities of wine and fine French cuisine, the conversation evolved into an alcohol-inspired lecture from Richard, about the tobacco industry. He started to reveal to Jim the future goals of the cigarette industry in America, as the lights of Paris innocently reflected off their wine glasses.

— — —

The lecture began as Richard told Jim, "…well, let me tell you cowboy. You know…or…maybe you don't. Oh, what tha hell…let me just say it. Jim, it's been recently reported… sensationalized…that people have been dying in increasing numbers after World War number Two from of all things - lung cancer. The big city boys and their newspapers, and… *Time…Newsweek…*you know, those liberal news rag mags are blaming it on cigarettes! They've managed to scare the be-jeeus out of the general public with stories from "experts" about unproven reported health risks associated with the so-called hazardous properties of tobacco, you know - saying there are nasty chemicals supposedly present in cigarettes that are contributing to this outbreak of lung cancer. Can't prove it as far as I'm concerned. It's pure bullshit I say - bullshit straight from a long horn's ass..."

Richard further elaborated, that because of this negative documentation, the cigarette industry, including *Teamspring*, had to counterattack by immediately discrediting these health reports and developing new marketing strategies to turn this threat to their advantage. They conspired with other US tobacco companies to development like-minded advertising that manipulated information to deceive the smoking and non-smoking public into believing that these adverse health claims had little basis in fact. Bradshaw sat in amazement - intrigued - as Mr. Runor discussed the projected evolution of the tobacco industry in its illusionary development of "healthier" cigarettes.

Richard continued, "...adding a filter to the cigarette gives the smoker the illusion of lessened health risks...you know, by cleaning up the smoke, but partner, filters realistically have little effect on removing any of tobacco's harmful shit, especially and luckily for *Teamspring*, its addictive nicotine properties. With the right advertising slant, smokers would feel safer, cleaner and guiltless...they all will be 'freed from the threat' necessary to satisfy their nicotine addiction..."

A low tar and nicotine cigarette, Richard indicated, was also being developed.

"...the beauty of this type of cigarette Jim, is that it will actually increase cigarette consumption. The lower amounts of nicotine will force smokers to smoke more cigarettes to satisfy their normal nicotine cravings. More cigarettes smoked, more cigarettes sold, and more profits made for *Teamspring*. Think about it...just advertising low tar cigarettes as 'healthier' will stimulate sales..."

To Jim, the tactics seemed endless; long cigarettes, short cigarettes, flavors, colors, and cigarettes created especially for women. There would be the introduction of cigarette packs containing coupons redeemable for domestic household products and sporting goods.

Jim listened intently as Richard continued.

"...sporting goods are targeted directly at the man, but attractive household products were specifically selected to entice women - the wives or girlfriends of their smoking male partners. As long as they benefited from acquiring free household merchandise, through the accumulation of hundreds of cigarette pack coupons, they wouldn't be worrying about any health risks resulting from their husband's or boyfriend's habitual smoking. It's also a good bet that they will take up smoking themselves to hasten the coupon collection process –"

"Holy shit! What a great plan! You get more women to smoke and there's no limit!" Jim said.

"You're right partner, but it doesn't stop there...not until the marketing geniuses get into the act. Marketing cigarettes will become extremely aggressive. More emphasis will be focused on television advertisements targeting women *and* teenagers. We will appeal to men's macho egos by hiring respected athletes and macho-men stereotypes to endorse their 'God-given' manly right to smoke...and billboard and magazine advertising, and free samples to our troops overseas would be increased dramatically...and I ain't finished yet –"

"There's more?" Jim said.

"Yup. Wait'll you hear this. We have employed doctors. Doctors, mind you, to endorse our cigarettes! That will put a lot of folks mind at ease. I helped out with that little advertising gem – "

"That *is* pure genius..." Jim said.

"Thanks cowboy. Yes suh - we have dozens of hard smoking MD's under contract. We're working out the ad campaign details. As for athletes, we have quite a few. We already have Joe DiMaggio under contract. Imagine that – 'Joltin Joe' a habitual smoker. What can I say? He likes money and women. Lots of it. We also have an actor playing a cowboy dude on a horse, riding among the cows in the wide-open spaces of somewhere with a cig hanging from his lip. He's probably a fag who's never been on a horse before. But what the hell, it's the image that's important, not the reality. He'll make us millions. Cigarette?"

"Don't mind if I do. Thanks. Say…these are *French* smokes."

"I know. I know. I apologize. Pure garbage, but what can ya do? Ran out of *Teamspring* smokes and you gotta take what ya can get. Light?"

"Thanks. That's some story, Richard."

"Oh, you all ain't heard nothin' yet. I've saved the best for last…"

"What's that?"

"Research and development, Jim - those chemical genius bastards over in R&D. Garcon!…More wine here please…"

Richard became more animated as he continued his discussion.

"…R&D is manipulating the cigarette's chemical composition, developing special tobacco blends that include additives and fillers intended to create a cigarette that is much more addictive, flavorful, burns faster, and is cheaper to produce. Do you believe that? Viva la science, eh, Jim? Whad ya think partner? You like? Ain't it ingenious? I'm excited about the endless possibilities. We'll make more money than God - all at the expense of those poor bastards – those tobacco addict saps. I almost feel sorry for them, until I check my bank account, then everything's okay." Richard laughed. "Where is that wine?…Garcon!"

The waiter approached the table of the two rowdy Americans, thinking he had every right to kill them and dispose of their bodies in the Seine if they sang another chorus of *The Yellow Rose of Texas*. Another bottle of wine was only going to add fuel to his justifiable desire.

"Can't you see our bottle's empty partner? We all want another bottle of the same vino, please. Great wine, eh Jimbo?"

"That's France. Great wine – lousy cigarettes," Jim said.

"Yeah. Wait'll they get a whiff of our smokes in a year or so. Heh! We'll get their asses too. The world is ours. *Teamspring* cigarettes shall rule the world!" Richard shouted.

"Amen to that! Yee hah!" a thoroughly drunk Jim echoed.

"Yee hah!" Richard returned the rebel yell.

With that last *yee-hah* the waiter was looking for any sharp utensil to forcefully insert into the bodies of these obnoxious American cowboys. Fortunately for the Texas duo, he reconsidered and reluctantly served them another bottle.

"Drink up cowboy! To our success! Remember the Alamo!" Richard said.

"Remember the Alamo!"

The Texans drank and, unfortunately for the waiter, broke into song again, continuing into the early morning hours in this Paris Café. It was to become an unforgettable evening for Jim, one that charted his path to a future without limits.

--- ---

Jim was always lucky – something that followed him around like it was his birthright. Richard's intoxication enabled him to lose all inhibition – clouding his judgment - allowing him to freely confide to a stranger the potentially harmful and ingeniously deceptive future sales strategies of *Teamspring*.

It was a good thing. Jim was fascinated. He was excited about the possibilities of making money this way. He wanted to know more. He wanted to be part of this endless insatiable conspiracy and get rich being part of it. He asked Richard, if there was any way he could get a job with *Teamspring*. Richard was impressed with *Texas Jim* and agreed to set him up with an interview when he returned to Raleigh.

At evening's end they shook hands, parting as friends, agreeing to get in touch when back in the 'States. Jim Bradshaw, the young confident college graduate, knew with Richard's help, he was on his way to fulfilling his dreams.

— — —

Jim got the job. He would not be denied this opportunity and his salesmanship, enthusiasm and father's influence were far too impressive for any hiring executive to ignore.

His rise at *Teamspring* was nothing short of miraculous. He was given a position in marketing and sales, successfully making the company millions in profits. He used every company backed cigarette promotion, gimmick, lie, and deceit tactic available to him to sell his company's product. He even introduced some of his own design, such as entire television shows sponsored by *Teamspring* and hosted by a *Teamspring* smoking emcee. His aggressive non-stop work style and results earned him notice and within his first five years he was promoted, as his father was, to Executive Vice President in charge of Television Marketing and Advertising. He was on his self-appointed schedule to become a very rich man.

However, that wasn't enough to satisfy his insatiable ambition.

He left *Teamspring* several years following his promotion and started his own privately financed tobacco company in 1966 that produced expensive designer cigarettes and ersatz "Cuban" cigars. One year later he purchased a small Kentucky distillery and added liquor, beer and wine products to his company's resume. His company, *Bradshaw Enterprises, Inc.*;

became *Bradshaw Enterprises International*, better known around the world simply as BEI. By 1970, Jim at thirty-seven was a multi-millionaire. Then, in 1971, his father invited him to be a member of the Board of Directors of *Vision Oil*. This time he enthusiastically accepted. Jim Bradshaw's millions, became billions.

— — —

Making his money was all about influencing people to consume an endlessly insatiable product. There was never a downside to this marketing strategy. It was all about consumption, and the insatiable consumption of oil, tobacco and alcohol, would never end, at least not in his lifetime.

The products he sold were addictive and he loved that quality in them. They were not only addictive but had the ability of giving the illusion of enriching and stimulating people's lives, but in fact did the opposite. Bradshaw didn't care; it was making him lots of money. Besides, he was a frequent user of these products and loved them. He would drink up to a quart of Scotch in a day and his three pack a day habit didn't even concern him. It was the fuel he used to get him through his insanely busy days.

Moreover, all the vehicles and equipment in the world that required oil and gasoline for their operation – *well- that was the pot of gold at the end of the rainbow. That was the ultimate money tree that would never die.* He was grateful for his father's contributions to this part of his rich and prosperous life.

CHAPTER 15

THE PHILOSOPHERS

JANUARY 1974

The Mr. Mogul traveling road show of prominent professionals, with Tony and Neil part of this gypsy caravan, somehow found their way to the city of Billings, Montana. The entire group of weary Chicago travelers would spend their first Montana evening at the Billings' *Cattle King Hotel*, a local establishment with great food and tons of personality. Part of the hotel's charm was its replica old west saloon. It was a charming place for this merry band of road warriors to celebrate the beginning of this great project before they separated and settled into their individually assigned Montana homes. They needed one last crazy night out before the cell doors closed behind them beginning their two and a half-year sentence of dedication and hard work. The saloon was used to its full potential by the Mogul party until its 2:00 AM closing time.

The next morning, foggy eyed and excited, they traveled to what was to be the exclusive Billings headquarters for the Mogul Skyscraper project team. It was a converted furniture warehouse, which had stood abandoned for many years.

The Mogul Company would occupy the entire three floors of this renovated twenty thousand square foot building until the skyscraper's completion. The "warehouse" would remain open twenty-four hours a day - seven days a week - to accommodate the non-stop production necessary to bring the two-thousand foot skyscraper to completion by its scheduled completion date.

When Tony and Neil arrived at the warehouse on this early winter morning, their first assignment was waiting for them. It was immediate and simple. They were to attend an informal "get acquainted" meeting at nine o'clock in the morning with the Crow Reservation Tribal Council. Wasting no time they commandeered a waiting company car and began their drive to the Crow Reservation and the city of Crow Agency. They had little time to prepare for where they were going or what to expect. Accessing US Highway 87-212, they started their trip east. After less than an hour of driving, the two men were experiencing the expanse of uninhabited real estate that surrounded the highway. Neil was both in awe and exhilarated. Tony was neither.

Tony was reflecting on his bus ride years ago to the Custer Battlefield. He thought during that trip...the *ranch was big and empty but it doesn't compare with what I'm experiencing on this bus ride...this was where empty went when it wanted to be alone...* It was unsettling to him at the time. He let Neil know of his feelings.

"Neil, do you realize if we ever get lost out here or our car breaks down, no one will find us for weeks? There is nothing out here! We'd be food for the coyotes or whatever animals they have out here that enjoy eating dead people from Maryland."

"I thought you were an experienced Montana Big Sky cowboy, Tony. You should be familiar with this wilderness. You've been out here before on a bus tour – remember?"

"It was different then. It wasn't freezing outside. It was summer. I was with a busload of people…and on the ranch…on the ranch…there was always someone around to watch my back. I was always with a bunch of other experienced cowboys. Right now, it's just you and me. You're no experienced Montana cowboy, Neil. No offense…"

"None taken. I *appreciate* the vote of confidence. Didn't think I appeared that helpless. In any event, I think you're overreacting a little. You have to learn to relax. People around here travel these roads every day and I haven't heard reports of anyone being eaten by wild animals."

"I hope you're right. Tell me we're almost there."

"We have about thirty miles to go. Hey Tony?"

"Yes."

"It's beautiful out here. Whad ya say? We have some extra time to kill before the meeting. How 'bout we take a slight detour on one of these dirt roads off the Highway and get a little closer to God."

"Are you serious or crazy or just seriously crazy? It's freezing out there. I left my Eskimo parka at home. Now I know we're gonna die."

"Take it easy. We'll be fine. We are *wearing* coats although yours may be a little light for this weather."

"What's wrong with a New York Yankees baseball jacket? It's all I have to wear until the rest of my stuff gets here."

"That's okay. I noticed some blankets in the car. That should keep you warm enough. According to the map we can work our way back to the highway a few miles up the road. Is that okay with you?"

"No."

"Come on. Aren't you up for a little adventure?"

"What part of *no* don't you understand?"

"Come on. Don't be a *wus*. Give it a shot. I'll be careful. How 'bout it?"

"You are a pushy guy, aren't you? *How 'bout it?* Does it matter? I thought I made it clear the thought doesn't thrill me. However, since it illogically appears you really want to do this Lewis and Clark *thing*, I'll reluctantly agree to go along with your insanity. You're the boss and as your humble employee, remember…I am putting my fragile life in your hands. Just don't get us lost. No one will ever find us."

"We won't get lost. Trust me. Let's go."

They pulled off the highway at the next exit. After a few minutes on an unmarked county dirt road that was slowly distancing itself from Highway 212, they decided to pull over to collect their thoughts and absorb their surroundings. The project's realities were being uncovered and thrust at them at an alarming rate. They both knew, they desperately needed time to reflect on the events that would soon be unfolding before them during the next two and a half years. This was as good a place and time as any to do just that.

They sat quietly in the car watching the road dust settle around them. After a few minutes of this unstructured meditation, Neil said,

"Let's walk a little. Is that okay?"

"Do I have a choice?"

"No. Grab those blankets and let's do it. We'll get to see how tough we are. Consider it project skyscraper basic training."

"Whatever you say, Sergeant Neil."

They left the warm friendly confines of their car and started to walk in no particular direction. After twenty minutes they halted their stroll and decided to sit on the cold hard ground, something their frostbitten butts would later regret. Sitting cross-legged wrapped in their blankets facing south on the great open plains that were part of the Crow Indian reservation in Montana, Neil and Tony began to reflect on the reality of the path they would soon begin to walk. Tony was the first to break the cold eerie silence.

"In your wildest imagination, did you ever believe that you would become involved in a project as isolated, advanced and imaginative as this?"

"In some obscure way, I did kiddo. I believe everyone, and that includes you and me, is born for that one event in life that is our legacy and our birthright to fulfill. Unfortunately, because of where we are in the evolutionary ladder of human existence, many of us go to our deaths under achieving and over indulging. It's sad. It's a waste of a life."

"That's interesting, Neil. Why so serious?"

"I know it's a little deep, but it's the only reason I can rationalize being here. Otherwise, why would I be sitting here in this place - so peaceful - so vast - so cold, so devoid of the unnecessary complexities of life? It's all because of the endless possibilities that this building will represent."

"I agree. It's all I ever think about. Think our building will be as beautiful and uncomplicated as this place?"

"That's the plan and you'll be a major contributor to its grand design. However, it's not our building – is it? Not yet anyway. It's still Mr. Mogul's. Although, he thinks of it as the world's building and if it's everything it's meant to be, then it will be part of this landscape in harmony with nature, not in opposition to it, like most everything we humans build. We are just the tools for its creation. I hope we can meet the challenge and the opportunities that it will present to us. After all, it's not really a building is it? It's an extension of humanity without the guilt of displacing nature or the reprisal of being dependent on environmentally unfriendly resources for its existence. It benefits all who are fortunate enough to experience it."

"Jesus Neil! You are being quite the philosopher today. I've never heard you so serious before. What's going on in that head of yours?"

"It's the way I feel right now. It's this place. It does something to me. That's how I know that this building will never fall short of its noble goals. It's part of being here in this place surrounded by its unlimited possibilities. I'm feeling so good, I wouldn't mind staying here forever."

"I knew it. You do want us not to be found. Let me know when you're ready to return to the real world. Okay? I'm just going to sit here until you become of sound mind. Hurry, because I'm about to pass out and freeze to death."

Wrapped in his blanket, a shivering Tony looked up into the clear blue sky

He looked over at Neil and started to speak his thoughts out loud.

"Hey Neil."
"What?"
"What do you know about this meeting?"

"Not much - other than a man named *Johnny Thunder Eagle* will be heading it. He's the reservation's project coordinator. I understand he is a full-blooded Crow. It'll be a short meeting - just a preliminary "kick-off" to introduce us to the reservation Tribal Council and a few other things. It should be interesting. I understand Johnny and Mr. Mogul have a close personal relationship. He didn't elaborate on the *how* and *why*.

"Everyone seems to know the Mogul except for me. Oh well. At least I get to meet *Johnny Thunder Eagle* – interesting name. A full-blooded Crow? How old is he?"

"Your age, I think."

"Interesting."

"You already said that."

"I know, but a Native American represents such a different culture. I get it now. This building is a marriage between our different cultures - the building's design - the reservation - the Native American connection. It's all so natural." Tony began to digress. "You know what doesn't make sense Neil, is the differences between the races here on Earth... Why are we physically different? Why isn't there a logical explanation as to *why*? On reservation land, we are designing a building to be constructed and occupied by a race of people we call Indians or Native Americans – the red man. They have been oppressed, murdered and subjugated to a life on a restricted area labeled a reservation by the very society in which we live. We have enslaved black people in this country. People of different races are fighting one another throughout the world and I can't understand *why*."

"Where in the hell did that come from? Now who's being a philosopher?"

"It's your fault. You're a bad influence."

"Yeah – right. Do me a favor for right now."

"What?"

"Let's just sit here and enjoy this moment for a little while longer before the cold air forces us to retreat back to the car. Tony, watch the sun in the sky as it smiles on us with its potential to provide us with a promising future and all the fuel we will ever need for living."

"Oh my God! It's back! Just when I thought it was safe, Neil the philosopher returns. I tell you what, leave your heavy thinking here for the day and when we get back to Billings, you can open a philosophy shop for your coworkers back at the furniture warehouse. Maybe we could invite some of the locals to attend so they can learn how to communicate with their cows."

"That's pretty funny! I guess you're saying you've had enough lectures from Professor Neil for today?"

"Yes. I've had enough of this deep freezer thinking. Can we get back to the car before you decide to walk into the wilderness in search of your true self."

"In a minute. Before we leave, there's something I need to tell you. I was going to wait, but this seems as good a time as any. I had a talk with Mr. Mogul last night. He finally let me know some of the mysteries surrounding the creation of this project. He also told me about your selection. I'm telling you now because I was ordered not to tell you until we were firmly planted on Crow Reservation soil. We're close enough. Now's the time."

Tony's eyes widened with anticipation. "Really? Okay, let's have it…"

"Are you ready for this? Mr. Mogul believes…now this is what he told me…he believes he was guided in choosing you by the Great Spirit – the *giver of all life* as believed by the Crow and Native Americans in general."

"The what? The *Great Spirit*?! Do you seriously want my head to explode? What kind of bizarre selection process is that?"

"He said you will understand it better in a few days."

"How? How will I understand in a few days? Tell me how."

"Can't do it Tony. I have been given my orders not to, under penalty of death."

"Come on Neil. Tell me!"

"Can't do it. Can't do it. You'll have to wait. It's only a few days."

"Don't be such an asshole! You know how I hate not knowing. It's driving me crazy. I should just run back to the car and leave you here to freeze. I know you can't catch me in time before I started the car and drove off."

"I knew I shouldn't have left the keys in the car."

"You should have thought of that before you decided to torture me."

"Just be patient. Give it a few days. Everything will be much clearer then."

"Okay. You're still an asshole."

"I love you too."

"Yeah. Yeah. Okay, I'll wait. Obviously, I have no choice. Can we go now or I *WILL* leave you here."

"Yes, we can go now. Don't get so excited."

"I'm still running back to the car. I'm beginning to lose all feeling in my butt. I'll have it started and warmed up before you get there - *turtle man*."

"Your butt?"

"No… the car, you moron."

"You run then. Run fast. Warm up butt. Warm up car. *Moron Turtle Man* will jog."

"Attempt a fast jog. I've seen you jog. It is turtle like. We have about a mile to go. We need to get there before sunset, so speed it up. One more thing before you eat my dust."

"What's that?"

"I'm looking forward to this meeting. I've never met a full-blooded Native American before."

"Me too. Me too. You can ask them about the Great Spirit's adopting you when we get there."

"Have I mentioned *asshole*?"

"Yeah, a couple times. If we can put your anal references on hold for now, let's proceed to our assigned destination. Our Native American project team is eagerly awaiting our arrival.

This has been a very rewarding adventure for me, especially my 'off-road' philosophy sessions…don't you think? Happy we took this break. See you back at the car in a few."

"Okay. I'm off. Watch my blanket fly in the wind."

CHAPTER 16

THE CANCER

One day in the spring of 1972, the workaholic profit centered world of Jim Bradshaw, changed forever. During an innocent business lunch with clients while discussing world politics, smoking his perpetual cigarette, and sipping his usual Macallan thirty year old on the rocks, he coughed.

It was an innocent cough, except this one had a unique result.

Covering his mouth with a white linen napkin as he usually did, he excused himself. As the napkin was lowered to his lap, he noticed a cluster of small red spots on it. It was blood. He had coughed up blood. This was cause for concern. His heart began to race as he imagined what it could be. He felt fine. He was experiencing no pain-no discomfort, but there was blood. *It was only a few spots. Maybe it was something I ate or an infected irritated throat. That was probably it. It was probably nothing.*

That *nothing* was investigated and diagnosed as lung cancer – an advanced form of lung cancer. The best and most expensive doctors in the world told him it was inoperable and not curable by any means known.

He was ordered to stop smoking and drinking. Most importantly, he had to immediately get his personal and business affairs in order. His life would soon be over. He did what he had to do. He revised his will. He began his travel around the country, reviewing his businesses and appointing new leadership that would follow him after his death.

His lung cancer was in its final stages and his life expectancy was estimated to be less than a year. He was coughing constantly. He had to be watched by his bodyguards continuously so he wouldn't try to sneak a cigarette or take a drink. His cigarette cravings or his desire for his precious Scotch never stopped consuming him. He couldn't understand what difference it could possibly make in his present fatal condition to smoke or drink, but he made every effort to abstain anyway.

― ― ―

It was on a flight to Denver months after his diagnosis that something happened to redirect his fate onto a different path.

Because of the weather, his company plane was forced to detour from its scheduled flight path. According to the instrument data, it was developing undefined mechanical problems. It needed to make an emergency landing at the closest airport able to accommodate its reported repairs. That airport happened to be in Billings, Montana. It was here, at this small insignificant airport, that Jim Bradshaw had his epiphany.

While sitting in the deserted airport's modest bar waiting for his plane to be repaired, drinking only a club soda, contemplating his last days on Earth, a person sat down on the bar stool next to him. This person, although a complete stranger to Jim, was not sitting next to him by chance. He was placed here deliberately. Jim looked over at the man with a feeling that he had met him somewhere, sometime before.

He continued to stare at the man. From his physical features it was obvious; this man was an American Indian, a Native American. He was young, tall and lean, with long braided black hair and dark toned brownish red skin. He was remarkably handsome and physically imposing.

The man felt the inquisitive stare from Jim, looked directly at him, and spoke.

"Hello. How are you today?"

"Hello. I'm okay… and you?"

"I am good. You are not from around here are you? Just passing through or planning on staying awhile?"

"Just passing through. I'm sorry, do I know you?"

"No you do not, and there is no reason you should, but let me change that by introducing myself. My name is *Johnny Thunder Eagle,* and by your stare I could sense you were wondering if I am an American Indian. Well stranger, I am. I am a full-blooded *Apsaalooke'*- which simply means '*children of the large beaked bird'*. Our tribal name however, has evolved to be more commonly known as the *Crow*. I was born, raised and live on the nearby Crow Reservation – the *rez* - here in Montana."

With that introduction, Johnny held out his hand in a traditional handshake gesture. Jim grasped Johnny's hand with a firm solid grip. Johnny's grip was just as firm but with obvious authority and confidence. As the two men shook hands, it would signify the beginning of a spiritual bonding that would last a lifetime.

"Pleased to meet you, Mr. Johnny Thunder Eagle," Jim said. "Sorry if my staring was so obvious. I didn't mean to offend you in any way. I'm Jim Bradshaw, an American businessman and white Anglo-Saxon Atheist, waiting for his private company plane to be repaired. May I buy you a drink?"

"Thanks Jim. I will take a Coke over ice if you are offering."

"Sure. Bartender, one Coke for my friend here."

The drink was served without so much as a moment passing.

"You are a very rich man, Jim?"

"Yes I am, but not for long."

"What does that mean?"

"It's a long sad story."

"I think my people are much accustomed to long sad stories. I do not mind listening if you do not mind telling."

"I don't feel up to it at the moment. Give me a little while to relax and maybe I'll fill you in on my situation later."

"That is okay. If you do not mind, maybe I can tell you about your situation."

"Oh really? You can? Okay Johnny, tell me about my situation. Entertain me. I have some time to kill. This should be interesting."

"Okay, I will try. We both know it is not a happy story. I know you are a wealthy man dying from an advanced form of cancer - lung cancer. Is that correct?"

The abruptness of the statement struck a very unfavorable defensive reaction in Jim.

"What? What did you just say? How the hell could you know that? It seems I underestimated you! I get it now; one of my crew planted you here. They put you up to this as some sick stupid joke to keep me entertained while my plane is repaired. Well it's not very funny or appreciated. When I find out who did it, they'll be looking for a new job. You know… you are one crazy sick Indian to try something like this."

Johnny didn't react to the obvious insult, instead he continued with his story.

"Sorry Jim, but it is not a joke. I have never been in contact with any of your people, or known about you before meeting you today. I was sent to meet you at someone's respected invitation. It was he who told me of your condition and where to find you."

"Who? Who told you?"

"Stoney Creek Smith."

"Who the hell is Stoney Creek Smith!?"

"Okay...relax. I can see that you are upset. I will tell you soon enough, but first, may I tell you a story?"

"I'm listening. You have exactly one minute. So it better be fast and it better be good."

"Okay, I will get right to the point. Another Coke and Club Soda please, bartender. Jim...Stoney Creek Smith, is one of the reservation's Holy Men, specifically he is a Shaman, or what most non-rez people would amusingly mislabel as a *Medicine Man*. A few nights ago Stoney had a vision. He does not have them often and when he does, he takes its message very seriously. In this vision he saw a rich, lost, and lonely man dying of lung cancer. He was told to find this man and invite him to the reservation to cure him of his disease. No answers were given as to why this particular man was to be found and cured, but the message was clear. *Find him and cure him.* Stoney sent me to find the man at this airport and return him to the reservation with this message; *The Great Spirit will guide you along the right path to find him and cure him.* That man is you and I am offering you a chance to recover from your cancer so you have an opportunity to accomplish something worthwhile for the Crow Nation and the world. That is my story. I am inviting you back with me to the reservation to save your life so you can fulfill your life's mission."

The information shocked Bradshaw into a coughing fit – a normal consequence of his lung cancer. After a few seconds that seemed to him like an eternity, it stopped. Catching his breath, he was speechless for a moment.

"Whew! Oh my God…thought that was it. Sorry about the coughing, it can't be helped, but your story…your story is quite a whopper. It really set me off. Let me ask you something Thunder Eagle. Are you nuts? Hmm? Are you sure there's no mind altering drug in that Coke you're drinking? Johnny, look at me. Look at me closely. What do you see? Do you see a fool? Do you?"

"No Jim. I do not. You know I do not think of you as a fool, but what I am telling you is the truth."

"Sure it is…Listen, I didn't become a very powerful and wealthy person in this world by being a fool. Now really, I appreciate your valiant effort, but I know when I'm being conned. What concerns me most is why are you pursuing this? I really want to know. Is your life that empty? What kind of perverted satisfaction do you gain by doing something like this to a complete stranger? Is this fun for you or is this some calculated payback toward the white man's injustices to the red man? Is that it?"

Johnny just remained quiet, letting this man vent his anger. He knew shortly Jim would be convinced of the truth and his quest. Jim received no answer from Johnny and continued his outrage.

"Mr. Thunder Eagle, or whatever your name really is, I don't know you or how you obtained this specific information about me, but I am sure about one thing. I'm sure as hell not going back to any Indian Reservation with you today or any other day. You got that? Now - I think you've had your fun. You can leave. I would like to finish my drink alone, forget this incident ever happened and get out of this cow town airport as soon as possible."

Jim looked over to his bodyguards seated at a remote table and summoned them to his location. The two very large men immediately got up and walked toward their boss. Johnny saw the two men approach as he spoke.

"I am sorry Jim. My intention was not to upset you. Stoney told me you would not believe me at first and would resist. He told me if you decided not to believe me that I tell you who contacted Stoney about you in his vision."

Jim looked up from his drink, felt his curiosity take over his better judgment, and said; "Jesus Christ…you don't quit do you? Okay, in order to shut you up, this is my last question to you. Who told Stoney?"

The bodyguards were standing directly behind Bradshaw, silently staring at Johnny, waiting for instructions to dispose of this intruder. Johnny looked up at the two men as if they were nothing more than two large trees. He answered Bradshaw's question.

"It was the spirit of Richard Runor, respected *Teamspring Tobacco Company* vice-president, who told Stoney to tell you to begin a new life with the Crow Nation and be cured of your cancer."

Jim looked back at his two bodyguards and held up his hand toward them in a gesture signaling them to not do anything - yet.

"How do you know of Richard? Jesus! You've really done your homework on me. You must have some of my best people helping you on this one. Am I right? I know I am right. Now please leave. I'll give Richard a call when I get home and tell him about you and your amazing story."

Johnny ignored the invitation to leave and simply stated, "Calling Richard won't be possible, Jim."

"And why is that?"

"Because Richard Runor is dead. He died several days ago."

And with that statement, Johnny handed Bradshaw a Billings newspaper that he had discreetly placed on the empty barstool next to him. In the business section, buried on page ten, was a paragraph on Richard Runor's death, ...*prominent Teamspring Tobacco Vice-President and cigarette marketing pioneer, dead at the age of 57, from unknown causes...survived by*...Jim read it in disbelief and mild shock. He sat back in his barstool nearly falling off, dropping the newspaper to the floor. His two large friends held him up and retrieved the fallen newspaper.

In reality and not reported was that Richard Runor had died of liver failure, heart disease and a form of cancer. He ended up a wealthy man, dead at an early age, a very wealthy man who left all of his assets to no one and devoted his life to the promotion of the products leading to his own death.

Jim started to cough again.

"Are you okay?" Johnny said. "I did not mean to upset you again, but believe me when I tell you that it is no coincidence that I sat next to you today. Finding you at a specific time in this airport would be next to impossible unless I knew exactly when and where to look and who to look for. This was done with help from the Great Spirit, who also forced your aircraft to land at this airport. Stoney's visions are never wrong and he believes in your destiny. Moreover, I know once you start to believe in your destiny that you too will accept it and return to the reservation with me. Your life and the lives of thousands depend on it. Believe me. Believe in the Great Spirit. Believe in yourself. Tell your people you will be going with me. It is only an hour's drive. You will have a life altering experience. And when you return home, you will be healthy again, ready for your mission."

Jim sat passively and began to feel a calm acceptance consume him.

"What mission?" he asked. There was no immediate response from Johnny.

He looked over at Johnny and stared him directly in the eyes. Johnny stared back with the message deeply conveyed in his own eyes. Jim nodded with approval and motioned to his bodyguards to back off, ordering them to never reveal this conversation to anyone - ever.

"Okay. You've got my attention. I need to satisfy my curiosity. I need to have a long conversation with this Stoney Creek Smith. I'll go. I need to tell the rest of my traveling group of my change in plans. They want'll have me committed, thinking I'm crazy, but I still write the checks so they can't do much about my decision to enter into this very strange arrangement. My bodyguards will accompany me to the reservation just to assure my safety. They may need to stay for a few days. Is that okay?"

"That will not be a problem, but once we get there, we abide by the rules of the reservation and the instructions from Stoney. Agreed?"

"Agreed."

"Okay then. It is time to go. Gather up your luggage and anything else you want to take with you and I will meet you outside the airport's main entrance. I will be the 'crazy' Indian waiting in a *Jeep*."

"Jeep?"

"Yes Jim. What were you expecting - a horse drawn wagon or a horse?"

"No…I was kinda hoping for a *Pontiac Firebird*."

"Funny you should mention that particular car. My cousin Vinnie Bear Claw has one. Maybe he will give you a ride sometime."

"That would be interesting. I'll look forward to it. I'll see you outside in ten."

And with that simple blind faith agreement, Bradshaw began his journey to the reservation.

Jim was informed just before leaving for the reservation that after an intensive search to find the source of the mechanical problems that forced his airplane to an emergency landing at the Billings Airport, nothing was found. It was a baffling mystery to both pilot and crew. Jim just shook his head when hearing the news and muttered, "Now this is beginning to become a little spooky...Great Spirit...??

CHAPTER 17

THE ARRIVAL

JANUARY 1974

Tony and Neil made it safely to the town of Crow Agency. As they rolled up to the Town Hall entrance and climbed out of their warm car, Johnny Thunder Eagle was waiting outside in the cold to greet them.

"Neil Hagman and Anthony Rullo...hello...the Crow Nation welcomes you. Thank you so much for traveling to our great land on such a cold day. It is a pleasure to finally meet you both. I am Johnny Thunder Eagle, your primary contact on this reservation during the building's construction. Mr. Mogul has told me many great things about each of you. I am looking forward to working with and helping you on this project. Please...follow me. The Council is assembled inside, awaiting your arrival."

The first thing that impressed Tony and Neil when they entered the Town Hall, was the pedestrian interior of this uninspired building - purely functional, nothing else. It was appointed with the most basic of interior finishes – vinyl floors, painted gypsum wallboard, two by four acoustical tile grid ceilings punctuated with diffuse fluorescent lighting, hollow core wood composite doors - the usual cheap basic construction that accompanied a lackluster government funded and constructed building. The BIA assured that their "people" were not given anything above the inexpensive and ordinary. There wasn't a choice, it was an accepted and approved policy.

Once the two travelers were seated among the Tribal Council members inside the building's austere meeting room, Johnny assumed his role as chairperson and moved forward with the informal meeting. He reviewed his assigned agenda from Mr. Mogul, before addressing his audience.

"Welcome to Crow Agency and our first *Mogul Skyscraper* project meeting. Thank you all for being part of this historic day. Before I begin with my obligatory presentation, I would like to introduce two principal members of our Billings' project design team. With us today, from the Baltimore, Maryland, architectural firm of *Neil Hagman and Associates*, are Mr. Neil Hagman Executive Project Manager *and* Executive Architect, responsible for overseeing and managing the design and construction of the reservation's skyscraper and Mr. Anthony Rullo, Solar Design Architect... Neil, Anthony, would you both stand please?...Did I get your titles correct, gentlemen...?

"Yes you did Johnny...thank you...but Mr. Rullo... Anthony...prefers to use the name Tony," Neil said.

"Good, then from now on we shall address Mr. Rullo as 'Tony.' Will the Council please extend their warmest welcome to these two fine gentlemen," Johnny said.

The Council responded not with the clapping of hands, but with an affirmative nodding of their heads accompanied by a personal Crow verbal greeting of acceptance. In spite of not understanding a word of Crow, Tony and Neil felt acceptance in the foreign words and smiled with appreciation.

Johnny then introduced every Tribal Council Government member by name to the two Baltimore travelers. When the formal introductions were finished, Johnny continued.

"Thank you Council," Johnny said. "What I have to say to you today is from the wisdom and vision of Mr. Mogul. Neil, Tony, and members of the Council, I know since your participation in this project began, you have been given discretely measured amounts of information regarding our mysterious skyscraper and its treasured goals. Today, I have been asked by Mr. Mogul to provide some additional pieces to this puzzle. Before this meeting ends, most of your questions should hopefully be answered."

"One of Mr. Mogul's goals is to have this building beget similar buildings, all capturing their energy from the wind and the sun, and constructed on Native American Reservations across the United States. Our skyscraper will represent the prototype from which many others will imitate. Additional buildings of every type and size will follow its lead, until hundreds of self-sufficient buildings will be constructed on reservation land. From these buildings there will be celebration and smiles on the faces of many Native Americans. This is Mr. Mogul's vision for America and for the original Natives of this country. For the first time in our history, since the white man took us prisoner in our own land, we will again be free. From the success of these buildings, a new economic base will be established. People from outside the reservation will come here to live and work. We will prosper and resurrect our identities as Native Americans. We will be reborn as honored children of the Great Spirit."

"It is imperative that our model skyscraper be a success. Mr. Mogul is financing this building using his personal corporate funds and loans from many anonymous private investors. The budget for this project has not been definitely established, but Mr. Mogul estimates it to be close to a billion dollars. Therefore, there is a tremendous responsibility affecting everyone involved with our skyscraper's future to not allow it to fail. With the talented and devoted people we will have working on this building, it will not fail."

"I must address one more unfortunate, but essential component of this project. It is the subject of security. Mr. Mogul will not to be compromised by anything or anyone who would attempt to threaten this project's success. If the primary tenets of this project are fulfilled, the major oil and coal companies in the years ahead will begin to feel the effects. The consumption of their products will decrease. They have seen this alternative future, and will do all they can to see our building fail."

"As most of you know, several members of our Tribal Council were approached by representatives from a few prominent Montana utility companies in an attempt to divert the reservation from this noble goal. These sources offered millions of dollars in the form of beneficial reservation economic opportunities, if the Tribal Council Government voted to reject the construction of this building. It has been a difficult process but the Council has unanimously voted to steadfastly refuse these 'beneficial offers.' We have made it very clear to these *benefactors* that the hopeful economic independence for thousands of our Crow brothers and sisters is not for sale."

"Make no mistake about it, this skyscraper is the portal to our independence. Therefore, during this project's duration, be cautious and aware of anyone who is not sympathetic to our cause. Do not discuss details of this building with anyone other than those on the approved list of project personnel. Keeping this information confidential, is essential to assuring this project's success."

"This concludes the extent of Mr. Mogul's message that I have been honored to share with you today. I know individual

Council members will have many more questions. I will answer as many as I can after the conclusion of this meeting. Neil and Tony, after I am through speaking with the Council, please meet with me. I have some things I need to personally discuss."

"In closing, allow me to remind you that our first in depth project meeting is scheduled in approximately three days. I will be contacting all members of the Council tomorrow to confirm the date and time. Thank you all. Fare well. Go forward in honor and peace."

After the meeting was adjourned, Johnny, Tony, and Neil met privately to discuss the details of selecting the site location for the reservation's grand building. Later, Johnny took them on a tour of the rez, showing them the sub-standard living environment that greeted his people every day. During the tour, the two men had very little to say, a lot to feel and many things wanting to improve upon in the lives of these people. After the tour, their earlier lighthearted attitude evolved into one dedicated to fulfilling every hope and dream that Mr. Mogul was promoting. With this skyscraper, his magnificent monument to truth, he was planting the seeds for the reservation's spiritual and physical renewal. Neil and Tony would return here in a few days to help select the site location for the building's permanent home. Only this time, their perception of the rez would have a more realistic perspective.

CHAPTER 18

THE CURE

JUNE TO SEPTEMBER 1972

Jim Bradshaw arrived at the Crow reservation's northern border in a little over an hour. Crossing this invisible barrier on his way to Crow Agency, he would soon witness the poverty and hopelessness surrounding the people living here. It made him sad and embarrassed to realize that all his power, influence and wealth did nothing to improve the quality of these people's lives.

His bodyguards followed and set up a watchful vigilance of their boss from a non-obtrusive distance as he was met and greeted by Stoney Creek Smith. Stoney was a noble man who looked to be in his mid fifties. He was stocky and muscular. He was of medium height and his hair was just below his shoulders and braided like Johnny's. He mentioned he was married and had a family – a boy and a girl, both married with children of their own. It was the only time Stoney mentioned anything about his family.

Johnny Thunder Eagle formally introduced Jim and his bodyguards.

"Gentleman, meet Stoney Creek Smith, our resident reservation Great Man. Stoney wears many hats for our Nation. He is a Holy Man, a Shaman, and a Visionary. He informs the Nation of all the life altering events that will impose themselves on our reservation. He is also a great healer -"

"Stop Johnny. Enough about me," Stoney said. "Who or what I am is not important. Jim, I am happy to finally meet you. The Great Spirit prepared the reservation for your arrival and your survival. Now, you need to rest and eat before we begin our healing journey. We must begin your journey soon, two nights from now during the new moon. My home will be open to you during your stay. I hope it meets with your approval."

Jim said, "Thank you Stoney. It is a very unexpected pleasure to meet you. I must admit this whole arrangement is extremely unsettling to me at the moment – very unsettling - but somehow I feel optimistic about the outcome. I don't know why, but I am allowing myself to trust you. You appear to be a man of honor. That attribute is very important to me in a person. However, I do need to talk to you for a very long time before I agree to put my destiny in your hands. I am, by nature, a very cautious man. If you are able to cure me of my cancer, then I will be indebted to you for the rest of my life. Do not be offended by my skepticism. I know I have everything to gain and nothing to lose."

"No offense is taken Jim. Without honor, man is just a hollow shell. Do not worry. I assure you, you have nothing to fear, only the opportunity to open your life to a meaningful purpose. Your personal quest will be answered in its time. Johnny, I will see you tomorrow. Thank you for finding Jim and convincing him to travel to the reservation. He is in the guiding hands of the Great Spirit now. Peace my brother." Stoney said.

"Thank you my brother," Johnny said. "It has been an honor to help fulfill the request of the Great Spirit. Jim, it has been quite an adventure and pleasure to meet you. We will most definitely meet again. You will fare well in Stoney's hands. Peace to you all. Good night."

Johnny left Stoney and Jim to prepare for their awaiting future.

"Stoney, if you don't mind, my bodyguards and I, sure could use a hot meal and a place to freshen up. It's been a long tiring day for everyone," Jim said.

"It will be my pleasure. If you would follow me, I will show you to your accommodations," Stoney said.

Jim and his bodyguards followed Stoney by foot the short distance to his modest home. There, they would share a bedroom in this small two-bedroom house. Stoney's wife was not at home. She had arranged to spend the next two evenings with her family a few miles away. Before she left, she prepared dinner for her arriving houseguests.

Jim and his bodyguards were pleased with their meal. There was nothing left over. When dinner was finished, a pleasant informative conversation developed between Stoney and Jim. Stoney assured Jim that his journey into the unknown was without question and it would be his path to a life devoted to the quest for absolute truth and harmony. He was impressed by Stoney's insight and knowledge and went to sleep from this exhausting day confident that a unique opportunity to open his life to a fulfilling future was awaiting him.

After two days of peace and tranquility, and Jim's safety obviously not in question, his bodyguards left the reservation. They were ordered to report back to the New York City office with instructions to deceptively brief his top executives about Jim's situation, and allow them to manage *BEI* without his input for an indeterminate period of time. Jim would prepare weekly updates on his condition and somehow transmit the information to his colleagues to assure them of his safety and progress.

In two days, as Stoney had predicted, they traveled by horseback to the predetermined healing location one day's ride south from Crow Agency. After arriving there and setting up camp, Jim went through a rigorous series of spiritual and physical rituals that he would never be afforded the opportunity to experience again.

Stoney took Bradshaw under his care, guiding him through many visions and ceremonies, providing him with herbs, teas, natural drugs and medicines, putting him on a special diet, all the while continually opening up Jim's inner spirit to the secrets of healing. In three months of this life ritual of living in a medicine tipi, sleeping on Mother Earth every night, bathing in hot mineral waters every day, meditating in a sweat lodge, and abstaining completely from anything that was his body's enemy, the cancer slowly disappeared from his body. He was cured. Stoney was impressed with Jim's success. He was confident it was the will of the Great Spirit to cure this man. From now on nothing will be permitted to block the path of this man and the fulfillment of *The Prophecy.*

During their three months together Stoney and Jim became close friends. Stoney was impressed with Jim's inner strength and his newfound conviction in the power of the Great Spirit. As they were packing up camp for their journey home, Stoney said,

"Jim, with thanks to the Great Spirit, and your faith in its power, you have been cured of your disease. Your body is cleansed. Today, you will leave this reservation, but later you will return, for a reason that I do not yet know, but you will return."

"Thank you Stoney. I know I will return. This was told to me in one of my visions during the healing process. However, before I return, there are major changes that I must make in my life before I can move forward on my new life path and return to the reservation."

While experiencing his many healing rituals, semi-conscious trances and visions, Jim was told what he must do with his renewed life. He must forever divorce himself from his oil, tobacco and alcohol business endeavors and reinvest the money acquired from their sale into the acquisition of steel mills, Portland Cement manufacturing plants, and alternative energy industries, such as solar and wind.

"Do what you were told to do in order to embrace your new life and prepare for your destined future," Stoney said. "The Great Spirit will follow you and guide you. Later, it will ask you to implement a great project for the benefit of the reservation and the Crow people -"

"What is it? What great project will the Great Spirit ask of me?"

"That is something I am not permitted to know. You will know soon. That I do know. Now…go in peace. Your people are impatiently waiting at the airport to take you back home."

"Stoney…I owe you my life and so much more. How will I ever repay you for this gift?"

"There is no need to repay me. Thank the Great Spirit for your life. I am just its messenger and servant. It told me I must keep you alive. I only did what I was asked to do. I am pleased that I was able to fulfill its request. You were a willing student and an honored guest. Good bye my brother."

"Good bye Stoney. Will I see you again?"

"It is most assured," Stoney said.

They embraced with a hug affirming their brotherhood. These two men, who were strangers three months ago, were now bound together forever through their common spirit.

— — —

With his future set before him, Jim walked away from Stoney and the Crow Reservation and into his new life. He walked toward and entered the red 1972 *Pontiac Firebird* driven by Vinnie Bear Claw that would take him to the airport and his *BEI* aircraft to New York City.

Vinnie had won the money for this car recklessly in a dubious Friday night high stakes poker game. He had bet everything he owned on drawing to an impossible straight flush. By some miracle and the fact that he was fairly drunk at the time and didn't know how impossible it was, he did it. He spent all his winnings on the car. It was the will of the Great Spirit he would later say. He loved that car.

However, the will of the Great Spirit went beyond just the car. Vinnie modified the "Screaming Chicken" decal on the hood to resemble an eagle. He nicknamed the car "The Screaming Eagle" or more accurately, "Vinnie's Screaming Eagle". The modified artwork on the car was legendary, so renowned that its reputation extended beyond the restrictive confines of the reservation.

Because of it, he was offered a temporary apprentice position with a graphic arts company in Billings. He accepted. He knew that his talent was a cherished gift given to him by the Great Spirit. It would assure him of a permanent position with his new employer. He vowed to honor it by never having an alcoholic drink or gambling for the rest of his life. He faithfully kept these promises to the Great Spirit and within a year was a respected permanent employee..

The ride to the airport was a blur of speed. The *Firebird* was cruising comfortably above ninety. It was an exhilarating ride on the winds of change, signifying the rebirth of James Jeffrey Bradshaw.

After arriving at the airport, Jim thanked Vinnie for the ride of his life. The two men had a good laugh about the crude thrill of driving fast on the open roads of Montana. But upon leaving the black interior of the Firebird, Jim's lighthearted mood turned serious as he realized all those things he needed to drastically change from those in his present life to the life chosen for him by the Great Spirit.

― ― ―

During his lonely introspective flight back to the City, he remembered that one infamous night, as a child of ten, something his intoxicated father conveyed to a group of *Vision Oil Company,* associates after a festive Christmas holiday party at the Bradshaw residence;

> *"...have them consume, consume, and consume until whatever it is they consume becomes an ever demanding obsession. Then, increase the cost of this product without actually increasing its performance or quality by advertising a falsely improved replacement product to enhance and renew the user's consumption habits. Always give them a little more – dangle that carrot at the end of the stick – again and again increase its price - and the illusion of improved quality -- ever so slightly – ever so subtly...*
>
> *...Continue this cycle of perpetual product consumption, improvement and elusive need. Make the consumer believe in their hearts and souls that they cannot live without it. Create an almost hysterical social and physical dependency...*
>
> *...Set up false supply and demand relationships to perpetuate an artificial growth of your enterprise at the expense of retarding humanity's evolving natural growth of a qual-*

> *ity life. This is the key to maintaining control over the consumer, power over the product, and endless profit. You will only get richer while your victims become more dependent in trying to satisfy their hunger, spending lots of money in their quest...*
>
> *...Constant consumption and dependency is the key to maintaining a profitable growth in our economy at the expense of extinction or eradication of the product or its consumers. The product can be replaced. The consumer can be replaced. They both can be replaced. They can always be replaced with someone or something else...The consumer is always fair game, even if it means compromising their health, financial well- being or welfare..."*

Jim did not understand what his father meant by these words at the time he heard them, until he himself walked through the eternal portal into the world of capitalism and profit without conscience.

He hated himself for what he had done to everyone who was consuming his products. He needed to do something to make amends. Now that he had his life back, he needed to help turn the world around. As the sunbeams streamed through the airplane's windows and washed across his face, he waited for the Great Spirit to give him his final answer.

On July 15, 1973, he was given that answer.

CHAPTER 19

THE BUILDING

Tony's second full day in Montana was occupied attending the mandatory design charette sessions with Neil, and the project's diversified professional staff. At these sessions, ideas for the skyscraper's design were proposed and discussed. There were many varied concepts and theories presented – some good, some not very good and a few highly imaginative ideas worthy of further investigation and development. Tony absorbed them all, took copious notes, and accumulated pages of sketches.

At the day's end, specialized design teams were organized and each was given an unique assignment. Tony's assignment was the exception. He was assigned an individual task, the one from which all the others would eventually evolve. He was to develop the skyscraper's preliminary design concepts, alone and without the assistance of his fellow professionals. He was confident he could do this, after all, he had been stockpiling ideas for buildings like this one ever since he was a child of ten. This attribute, however, didn't insulate him from being fearful of not being able to successfully deliver on this critical task. To add to his anxiety, every assignment, including his, was due by nine o'clock the next morning.

The brain storming meetings did not end until after nine. By the time Tony left the building and located his company assigned pick-up truck, his personal mode of transportation during the project's duration, it was nearly ten o'clock. Instead of remaining at the office to complete his work along with everyone else, he was ordered by Neil to his new home, a rented hunter's cabin located eighteen miles east of Billings. It was here that his personal solar research and design documents were delivered and waiting for his arrival. They were essential to assuring Tony's success. They were his Holy Grail – his portal to an enlightened architectural solar design. Without these pages of personal inspiration he could not succeed. They were his comfort, his security blanket, and his deliverance from his imagination filled world of dreams into the harsh world of reality. It was time for Tony to give reality a hard wake up kick in the ass. If only he could keep awake long enough to fulfill this desire.

A good night's sleep was a luxury he could not afford, not at the *Cattle King Hotel*, or anywhere else for that matter. He would need to remain awake throughout this night working on his design. It was the only way it could be ready by morning.

It was a lonely drive to the cabin. The temperature on this January night was somewhere south of freezing, with a threat of snow in the air. The heater in the pick-up was underachieving its ability to provide heat. Tony's was wearing his lightweight *New York Yankees* baseball jacket. It was ill suited in providing him with needed warmth against the cold.

...Where the hell is the heat in this truck...? Tony thought... *why couldn't my golden project be in Florida...?*

The company truck was a black 1972 *Ford F-100*, with a three hundred sixty cubic-inch, two hundred horsepower, workhorse V-8 under the hood. It was a lot more muscle than his underpowered Fiat could ever hope to provide, but it lacked the charm of his little red Italian "scooter". Before he left Baltimore, he safely transported his Fiat to Illinois, to be tended to by his loving uncle. It would be waiting there for him when he was finished with Mr. Mogul's magnificent skyscraper. He would miss that car and the love that surrounded it.

The truck's AM radio was not working. It was missing its antenna, but it didn't matter. All the local radio stations in the area were off the air until sunrise. Therefore, the ride was eerily quiet, except for the noise from Tony's insistent mutterings, and the F100's internal grumblings.

...just think...the Mogul empire will achieve through its research and development, automobiles powered by something other than an internal combustion gasoline powered pollutant spewing engine...what will it be...electric, hydrogen fuel cells, steam...?

Tony would confidently leave that problem to the Mogul engineers to solve. This morning his task was to design a solar powered, self-sustained skyscraper. For now, he would enjoy the ironic hypocrisy of driving a gasoline-powered pick-up truck while indirectly contributing in a dedicated effort to ending its dependency on fossil fuels for its power.

...Besides... pick-up trucks and cows out numbered the people living in this sparsely populated state....

Other than a horse, Tony knew it was the Montana rancher's choice for transportation over hundreds of miles of wide-open country. The truck was a welcomed change for Tony. The noise, the harsh ride, the no-frills interior all symbolized the beginning of a new adventure in a life that he had become accustomed to accept as ordinary.

This truck symbolized Tony's break from the ordinary.

Other than being incredibly cold, the night was darker than Tony had ever experienced. Clouds were covering any help from the moon's light. Stars usually visible by the millions were nowhere to be seen. There were no road signs or streetlights to help him find his way. All he had was a company prepared map that he had to read balanced on his lap, with a flashlight, while traveling most of his journey on five miles of poorly maintained dirt roads. It wasn't the easiest of tasks, but failure wasn't an option. Getting lost would result in failing to complete his crucial assignment before morning. He could never forgive himself if that happened. Worse than that, he would need to sleep in the truck with the possibility of freezing to death before sunrise.

He could see the headlines now.

"LOST ARCHITECT FREEZES TO DEATH IN TRUCK"

...How ironic would that be...here I am promoting the practical use of solar energy...stupidly getting lost...freezing to death...having no resources available to capture the sun's energy after sunset to warm my freezing body ...how do you capture and store the sun's power when it isn't there to capture...I need to work on eliminating that one minor defect in the practical use of the sun's power...

Putting his doubts behind him, Tony continued his drive on the only paved road he would see on this trip. At the thirteen-mile mark, it was time for his first turn, a left onto an unmarked road, dirt road number one. He was to travel 2.3 miles on this road and make another turn north for 1.7 miles on dirt road number two, ending with a right on dirt road number three for approximately one mile. The directions indicated the cabin would be straight ahead.

At the bottom of the map was written an interesting message,

"WARNING: Be aware of fallen tree limbs, standing water, and indigenous animal activity along the final approach to the cabin"

"*Great!*" Tony muttered. "*Either freeze to death, crash into a large tree limb, drown or get eaten by a bear. This adventure makes New Jersey seem like the Mecca of civilization to me right now. I know I wanted to get away from traffic, pollution and congestion, but this is not exactly what I had in mind.*"

Tony's previous road rally adventures with the local *Tri-County Sports Car Club*, on the back roads of northern New Jersey, enabled him to easily understand and follow the directions. Without so much as a distracting hic-cup, he successfully arrived at the cabin. He shut off the motor, breathed a sigh of relief, and left the truck headlights on so he could easily see his way up the gravel path to the front door.

Before he left the secure cold interior of the F-100, he grabbed a large lantern flashlight that was provided for him, along with a backpack containing a limited quantity of unknown food supplies, a first aid kit with snake venom vaccine, some emergency flares and his notes and sketches from the day's meetings. In the truck, there was also a gun rack holding a shotgun. The shells were in a box behind the front seat. Tony didn't like guns. Never the less, he shouldered the weapon and stuffed the shells in the backpack - just in case. This Montana wilderness truck was well equipped. It had just about everything he would need in an emergency, except for a heavy wool blanket and a bottle of whiskey.

As Tony approached the cabin, he instinctively started his flashlight survey of the structure and its surroundings. The cabin was located in a clearing surrounded by a light forest. He walked the cabin's perimeter. He could see it was constructed entirely from logs and stone, had only a front door and two windows on each of its four sides. Amenities included a woodpile, a remote storage shed, and an emergency generator. There was a six-foot deep front porch elevated two-steps up to its wood plank floor. The front door was prominent, a four by eight-foot behemoth, built from split logs and exactly centered in the cabin's front wall. It had no locking hardware. Thieves were apparently not a threat out here. There was also not an outhouse or water hand-pump to be seen. This, he assumed, meant the toilet facilities and water supply were conveniently supplied in the cabin.

Tony climbed the stairs to the front door. His hand went toward the latch handle. The door was heavy and the latch was secure. As Tony grasped the handle to open the door, he took a deep breath and whispered,

"This is it."

As he opened the cabin door, he laid his gear and gun on the floor just inside the entrance, using his flashlight to illuminate the interior. He searched for a light switch or a working light of any kind. His flashlight reflected off a surface mounted junction box with a light switch on the latch side of the door. He flipped the switch up to "on" and a lamp on a table next to a couch came to life, illuminating the cabin dimly with its warm incandescent glow. Other lights were discovered and switched on in rapid sequence adding to the cabin's artificial illumination.

With the cabin adequately lit, Tony finally saw what his home was going to be for the next two plus years. He was in one large open room, except for a small-enclosed area in the far corner, which he assumed was the bathroom. The bathroom was the only other "room" in the cabin. Opposite the bathroom was a small corner kitchen, furnished with a two burner electric range, a tiny oven, a refrigerator-freezer combo, a sink, and just enough cabinet space to store the essentials for one or two people for a long weekend. It was all Tony would need.

He estimated the interior dimensions of the cabin to be a little over twenty-five feet square. The interior walls were unfinished, exposing the natural characteristics of the exterior logs and stone. There was no ceiling, just the underside of rigid insulation covering the roof planks that were structurally supported with heavy rough sawn timber trusses. Two plumbing vents penetrated this roof, one from the open kitchen, and the other from the enclosed bathroom.

For heat, there were electric baseboards and a cast-iron wood-burning stove that was located at the cabin's center. Its flue was housed in a stone chimney rising prominently inside the cabin through the roof. Tony knew that this unique stove was going to keep the cabin very warm.

The cabin was well protected against the elements, well insulated, with all exterior penetrations and window frames adequately weatherproofed. As a bonus, all windows were provided with operable insulated shudders and the giant front door was equipped with a heavy bearskin rug that rolled down covering it like a shade. The cabin was a well-built structure and a good choice for Tony. It was simple, honest and very functional. It met with his approval. He was going to like it here.

Tony began his search for the location of his "stuff." Tony's belongings, his "stuff," had been shipped ahead to the cabin. He packed everything he was told he needed for his Montana adventure in boxes and duffel bags. Suitcases were something that Tony never had the money to buy or felt a reason to own.

He found the pile of boxes and bags placed in an open corner of the cabin next to an enormous king-sized bed with a handcrafted wood frame, headboard and footboard. It was a work of art. He almost succumbed to its beckoning call inviting him to enter its comfort zone to sleep. Tony resisted the urge with everything he had left in the way of will power. He had a job to do and there was no time to sleep.

He began sorting through his personal belongings until he located his special box. Tony held the box in his arms. It was a heavily duct taped Xerox paper supply box with a fitted lid. In addition to his cherished portfolio, the box held his life's work on anything that related to solar design. Hundreds of ideas, theories and sketches defining specific applications of solar design and self-sustained building architecture were in this box. Finally - he had the opportunity to use his ideas, among hundreds by others, and apply them to an actual building design.

However, before he could comfortably begin his creation, some warmth was required. The cabin was only a few degrees above the outside air temperature. Tony was shivering. He needed to get some heat flowing into this cabin. The heat from the electric baseboards and the wood-burning stove would have no difficulty in raising the temperature in the cabin to an acceptable comfort level. He laid his box on the floor, turned on the baseboards and went outside to gather firewood to fuel the stove, settling in for a long warm night of inspiration and creativity.

In the supplied backpack he found coffee, tea, bread, crunchy peanut butter, grape jelly, and cheese, enough food to help fill the void in his stomach until dawn. He started a fire in the wood burning stove. He prepared a pot of coffee. It was time to begin his work.

— — —

Mr. Mogul had specifically instructed Neil to assign Tony the overwhelming task of creating the building's design in less than eight hours. Tony was allowed the freedom to develop this design without any financial restrictions, but was restricted in allowing any outside influences to potentially distract him from his original thoughts.

Tony realized this difficult, nearly impossible assignment, was the first of many to follow, but it was the most important of any he would be given for the duration of the project. Of all the highly skilled experts out in the world educated on this subject, Tony had been given this opportunity. It wasn't logical. He knew he was about to wake up from a deep coma and discover that this entire experience was only an unbelievable fantasy housed in a dream.

Sitting on a heavy wool rug in an open area of the cabin, close, but not too close to the wood-burning stove, with his coffee, and peanut butter and jelly sandwich neatly placed by his side, he opened his special box and emptied his portfolio. He gathered up all of this information and together with the day's design notes and sketches, spread the entire contents across the floor in front of him. He began to read. He read for hours. It was difficult for him to believe that he was responsible for preparing these reports and developing these concepts. It was information he accumulated through years of research and original theories spawned from his inspired imagination. Some of these ideas, even to him, did not appear feasible, but this night they were going to be proposed regardless of any implied restrictions.

There was an eerie silence and calm entering the arena that was Tony's mind. He knew it was finally time to accept reality. His incredible journey was about to begin. He took a deep cleansing breath and relaxed his body. Everything was feeling so right.

It was the calm before the storm.

Suddenly, this calm transformed into panic. Tony's mind went void of all creativity and his thoughts were replaced by the fear of failing, of not being capable of accomplishing what he needed to accomplish. He began to feel nauseous and dizzy with anxiety. He ran to the bathroom, feeling the urge to baptize the toilet with vomit. He entered the room and stood over the bowl looking into the cloudy water, shaking nervously and breathing heavily. A few dry heaves were offered. He rested his hands on the walls above the toilet and waited for something else to happen. To his relief, nothing did. He stood there for a few minutes and nothing else happened. The anxiety attack had passed him by as suddenly as it had appeared. His breathing returned to normal. He turned toward the sink and looked into the mirror and said to himself,

"Well Tony, now that you've gotten that out of your system, let's kick some butt and get to work."

He bent over the sink, splashed some water on his face and drank a cold refreshing quantity of well water directly from the tap.

Returning from the bathroom to his great room, he again sat down, gathered all of his materials together and immediately began to write and sketch. The concepts for this building started to pour out from him like the beams of sunlight on a sunny day.

...This will work... This is how it will be...

As he was spitting out his ideas on paper, his mind began to wander into a stream of unconnected, but related thoughts. Tony gazed at the sketches in his hands. He was holding a small piece of hope for the future. He felt fulfilled and incredibly uplifted. This is what it is all about, finding the truth about our lives within our own hearts and souls.

> *...After all, wasn't life simply about love, love of humanity and the hope of a better future for all those who follow after our death...*

isn't the true evil in this world, the "bad" selfish people who retard this natural evolution and are motivated by achieving their personal goals at the expense of humanity... why is there always a smoke screen protecting these evil people as they perform selfish acts, hiding them so they can't be consciously held accountable for the world's evil...are the real villains in life the murderers, the thieves, the destitute ordinary people with no real influence over humanity except for their isolated acts of violence affecting only individuals, but who for the most part do not have any far reaching effect on society's future success...the real evil in life is found in those people who have power and are misguided in their thinking to perpetuate their power at the expense of the masses...these selfish people using ego driven motives, in the subtlest ways, limit humanity in its natural evolution towards perfection and purpose...

This monstrous skyscraper went against those who controlled society for their own financial and personal benefit. It will promote alternative energy resources, helping today's "modern" buildings decrease their consumption of more than half of the world's consumable energy thereby decreasing green house gases and improving the overall quality of the Earth's atmosphere. There will be little need for coal or nuclear powered electricity from a major utility company to power and light this building or fossil fuel to power its generators.

The major tenant of this building will be a powerful corporation. Its sole purpose: - to eliminate from the world the use of fossil fuels, and to develop and promote the use of renewable energy resources. The goal of this building is a definite threat to the future of the United States' petroleum and coal industries. This skyscraper corporation will be employing primarily Native Americans, a race of people who ironically had their culture, customs, food sources, and land taken from them by the same powerful organizations that will oppose this building. The intellectual energies and resources of these people will explore the development of solar power, electric cars, fuel cells, and the recycling of human and animal waste to produce methane gas to power motors for appliances and vehicles.

— — —

Tony's design started to unfold before him.

The building will be like no other on the planet. It will be an organic masterpiece. Everything in, on, and around the building would be working in harmony with nature while fulfilling the needs of its biggest challenge, the human element.

The building would follow Mr. Mogul's caveats that it be capable of self-generation and be responsive from the proliferation of an Architectural design that is totally governed by nature's laws. Its form would follow not function, but the natural evolution of life's cycles for birth, life, growth and death; naturally generating economic, social, and ecological advantages for the surrounding Native American communities and beyond.

Most importantly the building would fulfill these important goals directly from the sun by producing its own food, capturing oxygen from plants, recycling waste water, generating consumable nutrients and maintaining an on-site waste management system. Using regionally available building materials, it would be capable of absorbing itself naturally within its surrounding environment. In addition to the building producing its own power from wind turbines, solar cells and fuel cells, it will be capable of maintaining this energy efficiently by utilizing a super insulated and double walled exterior skin. It will use sunshades that will dynamically follow the altitude and azimuth angles of the sun, shading the occupants from the intensity of the sun's light while redirecting this light to the photovoltaic arrays and to naturally lighting the building's interior.

The building's birth would begin with its emergence from the womb of Mother Earth.

> *The site that will spawn the building would be filled with gardens and wooded areas surrounding it in a tribute to the early concepts of Frank Lloyd Wright, who envisioned a balance between technological man and nature. This was a most difficult balance to achieve, but once achieved, its very essence gave life a true harmony between the contradictory complexities of human intelligence and the always honest simplicity of nature's laws, providing an exhilaration beyond what could previously be felt by anyone ever before. It was truth.*
>
> *At the building's base would be a series of simple paths and footbridges connecting it with the Crow villages that would eventually surround it. The building's materials and colors would contain rich natural hues that would blend harmoniously with the colors of the surrounding land. It would not, like most commercial buildings in the big cities of America, be divorced from its surroundings.*

It would have sky gardens, botanical gardens with waterfalls, every ten floors as the building climbed toward the heavens. There would be outside observation decks and grass roofs and at the 100th floor, a Native American history and world science museum.

It would be built with operable windows and louvers that would use natural ventilation to supplement air-conditioning and enhance air circulation. It would incorporate selective passive heating and cooling technologies coupled with energy efficient mechanical systems and use all natural non-toxic interior materials.

The design details of the security, internal and external telecommunications, lighting, heating, and cooling will be assigned to the engineers for development within the parameters of Tony's design and the building's intent.

Tony began sketching the container in which all of these functional elements would be housed.

The building's footprint would effectively be a two-thirds circle derived from two graceful arcs, each starting due south and arcing east and west, each at 120º, representing the sun's complete 240º azimuth from sunrise to sunset on this latitude's longest day of the year- the Summer Solstice. This sun capturing elevation would encompass full east, west, and partial north exposures. The remaining 120º of the building, its "back triangle," would be partially filled with a straight north wall section without windows. It would provide no sustainable energy attributes to the building. Instead, this area of the building would house its utility and vertical transportation elements. Elevators, stair towers, mechanical equipment, toilet rooms, electrical and telephone closets, generators, storage and anything else the engineers would require to sustain the energy captured by the sun and the wind will be located here, in the "dead zone," as Tony decided to label it.

Tony envisioned the building as being segmented into four specific vertical sections.

The maximum floor-to-floor height of each floor, for now, would be limited to approximately twelve and a half feet. This height would be finalized to its most efficient dimension as the design evolved.

The footprint of the initial section of sixty-four floors will occupy the largest ground area. The first five floors will contain a grand entrance lobby to showcase the building's innovative design. The next block of forty-two floors will begin atop the first sixty-four in a thirty-three percent smaller area. The third block will again be one third smaller and contain the remaining thirty occupiable floors. The building's final twenty-four floors of three hundred feet, would be devoted exclusively to wind turbine placement, communications equipment and an observatory.

This last section was the very heart of the building, the physical part of the building that would give it life - its heart. Approximately two hundred fifty feet of the remaining three hundred foot building height will be exclusively devoted to wind turbines, each turbine housed in its individual structural grid. The engineers will determine the most efficient size, quantity and configuration of these turbines in order for them to provide maximum power to the building. Their power output combined with that produced by the solar cells, fuel cells, hydroelectric generators, and if required, remote wind farms, would supply the building with all the energy it would need to power its attributes.

The wind currents flowing through the turbines will freely exit from the building's open north facade, but first would be channeled to dampers to counter the wind's forces with an opposite force to minimize the twisting and turning of the building's structure due to the wind's velocity. These counterweights or dampers would be contained within each wind turbine's structural framework. The use of cylindrical or directional turbines enabling the wind to be captured and utilized from any compass direction was also proposed.

For wind turbine maintenance, dedicated elevators would safely transport maintenance personnel to catwalks and ladder stairs for routine servicing and inspection.

At Mr. Mogul's request, the remaining fifty feet of the building would be devoted to an observatory and the installation of satellite communications equipment enabling communications with the rest of the world and beyond.

Finally, as promised to Johnny Thunder Eagle and the Crow Nation, a white marble eagle statue with a myriad of white laser beams emitting from its heart and aimed toward the Milky Way and the constellation "Aquila," the Eagle, and its brightest star, Altair, would be placed at the building's apex, above the observatory. It would signify a spiritual and cultural rebirth and unification between men of nature and technology, a symbiotic marriage between the Native American union with nature and the white man's misguided, but advantageous and usually well-meaning technological world.

The successful completion of this building, Tony hoped, would make distant memories of oil spills, air pollution, and the destruction of the atmosphere from the adverse chemical by-products of fossil fuels. After construction of this building, with the promise of hundreds of similar buildings following its advanced sustainability concepts, those unfortunate events, eventually, will dissolve into distant memories.

— — —

Tony was writing and sketching his concepts through the night for almost five hours. The sun would soon rise for the dawn of a new day as he reviewed his night's work. His food rations were exhausted. He felt as if he had just crawled out from under a rock. He needed to sleep for a couple hours before his nine o'clock morning meeting in Billings.

Today's pace was insane. He didn't know if he could survive many more days like this. He looked over at the giant bed with its fresh sheets and comfortable mattress, got up from his seated position and walked towards it with a purpose. Before allowing his head to rest on the bed's large pillow and closing his eyes for a much needed nap, he needed to perform his nightly ritual, something he did every night since his mother's death.

Searching through his duffel bags, he found and carefully unwrapped two candles, one a cream color, the other light pink. These two objects represented his unique path to a private spiritual comfort. He set them in their brass holders, side by side, on the nightstand next to his giant bed. He shut all the lights in the room, save for one dimly lit bulb in a far corner of the large room. He knelt down in front of the candles and lit their blackened wicks. He said the words, the words that were music to his restless soul for the past four years.

"Mother and Father, I ask your loving watchful eye to guide me through the new day tomorrow and I thank you for guiding me safely through today. May the love you eternally share for each other be the strength that I carry within me to battle those who do not understand the value of truth and love. Maria and Louis Rullo may the higher power of life's creator bless your souls and may you rest in a peaceful embrace."

He blew out the candles and purposely squeezed the hot wicks with his fingers to experience a brief moment of pain in his parent's memory.

He stood up emotionally drained from his long day. He checked his wristwatch for the time. Then, he pulled out an alarm clock from one of his duffels, wound it up, set its time and alarm, and gratefully collapsed on the bed fully clothed. He slept peacefully and without dreams.

———

The obnoxious sound of the alarm clock's ring woke Tony at 8:00 AM. His milestone day was about to begin. He took a brief, almost warm shower, shampooed his curly Italian head of hair, quickly shaved, threw on some clean clothes captured from his bags of stuff, grabbed every piece of information prepared only a few hours before and bolted out the door to his truck, only to be reminded how cold it was.

...Thank God, it didn't snow...

He immediately went back inside removed his baseball jacket, threw it on the floor, grabbed a wool sweater, and the heaviest coat he could find, along with a scarf, gloves and a wool cap. He was now ready to roll out the door safely insulated from the cold.

Tony threw his stuff in the truck, sat himself down in the driver's seat, placed the key in the ignition, turned it to start the truck and heard nothing. He turned the key repeatedly and still heard nothing. Then, he remembered. He had left the truck's headlights on all night and its battery was stone cold dead. It was eight-thirty in the morning. He had to be in Billings, which was eighteen miles away in thirty minutes.

He couldn't call the office for help since telephone service in his cabin would not be available until the week's end. He was in an unfortunate position. There were over forty very important people patiently waiting for him to make his presentation, people whose assignments for the day were dependent on the content of Tony's work.

...This is not a good way to make a first impression....

Tony thought of a possible solution to starting the truck - push it up to a sufficient speed to pop the clutch and turn the engine over. This was not a possible. Tony wasn't strong enough to push the truck to any appreciable speed, since it was facing the wrong way on a gentle downhill slope. His other option was to start walking and running to Billings, as fast as he could. At a brisk pace he probably could get there in three or four hours sweaty, frozen and exhausted. It would be awkward, slow and cold. He would have to carry all his drawings and materials. If he was lucky, when he reached the main road he may be able to hitch a ride. That was probably his best possibility, however unfavorable, to reach the office sometime before noon. What he really needed was a search party from Billings to rescue him.

Then, Tony thought of something else that might work. He switched off the headlights allowing the battery to minimally recharge and got out of the truck. He went inside the cabin to find his trusty Volt-Ohm-Meter, or VOM, a meter he had had for years and used often. It took him a few minutes of searching through his bags of stuff until he finally found it, watching it fall from a gray duffel bag, bouncing and sliding its way across the wood floor. His foot blocked its unimpeded romp and he picked it up, checked it for continuity and ran out to the truck.

Reaching the truck, he popped its hood, located the battery and his VOM observed its voltage at slightly above ten volts. This was not good. It would take at least twelve volts to crank the starter. He had to find another twelve-volt battery or one that could add three or four volts. He sat on the truck's cold fender feeling defeated and without hope. He stood up and turned toward the cabin to search for something inside that could work. His eyes fixed on the emergency generator. He apprehensively walked toward it hoping against hope that it had the something he needed. Reaching his destination, he inspected the generator. It had a battery-powered ignition.

...This could work...the generator has a small six-volt battery, unfortunately a battery that's been sitting outside in the cold holding its charge for God knows how long...

He measured the generator's battery voltage. It was 5.3 volts. Using the wrenches from the truck's on-board toolbox, he hastily removed the battery from the generator's frame and carried it back to the Ford.

The sun was shinning brightly this morning. Its beams of radiant energy were shining directly on the truck's engine. Tony welcomed all the heat he could capture. By wiring the two batteries in series, it should total over fifteen volts and may provide sufficient power to turn the engine over on this cold morning. He was aware that their potential differences could result in a chemical imbalance and a possible explosion. Under the truck hood with jumper cables found in the truck, Tony quickly fabricated his hybrid fifteen-volt battery. He stepped back from the truck, apprehensively watching the batteries for any signs of distress. A few seconds went by. Nothing happened. They didn't explode.

Feeling safer now, he quickly walked back to the truck and measured the combined voltage of this emergency battery. The meter recorded over fifteen and a half volts. *This is encouraging.* He sat in the truck behind the wheel, pumped the gas several times and pulled out the choke. He put the key in the ignition and turned it to start.

After several uncooperative engine grunts, the V-8 engine made its starter induced revolutions, shuddering and shaking its way into Tony's heart, as it coughed itself to life. Tony revved up the engine and breathed a sigh of relief.

...Innovative solutions to seemingly impossible problems were the key to living a successful and fulfilling life here on Earth, especially when it involved starting a truck with a dead battery on a very cold Montana morning...

He disconnected the emergency generator's battery, being very careful not to touch the truck's steel frame and run fifteen nasty volts through his body. He reconnected the battery cables and closed the hood. Success! Everything was right with the world. The Ford was warming up, sounding smoother and happier.

He checked inside the cabin to make sure he didn't forget any of his design concepts and plans, ran to the truck, put it in reverse and started his journey toward Billings. It was nine-ten. He was late, but had a great story to tell everyone at the office, that is, if he still had a job.

Then he remembered, in the cabin were the directions back to Billings.

He could take the chance on remembering his way back, but decided it wasn't worth the risk. He drove back to the cabin, retrieved the directions and flashlight, got into the truck, and headed to the office.

He was driving as fast as the bumpy dirt road would allow. Dust was flying up from the road and Tony was bouncing around the cab like a rodeo bull rider, but he didn't care. He didn't care. He was starting to feel good, no incredibly good as if he were on a drug induced high.

He couldn't wait to get to the office and start the creative energies flowing.

Tony put on his sunglasses looked up at the sun and smiled.

…This is going to be a good day….

CHAPTER 20

THE PRESENTATION

To Tony, the time traveling the eighteen miles to the office lasted only a few moments as his mind was floating in the undetermined fluid of space that had no conception of time. It was nearly ten when the wheels of his truck came to a screeching halt in front of the furniture warehouse. He parked his truck close to the building's entrance. A convenient parking space was not a rare find in this small western town.

Ironically, he rationalized; being late for this meeting was caused by a personal energy crisis; a self-inflicted one, but one never the less. It was exactly what the skyscraper was envisioned to eliminate by providing its own power using the latest state of the art renewable energy technology. Tony solved his energy crisis by using a crudely fabricated spare parts booster battery.

Gathering up all of his drawings, notes, and files, he made his way from the truck to the warehouse lobby to Brenda, the awaiting receptionist. As he reached her desk, she greeted Tony.

"Good Morning Mr. Rullo. Are you okay? Did you over sleep? Oh my goodness, we were so worried you may have had some a problem getting here from that old cabin. We were about to send someone out there to check on you. It's so remote. I know you'll be happy to finally have a telephone there. Anyway, I'm happy to see you're okay. Don't worry about being late. They are all patiently waiting for you in the main conference room. I have a cup of coffee for you, if you like. Is that okay?"

"Good morning Brenda. I'm so sorry for being late. Thank you for worrying about me. Yes, a cup of coffee will be great. I don't think I have any free hands to carry it to the conference room. Would you mind giving me a hand?"

Brenda was a Billings local. She was a down-home friendly, pleasant and attractive person - a welcomed addition to the office environment. Her response to Tony was typical Brenda.

"Of course Tony. I'd be happy to carry your coffee and anything else you may need to take to the meeting for you."

"Thanks. I really appreciate it. You know, I do have a pretty good reason for being late. You'll be sure to hear about it after the meeting. Unfortunately, right now I have to concentrate on convincing the people in that room that I'm not a total screw up. I wish they were all like you."

"Oh Tony; don't worry about a thing. I'm sure they are as concerned and worried about you as I was. Just be yourself and give them a chance. They'll understand."

"I hope so."

"We better get going."

"I know. I'm late enough for my show."

As Tony was walking down the hall, he took several sips from the coffee held in Brenda's helpful hand, stopped at the water cooler for a quick drink to cool his palette and began to contemplate his entrance.

THE PRESENTATION

The doors to the conference room were closed. Brenda extended her free hand to open them. Tony and Brenda made their apprehensive entrance into the large room.

Tony knew that whatever awaited him beyond these doors could be an uncomfortable embarrassing experience. The attendees at this landmark meeting would be critically focused on him, anticipating an acceptable explanation for his late arrival, and likely to be very skeptical as to the merits of his proposed design. He dreaded the pending assumptions of irresponsibility and incompetence from those seated in judgment. Nevertheless, he was prepared to handle the pressure. He had programmed himself during his eighteen-mile trip to impose an overwhelming positive energy unto a potentially skeptical crowd and present his design concept with undeniable confidence and conviction. However, he was not prepared for the surprise that awaited him.

"Good luck," Brenda said, as she placed the coffee on the large conference room table at Tony's assigned seat. She immediately left the room.

Sitting there were forty-three professionals patiently waiting – and Neil.

Neil broke the silence.

"Tony! Welcome! We are very honored that you finally decided to find time in your busy schedule to attend our meeting."

"Thank you Neil. I'm sorry I'm so late. I have a good excuse – honestly I do. It's rather amusing."

"I'm sure it is. Tony, before we get to your 'rather assuming' excuse, and I know we are all anxious to hear it, there is something I need to tell you. We have discussed it with all those in this room and have reached an unanimous decision."

"What's that?"

"Tony, regrettably you failed your first and only test. You were late. There is no excuse for it. You have inconvenienced too many people on this very important day. And since Mr. Mogul has zero tolerance for this type of behavior, pack up your things. You're fired," Neil said, with all seriousness.

The words hit Tony with an unsettling impact.

*…I knew it…*he thought…*my dream has ended…it's finally over…one mistake…that's it…I can't be trusted…I don't blame them.*

He looked over at Neil. Neil stared back intently. After a few seconds of this icy stare, Tony managed an embarrassed smile and started to apologize, hoping for a reprieve, but before any words could leave his mouth, the room's silence was broken by spontaneous applause and the sound of laughter. Everyone was clapping and yelling remarkably encouraging things at Tony. Totally confused, all he could do was produce a moronic grin.

…Was this a joke?…am I actually forgiven…?

Neil shouted through the noise.

"Okay. Okay. Everyone calm down," Neil said. "Sorry Tony. We just had to do it to you. We were getting bored waiting for you to show up. We decided to mock fire you as punishment for being late. By the expression on your face, I think it made quite an impact. We were worried about you. We're happy to see that you're okay."

"Well it worked. You scared the crap out of me. I need a drink."

Neil walked over to Tony. He placed his hands on Tony's shoulders and whispered, "Relax, we know we went a little overboard with our little joke, but it did get your attention. It's okay. Take all the time you need to get ready for your presentation. We'll wait."

"It's okay. I'm ready."

After a few more sips of his coffee, Tony tacked up his sketches and assembled his written information.

"Okay Tony, we're ready too," Neil said. "Now show us what you've prepared and it'd better be great or I may have to reconsider my previous decision. The room is all yours. Impress us with your inspired design."

Tony took a deep breath. It was time.

"Thank you, Neil. Gentlemen, and ladies…good morning. I sincerely apologize for being late. After my presentation, I'll enlighten you about the unfortunate self-inflicted incident which caused it. Consider it as post-presentation entertainment. Before I begin, I want to complement all of you for that convincing attempt at firing me. Well done. It's something I will never forget – believe me. Now, with that adventure behind us, I will enlighten you with my noble effort in designing the greatest building in the world."

Tony enthusiastically began his presentation. It took him over an hour to present every detail and concept of his proposed design. Neil and the project team listened and absorbed every intimate detail. They were excited by the possibilities and unlimited potential that Tony's design had to offer.

The electrical engineers were anxious to begin their work on the design of the wind turbines and photovoltaics. Every discipline of technical expertise grabbed at their piece of the building's conceptual pie. The opportunity for breakthrough innovation was evident in Tony's design and it wasn't going to be denied.

— — —

The meeting lasted over six hours. It was a non-stop activity of comments, criticisms, planning, and coordinating. Design schedules were prepared and the fast track road to design development was now officially opened for business.

At the end of the meeting, while the attendees were distributing themselves to begin their personal assignments, Neil grabbed Tony, put his arm around him, and said, "Tony...let me say with all seriousness, and with the utmost sincerity, that I am very proud of you today. You stepped up to the bar and you met the challenge like I knew you would. You put together an excellent and innovative design in a very short time. Thank you. It's going to work and it's going to be great. I'm excited about the possibilities. Can't wait to tell Mr. Mogul. Are you ready to talk to him?"

"What do you mean?"

"I mean we're going to have a conference call with him right now. How do you feel about that?"

"I think I'm going to be sick."

"You'll be fine. Just repeat everything you said at the meeting. You'll see he's very easy to talk to. Come on. We'll do it from my office. He's waiting for our call. There are a few things you have to promise me before we speak with him."

"What's that?"

"Do not ask any personal questions or how the Great Spirit used him to select you. He won't answer you anyway. Okay?"

"Okay. I promise. Let's do this before I pass out from fear," Tony said.

--- --- ---

The introductory call to Mr. Mogul went well. Mr. Mogul enthusiastically approved Tony's design and let him know this - without pretense - without hesitation. Tony was discussing the call with Neil - walking with him to the warehouse's exit – proud of his work for the day and embracing the thought of an easy day tomorrow.

"Well I guess that's it," Tony said. "Thanks Neil. That was an awesome experience. You're right, Mr. Mogul is a very captivating individual. Can't wait to personally meet him."

"I'm sure the feeling is mutual. Did you have a good time today?"

"Are you kidding? It's been unforgettable. Without a doubt, the greatest day of my life, but right now I'm too exhausted to feel any emotion. I really need to go home and get some sleep. I plan on sleeping late tomorrow if that's okay with you."

Neil looked back at Tony with a pained, questionable expression. Tony caught the look and knew he was in trouble.

"Oh no," Tony said. "Tell me you don't have something tediously important for me on your schedule for tomorrow? Did I mention the word *exhausted*?"

"Yes you did. Don't worry. You're young. You'll recover. You're right - there's something on our schedule for tomorrow, but it isn't a major deal. You can handle it. I know you worked very hard last night pulling this design together, and your *electrifying* adventure with the truck, that was a classic-"

"Okay Neil, quit stalling. What's going on tomorrow?"

"Remember we discussed with Johnny the selection and surveying of the building site on the rez…?"

"Yes, but—"

"Surprise! That's tomorrow."

"I should have known."

"Relax. It'll be hardly any work at all. We'll take our time, walk the area, and designate the actual site perimeter for our skyscraper. If we have time we'll work out a few site details for your design too. Johnny'll be with us. He'll take us to the area designated by the Tribal Council and Mr. Mogul for the building's construction. Be at the office at eight."

"Is that it? No more surprises?"

"No. That's it. See you tomorrow?" Neil said as he crossed his fingers behind his back.

"I guess, but why are you telling me this now? You must have known about it for days. Why now…with no prep?"

"I had to do it this way Tony. Otherwise you would have been distracted from devoting one hundred percent of your energy to your design. I couldn't allow you to become distracted. I needed you fully focused on this building's design. You understand."

"I understand I was manipulated, if that's what you mean. By the way, your idea of walking the site all day tomorrow in the early morning hours is not my idea of relaxing and taking the day off. You're without mercy."

"Merciless Neil – that's me - so quit your complaining. It won't work. Anyway, don't hate the messenger. It's not me that's merciless - it's this project. You knew it was not going to show anyone any mercy. We have direct orders to get this site defined and selected by close of business tomorrow. We aren't permitted to waste a single day. Don't worry. You'll learn to adjust to this insane pace. Listen…if it will make you feel any better, look at our task tomorrow as a fun filled field trip. It'll be fun. I'll drive. You can rest. To make up for it, I'll treat you to dinner tonight. After that, you can go home with a full stomach and get to bed at a decent hour. Come on…"

"That's the least you can do, since I'm ready to pass out from starvation and exhaustion…"

CHAPTER 21

THE SITE VISIT

At nine o'clock in the morning on a cold January Montana day, Tony and Neil arrived at the home of Johnny Thunder Eagle in a four-wheel drive faded gray 1973 GMC *Suburban*, a large truck-like passenger utility vehicle that could seat nine. It resembled a station wagon on steroids. Tony hated this "thing". It was big, slow and consumed large quantities of gasoline. It had no personality and handled like a spastic truck

...The anti-Christ of energy efficient transportation... Tony thought.

He was hoping the future of automobile production in America would produce more environmentally friendly vehicles than this *Suburban*. Its one redeeming quality was that it did serve its purpose well over the wide-open country of Montana. He would appreciate its functional attributes in a continuing love-hate relationship as the project evolved over the next few years. He concluded that his pick-up truck was a utility vehicle with a more endearing reputation.

— — —

Johnny was waiting outside his small house in an unzippered heavy wool coat, no hat, no gloves, seemingly oblivious to the cold. He was shouldering a backpack. In it were packed sandwiches and a large thermos of coffee. He was prepared for a long day of site hunting with Tony and Neil.

Johnny's house had all the essentials required to make it a comfortable home. It was a simple aluminum clad, wood frame box, with an asphalt-shingled roof. It housed all the basic needs on one floor. It was similar to Tony's cabin, but without the personality and warmth. Unlike Tony's shelter, it had two separate bedrooms, a bathroom, a living room and a kitchen large enough to accommodate a dining area. It sat in a long row of homes, all similar, all wanting; all occupied by Crow families in various stages of their life's journey.

Neil and Tony waited in the *Suburban* for Johnny. Since their initial meeting with him, they were curious to know more about this prominent member of the Mogul team. Today, they would have that opportunity.

Tony had a special interest in Johnny's personal history. When he was first introduced to him, it brought with it a certain sense of familiarity. Tony felt something, a connection, as if they had met before. He needed to find out if Johnny shared the same feelings and if he did, did he understand what they could possibly mean.

...What on Earth do I have in common with this man?...

The three of them sat comfortably in the front seat. Tony, being the smallest, occupied the middle. He was the little kid in mom and dad's station wagon. The thirty-minute drive to the site's location allowed for a casual conversation to develop. Tony resisted the urge to immediately satisfy his curiosity about Johnny by asking him personal questions. Instead, he decided to say little and allow Johnny the opportunity to open up. It was the safe thing to do. After all, Johnny represented someone from a sensitive culture and history. Tony was ignorant of this culture and was not about to add to that reality with any inappropriate comments. After a few minutes of idle chatter, the conversation was dominated by Johnny, as he offered an uninhibited account of his life on and off the reservation.

After a few minutes of Johnny's stories, Tony realized whether it was his life in New Jersey or Johnny's life on the reservation, life experiences were universally human, and at the moment, universally shared. Tony embraced the details of Johnny's life, so much not like his, so much not like anything he knew.

The men exchanged personal information in rapid-fire sequence trying to satisfy their mutual curiosities and interests. They discovered fascinating new things about one another. However, there was one question Tony could not wait any longer to ask Johnny.

"Johnny, I need to ask you something. It's been on my mind since we first met at the Tribal Council meeting," Tony said.

"What is it Tony?"

"Is there some remote chance that we've met sometime, somewhere before? I feel like I know you in some obscure way. Is that possible?"

Johnny smiled and looked at Tony and answered. "You have never met me, but I have seen you before - from a distance, a few years ago."

Tony's eyes widened. "Really? I had a feeling. When? Where?"

Johnny continued to smile, eager to explain.

"About three or four years ago, during the summer - here on the rez - you were traveling with a group of tourists on a guided tour of the Custer Battlefield. Am I Correct?" he said.

"Yeah. I think it was four years ago. But how -"

"I was there that day guiding a group of teenagers, seniors from a Hardin High School class. They were on a field trip gathering information about the battlefield for a Native American history assignment. I saw you. Just for a few seconds. Did not give it a second thought. You were just another tourist on a bus tour, but something about you made you stand out from the rest. I could sense that this stranger was to become part of my future. Your face has been permanently etched into my mind since then."

"The dream Tony…," Neil said.

"Yeah Neil…the dream."

"What dream?" Johnny asked.

Tony then told his "dream" story to Johnny along with his varied experiences, living on a working ranch in Montana. Johnny just listened and nodded with approval. When Tony finished his story Johnny said, "Stoney was right again."

Tony looked at Johnny with a puzzled look. "Who's Stoney? What was he right about?"

"Stoney is our reservation Shaman, our holy man, and he predicted someone like you would be included in my life someday as part of a grand plan by the Great Spirit. Your dream was your vision to your future. You just did not understand its meaning," Johnny said.

"I guess not, but at least I tuned in to previously meeting you. What does this Great Spirit *connection* have to do with me?" Tony said.

"Tony, I mentioned to you before that Mr. Mogul was guided by the Great Spirit in your selection as the primary solar design architect for this building," Neil said.

"Yeah. You told me," Tony said.

"Well, Johnny is part of that process. It's a very interesting and enlightening story and I know you are anxious to discuss it in more detail with Johnny, but it will have to wait.

We don't have the time right now. We need to immediately begin our work. You can continue this conversation later. I'm curious about it myself. Okay Tony…Johnny?"

"Wait a minute! Not so fast Neil. There's a lot of curious stuff going on between Johnny, the *Great Spirit,* and me. You said I would understand how I was chosen in a few days. Now that I'm finally getting a little info on the subject, you want me to stop?…don't think so."

"Tony, listen. There are many things about this project that are going to make your head spin. You'll have hundreds of questions. At the moment, I don't want to get sidetracked from our mission here. For now, let's try to stay focused on what we need to do today. We'll talk more about your connection with Johnny and the Great Spirit later, I promise. Please... Try to understand. Okay?" Neil said.

Johnny added. "It is okay Tony. We will talk later."

Tony exchanged glances with the two men. He knew there was a lot that they were not telling him, but he also trusted their judgment and surrendered his curiosity for a later time.

"Okay guys. I'll wait. Looks like I have no choice. Let's get to work."

Any further conversations about the Tony-Johnny connection stopped simultaneously with the *Suburban* as it arrived at the designated area assigned for the building's construction. It was in the middle of nowhere, but part of somewhere very specific. It was considered by the Crow people as chosen holy ground. It was the only location where the Tribal Council would allow the proposed skyscraper to be built.

Neil and Johnny reached for the door handles, but before they had a chance to open the car doors, they were halted from their exit by the ground shaking beneath them. They sat in the vibrating truck; stunned, rigid, white knuckled onto anything that would keep them secure, unsure of what to do or how they were expected to react to this tremor. After about ten seconds the Earth's trembling stopped. The men however, did not. They were still shaking. Tony took a deep breath and looked over at Johnny.

"Holy shit! What the hell was that?" he said. "Was that an earthquake? Is that something that happens often around here, Johnny?"

"No. No. Not really," Johnny said. "At least I do not think so. It is my first. This area is not known for earthquakes. We have had some minor ones through the years and a major earthquake, a 7.4, was recorded in 1959 at West Yellowstone, but that was a very rare occurrence. I do not think this will happen again at least not for quite a while. Let us pray it does not."

"I hope you're right. Our building can't be built on potentially unstable ground. What do you think Johnny? Are we goin to be okay? Is it safe here?" Neil asked.

"That, I honestly do not know. Let us be thankful that it was only a minor tremor. If it is any consolation, I would prefer to think that we are safely in the protection of the Great Spirit. Maybe, it was just its way of letting us know that this place is a great source of energy and power for our new building," Johnny answered.

"No offense, but I think you're reaching a little there, Johnny. Do me a favor, will you? Since you seem to have a direct line to IT. Will you let the 'GS' know I don't appreciate ITS *subtle* way of showing us ITS approval," Tony said.

"The Great Spirit has many ways to convey its messages, Tony. If you become aware of its methods, there are specific interpretations about the meanings behind its actions. You should not feel afraid," Johnny said.

"Well, with knowing that, I hope that will be the end of its intense messages for today. You can explain to me later what they all mean. I'm certain it will be a rewarding experience for me to understand the power and guidance of this Great Spirit. It's not something that is discussed much in 'Jersey. By the way, I'm not afraid, just a little concerned," Tony said.

Johnny laughed and said, "I will be happy to enlighten you about the Great Spirit. However, I can assure you; your guess is as good as mine about its reasons for having us experience this earthquake. I do not know what it could mean. Not even Stoney predicted this one."

"I guess the Great Spirit wanted it to be a surprise." Tony said.

Neil replied. "It's nothing to worry about. We'll report the earthquake to our geologists and structural engineers. They'll review the seismic charts and maps, do their surveys, and investigate the potential for earthquakes in this area. They'll design the building's structural system to accommodate whatever it requires to resist an earthquake of any magnitude. No worries. Everything will work out to the building's benefit. Okay guys? Feeling better? I think we're safe now. So let's get our asses out of this truck and get to work."

— — —

After Neil's reassuring comments, the three men gathered their gear and attempted to exit the truck. As they opened its doors, something else stopped them in their tracks. They sat and watched as the sky turned black with a suddenness that defied logic. It was as if the sun suddenly had left the sky. It was a thunderstorm in the making, only without the thunder and without the storm.

"What the hell's happening now?" Tony said. "First, the earthquake and now this. What's next - the Earth suddenly opening up and swallowing us?"

Johnny remained silent trying to understand what this new phenomena could mean. Neil again tried to rise above this unexplained event of nature. He ignored Tony's outburst, deciding instead to divert Tony and Johnny's attention from the blackout to the work.

"All right gentlemen. Calm down. Calm down. Don't worry. I think it's safe to assume that the sun disappearing from the sky doesn't mean our world is coming to an end. It's probably just a side effect of the earthquake. I vote we ignore it and concentrate on beginning our task at finding the perfect location for our building's birth. So, if neither of you have any objections, let's go…but just in case… I'll leave the lights on and the motor running."

Johnny and Tony nodded reluctantly in agreement.

The three men carefully departed their steel encased protection, allowing their feet to cautiously probe the ground as if this action would somehow keep it from moving again. Confident that Mother Earth was not going to shake her bosom for a second time, they began their exploration of the area. They walked over its lightless vast expanse, slowly, in silence, with flashlights at the ready, the only sound being their footsteps compacting the turf below them. In all this subdued light and solitude they were attempting to find and designate a specific area that would be the perfect location for the skyscraper. They scanned the area – then they saw it. It was indisputable and obvious. In the darkness they witnessed an area the size of a truck tire glowing with a phosphorescent yellow light. The earthquake had brought to the surface something very special.

"Do you see that?" Tony said.

"Yeah. I see it. We all do," Neil answered. "The Earth is glowing. I've never seen anything like this before. Johnny, any ideas?"

"Yes. I have one. I believe that glow is being created from a disturbed phosphorus mineral deposit," Johnny said. "We should not get close to it. It needs to burn itself out. Its smoke is poisonous. I have witnessed this before on the reservation. My people call it the *phosphorous sun*."

Johnny then realized the importance and hidden meaning of the glowing phosphorous. It was purposely uncovered by the earthquake's disruptive force and made visible by the blackout.

"This must be another message from the Great Spirit. We are to build our building over a phosphorous mineral deposit, an element that is essential for the growth of all life. No plant or animal can exist or live without it. It is used to make sodas, fire, grow plants, and develop bones. It is an abundant mineral on our reservation."

"How do you know that?" Neil asked.

Johnny explained; "Many years ago one of Montana's largest mining companies wanted to strip mine coal from our reservation. They wanted to lease from the Crow Nation mineral rights to our land to extract this coal. The Tribal Council Government conditionally agreed to the lease. They charged them large fees to survey our land for coal. In the process they found enough coal reserves on the reservation to warrant a full mining operation. We allowed them to mine coal for a few years until we saw the uncompromising devastation and destruction of our lands from their strip mining. The Tribal Council finally revoked their lease on a legal technicality and refused any future requests by them to continue mining. What makes it so additionally difficult for the reservation today is that because of the Federal Government's energy policy influencing mining conglomerates to initiate mining operations to extract as much coal from Montana's eastern coal reserves as possible, the Crow are in a constant legal battle to prohibit coal mining on the reservation."

"The mining company tried to legally overturn the Tribal Council's decision using their influence with the BIA, but through several ugly and expensive court battles, they were eventually denied access. They left the reservation defeated and very angry. However, a by-product of their strip mining was the discovery of large deposits of igneous rock containing phosphorus. The reservation wanted to mine these phosphate rock deposits to extract, sell and use the elemental phosphorus for fertilizer and nutritional supplements for livestock. We tried to acquire government loans to buy equipment to develop our own environmentally friendly mining operation, but have been stonewalled with Government bureaucracy for years - now this."

"If we site the building here where the phosphorus glows, the excavation and site development will most probably yield high deposits of phosphorus. These deposits can be used by the reservation to our advantage. It appears to be part of the Great Spirit's plan. It also is a symbolic representation of a fertile area from which this building will grow strong. The glowing area is the predestined location of the building's heart and soul."

"The Great Spirit is telling us to dig here since the phosphorus that we excavate for the building's foundation will go back into the Earth to grow crops and help feed our people with a bountiful harvest fertilized from this site. This is our new home. It is blessed. It is in balance with nature. It has been given to us by the Great Spirit."

Tony and Neil just stood passively listening to Johnny's amazing story. They didn't respond, but both knew the events of the day were so far removed from the ordinary that they were not meant to be argued or discussed, just accepted. The powerful force that was controlling this project was not to be denied.

Johnny continued. "What do you think, Neil? Tony? Is that not the womb for our building's birth?"

Neil never had to make a site decision based on a glowing burning spot imposed directly from Mother Earth, but this was no ordinary site and this was no ordinary building. Neil pondered this unique series of events for a moment and made his decision. "I don't think I have any other choice, Johnny. I don't want to experience another 'natural event' if we say 'no' to this sign. I agree, this is the spot that will represent the center of our great building," he said.

There was no verbal response from Tony or Johnny, only physical affirmation. This was without a doubt the building's birthplace. It was here on the highest elevation in the immediate area amidst a phosphorus glow that the building would sit in prominence over the sea of green that would surround it.

The darkened sky began to lift its veil and lighten. Tony removed his Nikon SLR from its case, mounted it on its tripod, and began taking dozens of photos of the chosen site and the surrounding area, his 28-millimeter lens capturing as much of the panorama as possible with each exposure. Before Tony was through his second roll of film the sky was a stunning blue and the sun was shinning. The Great Spirit had stopped working its magic over this land of the "great teepee" as the Crow had light heartedly named this new skyscraper of freedom.

With the building's location obviously selected by the Great Spirit, the men established a benchmark to begin the survey. Each man walked a line that would define the site's perimeter. This perimeter enclosed an area covering roughly two hundred acres or about one-third of a square mile of land. They set wooden markers in the Earth representing the four corners defining the site's boundaries. The corners formed an irregular square. They planted a handmade white flag in a crudely measured site center close to the previously burning but now glowing crack in the Earth, signifying the building's heart. Their assignment for the day was now complete.

———

It had been a long day of walking miles and working almost six hours. The men sat near the building's proposed heart, rested, and thought about what they had seen, felt and accomplished. Johnny reached into his backpack, handed out the prepared sandwiches, and from the thermos, poured a hot cup of coffee to be shared with his friends. They began eating their lunch when it was almost time for dinner. Their work for the day was done, but their work for the next two and a half years was just beginning.

Neil said, while biting into a chicken salad sandwich; "These sandwiches are great Johnny…delicious. Thank your wife for me." He held up his sandwich in mock salute. "Great work everybody. We worked our butts off today. What an unforgettable day! Now we'll let the Civil Engineers professionally survey the site and correct our crude attempt at defining its boundaries, that is, if the Great Spirit is finished messing with us."

"I believe the Great Spirit has said all it needs to say to us for today. I do have a curious question for you Neil. Why are we setting site boundaries? Are they necessary? We are not imposing on anyone else's property other than Crow. Look around you. It is quiet country - wilderness. There is nothing or no one out here to disturb. You white people and your restrictive exploitative concepts of land ownership," Johnny said.

Neil laughed and said; "Okay Johnny. I know you've been through all this before with Mr. Mogul. You know the reasons. It's in our lease agreement with the reservation, which is part of a contract mandated by the Federal Government. We need our property lines, square footage and boundaries. That's how they know what to charge Mr. Mogul for the land use. They insist, even if all these boundaries become imaginary to everyone else. If gives our designers that invisible envelope from which to design."

"I know, I could not resist," Johnny said. "It is an 'Indian' thing. We will never convince you whites otherwise. Mother Earth should be free to all her children."

"I wish that were universally believed by everyone," Neil said.

Johnny shook his head in bewilderment letting the subject disappear into the cool air. He began to speak about what was spoken of before.

"So Tony, Neil has mentioned to you that Mr. Mogul selected you with guidance from the Great Spirit."

"Yes, that's what Neil told me. How he managed to pick me out of a crowd as 'The Architect' for this project is a mystery to me. I imagine supernatural guidance is as good a reason as any. What do you know Johnny? Did the Great Spirit single me out among the bewildered mass of humanity?"

"Yes. I was told by Stoney and Mr. Mogul that it did. I believe it was the same way I was chosen, through the spirit of a great white eagle."

"Great white eagle?" Tony said.

"It is one of the Great Spirit's messengers. Accept it for now. In the future you will personally experience and understand this messenger. It watches you. You are under its protection and guidance. This entire skyscraper project is under its protection."

"Really? Thanks for clearing that up for me," Tony said.

"You will understand better in time. Soon you will understand how we are part of the Great Spirit's great plan. The three of us are part of its great plan," Johnny said.

"If you say so. Maybe someday this will all make sense."

"Tony, are you okay with what I have presented to you?" Johnny said.

"I guess. I just need a little time to absorb and accept it."

"That is good. I will look forward to us walking together on the same path. We all have had a lot to experience this day. We must now allow the natural forces of the Great Spirit to guide us along the right path," Johnny said.

The three men sat on the ground continuing their discussion for hours about the Great Spirit, Mr. Mogul, and the building's promising future. Their conversation would end, as the day naturally began to darken, signifying the time for the men to pack up and head home. The *Suburban*'s passengers climbed into the truck to begin their journey back to Thunder Eagle's home. During the day Tony and Johnny had given birth to a friendship. Neil witnessed the two young men from different cultures, races, and religions, bond into a relationship that would transcend these inherent differences.

— — —

After arriving at his home, before Johnny removed his tired body from the truck, he asked Tony the question he had reserved all day for just this moment.

"Tony, I need to propose something to you at Stoney's request."

"Stoney's request? What's that?"

"I am proposing that you honor Stoney's request to participate in a Crow honored sacred ceremony - a Vision Quest."

"A Vision Quest? What do you mean?"

"It is something that was requested by Stoney. He has a very good reason for asking you to participate, otherwise, he would not impose on you something that didn't have a worthwhile purpose. It is not his way. The experience will help you understand some of the hidden meanings surrounding your future. It will be an enlightening experience for you. I will be with you throughout the ceremony, assuring your journey is a safe one."

"When?"

"Stoney would like to arrange it as soon as possible, perhaps in a few days. I will explain to you then, how your Vision Quest will be performed, and what you can expect while experiencing its influence. Will you accept?"

"Don't know. This is so unexpected and highly unusual. I don't deal with surprises well. I need some time to think about it. My work on this building requires every minute of my time, especially now at its inception. I don't think I can fit it into my busy schedule for a while – maybe I will have some free time in a few months. Neil, what do you think? Can I spare any time for a quest of my vision?"

Neil answered. "You're covered Tony. Mr. Mogul has already given his blessing. We can work around your schedule. He didn't say why, but he wants you to experience what he's experienced. In fact, he's practically ordering you to do it. If it's okay with you, it's okay with him. However, the final decision is yours – no pressure."

"No pressure – my ass. This sounds like another - *offer I can't refuse* - decision. So, this bizarre request has been discussed before Johnny's invitation? Neil, you know, I'm getting a little tired of these 'little' surprises. This is the second one in two days…please – enough is enough."

"Sorry Tony. Again - it's your boss' idea - not mine. You'll just have to adapt to his unusual methods, just like everyone else working on this project. Believe me, he has only your best interests in mind," Neil said.

"Okay. Okay. I accept. I'm too tired to argue. If Mr. Mogul *and* Stoney want me to do this, so be it, I'll do it. Just let me know the *when* and *where* and I'll be there. Don't know what else to say. Need to know a lot more about it though. There's a lot I don't know - a lot. Johnny?"

"Do not worry," Johnny said. "I will explain everything you will need to know during our travel to the sacred site. We will begin our journey from my home in three days beginning on Friday before sunrise. The entire event including travel time will require most of the weekend. We will return Saturday evening. You will have Sunday to rest – at home. Friday, we will have a few hours drive ahead of us. Are you comfortable with riding there in my jeep? It has no top. It will be cold…or should we take your truck?"

Tony replied. "My truck…definitely my truck, although its heater doesn't seem to be working. At least, it'll be a little warmer. I'm okay with that. I have a question for you Johnny. Why is everything at sunrise with you people? Don't you ever sleep late and begin your ceremonies in the 'noon? Ever since this project started, sleep seems to be something that is in short supply. But for you, and only you, because I like you, I will drag my tired little body to your home - Friday morning at sunrise. Just let me know what you want me to take with me…Neil?"

"What?"

"What do you think?"

"Like I said before, everything has been approved. It's all good Tony. Don't worry about anything. But remember, I want to hear all about it when you return. Work hard the next few days, and then let yourself fly free for your enlightening weekend. By all means, enjoy yourself," Neil said.

"Okay. I can do that," Tony said. "So far, this project has been one non-stop barrage of the unexpected." Tony held out his hand to Johnny. "Johnny, thanks for everything. I will see you Friday morning."

"Tony, it has been a pleasure," Johnny said. "Thank you for a fine day. The site we selected will make a perfect home for our new building. I will give you a call at the office tomorrow to let you know what to pack and what to expect. I will see you on Friday."

"Okay. That sounds like a plan I can live with," Tony said.

After the three men said their "good-byes," Johnny left the *Suburban* for the short walk to his front door. He waved at Tony and Neil as they began their drive back to Billings. Tony thought about the day and knew that he and Johnny Thunder Eagle were destined to become lifelong friends. Their connection was real. He wasn't concerned as to the *why*. He would find out in time.

Sitting passively in the now roomy front seat, Tony looked over at Neil and said, "Neil, it's been a very strange day, but I wouldn't have missed any of it for all the buildings in New York City. Although, I wish you would have given me some advanced warning about this *Vision Quest* thing. First, the site visit surprise, and now this? Any more surprises for me down the road?"

"Not that I know of…honest. That's all of it. Like I said before, none of this was my idea. Stoney and Mr. Mogul wanted it kept a secret. They felt it was better if you didn't know until today. Don't worry about it. It'll be okay."

"So this was the - *I'll know in a few days* - thing?

"I certainly hope so, for your sake. We've put you through a lot…and it's only been a few days…"

"I know…any *crazy* plans for tomorrow?"

"All I know is that you'll get back to work on your design. Oh…don't forget to get all the film to Brenda for developing ASAP. Have her get two copies of each photo. Your project team will meet with you tomorrow morning at nine to discuss the details and development of your design. Schedule a site visit with them as soon as possible. Don't let any of them influence you against your better judgment regarding the building's design or the site. Many of them are jealous. They think you're too young and inexperienced to be in charge, but if any one of them gives you problems, let me know, I'll relocate them. There are ten others waiting to take their place. I've made that clear to everyone on your project team," Neil said.

"Yes Neil. You've reminded me of that over a hundred times, but understand, I'll always listen to what anyone has to say. I want to keep an open mind. This building is important to me. I want to get it perfect. I don't want to miss any critical details."

"Didn't mean to imply otherwise. There's just so much work to do and we're on a very tight schedule. I'm personally beginning to implode."

"I know the feeling. See you at tomorrow's meetings?"

Neil paused for a moment before answering and looked at Tony as if he were trying to read his mind.

"No. I'll be picking Lisa up at the airport. She's finally making her way to Montana. Can't wait to see her. It's been only a few days, but I really miss her. We'll grab a bite, stop off at our apartment, and after she settles in, I'll take her to the office and introduce her to all the worker bees. So, I won't see you until after lunch. I'll give her time to rest before she gets involved full time on this project. Her being here is important to me."

...Important to you...and a big problem for me...! Tony thought.

Neil noticed Tony's facial expression had changed to one of concern.

"What's wrong, Tony? Are you okay? Tony!" Neil said.
"What!?"

"You looked worried. Are you okay? Did you hear anything I just said?"

"Yeah. I heard you. *Lisa's coming to Montana.* That's great. Can't wait to see her too. Sorry. I was just thinking about all the work I have to do on this project - trying to filter it all through my mind in some rigid logical sequence. You know what? It doesn't work. I'll just have to let this project flow through me naturally as Johnny said..."

In fact, Tony was lying. Every time Lisa would enter his life in thought or action he would have to fight every impulse to not react to his honest feelings. It was interfering with his concentration on the job. Perhaps the Vision Quest would help ease this tension. He needed something.

"...Neil, is it okay if I jump in the backseat and take a short nap? I need to rest for a little while. It's been a long day at the end of a long hard few weeks," Tony said.

"Sure. It's okay. Sleep. You deserve it. I'll wake you when we get to the office," Neil said.

The *Suburban* rolled onto the state highway to Billings. Tony sprawled out on the backseat and gently closed his eyes. Neil drove back to the office with his own disturbing thoughts about Lisa and Tony.

CHAPTER 22

THE ARRIVAL

The ride from the office up North 27th Street to the Rimrock location of the Logan International Airport, took less than ten minutes. The airport was an easy commute and once there, the parking and access were not much different from that of a small retail shopping mall. It was that easy; unlike the chaos experienced by Neil at the BWI or Newark airports. Neil liked this airport for its convenience and friendly western hospitality.

It was the home of Jim Bradshaw's rebirth and the fascinating chain of events that transformed him to the benevolent Mr. Mogul, the anonymous contributor to the Crow Nation Skyscraper.

Neil eagerly waited at the arrival gate for the love of his life. He watched for Lisa as dozens of passengers filtered through the narrow exit corridor. Through this crowd, he saw a sudden flash of shiny blond hair, and soon after, the complete package. It was Lisa. She looked very stylish, wearing blue jeans held up with a large buckled hand tooled leather belt and a white western shirt accented with a turquoise slide, bronze leather, bolo tie. She had dressed for Montana. She knew the outfit would result in a big smile from Neil. It did, as Neil produced a toothy grin that extended from ear to ear. He was ecstatic. He held his arms outstretched and open for his greeting.

"Lisa! Great outfit! You look fantastic! I'm a lucky dude. I have my own Montana cowgirl! Welcome to the Wild West. Whad ya think? We've sure come a long way since Princeton? Man, it's great to see you. How are you?"

"I'm fine. Great to see you too, Babe. I thought you would like the outfit. Got everything in Baltimore," Lisa said.

"It looks like it's right from Billings'. Can't wait to see it on the floor of our bedroom! Oops. Sorry, Lisa. Gettin' a little ahead of myself here. I just missed you so much. Let me rewind. How was your flight?"

"Slow down partner. Give me a little time to parade the goods. The flight was fine…a little bumpy."

"Missed you."

"I know. You mentioned that already. Missed you too."

A massive embrace and a long intimate kiss followed.

"Wow. You feel great. Can't wait to get you home," Neil said.

Lisa laughed. "I gathered that from your previous comment. We'll get there in time. I am looking forward to *breaking in* our new apartment too."

"I know what you mean. You'll love it. It's waiting for your interior design talent to make it our special place. But before we go anywhere or get busy with work, let's get something to eat. Hungry?" Neil said.

"Starved."

"Thought you'd be. That airplane food is something to avoid. There's a great place in Billings –*Kelsey's* – an All-American restaurant and saloon. Great food –drinks - atmosphere. Its architecture and interior design isn't bad either. Interested?"

"You bet."

"By the way, how's the Baltimore office doing? Leave it in good hands?"

"Don't know. Some of the 'left behind' staff are jealous. Want to know when they can come to Montana to help out. I told them if we need them we'll let them know. They're not happy. Hope they won't trash the place."

"You left Mike in charge?"

"Yup. Mike's a good man. He'll keep them in line or he'll kick the shit out of them."

"That's Mike. He's a big guy – ex-Marine, you know."

"Yeah, I know. Did all my stuff get here?"

"It's all here. Safe and sound. Arrived yesterday."

"Good. That's good. Let's get some food."

Their drive from the airport was filled with playful conversation. They held hands all the way to *Kelsey's*. They were happy to be together again.

Seated comfortably at their booth, Lisa's conversation shifted to the unexpected.

"How's Tony doing?"

"Tony? Not too bad. We're really working him hard. He's been super busy since he's been here. We walked the site yesterday. Wait till I tell you about that adventure! The night before, he put together a fantastic design. That kid's got talent. Mr. Mogul and the Great Spirit really knew something when they picked him."

"You told him all that stuff about the Great Spirit!?"

"Sure did."

"How did he react to *that*?"

"He flipped - like I knew he would. Didn't surprise me. Johnny Thunder Eagle was great with him. Calmed him down – as best he could. Helped him understand. You know, he's going on a Vision Quest."

"When?"

"In a couple days."

"Oh my God! That poor kid! I bet he's wondering what he's gotten himself into. Mr. Mogul's idea, huh? Johnny's the Crow project coordinator you told me about?"

"Yup. He's quite an interesting person - Mr. Mogul's savior. Never know what to expect from him next. He's really got his act together. Can't wait for you to meet him."

"Me too."

The waiter approached the table.

"May I take your order, sir?"

"You can start with two single malts, any kind, and soda... on the rocks with a twist. Give us a couple minutes to order."

"Yes sir. Be right back with your drinks."

"Thank you," Neil said.

Kelsey's was a renovated feed and grain store. Its interior was innovative for its day. It was a style of architectural design that was making its presence known throughout the country. The interior was stripped down to its bare essentials, exposing structure and function as essential design elements. The ceiling was open, displaying the heavy timber structural framing that was prevalent in Billings at the turn of the century. The added heating and cooling ducts were exposed and painted black, so they practically disappeared in the dark and open space above. It was simple, functional, and honest, and it suited its purpose well. Neil liked this place for its architectural style and atmosphere, but knew, after his skyscraper was completed, ordinary buildings like this could never again be designed in the same way. Lisa enjoyed its interior appointments too, and decided with Neil, to make it *their* place while living in Billings.

"Lisa, how 'bout a couple of Montana's best steaks to celebrate your first day here? Not too early, is it? "

"Not at all. I'm still on EST."

"Thought so. Then steaks it'll be."

During lunch the course of conversation covered mostly everything but eventually Lisa's attention turned back to Tony.

"Has Tony met anyone since he's been here?"

"Geez Lisa, the guy's only been here a few days. He hasn't had any time to himself. I've been working him to death. I know he's a handsome kid, but it would be next to impossible for him to meet anybody yet. Give him a few weeks. That's a strange question coming from you. Why'd you ask?"

"Don't know. Guess it was a stupid question. Forgot how busy you guys have been. I worry about him though. He seems so detached, in his own world, almost lonely at times. Don't you think?"

"Haven't given it much thought. Been too busy working on the building to wonder about Tony's personal life. Anyhow, I'm sure he'll get his chances at love while he's here, that is if I ever give him any time. It's going to be crazy busy around here the next two years. Besides. I don't think he's detached. His head's been constantly into this project. There's so much for him to do. I know. It's driving *me* crazy."

"That's for sure."

"Oh really? I thought you liked *crazy*..."

"I like *you*. Crazy comes with the territory."

"You bet it does. Lisa…do you like Tony?"

The moment had arrived for Neil to ask the question that was beating him over the head for weeks.

"Sure. I like him."

"No…I mean…are you attracted to him?"

"That's a bizarre question. Where did that idea come from?"

"I don't know. Ever since you two first met, it's something that's been bothering me. I sense this strange connection - a really strong connection. The two of you get along so well. He seems happy when he's around you - a little nervous – but happy. Hey…I'm not worried. I know you would never bail on me, but it all seems like there's something about you two that's coming from a very unique place."

"There's nothing to worry about Neil. I admit…I had a strange feeling about him when I first met him too, but it was the type of feeling that wanted me to look after him – kind of a 'mother hen' thing. For some reason, I worry about him being happy – but that's as far as it goes."

"Are you sure?"

"Very."

"Okay, but if anything changes - you know, if 'mother hen' wants to lay some eggs…"

"Jesus Neil! Stop it! What the hell's gotten into you? That's gross! I've never seen you act like this. Are you okay? Is this project messing with your head? What's gotten into you?"

"Sorry Lisa. It's just something that's been bothering me for a while. You're right. I am overreacting, but there's something about Tony – something about that guy. He has a particular aura around him, an unusually strong presence. Can't exactly figure it out, but it's something special. Listen… for my sake and sanity, if you have any doubts, any doubts at all, let me know. I'll understand. I promise. You know we can talk openly about anything."

"I know, Neil. I know, but don't worry. Everything's okay. My love for you is without question. You're not only my husband, but my best friend. Tony's a very likeable person, but to me – to us - he's just a close friend and a very talented employee. We'll both see to it that he does well on this project and look out for him. Okay? Now for god's sake, enough about Tony. I want to know more about this Johnny Thunder Eagle…"

CHAPTER 23

THE VISION QUEST

Following a hard bumpy truck ride and a two-mile hike, Tony and Johnny, arrived atop a remote location in the Pryor Mountains, historically used by the Crow for Vision Quests. This reservation site was deemed sacred and blessed. It had an overwhelming sense of peace. It was serenely quiet except for the sound of bubbling water from a nearby ground spring.

After setting up camp, Tony and Johnny relaxed by the campfire witnessing a beautiful sunset. They watched the sun disappear over Montana's southwestern plains, which seemingly flowed to infinity. There was nothing here to block this magnificent view. The horizon was a straight line that conveyed the impression the Earth ended somewhere just beyond this horizontal boundary. This indeed, was "Big Sky" country.

Tony thought…*this is so beautiful…a simple sunset, a daily occurrence available for everyone…but an experience not noticed and unappreciated by most…why?…*It wasn't important. Right now, all he wanted to do was watch the sun set lower in the sky, not wanting to miss a second of its beauty, its wonder, and its purpose.

Johnny pointed up to the fading blue sky. Tony responded to Johnny's gesture, looked up and saw a large bird flying about fifty feet directly above them.

"That is a bald eagle," Johnny said. "Notice its white head, and black and dark brown-feathered body. It appears to have a wingspan of about six feet. That would make it several years old. It is a great bird. One of the Great Spirit's messengers."

"I know. You've mentioned that."

"My name is in honor of its message to my mother."

"Really? What message?"

"Sorry Tony. I cannot say."

"Okay. I understand. Maybe some other time. So - it was the Great Spirit using its eagle to choose us both for this great project?" Tony said.

"Perhaps," was all that Johnny offered in response.

"Perhaps...*aquila*..." Tony said.

Tony's mother, as part of her futile efforts to teach him the most rudimentary Italian, had included in her teachings the Italian word for eagle - *aquila.* Her efforts went mostly unrewarded, as Tony's command and need for the language vanished with his advancing years. He recalled from his high school Biology, the bald eagle's formal Latin name was quite different, *haliaeetus leucocephalus,* and that these birds of prey were not "bald" at all. The name was derived from the Old English word "balde", which simply means "white." The original meaning, as in most word derivations, became distorted through time. Tony had conveniently forgotten the Latin descriptions of just about everything else he studied in Biology, but he remembered this one. He was always interested in the bald eagle and the majestic almost mythical image it conveyed. He always felt connected to this bird, but could not imagine why, until now.

He thought...*perhaps my mother knew something that I didn't...perhaps...*

He watched it fly higher and higher in the sky, until it was a distant undefined black speck, beginning its journey south to another destination. He thought...*what was it doing out here...it's not hunting for food...no fish here...shouldn't it have migrated to a warmer climate by now...do eagles migrate...?*

Then his thoughts abruptly shifted... *haliaeetus leucocephalus...where did that name come from...who were these people who defined and classified the thousands of animal and plant species in this world...who devoted their life to finding and classifying the different species of animal, vegetable and mineral...who assigns, approves and records these formal biological Latin names...why Latin...when did all this happen...where did this all happen...who personally knew anyone who did this as their life's vocation...why am I so ignorant of this process...?*

Tony turned his attention to Johnny, with the purpose of suggesting these questions to him, then wisely decided... *no reason to disturb the serenity of the moment or Johnny with these absurd questions...that's not why we are here tonight at this special place...*

As dusk slowly evolved into night, it was time for Tony to put these thoughts behind him. It was time for his Vision Quest.

— — —

In the past, a traditional Crow Vision Quest required four days and nights of fasting. This was the most meaningful religious experience of any Crow fortunate enough to endure its physically demanding ritual. During the Quest's duration, prayers were offered to the "Great Spirit" or as the Crow would name the creator, "First Maker," for guidance. To further amplify the experience, the seeker would cut off part of a finger or induce superficial wounds to experience the pain, euphoria, and unconsciousness that followed from the loss of blood and fasting. From this physical trauma, many would experience "visions" with prophetic messages. These messages helped them to understand their purpose through life. In the past, before many a major battle, warriors were provided guidance by the spirits on how to gain certain victory against their enemies.

Over time, changes were made to this traditional ceremony. The Crow began to use natural drugs as a substitute for the extended periods of fasting, self-inflicted wounds and sensory deprivation. Historically peyote was the first drug used, but in this century there were other drugs derived from natural plant sources growing on the reservation. Only honored Crow holy men were permitted to know of their identity and location.

Tonight, Tony was being introduced to a secret mixture of these drugs as part of a specific ritual that would provide the guidance for him to seek the truth and acquire the knowledge needed to design the world's tallest and completely self-sustained building. He hoped it would also help him understand his failures at love and his unquenchable passion for Lisa. Most of all, he was seeking relief from all the inner turmoil that was part of who he was.

In a chiseled stone bowl, using the fresh flowing spring water found at the site, Johnny added the chosen ingredients, heating it over the open fire. He chanted aloud a series of prayers, while stirring the potion, stopped, took a cleansing breath, and silently recited a closing prayer. Johnny slowly poured the potion into a blessed stone cup and handed it to Tony. He instructed Tony to recite the same prayers before drinking. Tony complied. When the prayers were finished, Tony was permitted to drink the hot sticky-sweet liquid. He closed his eyes and waited. He gave thought to his mother and father's love and everything that was now part of his life. Within minutes he began to fall into a deep awakened sleep, which slowly evolved into a trance. Once in this trance, Tony began to hallucinate and illogical dreamlike visions emerged from his subconscious.

> *Tony found himself in a very bright place devoid of any sound or substance. He was suspended over the reality that was conceived to be an empty lifeless Earth below. He was only two to three hundred feet above its surface, but at this height he could easily see into the future beyond the boundaries of his mind. He discovered his suspended state was not without movement and his body could easily be accelerated into flying, so he started to fly, ever so gently, ever so cautiously. While flying slowly over the Earth's surface for what seemed like an eternity, he could see the lifeless flat landscape below him begin to change into something else.*
>
> *He witnessed the emergence of life giving forms, as they spread their existence forcefully, creating endless grassy plains, sporadically swelling over miles and miles into small grass covered hills and large snow spired mountains - their melting snow gracefully flowing into awaiting voids below. Tony was witnessing this creative chaos so fast and randomly, that he was unable to focus on anything for any length of time before it would change into something else – something more dramatic and beautiful.*
>
> *It was a place empty of human or animal life. It was not without civilized human structure however, as popping up out of the ground like mushrooms, were countless numbers of small mud and straw shelters of every imaginable descrip-*

tion rigidly placed to form small deserted villages. These villages evolved magically from blurs of indecent, unplanned conglomerations into small towns built from wood and stone. These towns disappeared and reappeared faster than Tony could absorb, as they became large empty peopleless cities. These cities with buildings of brick, concrete, granite and steel, were undefined, without purpose, perceived as a unified mass of unrealistic dreams. These dreams evolved into unfulfilled promises. Unfulfilled promises found residence in his mind and haunted him, until he could not stop wondering how could he accept the unimaginative conformist thinking of the masses? Was this required for his survival and success? Could that be success? What was success?

He was not given time to search for an answer, as everything around him was becoming a dizzying blur of non-conformity. Then, it all stopped, forcing him to fall ever so slowly, ever so softly to the ground, alone in an empty grassy meadow among the clover, flowers, and bees. The sky was a brilliant blue. It was hot, but no sun could be seen. Rain clouds suddenly formed. It began to rain. A flash of light filled his eyes blinding him for a moment, as he lie motionless on the ground. His eyes cleared and focused on a seed falling from the sky, settling into the ground. From it a tree immediately began to grow, slowly at first, then faster and faster, taller and taller until its topmost branches could no longer be seen as they disappeared into the clouds.

This first seed was followed by countless others falling from the sky, spawning more and more trees until the flower covered meadow was transformed into a thick forest of green and brown.

Treetops were lost in the clouds. Suddenly, it stopped raining. The trees stopped growing.

Tony watched all that was happening around him in amazement, until he realized that he was trapped, completely surrounded by this forest, with no apparent way out. He was not concerned. He felt secure and safe within the forest until he heard a loud crashing sound from above, abruptly destroy the calm. It was the trees. Looking up, he could see, just as suddenly as they grew, the trees were beginning to die, toppling to the ground, piece by piece, branch by branch, in a massive display of Mother Nature's power. The sounds from thousands of self-destructing trees, was deafening and their impact as they fell to Earth, violently shook the ground. Tony realized the falling debris would soon find him. He had to immediately escape from this chaos or be crushed to death. He started to run. He ran for miles, narrowly avoiding death. until he reached exhaustion and could run no more. He peacefully sat on the ground with his face buried in his hands, waiting for death to arrive.

Death however, was not given its chance to capture him. Before the avalanche of branches and limbs buried Tony, ending his life, a great white eagle swooped down from the heavens, flying through the devastation unharmed, and captured Tony in its talons carrying him thousands of feet above the ground to safety on a distant mountain ledge. It gently released Tony and assumed a position perched at his side. Tony was in shock. He couldn't speak. He simply stared at the eagle wondering what was to happen to him next.

The eagle was massive- more than five times Tony's size. Its feathers of gold and white glowed. Its head was regal and perfect in shape. Its razor sharp vision surveyed the creation of its peaceful domain. It would occasionally look over at Tony and seemingly smile. Tony could only smile in return and gaze upon the beautiful green Earth below him. With this great eagle at his side protecting him, he was safe again.

The eagle broke the silence and spoke. "Do not be afraid Tony, I am your protector. I am your guardian angel. Your spirit will remain free. It is time for you to go now. Go. I will await your return. Go. Return to your home and think of me whenever you are afraid. Your future is not clear. Your future is not here, but the answers will come to you in time. Go now."

Tony looked over at the eagle. He did not understand. What was the eagle saying? What was he supposed to understand from this eagle? He tried to respond, but the thoughts in his head could not be spoken.

The eagle did not offer Tony any further explanation. Instead, it spread its magnificent wings and flew over to Tony lifting him in its giant talons. It carried a helpless Tony higher and higher toward the sun. Then, without warning, the eagle released him. As Tony fell, the Eagle said, "Let yourself fall free. Do not be afraid. You will not die. You will live forever."

Tony tried to understand and believe, with absolute faith, the eagle's commands, but he could not convince his mind and body to obey. He continued to fall out of control. He panicked and lost consciousness falling through a fog of blue mist. His body hit the Earth gently. He began to understand. The time to end this journey had arrived.

A haze filled his eyes and the smell of lilacs filled his nose as Tony awoke from his vision next to a fire, wrapped in a buffalo robe under the watchful eye of Johnny Thunder Eagle.

"Welcome back from your journey. I hope you fared well," Johnny said. "You have been away for several hours. Here... drink this tea. It will clear your mind and relax your body. Do not be concerned with what you have just experienced. Tomorrow, we will pursue talking about the messages offered in your vision. For now, it is very important that you allow yourself to slowly return from your journey. Drink. Flush the blessed potion from your system and you will feel as you have never felt before. Drink..."

After Tony drank the cleansing tea, and slowly settled back into reality, the surrounding plains emitted a peaceful and sensual rapture. The air had a smell of freshness that became intoxicating in its embrace. Each sound of nature had a purpose. Each one linked itself to the next in a symphony of sound that was as single in its purpose as it was in composition; a symphony never to be heard again in the harmony that was of that moment. It was a feeling that Tony wanted to keep forever. It was a feeling of the ultimate link to life and this Vision Quest was responsible. The only question was, was this feeling real or was it one of illusion? It felt too overwhelmingly honest, to be anything other than real.

A fog had been lifted and what was once covered in a shroud of mystery to Tony was now finally available to be viewed by his eyes in all its beauty and majesty. Awakening the deepest innermost desires of his soul, it had become a personal experience that equaled no other in his life. In that respect it was unique. In that respect, it was never to be equaled again in his life. In that respect, it was here only for this moment.

Tony and Thunder Eagle slept that night in a canvas tent next to the campfire. It was the deepest and most satisfying sleep of Tony's life. In the morning, at sunrise, he awakened to the bright sunlight, with a feeling of complete freedom and purpose. This feeling would eventually be taken from its rightful place in Tony's mind, as soon as he confronted the real world, and it was painfully replaced with the overwhelming human influences of ignorance, greed and violence - influences that Tony was destined to encounter again and again, blocking his rightful path to the truth.

CHAPTER 24

THE EXCHANGE

It was the beginning of a cool peaceful evening in September. In Billings, autumn nights varied from mildly hot to pleasantly cool with a gentle breeze. Tony managed to pry himself away from the drafting table to get a needed cup of coffee from the break room. It was almost four o'clock. The Furniture Warehouse was always busy with activity. It never slept. The production pace was frantic, but Tony was pushing himself to keep up with the demands. He sat at his desk, reading the telephone messages taken by Brenda that he had conveniently managed to ignore for the day. None of them needed immediate attention. He would answer all of them tomorrow. Then came that sound, a sound that broke the silence like no other. Tony looked over at its source, reached out and stopped the ringing.

"Hello, Tony Rullo, Project Architect."

"Hello Tony. It's Neil. Are you busy?"

"I'd better be, otherwise we're both in big trouble. What's up boss?"

"Today, I received a call from Harry Barnes, of Germany's *Sunflex*…you know geeky genius Harry…their solar cell rep. He indicated there were problems with Mr. Mogul's silicon refining factories supplying *Sunflex* the essential materials for the photovoltaics. Bottom line is this could result in *Sunflex*'s inability to manufacture the quantity of cells required for the building in our scheduled time frame. This could seriously impact our already impossible construction schedule. We need to work on a few alternative schedules with other materials suppliers to supplement Mr. Mogul's refined silicon, just in case it can't be delivered on time. Tony…listen…I'm at the site now but I'll be back at my apartment in an hour or so. We need to get a handle on this as soon as possible. We can't afford to allow this minor glitch to cause the project any unnecessary production delays. Why don't you stop by with the necessary documents and we'll review our options at my place over dinner. Lisa's cooking. I know you could use a home cooked meal. Why don't you show up at six? Will that work for you?"

"Of course. No problem. I can be there at six. By the way, thanks for the dinner invitation. I am looking forward to it. See you in a couple. Bye..."

"Thanks. See ya later buddy."

Distracted by the unexpected invitation, Tony couldn't concentrate on work. He decided to call it a day and pass the extra time before dinner by taking a two-mile run followed by a refreshing shower at the local health club. He needed to relieve his Lisa pre-dinner anxiety. Unfortunately, in his preoccupied state of mind, he underestimated the time it would take to finish his run, shower and change his clothes. He was late. Embarrassed, he did not want to call Neil to explain. It was better to just show up and ask for forgiveness, so he went directly to the Hagman's apartment as quickly as he could.

— — —

Neil and Lisa rented a large two-bedroom unit in an apartment building that was less than a ten-minute walk from the office. It was over two hours since Neil's call. Tony looked at his watch. It was twenty minutes after six when he reached the entrance. Among a matrix of others, he found the one security intercom labeled "N&L Hagman" and pushed the button.

A voice responded. "Yes?"

"Hey Lisa. It's me…Tony. I'm late. Tell Neil I'm very sorry. He was expecting me at six. I hope I haven't messed up your dinner plans. Neil and I have some work to discuss after dinner. Hope he mentioned it to you."

"Oh…Hi, Tony. Yes…Neil told me, but unfortunately he's not here. He's on his way to Chicago to meet with Mr. Mogul. He was called away at the last minute. Mr. Mogul's private plane was waiting for him at the airport. It sounded urgent. We tried to call you at the office, but you weren't there. No one knew where you were. It's okay though. You can come on up anyway. Dinner's still waiting for you."

"Are you sure? I don't want to get in the way of any plans you may have for the evening. I can let you have a quiet evening to yourself."

"Don't be silly. Get your butt up here. Dinner's already prepared and I would enjoy your company."

"Okay, if you insist. Be right up."

Tony heard the door unlock. He entered the building. Its lobby was quiet, unassuming and deserted. Tony wondered how Architects, working on the most aesthetically inspired projects, end up living in the most bland of buildings designed by uninspired Architects or worse, Developers. This building was strikingly bland, but it was one of the better ones in Billings and the tallest, topping out at six floors.

Tony was happy with his small rented cabin away from the city, but Neil and Lisa wanted a little more comfort. They enjoyed the urban pace of a city, even if it was the subdued pace of Billings.

He entered the tiny elevator and pushed the button for the sixth floor. The ride up was brief. An illuminated number six above the elevator doors was followed by a distinctive "ding" of a bell, signaling that its destination had been reached. The elevator doors opened. He walked down the corridor toward the familiar brown door of apartment 6-G. He knocked. Tony saw the shadow of Lisa's eye peek through the peephole. She unlocked and opened the door.

As the door opened to reveal Lisa, Tony reacted as he always did when first seeing her. He presented a quiet calm presence on the outside, but on the inside trapped within his mind and body, there was a nervous ambiguous mix of attraction, desire and resistance. He tried to control it. He desperately wanted to avoid any personal embarrassment, but he knew the routine. All he could do was wait it out, wait until his feelings subsided to a comfortable manageable level.

"Hi Tony. Always a pleasure to see you away from the office," Lisa said. "You look good. Hair's a little damp. Just get out of the shower? Don't just stand there, come on in." Lisa held the door open, lightly grabbed his collar with her free hand and playfully pulled him in. "Sorry, about Neil's unexpected trip. He told me to offer his apologies and to invite you in for dinner. He promised to call later after his meeting. You can talk with him then."

As Tony entered, he noticed the apartment was as usual, impeccably clean and tastefully furnished using a mixture of modern and traditional furniture. Lisa had a knack of combining the old and the new in a seamless transition of time and taste. Her interior design background, coupled with her knowledge of historical and modern trends, made the final result extremely satisfying. On the walls, hung paintings in various styles, original photographs, and a few architectural renderings by Frank Lloyd Wright and Le Corbusier. Their placement was deliberate and in keeping with the style of the room in which they were placed.

Tony never had been alone with Lisa away from the office. He didn't know how to react to this new experience. It was awkward, so Tony decided to channel his apprehension through casual meaningless conversation.

"Hey Lisa. Good to see you too. I guess I can hang out here for a while. Are you sure you don't mind?" He set his documents on the coffee table.

"No. I don't mind at all," Lisa answered.

"Okay. You've convinced me to stay…guilt free."

…guilt free?…why the hell did I say that?…

"Okay, it's settled," Lisa said.

The enticing aroma of dinner filled the air. Tony walked into the kitchen and saw the reasons for the wonderful smell. It was Lisa's simple, but elegant specialty - Chicken Marsala, fresh cut green beans with a hint of ginger, and creamy mashed potatoes. The mashed potatoes would be blessed with her delicious secret chicken gravy whose ingredients she was happy to keep selfishly to herself. He also noticed a fresh Caesar Salad begging for attention over the imposition of the main course. Lisa had cooked this meal for the three of them, many times before. Tonight, it was a meal waiting for an invitation.

"Thanks again. Dinner looks and smells great," Tony said.

"Thank you. I know you love my Marsala. Why don't you find a comfortable spot to sit? We'll relax for a little while before we eat. I'll fix us some drinks."

Tony found the living room. He chose the only single chair in the room. He didn't want to give Lisa any opportunity to sit next to him.

"Lisa, the place looks great, as usual. You are a very talented lady. I feel like I'm sitting between the pages of *Interiors*

Magazine. It feels good to just sit and do nothing for a change. How are you handling this insane project?" he said.

"I'm hanging in there. Everything's good with me, but you know that. What about you? You okay? Seem a little troubled. Is something bothering you?" Lisa shouted from the kitchen.

...Busted!... Tony thought...*Yeah - something is bothering me – you!! ...*

"You're very perceptive. Something *is* bothering me."

"Well let's hear it. Tell it to Doctor Lisa," she said as she entered the living room and assumed her position on the sofa opposite Tony.

"It's just lately, I've been having feelings of inadequacy. I've been questioning my ability to adequately perform on this project."

...that's good Tony...get the sympathy vote even if what you are saying is somewhat true...keep going... I'm even starting to feel sorry for myself...

"I compare myself to Neil and most of the other talented people on this project and I feel unqualified. Isn't that strange? Then, to make me feel even more inadequate, add to all this talent, the imagination and vision of Mr. Mogul and I feel even worse. His ideas are so far ahead of their time," Tony said.

"Yes they are. He's quite the renaissance man."

"I know. I know. And every time I think about his extraordinary vision and what he hopes to accomplish on this project, I feel like a caveman. According to Johnny, he even has some special connection with the Great Spirit. The man is a god. I know I must sound a little naïve and immature…" Tony was babbling. He knew it. He just needed to say anything to get his mind detoured from his feelings for Lisa.

"Tony…stop. You're being silly. Don't you believe for one moment that you aren't as or more talented than anyone else on this project. I know you don't believe that. No one does. I don't think you fully realize how truly creative you are. You are greatly admired."

"Think so? You're not just saying that? Sometimes... sometimes...I don't know. Sometimes, I'm just not so sure about my self-worth," Tony said.

"Of course I meant it. I would never lie about something like that, and as for your 'self-worthiness', trust me, everyone is impressed with your work, especially Neil. Me too. Face it, you wouldn't be in this position if you didn't possess an exceptional talent."

"Thanks. I appreciate the vote of confidence. Means a lot to me. It seems I'm always questioning my abilities. It's a low self-esteem thing - built into my DNA, I think."

...okay Tony it's time to give this sympathy bullshit a rest...

"You're fine," Lisa said. "You've just been working too hard. You must be exhausted. How about we change the subject and talk about anything except work?"

"Okay, but I want to talk a little more about Mr. Mogul."

"Why"

"Because I'm curious. I need to know more about the man. I know Neil's relationship with him, but what about yours? Have you ever met him? Seen him? Do you think I'll ever meet this curious super-man before the completion of this skyscraper?"

"As far as I know, you and I will not meet him until the project's completion." Tony's questions unsettled Lisa. She paused before continuing, electing to take her response along a well-guarded path. "Tony, I need to tell you something important, something very important about Mr. Mogul and this project," she said.

"What's that?"

"Were you ever told why no one could ever know Mr. Mogul's identity before the project's completion?"

"No. Neil never went into detail as to why. I just accepted it. Haven't given it much thought…'til now."

"Well…to put it as simply and directly as I can, knowing Mr. Mogul's identity has to remain a secret. It's not safe for you, me or anyone else working on this project, including Neil to know his real identity. I worry every day about Neil's safety. He assures me that he is out of harm's way. It's Mr. Mogul that they want. Neil's been very honest about this with me. There is no one else he can share this information with. Now against his wishes, I'm sharing it with you in complete confidence. Promise me you will keep this information between us Tony…promise."

Troubled by this revelation, Tony answered in the only way that he could.

"Of course I will - of course. You know you can trust me. Why is Mr. Mogul's identity such a danger? Who wants him? Why do they want him?"

"Since you asked, here it is, wrapped in the proverbial nutshell. Neil has made it clear to me there are many people – no - make that many powerful special interest groups hidden inside large corporations, that want to see this project fail. There are rumors circulating that they want it stopped dead in its tracks. To assure this, they want Mr. Mogul and his millions, permanently removed from the project, if you know what I mean. This project could potentially take millions of dollars from the pockets of a great many, whose profits are made from the sale of oil, natural gas and coal. These leeches are hell-bent in creating trouble for our skyscraper – lots of it - so Neil needs to be introduced tonight to the heightened security measures that need to be in place during the building's construction. The entire project team will be briefed when

Neil returns from Chicago. That's all I know. You understand the need to keep this confidential, don't you?

"Yes Lisa, I understand. It's our scary secret."

Lisa smiled. "Good. That's good. I'm relieved to be able to tell you this stuff. It's been driving me crazy trying to keep it to myself. I'm sure it appears worse than it really is. Can't be too careful about something as innovative and expensive as this building. The good news is that Neil has assured me that after the building is completed and the dust settles on the 'dawn of a new age,' as he puts it, you'll have the opportunity to meet Mr. Mogul, everyone will. It will be the party to end all parties. So for the time being, let's put this behind us, relax and have that drink."

"That party cannot come soon enough for me. Now, about that drink, isn't drinking alcoholic beverages still a 'no-no' with Mr. Mogul on this project?" Tony said.

"I won't tell, if you won't, but technically, we're not working on the project right now. Besides, you need a drink to calm you down – to calm us both down. It's purely medicinal," Lisa playfully said.

"Okay, if you insist. I can sure use one after hearing that stuff about Mr. Mogul," Tony said.

Tony studied Lisa as she walked to the bar. She had removed her shoes and glided effortlessly to the bar barefooted. She was wearing a simple black skirt hemmed just above her knees, accenting her shapely bare legs, and a white blouse that was barely opaque. It was a provocative, hard to ignore outfit, especially when it was flowing over Lisa's hard to ignore body. Lisa was about three years younger than Neil, and eight years older than Tony. An older attractive woman was always one of Tony's favorite objects of desire. He had admired her from a distance, many times before, but tonight, her presence was magnified by the imagination of the moment.

...just bring the bottle over here...I'll drain it and put myself out of my misery...

Lisa fixed them both a single malt Scotch and soda with a twist of lemon, "on the rocks." It was Tony's preferred drink and hers too. She acquired the taste during many after dinner drinks with Neil.

She handed Tony his drink. They clinked glasses. Tony offered the mandatory *...best of health, happiness and success...* toast.

"You know...the more I think about it, the more gruesome that Mr. Mogul scenario becomes," Tony said. "It's too bad our country is filled with rich and powerful people promoting, at any cost, their personal self-serving greedy agendas. I'm very fortunate. I'm involved in the most amazing building in the world with the most amazing group of people ever assembled for one project, including you, of course. I know we're going to beat those bastards at their own game. I know it. We can't lose with truth, talent and of course lots of money."

Tony held his glass up and Lisa responded, acknowledging the compliment. She smiled.

"You know, Mr. Mogul has given me a once in a lifetime opportunity," Tony said. "It will probably be the greatest work of my life. I can't disappoint him. If I fail, I think I'll jump off a bridge or from the top of the building. I couldn't live with the failure. I couldn't. I know me."

Tony gulped his drink and drained his glass. He was beginning to feel a little light-headed. Too many hours in front of the drafting table and the constant research, the constant phone calls, the design's constant fine-tuning, all were taxing his endurance. The pace, details and coordination, all were beginning to take their toll.

"Don't ever say that Tony! I know you don't mean it, but I don't ever want to hear you say anything like that again. Promise me. Promise!" Lisa said.

"Okay. Okay. I promise. I was just making a point. I wasn't serious."

"Sorry I yelled at you."

"It's okay. I deserved it."

Lisa noticed Tony's empty glass.

"Do you want another drink, Tony?"

"Please."

Lisa fixed them both another ill advised Scotch and soda. She handed Tony his refreshed drink. Tony decided to change his seating assignment, and sit next to Lisa on the sofa. Tony had unknowingly let his guard down. This was not good. He didn't know what to do. He had made a mistake. He said nothing and tried to think of a way out of this awkward situation. Lisa looked over at Tony.

"Hey. Hello. Tony, are you there?" she said. "Why so quiet? What are you thinking about? I hope it's not work related. I remember when you told me during your first few days at *Hagman's* that this was definitely a 24-7 project and you were just the type of 24-7 guy to carry it through to completion. I think you were trying to impress me at the time. I thought you were kidding, but now I'm not so sure. You're really crazy enough to have meant it. Well, my advice to you is - either you're going to relax here with me and put work on the back burner or I'm kicking your ass out the door. You don't have to be so up-tight when you're with me. I won't bite. Loosen up and show me your charming and witty side. I've seen you carry on like a nut at the office. You joke around. You laugh. You smile. What happened to your sense of humor and smile? Leave it back at the office? You know, it's okay to smile."

Tony laughed. Lisa always managed to make him laugh. He loved being around her, even if it meant the torturous reality of abstaining from his true feelings.

…if you only knew how much I want to kiss you right now…you wouldn't wait to see me smile… you would immediately kick my ass out of here…no question about it…

Tony kiddingly replied, "Okay. Okay. You're right as usual. This project *is* kicking my butt. But tonight, just for you, I will shift gears and take a break from thinking about work. I will even smile. See?" Tony attempted to smile.

Lisa looked at Tony and said, "Oh, was that a smile? Is that the best you can do? You can do better than that!" Lisa laughed.

It was a laugh that gave Tony an uncomfortable warm fuzzy feeling.

…was there anything that this woman did that irritated me?…maybe…but I can't think of anything right now…if I did I would just make up an excuse as to why I was mistaken…

Tony smiled again. This time it was better. It was a good smile – a happy smile. This happy feeling was beginning to become contagious. There may not be a cure. Lisa was infecting him with genuine happiness. He started to relax and his ability to resist Lisa was rapidly losing its foothold on Tony's emotions.

Lisa reached out to touch his cheek.

"There's that Tony smile," she said. "I knew it was in there somewhere. You're such a mess. What am I going to do with you? I guess Neil and I will have to put up with you just as you are, which isn't too bad. After all, you're an excellent architect and a terrific person, despite what you think." She touched his cheek again. Tony didn't react. He just kept smiling.

…touch me again Lisa, and I'm going to faint…

"You have no choice," he said. "You to have to put up with me until the project's finished..." Tony paused and said something that took him completely by surprise.

"...Lisa, do you have any idea how beautiful you are?" He heard himself say it but he couldn't take it back. The Scotch, that unconscionable Scotch forced those words from his lips. But Lisa's touch - that touch was something he wasn't able to ignore. It caused him to say something he had wanted to say ever since Lisa's image was permanently etched into his mind. Now maybe because he was overworked, mildly delirious, and a little drunk, he finally said it. He wondered if there was anything he might do to redeem himself from his ill-advised remark.

Fate had other plans.

Lisa was surprised. "Really? You really think so? Thank you. That's a precious compliment, but I think I need to limit your drinks to two before you get really silly on me. I'm not so sure you meant to say that."

Lisa looked away. She was embarrassed but confident that her making light of the moment would enable it to pass. She could forget it meant anything, but it didn't pass.

"God Lisa, I'm sorry. That was so inappropriate. You're Neil's wife for God's sake. What's wrong with me? Listen, I didn't mean anything by it, other than it being a simple honest compliment. I wasn't trying to flirt, embarrass or come on to you. Honest."

"Oh shut up. It's okay. You don't need to apologize. I'm flattered to know you think I'm attractive. However, so that you too may feel a little uncomfortable… I am required to let you know what I think of you. I think you're a very handsome man. I've always liked your eyes. You have pretty hazel eyes. I think they really reflect what a warm hearted person you are. There - I said it. We're even."

"*We're even?* That's a strange comment. Now I'm off the uncomfortable chart after that compliment. How am I supposed to react to that?"

"Don't. Don't react. Just accept it. Okay? Incidentally, Neil and I always wondered why you weren't involved with anyone. You've been here in Billings for months and we can't understand why you haven't become involved with or at least seriously dated a local. There are a lot of women in this town who are asking about you. I can always fix you up with someone if you want..."

...talk about a well-placed ass kick back to reality...

"Please, don't ever do that," Tony said. "That's so not necessary. I'm just too busy to get involved with anyone while I'm working on this project. There just isn't any time. You know that. You know the crazy workload. Anyway, it's not your job to worry about my love life. I am capable of finding my own women. I'll meet someone when the time is right, then everyone – including you – can stop bugging me about my personal love life."

"Uh-oh. Seems like I struck a sensitivity nerve here. Sorry, I just thought it was okay to interfere in your life a little. After all, you're practically family. Wouldn't it be good for you to meet someone - loosen up a little - have some fun? You shouldn't let your past keep you from moving forward because you've been hurt so many times before. You know... Neil and I always thought, and Tony please don't take this the wrong way, we thought maybe you're too sensitive. You find it difficult to hide your true feelings. So when you're involved with someone you really like, you have a tendency to frighten them away with a little too much emotional intensity. Some women can't handle that. I think it's the *Italian* in you."

...where the hell did that psycho-babble bullshit come from?...what happened to my sexy Lisa – my fantasy?...she was here a moment ago...too sensitive?...Italian in me?...

Tony's heard a loud - POP! - from the sound of his infatuation balloon bursting. Lisa's remarks offended him. He was being judged. This woman, whom he adored, was judging him, criticizing him about his sensitivity. He hated that.

"Really? I wasn't aware that my personality dynamics were under a microscope, but that's okay. I know you're just trying to help - I think. Please...stop worrying about me. I told you...I'll find someone when I'm good and ready. In my life, in any serious relationship I've been involved in, I've always experienced a combination of bad luck, bad choices and bad timing, my *trifecta* for failed relationships. I've become very cautious...very cautious. Please...no more advice. I'm not ready for a relationship. Let me handle my personal life in my own time – in my own way. Okay?" Tony said.

Lisa felt the frustrated emotion in Tony's guarded reply. "Okay. I understand. I'm sorry I hurt your feelings. I know you've tried and I've heard some of your relationship horror stories. It's just that I care about you a lot and only hope that you will find someone you can love and share your life. You deserve it. That's all. Don't be offended if I tend to be too much of a 'mother hen'. I'm only trying to help."

Tony heard the words, *care about you a lot,* and couldn't let these words pass without asking, "What did you mean about *caring* about me Lisa?"

"I don't know exactly. What I do know is I sense there is considerable tension between us right now and I don't like it. So, let's start over. Please don't take anything I've said the wrong way. I didn't mean to offend you in any way. I thought I was helping."

"I know that. I also know you evaded the answer to my question. You know what…if you don't want to tell me, I don't care. Besides…I'm very tired and feeling really uncomfortable with this whole conversation. I think it's best if I take my *Italian sensitivity* and go. I should get back to the office for a few more hours of work. Tell Neil when he calls, that I'll talk to him tomorrow, or he can try to catch up with me at the office tonight. Sorry about dinner."

Lisa was offended by Tony's decision. Her wounded pride was not going to accept his decision to leave.

"Tony…please…I understand how you may feel, but don't leave because of my misguided remarks. Stay. I have dinner for three that's going to go to leftovers if I try to eat it alone. Forget what I said before. It was unfair and probably it was me who's feeling a little guilty and overly sensitive. You're a terrific person. Neil and I both adore you. Please stay for dinner. I really would enjoy your company."

"No. I need to go."

Lisa held Tony's arm to keep him from moving away. She then said something that didn't need to be said.

"Tony…Neil's not coming home until tomorrow evening, but he'll call tonight. You can talk to him while you're here. I'm sure he'll appreciate the opportunity to talk to you and I'm certain he'll want to share with you the results of his evening with Mr. Mogul."

Tony looked at her. He heard every word she said and wanted to reply, but he couldn't. He just stared and all his inhibitions, all his resolve to not give in to his desires, his love for this woman, began to dissolve until there were no barriers. He was possessed with an overwhelming passion and purpose. He resisted.

"What's wrong? Did you hear anything I just said? Can I set your place for dinner? Are you all right? Say *yes*. Say you'll stay for dinner. Say something," Lisa said.

Tony answered in the only way he could, "Sorry Lisa, I can't stay. I've got to go. Tell Neil to call me at the office." Tony turned to leave. He started for the door.

Lisa reached out again grabbing his arm, this time with a stronger grip.

"Lisa, what are you doing?" Tony asked. "Please, let go of my arm."

"Don't leave," she insisted.

Her insistence and her hand on his arm triggered in him a response that he was powerless to resist any longer. He turned and faced her - stared at her for an instant that felt like forever. His eyes became locked on the deep blue of hers. He reached out to hold her and felt himself slowly bringing her closer to him. There was no resistance offered. He perceived his actions in slow motion, isolated freeze-frames of time. None of what was happening seemed real. None of it seemed real except for the feelings Tony felt inside his heart. Lisa's blond hair flowed casually in front of her face as he drew her still closer to him until their bodies were almost touching. And when their bodies finally did touch, their breathing became the only separation between them, forcing their lips to respond in the only way that they could. Tony knew that this was the final moment before the answers to many unanswered questions would be revealed. It was the point of no return. There was no turning back.

He kissed her softly on the lips, gently, just a whisper of a kiss. He felt Lisa respond softly and tenderly. He kissed her again. This kiss was deeper, more responsive, warmer and giving. After that, what followed was a sea of passion that knew no boundaries. They were lost now in that timeless ebb and flow of desire that only engulfs those who are destined to be part of its mystery. Their flesh became consumed by their passion. Their bodies felt as one and what followed next was an act of love that would be their legacy and their history for the rest of their lives. They made love throughout the night, interrupted only by Neil's call.

Lisa told Neil that Tony had left hours ago and she had no idea where he was. She told him to call Tony at the office tomorrow morning. Lisa lied to Neil. She didn't know what else to do.

Throughout the night, Tony and Lisa could feel the guilt spread throughout their being, but it made no difference to either of them. In the morning they would wake in each other's arms with the guilt, but not the shame. Neither of them were ashamed. Their problems however, were just beginning, and Tony and Lisa did not know how they were going to respond to each other, to Neil, and to life from this day forward.

The dinner remained on the stove - cold, uneaten and forgotten.

CHAPTER 25

THE MORNING AFTER

It was nearly six in the morning. Tony's eyes opened from a deep exhaustion induced sleep. In his arms, directly by his side, in her marital bed, was Lisa. Having her next to him was everything he imagined it would be, and more. Making love to her through the night was magical. Only now, on this morning after, his emotions were struggling through a maze of conflict. He was emotionally and physically satisfied, happy, shocked and sickened all at the same time. He was not able to sort through all these ambiguities now. What he must do is compose himself and be as rational as he could be under the circumstances. He gently shook her.

"Lisa. Lisa honey, wake up," Tony said.

"I'm awake. I'm awake. I've been awake for a while just lying here feeling you holding me, thinking about last night. I didn't want to wake you. Good morning."

"Good morning. How are you? Are you okay?"

"About as okay as I can be under the circumstances. Oh God Tony, what did we do? I'm so sorry."

"Sorry for what?"

"For the whole thing. I shouldn't have let it happen. I should have let you leave when you wanted. I shouldn't have pulled you back. That's what I'm sorry for. Because of my weakness I've compromised your life…your future…your integrity…my marriage, and God knows what else."

"Lisa, I…"

"Please, Tony, let me finish. You know - I've been married nearly fifteen years and not once did I ever think of being unfaithful to Neil, not once, until last night. It was strange how it just happened like it did, all of a sudden - without any pretense – without any warning. It just happened. You were here. You were here in my home, in my arms, in my bed and I did nothing to stop it. And I'm sick about it – just sick. I'm sorry. I need you to go now. I need time. I need time to think, time to understand what the hell just happened here. I need to be alone. Please understand. Can you just go? Just go. Okay?"

"Lisa, don't do this to me."

"Do what?"

"Shut me out. Don't shut me out. It happens to me all the time. After what we've both been through last night, I need to know from you that you care enough about me to work this out. I need to know that whatever happens between us from now on, will be something we can mutually accept. Listen…I know what we did last night was wrong. I know it can and probably will cause us serious problems down the road. But you know what? Last night making love to you is something I'll never forget and never will regret. My feelings for you go deeper into my heart and soul than they have for anyone else in my life. I knew that from the first time I saw you. I want you to know that whatever you may think and whatever you may feel, I did not want this to happen. But since it did, can we try to understand what it could mean to both of us in some future obscure life plan? Can you do that for me? Just try to do that for me and don't shut me out of your life, not yet, not now."

Tony's words made Lisa realize how harsh and detached she must have sounded.

"Tony, I'm so sorry. I didn't mean to give the impression that I don't care about what happened last night. I wasn't trying to shut you out. It's just so difficult for me to understand what just happened between us, especially when I look at you here next to me. You're pretty difficult to ignore. When I look at you, it makes what we did seem okay and it's not. Your being here makes it too easy for me to rationalize a justifiable reason for us sleeping together. Please understand. For right now, I just need to put some distance between us so I can think this through. Tony, I promise we'll work this out together as soon as we can - "

Tony wasn't content to let Lisa's response go by unchallenged.

"God...Lisa, don't you think I feel the same as you?" he said. "The only difference between you and me, is what *I* want to do about this *thing* between us right now. Right now, I don't need distance. Right now, all I need is to hold you for a little while longer. It's the only thing that makes any sense to me. It's the only way I can keep from losing my mind. I know you're upset and obviously don't feel the same, but please, please do this one thing for me."

"I don't think I -"

Tony ignored Lisa's weak attempt at resistance and reached for her, pulling her closer. Lisa tried to resist, but eventually gave in to her honest feelings. As they drew closer – naked body to naked body, Lisa began to cry.

"I'm so worried. Tell me everything is going to be okay," she said.

"Sshh. Stop crying. Don't worry. We'll fix this. Everything's going to be okay, I promise."

They held each other tightly, both knowing that this moment would soon end, both slowly accepting the reality that fate had dealt them, both knowing that whatever happened between them, had no simple answer or solution. Tony released his hold on Lisa to give her one more kiss before leaving her side. The kiss was brief, but conveyed every emotion that Tony had trapped inside his captured heart. Lisa responded in kind.

As Tony left her bed, he couldn't keep his feelings from taking over his better judgment.

"Lisa," he said. "I'll never forget this moment and how beautiful you look. You know that if I could, I would stay here with you forever. Last night was unforgettable. You know that. You also know my feelings for you. Don't ever forget that. I'll give you your space. I'll leave, because I must, but you need to promise me to call later so we can talk this through. Will you do that?"

"Yes. I'll call. This may sound a little strange judging by my response this morning, but I want you to be sure about something too. I feel the same about you. Surprised to hear me finally say it? Don't be. It's true. Unfortunately, these feelings have been with me for quite a while. For obvious reasons, I've been keeping myself from acting on them, until now. That's all I'll say about it. So please remove that body of yours from here before we get into more trouble. The best thing for both of us right now is to separate and go on with our normal day as if nothing ever happened between us. Okay?"

"Okay."

Lisa watched Tony get himself quickly dressed and begin his exit from the Hagman's bedroom. She said before he left the room, "I'm going to lie here for a few minutes and attempt to get myself back to something resembling normal. Let yourself out. It will be easier on me if I don't see you leave."

"I understand. I'm sorry I complicated your life and Neil's this way. He deserves so much better from me. I owe him so much and look how I repay him…I sleep with his wife. I don't think much of myself right now."

"Shut up. Don't say that. It's not your fault. We both made a mistake, but we'll make it right. We'll talk. Now, get that nice butt of yours out of here and go home. I'll catch up with you later."

— — —

On the drive to his Cabin, Tony's mind started its futile exercise to make some sense about what had happened to him and Lisa last night. It wasn't supposed to work this way. True love was not supposed to be with another man's wife…*What the hell was going on?…Why wasn't he just a normal person with a normal love life?…Why all this personal drama?…* He hated to have to live with the memory of cheating on his friend – someone he loved as a brother. Nevertheless, through all this guilt, he couldn't ignore his feelings for Lisa. He truly believed he loved her, but he knew this wasn't the path love should take. Love shouldn't feel this wrong. He felt dirty. He felt weak.

This problem had only one solution; one painful solution only. He could never allow himself to be with Lisa in that way again. In fact, he may have to disappear from her life permanently. He would have to abandon a once-in-a-lifetime project, because of his feelings for this woman, someone else's woman.

— — —

As Tony washed up in robotic fashion getting ready for work, he imagined his first encounter with Neil after his affair with Lisa as being a painful and embarrassing confrontation. It was one meeting that he wanted to avoid forever.

Looking at his reflection in the bathroom mirror, he tried to understand. Why was making love to Lisa the most gratifying physical and emotional sensation he had ever experienced? He felt at the moment of orgasm as if he were floating through the universe on a cloud - safe, loved, and contained in a tidal wave of passion and immortality. How could something that felt so right, be so wrong?

A strange sound from outside the cabin startled Tony. He raised his head, turned and looked through the bathroom window, where he saw the reason for the noise. For the first time since living here, he saw a bear, a black bear casually walking across his yard moving aside any obstacle that attempted to block its path. The bear stopped directly in front of the window, about sixty feet from the cabin. It raised its round furry seven-foot frame on its hind legs, tilted its head and began to sniff the air. It remained in this position for a few seconds, its front paws tucked neatly into its chest. Then, it opened its mouth and let out a soft grunting growl. It was almost as if the bear were singing. Without any apparent reason, the bear lowered its head, looked directly into Tony's eyes, and began its singing again. Tony stood motionless, hypnotized, strangely drawn to this bear. He wanted to leave the cabin walk up to it and embrace it with a hug, a foolish thought that he wisely dismissed.

After a few seconds, the bear finished its personal song of mystery, dropped its stance to all fours and continued to stare at Tony. Tony continued to stare back. The bear let out a final growl, a roar, more forceful and angrier than any before it. Finished with its performance, it turned its back to Tony and slowly walked into the woods, disappearing among the trees quickly and without a trace. Tony continued to stare at the empty space that once was occupied by this bear and was convinced he saw it now filled with the glow from the bear's spiritual energy. The bear had delivered a message. What the message was, Tony did not know. He would ask Johnny for help in understanding its meaning. Hopefully, it was a message containing a simple solution to the trauma that was suddenly thrust into his life this troubled morning.

Living in Montana, had given Tony a heightened awareness of nature and its relationship with that of being human. It wasn't an acquired feeling. It was a consequence of living in an environment that allowed the opportunity for nature's energy to flow unencumbered, transcending the influences of the confused concentrated masses of humanity. Still, it was a constant struggle to rise above the trash in his mind, and become pure in thought, as he did immediately after awakening from his Vision Quest. But now, in this isolated moment, he could feel his thoughts becoming free from his everyday distractions. This freedom was not permitted to continue for very long. It was buried by the ring from the telephone, a perfect example of the type of human interference that constantly disrupts the natural order of life.

Tony walked apprehensively to the wall phone and lifted the receiver from its cradle.

"Hello," he said.

"Tony? It's Lisa. I'm sorry to bother you now, I know you're getting ready for work, but I'm going a little crazy here and I couldn't wait any longer to talk to you."

"It's okay. You're not bothering me. I'm happy you called. I'm still not handling this too well either. What's wrong besides the obvious?"

"We need to talk soon. We need to get this fixed, so it doesn't hurt anyone, especially Neil." Lisa was talking calmly, but Tony could sense that she was close to tears.

"You're right. I agree. When do you want to get together?" Tony asked.

"Tonight. I want to see you tonight, before Neil comes home from Chicago. His plane arrives at eight. He'll be driving himself home from the airport, so we'll have an extra cushion of time. Let's meet at *Kelsey's* for a drink, and maybe a bite to eat around five. Is that okay? Can you make it?"

"I'll be there. Lisa…I can tell from your voice that you're upset. I wish I could be there to make things better for you, but knowing me, I would probably only make things worse. For today, try your best to take it easy on yourself. Take care of you. I will keep my distance. I have meetings most of the day and I have to make a quick visit to the site, so thankfully, I won't have many opportunities to interact with you at the office. I will be calling Neil later today. Since he called you last night, he probably tried to call me at the office. I just hope he didn't try to call me here or I'd have a lot of explaining to do. The sooner I call him the fewer questions there will be about my whereabouts. So for now, we will do our best to avoid each other and save our energy for tonight. Is that okay with you?"

"Yes. That plan works for me. Tony?"

"Yes."

"I wish it were different between us. I wish it wasn't like it was."

"I know. Me too. Unfortunately, we have to deal with the reality of the situation and it is what it is."

"Tony?"

"Yes."

"You don't think I'm a bad person for what happened last night?"

"No. If anyone is to blame here, it's me."

"I knew you'd say that. That's not true."

"Listen, it doesn't matter. It serves no purpose for either of us to assume blame. Right now, we need to find a way to fix this. Okay?"

Lisa ignored Tony's question and just said what was immediately on her mind and in her heart. "Tony…I love you."

"Oh God, don't say that now Lisa. I can't handle that reality. I just can't. Please understand, I need to stay focused on our problem, which right now doesn't include expressing how we feel about each other. Okay? We'll talk more later. I need to hang up before my head explodes. Please understand."

"Okay. I'm sorry. That was not fair. I know it's not the right time to tell you how I feel. It may never be the right time."

"I know. Don't worry about it. We'll fix this mess. See you at *Kelsey's*."

Tony hung up the phone more emotionally confused than before Lisa's call.

…this can't be the will of the Great Spirit…there's something wrong…this shouldn't have happened…it can't be part of its grand plan…

He wished earlier he had let the bear give him a great big hug of death. He felt alone now. He couldn't share this experience with anyone, not even Johnny. He would ask him about the bear though. The bear was a sign that may have a reasonable and fortuitous explanation.

CHAPTER 26

THE PLAN

The workday flew by without incident. Tony barely caught a glimpse of Lisa during the day, as they flawlessly worked their evasive maneuvers. At four forty-five, he ended his work for the evening and made his way to *Kelsey's*. Upon arriving, he requested a remote intimate table for two, ordered two drinks, and waited. He asked the waiter to show Lisa to his table as soon as she arrived. She arrived in less than five minutes. They both ordered dinner and before it was served, it was time for their talk. Tony was first.

"Lisa…I've been thinking about this all day…thinking about last night. What happened last night…what happened, was so unexpected and incredibly wrong. It felt like it was a ride on some ill-conceived morality altering fantasy cloud. Let's face it; we were oblivious to the consequences of what we were doing. We allowed our emotions to run free, unimpeded by the realities of today., fueled by the reckless desires of intoxicating passion - so unfair - so without a conscience. My question is; why did we allow this to happen?"

Tony surprised Lisa with his unexpected and stilted analysis. She took a sip from her drink followed by deep calming breath.

"Wow. That was a little off subject. I don't know why this was allowed to happen, Tony, I really don't. All I know is that we are strongly attracted to each other, and we are here to arrive at a mutual agreement on what we should do about it. Believe me, I feel the same as you. It was a wonderful experience for me too. That's not what we should be talking about now. We don't have time to discuss the *us* or the *why*. We need to talk about finding a way out of this dilemma. I have some ideas on what I think we should do, but first I want to hear what you have to say. We don't have much time."

"I'm sorry. You're right. I got carried away. I've just been thinking about this all day. It's driving me crazy, but I do have a plan…" Tony said.

"Let's hear it," Lisa said.

"Okay. Here goes. I know that 'we' cannot happen. That's a given. What we did last night was wrong and we both know it. What happened last night, stays with last night. We need to promise each other that. Most importantly, I can't let my feelings for you control my decision. I care about you and Neil too much to mess up your lives. I've decided I can't keep working here with you on this project. My feelings for you will affect my work. I've decided to resign my position here and try to find another less responsible position with Mr. Mogul's company in New York or Baltimore. By doing that, everyone's protected. That's my plan."

Lisa shook her head in disapproval.

"No…no Tony. You can't do that. I won't allow you to do that. It's just so unfair to you."

"You're wrong. I need to leave this project and you. I've never felt this way about anyone. It's the only way I can realistically bury my feelings and protect you. It's the only way."

"No. There's another way," Lisa said.

"Sorry, my mind's made up."

"Just shut-up, and stop being so stubborn. Listen to what I have to say for a minute. Okay?"

"I guess."

"Tony, you don't need to transfer - I will. You're much too important to this project to not be an integral part of it here in Billings. I'll go. I'll tell Neil I need to get away from the insane pressure. I'll relocate to Baltimore until the project's completion. I'll make myself inaccessible to you. You have to stay. I won't allow you to leave. Let me go. My not being here isn't going to make that much of a difference. It's what I want to do -"

"You honestly would do that for me? You would choose to abandon an opportunity of a lifetime to accommodate my future success? You could stay. I would completely understand your decision to stay."

"No. I can't do that to you. I'll leave. It's the only plan that makes any sense."

"I understand now why I love you so much. Okay, I'll reluctantly try to accept your decision, but only if you honestly believe in it. Think about it carefully. Let me know what you decide in a few days. Other than that, please don't waste any more time or thoughts on me. I don't want to ruin your life any more than I already have."

"Are you crazy? You haven't ruined my life, you've enriched it in so many ways, despite what you may think. Please understand that. I'll always have feelings for you. You're a very special person to me. Unfortunately, that doesn't mean anything in helping to fix our present situation. We need to put some safe distance between us as quickly as possible. Tonight, I'll start planting the seed in Neil's mind about my desire to transfer. The sooner I can resolve this, the better it will be for the both of us."

"Thanks. I don't know what else to say."

"You don't have to say anything. Just sit back and let me take care of it. It'll be okay. I promise."

Tony and Lisa continued their conversation saying just about everything that had to be said, eventually sitting at the table in silence, their eyes fixed on each others, trying to understand without words what they were honestly feeling. As the smoke-filled room started to clear itself of people, the solitude between them increased until only their eyes conveyed what meanings were in their hearts. The candle on the table burned slowly down to a hot pool of wax, dripping on the tablecloth with the carefulness and deliberateness that was the evening.

Lisa grasped Tony's hand and said something she did not mean; "Tony, I want you to know something. I will try to stay out of your life. But, if you need me for anything, I'll be around. Honestly. I'll always be here for you."

"Thanks, but you don't have to say that. It'll only create more problems. We're not meant to be, at least not in this lifetime. Just leave it alone. Let it go. It's getting late. You need to go home now. You need to be there when Neil arrives."

"Okay." It was all Lisa was capable of saying. She wanted to say so much more.

Their dinner was over. Tony's tip was generous. Lisa remarked on his thoughtful gesture. These were the last words they spoke to each other until they exchanged "good nights" and unexpectedly kissed for probably the last time. Tony silently told her he loved her. He wouldn't allow the words to pass from his lips and destroy the finality of the moment.

The trip home for Tony was fast and vigorous. When he arrived at his cabin, he collapsed on his bed in his clothes. He stared at the roof beams until his eyes blurred and closed. He fell to sleep with dreams of comfort helping him feel safe and secure until the morning arrived, to shake his crystal cover of protection.

PART 2: DEATH

CHAPTER 27

THE ACCIDENT

Over two months had passed since Tony and Lisa's memorable night together. In all that time, Lisa never mentioned to Neil her intentions to leave Billings for Baltimore, as she promised Tony. The longer she waited to pursue the subject with Neil, the harder it was for her to break free from her self-absorbed responsibilities and the easier it was for her to ignore doing anything at all. During this time, Lisa made a conscious decision not to call or talk to Tony. She made no attempts to let him know what she was thinking, feeling or doing. After her promise to not shut him out of her life, Lisa was doing just that.

Tony became distraught and confused over Lisa's decision not to leave Montana or contact him. He understood her conflicting feelings and how difficult it was for her to leave Neil for reassignment in Baltimore. Nevertheless, it only served to cheapen the emotional significance of their one night together. He readjusted his emotional attachment towards her. He became detached from any reality of their ever being together. It was now his isolated problem. It was now his emotional baggage. He would deal with it on his own terms, in his own way.

He retaliated in the only way he knew. He purposely avoided Lisa at the office unless it directly involved work. He declined all invitations offered by Neil to stop by for dinner or a drink. It was becoming easier for him to accept the disappointment of her actions. He was familiar with dead end relationships and broken promises.

Tony had discussed the Lisa encounter and the significance of the bear with Johnny Thunder Eagle. He tried to keep the affair to himself. It was the prudent and safe course of action. Despite all his fail-safe logic, he could not allow himself to suffer in solitude. He recruited Johnny to help him with his problem. He needed closure and Johnny was the only person that had the wisdom to help him through this experience as painlessly as possible. However, much to Tony's dismay, Johnny offered little advice or direction. He only listened. He would leave the matter in its natural state, not wanting to disturb its predestined path. He advised Tony to do the same. The bear's visit however was a story Johnny was happy to entertain. Johnny told Tony that the bear would reappear to him again in the near future, in a dream or a vision. It represented Tony's inner spirit – a universal bond with the bear. At that time Tony would know the bear's message. That is all Johnny knew.

— — —

Tony had spent another twenty-four day at the office nearly working himself to exhaustion. The sun was rising on another day. The phone rang. Tony ignored the ring. He was face deep in his work, half asleep from his second consecutive all-nighter and definitely not being productive. He needed to go home and get some sleep. Why was he pushing himself on a job he knew he had so many doubts about finishing?

The phone rang again. Annoyed, Tony searched to find it. The phone rang again. When he did find it among all the chaos, probably buried under piles of drawings and files, he was going to destroy it. The phone rang again. Finally, there it was, on the floor next to his drafting table. He grabbed it and in his half awake stupor answered it.

"Uh…Hello. This is Tony…Rullo, Mogul Enterprises - Project Architect," Tony mumbled.

"Tony, it's me."

"Lisa?…" Tony asked in shocked relief. His heart seem to stop for an instant and then started to beat rapidly from this emotionally charged contact.

…She finally called me…was it because she told Neil she was leaving?…am I going to get relief from this mess?…

"Lisa?…It's a relief to finally hear from you. Why did you wait so long to call me? Why did you shut me out? I asked you to not shut me out. I miss you, more than you know, more than I thought I could. I miss not talking to you, not being with you every day. It's been driving me crazy..."

Tony couldn't believe he said that. He remained quiet and waited for a response to his awkward outburst. None came.

"…Lisa?…" he said. Lisa said nothing.

Annoyed, Tony continued. "…Don't you have anything to say to me after all this time - anything? You can't just call me out of the blue and have nothing to say…"

Lisa was still silent. Tony's frustration was increasing.

"…There's no excuse for you not contacting me in all these months. What's going on with you and Neil? What happened to your plan? Are you leaving or staying? I need to know. You owe that to me. For God's sake talk to me!…"

Lisa was silent for a moment more, completely detached from Tony's ranting. She ignored Tony's frustrated ramblings and continued to the purpose of her call.

"Tony, I have some horrible news to tell you. Minutes ago…I received a call from the site…oh Tony…"

Lisa's hysterical tone instantly made Tony aware that this call was not about them. It was about something else – something beyond his selfish emotional interests.

He asked apprehensively;

"What Lisa? What is it? What happened at the site?" His mood shifted abruptly from angered lover to concerned friend.

"Neil's dead…at the building site…there was an accident…something about the freight elevator falling. The cable snapped or something. I don't know. Or the brakes failed. Maybe faulty brakes, they said. It doesn't matter. It fell. He's dead. Oh Tony, please. I need you to come over here right away. I don't know what else to do. They want me to formally identify his battered body. It's making me sick thinking about it. There was no one else I wanted to be with. There was no one else I wanted to call, except you. I need you here with me now. I can't do this alone. I'm too upset to drive. I'm feeling sick to my stomach and can't stop shaking. I need you to take me to the Billings' morgue. Please…I need you to come over now!"

Tony dropped the receiver to his side and it fell from his grasp hitting the floor.

…Oh my God!… No!… This can't be true! Jesus Christ!… It can't be true…It can't be true…Neil can't be dead…Oh God this can't be happening… What am I going to do now?…

What cruel insensitive joke was life playing on him? Where was his guardian angel, his giant eagle now? Where was Neil's? Why didn't the Great Spirit protect him from this evil?

The receiver was on the floor. Tony was in shock, talking to himself, oblivious to what was happening around him and

Lisa's call. The muffled hysterical cries of Lisa could be heard reverberating from the receiver's mouthpiece.

"Tony! Tony, are you there? Tony! Did you hear me? Neil's dead! Please answer me! Oh my God, don't leave me alone like this. Please answer me!"

Lisa's sounds slowly started to evolve themselves into the recesses of Tony's unsettled mind. They gradually pulled him back from his shock. His emotions began to settle back to a manageable level. He realized what he was doing and quickly pulled up the cord of the receiver gradually lifting it off the floor. He needed to stay calm for Lisa. He couldn't allow himself to react to this tragedy. He could hear Lisa's screams and cries from the receiver getting louder and louder as it slowly made its way to his ear.

"Lisa? Hello. Hello. I'm sorry. I'm back. I'm back now. I'm so sorry. I just reacted. I dropped the phone. I'm trembling here. I'm in shock. I can't believe that Neil is dead. Are you sure? Is Neil dead? Are you sure?"

Lisa sobbed. "He's dead Tony. He's dead. I can't talk about this anymore. I need you here. I need you."

"Of course. Yes. Of course you're sure about this. I'm so sorry. I'm so sorry. I'll be there as fast as I can. Don't do anything or go anywhere until I get there. Do you need me to do anything or call anyone for you before I leave?"

"No. I just need you to get here as fast as you can."

"Okay. I'm on my way. I'll be there in a few minutes."

Tony could feel his heart sink into his stomach. His eyes filled with tears. He began to cry. Neil dead? What could this mean to Lisa? What could this mean to him? His best friend is dead. What about the project? What will happen to the building, Neil's skyscraper, Neil's dream and Mr. Mogul's vision? He couldn't bear this burden alone, but right now he needed to be strong for Lisa. It was Lisa's time. She needed him and

THE ACCIDENT

he had to be there for her, even if he didn't know what he was supposed to do, or how he should feel. With his feelings for Lisa so strong and suppressed, the disgusting thought surfaced briefly, that with Neil gone, they could begin a relationship. The thought sickened him. It made him angry and disappointed.

As soon as he hung up the phone, he could hear the sounds of chaos break loose throughout the building as the news of Neil's death had obviously found its way to Brenda and was quickly being circulated. Everyone would soon know. Tony needed to leave immediately before this wave of grief unmercifully consumed him.

― ― ―

Tony put all of his emotional baggage with Lisa in storage. He arrived at her apartment to begin the usual activities that follow the death of a close friend and loving husband.

Lisa personally identified Neil's body that day, with Tony bravely but tenuously standing by her side on the verge of tears and nausea. The next day, the ordeal of Neil's funeral arrangements were managed and organized, with Lisa's input, by the Mogul organization. The services were to take place in Billings. It was Neil's request, according to Lisa. Ironically, it was to be held in a Roman Catholic Cathedral, not because of Neil's reverence or allegiance to this religion, but because it was the largest church in the city and an architectural treasure, the primary reasons for Neil's choice. It also was large enough to hold the hundreds of mourners that would be attending the funeral.

Just about everyone associated with the project attended. Neil and Lisa's parents were there, along with Neil's brother and Lisa's sister. Johnny Thunder Eagle, Stoney Creek Smith, and members of the Tribal Council all attended. The office was closed and all work stopped for three days in tribute and respect to a great architect and human being. It was a solemn and sad event.

A speech was written by Mr. Mogul and read by Charlie. Even at Neil's funeral, Mr. Mogul could not take the chance of having his identity known. His security, now more than ever, was a concern. His speech reflected the goals of Neil as it related to his life, his love for Lisa, and his undying devotion to the skyscraper's success. It emphasized the undeniable fact, that Neil was a good man, who died too soon and too young, his life stolen from him, denying him the chance to witness the fruits of his efforts.

There were local priests and ministers there in Neil's honor, but they were not invited to speak. Only the words of Mr. Mogul, Johnny Thunder Eagle and Lisa were allowed to echo through the cavernous confines of this sacred Cathedral. Tony could not and would not say anything at Neil's funeral. He was overcome by grief and guilt. Neil's death was something he still could not accept. Neil was his mentor – his brother. He was the rock he could lean on when he had any problems. Increasingly, Tony doubted his ability to successfully continue on the project without Neil's guidance.

— — —

After the completion of Mr. Mogul's eulogy, there was a moment of silence. The serenity was broken by Johnny Thunder Eagle's quiet appearance at the pulpit. It was his opportunity to speak to the assembled crowd. The people who knew Johnny, noticed that his hair was much shorter. Johnny and Stoney had cut their hair in honor of Neil's death. They were following a traditional Crow custom, signifying the beginning of a period of mourning.

Johnny spoke from the depths of his Native American roots, confining his words within the traditions of his heritage, and not allowing his emotions to transcend the purpose

THE ACCIDENT

of his message. He spoke of the circle of life and the beliefs of his people. He spoke of Neil's death as welcomed by the Great Spirit. He spoke of Neil not dying in vain, but with a great honor and purpose. He spoke of him as a brave warrior. He spoke using a simple Crow prayer. "You are gone. You are young. Do not turn back. We wish you to fare well. Eternal are the heavens and the Earth. Old people are poorly off. Do not be afraid." The prayer was well received for the simplicity of its profound message. After his message was finished, he and the attending Native Americans performed a traditional Crow burial song asking the Great Spirit to welcome Neil into its world and to keep him safe and well.

Johnny then escorted Lisa to the pulpit. It was now Lisa's turn to speak. She was tastefully dressed in a black dress, her body adorned with not a single piece of jewelry. She was hatless and without make up. She was without expression or emotion. The crowd sat quietly awaiting her words. The words came - slowly, deliberately, in a whisper.

"Thank you, Charlie, Mr. Mogul and the entire Mogul Organization. My words cannot express how grateful I am for all you've done for Neil and me. Thank you Johnny, the Crow Nation and all your Native American brothers and sisters, for honoring Neil in that way. It was beautiful. He would have loved it. Everyone, thank you so much for honoring Neil today. I know he cared for you all and would feel guilty about taking your valuable time away from the important things you need to accomplish in your lives today. I do not have much to say, Neil wanted it that way. He was a man of few words and strong conviction. He asked me only to read something in the event of a premature death, one thing and one thing only. I only ask that whatever your beliefs, or religions are, that you make this reading universal. Have it embrace your personal beliefs and needs at this time. This reading is in honor of

Neil's life and death, as he walks now in the land of the other reality. We were not practicing Christians, but Neil believed in extracting the best attributes of all the religions of this world. Now, he is experiencing the absolute truth and is part of the 'Great Spirit's' world. I'll begin. Please bear with me." She surprised everyone by saying nothing about Neil or the circumstances of his death; instead she simply and eloquently recited from the Bible, the 23rd Psalm.

> *"The Lord is my Sheppard;*
> *I shall not want.*

She paused briefly, her composure near its breaking point.

> *He maketh me lie down in green pastures.*
> *He leadeth me beside still waters.*
> *He restoreth my soul."*

Lisa paused again for a few seconds before continuing. She took a deep breath and whispered, "His soul shall live forever". She continued.

> *He leadeth me on the path of righteousness*
> *For his name's sake.*
> *Yea, though I walk through the valley of the*
> *shadow of death,*
> *I will fear no evil.*
> *Because Thou art with me;*
> *Thy rod and thy staff shall comfort me.*
> *Thou preparest a table before me*
> *In the presence of thyne enemies;*

Another pause, with her saying, "His enemies shall find the truth and be saved," and finished the final few lines;

> *Thou anointest my head with oil.*
> *My cup runneth over.*
> *Surely goodness and mercy shall follow me*
> *all the days of my life,*
> *And I shall dwell in the house of the Lord forever."*

After her reading, she told everyone it was one of Neil's favorite Christian psalms. She also said it was one of his prayers that he recited daily for the project's safety and success. He had several he used, assembled from different religions of the world. Lisa was in tears, as she tried to keep all the composure that she could manage while trying to finish her remarks, but it was not to be. She broke down at the pulpit. Tony walked up to her and graciously escorted her back to her seat and her family. The church was silent. Nothing more could be said. Charlie thanked everyone and the service was over.

Neil's casket was carried from the church and transported by hearse to the building's site. Once there, it was placed in a horse drawn wagon and traveled the short distance to one of the reservation's sacred burial plots. His body was not placed atop a scaffold supported by four forked poles, as was the Crow tradition. Instead, the casket was buried under the scaffold, with Neil's feet facing east. It was as Neil desired and as requested by Lisa. He was the only non-Native American person in Crow history allowed to buried here.

Lisa and Tony spent as much time as they could together at the funeral. They hardly spoke; instead they held each other's hands tightly sharing the security and comfort it gave to them. The only time Lisa left Tony's side, was to accept condolences from the hundreds of mourners. When the ordeal was over, she was exhausted. She used her final reserve of energy to be with her parents and sister, and Neil's parents and his brother. She stood with them as Neil was buried.

Tony was standing next to Johnny Thunder Eagle and Stoney Creek Smith as he watched Neil's coffin slowly enter the hole in the ground. He became paralyzed with grief. Tony thought…*why bother moving on?…I can't do this anymore…how much more can I take?…first my father, then my mother, and now Neil…between all of this…Lisa…all I wanted was a chance to help make a positive difference in this world…I was given that opportunity and I screwed it up…*He looked sorrowfully at Johnny and began crying. He looked over at Lisa…*what happens now?…*

— — —

With the service over, Lisa excused herself from her family and walked over to be with Tony and Johnny.

"Hello, Johnny. Good to see you. Haven't had much of a chance to talk to you today," she said.

"Hello, Lisa. How are you holding up?" Johnny said.

He gave her a hug, stepped back and waited for her to respond. Lisa appeared very calm.

"I'm okay, I guess…There's not much more to say or do. Death is so final. Life is so fragile. That's about it. Time to get back to living out our lives. I just need to find the strength to help me get through this dreadful day. How are you?" she said.

"I am doing well, but I am not so sure about our friend Tony here. The Great Spirit will give you your strength Lisa. If there is anything we can do for you on the reservation or anywhere else, just let us know. We are your family."

"That's very kind of you. Thank you. I'll let you know if I need anything. Excuse me Johnny, may I talk to Tony alone for a moment?" Lisa said.

"Of course. You do not need my permission. I will leave you two alone."

Johnny looked over at Tony and shook his head.

"Go easy on him, Lisa. He is not doing well," he said.

"I know. I'll see you in a little while," Lisa said.

Johnny walked away, leaving Lisa and an unsettled Tony alone. Tony looked up from his troubled thoughts and focused on Lisa.

"What?" he said.

"Tony?" Lisa said.

"What?"

"Can I talk with you? It's important. Let's find a place to sit. I'm exhausted. I need to sit down."

"Sure. What is it? What's this about?"

"Just a minute. Let's sit first."

They walked over to three vacant folding chairs at the burial site. Many curious eyes were watching them as they sat down. Tony thought of the first time he met Lisa and Neil, the time when they all sat together on folding chairs in front of a card table. It was Tony's initial interview with the Hagman's; the one event in his life that started the most fantastic ride of his life. Now one chair was empty. Now one life was gone. Tony's eyes again filled with tears.

"Lisa…excuse me…give me a minute…I'm sorry..."

Lisa put her arm around him.

"It's okay. It's okay. I know how you feel. Believe me, I know. I'm still numb from Neil's death. I'm still in shock. Any minute now it's going to hit me and I'm going to collapse and pass out from grief, so be ready to catch me when I fall. Okay? Don't let me fall. Hey. How you doing? Better?"

"I'm okay now. I'm okay. God! It never ends does it? When are the happy days coming? I missed you while you were busy being gracious. I needed you. It's good to be sitting next to you again. ... okay, I'm better...I'm ready. Talk."

"Johnny knows about us, doesn't he?" Lisa said.

A startled Tony answered, "Yes. Is it that obvious? I'm sorry. Is that a problem? I needed someone to talk to about us and he was the only one I could completely trust. Don't worry. He won't mention it to anyone. Is this what this talk is all about? You're upset because Johnny knows?"

"No. It's okay. I'm not upset about that. If I were you, I would have done the same thing. Johnny's a wonderful person and a true friend. I just brought that up because I could sense that he knew something about us. That's not what I need to talk with you about. That's not what's important to me right now. I don't want to talk about me or us. I want to talk about you."

"Me? Why me? Now? Can't it wait? Don't you have more important things to worry about today?" Tony said.

"No, I need to discuss this right now." Lisa looked directly at Tony.

"What?"

"Tony, don't do it."

"Don't do what?"

"I know you Tony. I can feel your pain. You're beginning to harbor doubts about yourself, your life and the project, aren't you? You want to quit and isolate yourself from everything. You want to quit life, don't you?"

"What the hell...how could you possibly know that?"

"Come on. Don't you think I know you by now? I know what you're thinking. I know what you're feeling. I think I know you better than I knew Neil. There's something about our connection, something that enables us to share each other's feelings. I can sense it with you. This tragedy is not letting go of you. Whatever you're feeling right now, whatever it is, it will pass. Trust me. It will pass. You have to let it go. It's not your fault. Let this tragedy pass and get yourself together enough to rebuild your confidence, trust in your ability, and accept your destiny to continue contributing to this project. Do it for you. Do it for Neil. Do it for me. Don't get down on yourself. None of this is your fault."

"You are something. You really do know me. You're right. Life just seems so empty and pointless to me, especially today. I don't know what to do. I need help, but that's not important. You shouldn't be worrying about me today, not at Neil's funeral, not now."

"Tony, Neil is dead. Nothing can change that. You're not. It's my job to worry about you. I want what's best for you – always did. That's why I couldn't leave you or be with you all those months I stayed away from you. I was in an emotional limbo. It was painful for me. It was a selfish decision. I cried a lot, but it was for the best."

Lisa reached out to hold Tony's hand. Tony didn't react. He couldn't.

"How did you get so smart and so amazingly strong?" he said. "You just buried your husband and you're worrying about me, worrying about how *I'm* doing, telling me to get over this tragedy? You're so right. I am feeling down on myself. Can't help it. I really miss Neil. He was like a father *and* a brother to me. He was such an amazing person – a wonderful human being. I can't let him go and of course - there's us, which really messes up my head. It's all very confusing. You know that. Give me a few days. I need time to be by myself and think. I promised myself I would try to understand how to deal with this. In the next few days, if I need your help, I'll let you know. In the meantime, I won't do anything drastic. I promise."

"That's what I want to hear. You know I really miss Neil too - very much. I am feeling his death on so many levels that it's driving me crazy. We need to be available for each other until we can come to a comfortable place in our hearts concerning Neil's death. Okay?" ... Lisa paused.

She apprehensively glanced over at the few remaining mourners.

"...Looks like people are starting to get curious about our little talk. Let's end it for now. We need to catch up with the others. My family and Neil's are staying with me tonight. Stop by anytime or call me if you need to talk. Let's go..."

The day had turned cold and dark. It was not the prettiest of days to be outside for a funeral, burying your best friend and husband. A sorrowful wind blew from the west and carried with it the lasting memories of Neil Hagman. This mournful day was over.

CHAPTER 28

THE EXPLOSION

There was an investigation into the circumstances surrounding Neil's death. Construction was halted for five days. After an intensive inspection of the fallen construction elevator's transport system, no evidence was found suggesting that Neil's death was other than an accident. A defective cable and improperly installed brake linings were determined as the cause of its plummeting ten floors to the ground, killing Neil. A conclusion that did not make sense, however, was why Neil was using this untested death trap – alone – in the first place. He was much too careful and aware not to have known that this particular hoist was not fully tested.

Even though Neil's death was ruled an accident, Bradshaw initiated increased security protocols at the site. Immediately following the accident he instructed Johnny to organize a Crow security force for the select purpose of securing and policing the site for any suspicious or threatening activities. Johnny handpicked fifty of the reservation's noblest and must trustworthy brothers to be part of Mr. Mogul's army. They would live at the site until the building's completion. He also began an accelerated process to issue personal photo identification badges to every employee, have visitors badged and escorted, and deliveries carefully screened before being allowed onsite. Surveillance equipment ordered over two months ago after the infamous Chicago meeting between Neil and Mr. Mogul, still had not arrived. Since Jim Bradshaw's desire to purchase a system that used the latest state of the art technology, the cameras, monitors and videotape recorders were in limited production and not readily available. The much-needed equipment would not arrive for another six weeks.

Jim was cautious in immediately finding someone to replace Neil. He needed to assign a person he could trust completely, as he did Neil. Until he could make a decision and appoint a suitable replacement, everyone previously under Neil's supervision was ordered to complete their respective assignments and report directly to Charlie Wilson.

Meanwhile, Tony managed, with the help of Johnny and Lisa, to lift himself out from his deep pit of self-doubt. He was working again, focused more than he was before Neil's death. As for Tony and Lisa, they began seeing each other as friends, ever so carefully, ever so cautiously – while maintaining a close working relationship. They often discussed a possible future together, and its potential to evolve into something normal and uncomplicated. However, the reality of Neil's death and the project's overwhelming responsibilities, put their emotional future firmly on hold. They assumed the bulk of Neil's workload, although they were not granted direct access to Mr. Mogul, as Neil would have had, frustrating them and their ability to efficiently process their work.

— — —

Three weeks had passed since Neil's death.

Today, Tony was scheduled to visit the building's fifth floor to inspect the installation and operation of his favorite subject - solar cells. Each time he visited the site he was always impressed by how fast the building was climbing skyward. The building's structural frame had reached fifty floors. Only one hundred more floors to frame, and the building's steel skeleton would be complete. It was magnificent to see this vision rise into the sky - a monument to everyone's talent, hard work, and dedication.

The passenger elevators were in place to serve the first twenty-five floors, but not approved for occupancy. Tony would normally use one of five construction elevators, *hoists,* to access the unfinished floors of the building, similar to the one that plummeted Neil to his death. Tony was being extra cautious, wearing his mandatory hardhat, safety glasses and steel-toed shoes, forgoing the elevators and using the stairs to access the building's enclosed fifth floor. On this floor the interior finishes and specialized solar applications were nearing completion. Solar cell panel arrays were being installed in conjunction with the window frames. The sun was shining. It was the perfect day. Tony inspected the completed solar cell installations and tested the voltage output of a typical array. It was performing according to its listed specifications. He tested several more arrays – all functioning perfectly.

The site appeared secure. Despite this appearance, Tony did not feel safe. He was suspicious about the circumstances surrounding Neil's death. He was certain it was not an accident. Neil was much too careful to ride in an untested construction elevator. Tony concluded, Neil was led to believe that it was safe by someone he trusted. In his gut, he knew there was a person or persons on site who were assigned to murder Neil, and destroy this building, especially after the horror story revealed to him by Lisa several months ago. He was positive of that as was most everyone associated with the project.

— — —

Tony had an appointment at the site with Harry, the *Sunflex* solar cell engineer, and Martin Smith, the project's senior electrical engineer. He surveyed the floor. He didn't see them among the dozens of workers.

There were hundreds more throughout the building's shell. This project never slept. Three shifts working as a well-oiled machine, twenty-four hours a day, seven days a week, to build the greatest building in the world - everyone in harmony - everyone working together as bees in a hive. Every part of this building was being assembled like it was an expensive Swiss watch.

A group of workers across the floor whistled and gave Tony a wave. Tony waved back. The group started walking toward him. He noticed that good ol' Harry and Martin were with them. Harry was one of the smartest people that Tony had ever met, although on this project, meeting a technical genius was not uncommon.

Tony's pace quickened as he excitedly closed the gap between him and the group. He started thinking about the unfortunate death of Neil, and how disappointed and sad he was that Neil would not be here to see the building's triumphant completion.

Before these thoughts in Tony's head cleared, he saw a blinding flash of light and felt the floor shake. He then heard a sound so loud that he instinctively covered his ears shielding them from the pain, and felt a force so great that it forced him to helplessly fall to his knees.

What happened next filled Tony's mind with a fear that was telling him he was soon to die. The destructive sequence of events started to unfold before him in fractions of a second.

Glass blew out of their window frames shattering into thousands of pieces. The floor shook violently. Exterior walls began to crumble. It appeared the building was beginning an unimpeded journey towards total collapse. Tony was trapped. He knew that his death would soon arrive. There wasn't anywhere he could escape. Nowhere to run, nowhere to find refuge, only total destruction surrounded him. He thought, first the beams, then the girders and finally the columns, floors, walls and everything that was part of the building would end in a mass of rubble on the ground with him buried and crushed beneath it all.

That was intended to be the natural order of this building's collapse, but this building was not following order. It was fighting back and would not allow itself to die. It was resisting death in any way it could with Tony embraced inside its determined resistance.

Tony couldn't see. He was blinded by smoke and debris. It engulfed him. He couldn't breathe. He tried to stand up, but fell to the ground as he began to lose consciousness knowing that these were his last thoughts and his last breaths. The noise was deafening. He managed to crawl to the building's exterior edge trying to find any way to escape.

He heard himself say without any pre-thought:

"...Mom...Dad...Help me...I need you...don't let me die yet...I'm not finished...I need to finish...Help me..."

There was the sound of another explosion. He reached out and felt a wall as it collapsed in front of him.... *Oh my God... my Vision Quest...* Suddenly, he felt himself fall and float and then nothing.

— — —

It was nearly two hours since the building was hit with this insulting blow to its existence. No one not officially included in the rescue operations was permitted to be within one-quarter mile radius of the building site. The site was secured. Hundreds of fire and rescue volunteers, law enforcement and project personnel were there investigating the explosion, searching for survivors, and anything that could shed some light on the how and why of what happened. They sorted through the rubble, sadly discovered the bodies of the dead, and attended to the injured.

Dozens were patrolling the area around the building on horseback and on foot. Johnny Thunder Eagle was part of this patrol, riding with three Crow brothers looking for anyone who might have fallen outside the building's walls. Johnny rode over to a large green rectangular garbage dumpster. This particular receptacle was filled with fiberglass insulation, cardboard boxes and packing, everything that could be soft and recyclable was in this dumpster. It was one of the many recycling programs that Tony had implemented during construction. Johnny was thinking this as he looked inside its boundaries. Horrified, he saw a body sprawled across this mountain of trash, unconscious and bleeding. It was Tony, barely alive. The recycled garbage most likely cushioned his fall and saved his life.

Johnny shouted, "Over here! Anyone! Over here! Get the ambulance. I found Tony. He's alive. Hurry…"

Johnny climbed into the dumpster and cradled Tony's blood soaked body in his arms. He then chanted a Crow prayer asking the Great Spirit to spare Tony's life. For today, Johnny offered to the spirits above, was not Tony's day to die. This brave warrior was not going to die today. That day, Johnny knew, was one reserved for a future moment, a moment that would have a special purpose for Tony, this skyscraper, and the world.

He wrapped Tony's head and body in rags and tried to keep the obvious wounds from bleeding. Tears started to well in Johnny's eyes as he held the almost lifeless body of Tony in his arms. The history of his people, of the Crow Nation, was filled with the overwhelming forces of greed and dominance by the White people, the intruders upon his land that resulted in the deaths of many innocents. Johnny understood the bombing was a deliberate attempt by these same greed and dominance driven people to stop a worthwhile project from succeeding for the simple reason that it would take money from their pockets, and power from their lifeless souls.

Holding Tony, he continued to pray, and waited for the ambulance. It seemed like hours to Johnny before the ambulance arrived, but in fact it was only minutes. All available lifesaving assistance from Harding and Billings was on site, summoned minutes after the explosion.

The paramedics carefully secured Tony to the stretcher for transport to the Billings hospital, and used every means at their disposal to keep him alive. They tended to his wounds, stopped the external bleeding and set his broken leg and arm. They wouldn't know the extent of his injuries until he was examined and X-Rayed at the hospital. As the ambulance headed toward Billings, Johnny was there at Tony's side, reciting his prayers to the Great Spirit. One of the paramedics was a fellow Crow brother from the reservation. He looked at Johnny, nodded his head in approval, and smiled.

"He's going to make it, Thunder Eagle. He's going to make it. He will not die today," he said.

"I know, Little Sparrow. I know..."

— — —

When Tony arrived at the hospital, the doctors discovered, in addition to a broken leg and arm, he had a concussion, two broken ribs, a collapsed lung, and a severely bruised back. His body had experienced severe trauma, with many surface abrasions. Still, he was lucky to be alive. He was rushed to the operating room and the parts that could be fixed would be fixed.

The Great Spirit's guardian eagle would watch over him now.

At the end of the day, the final count was fourteen people dead and thirty-eight injured along with millions of dollars of damage, and thousands of solar cells destroyed. The building's fifth floor suffered the heaviest destruction. The fourth and sixth floors incurred minor damage. The remaining floors were relatively unaffected by the explosion. There was a giant hole in the building's skin that encompassed about twenty-five percent of the south wall, and small portions of the east and west, between floors four and six. The building's structural frame, its columns, girders, beams, its entire vertical support system for all floors, remained intact. Its superior and innovative earthquake resistant structural frame enabled it to withstand the onslaught of this ill-conceived attack.

The Great Spirit had assured that.

After assessing the extent of the damage, it was concluded the fifth-floor bomb assault was not intended to destroy the entire building. For that goal to succeed, it would have required hundreds of additional bombs strategically placed on all of the exterior columns below the fifth floor, each bomb wired to explode sequentially, floor by floor, essentially collapsing the columns and with them most of the building's structural support onto itself. No additional bombs were found on any other floors of the building. It became apparent then that the bombing was not an attempt to achieve the building's total destruction, but an exercise in destroying it by inflicting extreme financial hardship for its reconstruction, essentially detouring it from its noble goals and keeping it from meeting its already impossible scheduled completion date. This project, this skyscraper, was in danger of not being completed on time, if at all. It was now in a battle with an unknown enemy, just to stay alive.

THE EXPLOSION

— — —

News of the bombing spread throughout the wire services and immediately erupted into a national media event. The major TV networks, local news reporters, and the curious, interested only in the sensationalism of this event, were traveling to the site to report and witness anything that would be deemed controversial and ratings worthy.

Soon, the site would be overrun with dozens of reporters with no connection to, or understanding of, the project or its goals. This quiet revolutionary skyscraper was now the target of an opportunistic media, riding on the coat tails of the high television ratings that the 1973 "Siege at Wounded Knee" takeover received. It would only be a matter of time before Jim Bradshaw's, well-guarded secret was exposed to all.

CHAPTER 29

THE PROTEST

The explosion's cloud of dust and debris had settled like a dirty blanket over the building site. Dedicated crews worked continuously for forty-eight hours through the bitter cold nights in an attempt to get the building back to a point where safety was assured and construction could again begin.

It was almost noon.

The sun was poised in the cloudless blue sky at its maximum apex. Its low winter angle from the horizon caused its illuminating beams to cast long shadows on anything blocking their light path. The hint of a winter breeze infused the air with an intoxicating freshness. It was on this cold clear day in December, that an unexpected gathering storm was engulfing the skyscraper's home. This storm was taking its form not from Mother Nature's palette, but from the gathering of hundreds of energized and spiritually driven people united in protest.

These protesters represented a potpourri of people, people previously active against the Vietnam War, presently active in the American Indian Movement - AIM, and newcomers suddenly married to a new cause. This gathering however, was not a protest against an unjust war or denied human rights, but a protest to not allow a dream to die an unjustified premature death before it could have its opportunity to literally shine in the sun. Now, hand-in-hand, in a giant protective circle, these people had the battered skyscraper surrounded.

The fuel that launched this protest evolved from the abrupt actions of the predictably uninformed but politically driven self serving interests of the BIA. From the project's inception, the BIA felt ignored, powerless to control the imposing multi-billion dollar organization behind this project. It was never in favor of the skyscraper succeeding without substantially benefiting from its existence. Now it was seeking retribution by any means at its disposal.

The BIA immediately implemented appropriate legal action with cooperation from the Department of the Interior, to halt further construction of this bicentennial skyscraper. They received justification through hastily conducted superficial investigations, into the bombing by the CIA and FBI. From these investigations unproven theories were formulated, circulated within the Department of the Interior, and leaked to the media, linking the bombing and the "accidental" death of Neil Hagman to an as yet unidentified Middle Eastern terrorist organization, supposedly financed by OPEC. Hypothetically, the underlying purpose of this organization was to destroy the building and thereby symbolically destroy all it would potentially represent in ensuring a diminished economic future for the world's petroleum industry. This suspected terrorist act was sufficient reason to classify it as a potential threat to National Security, a threat if not immediately exposed and deterred, would eventually escalate into a systematic destruction of other targeted sites, and the deaths of many innocent Americans.

The United States Government could now legally assume jurisdiction over the building and the site, effectively assuming control from BEI and the Crow Nation. Government officials attempted to defuse this awkward situation by immediately meeting with the Tribal Council Government, assuring them that these invasive actions were only temporary, the government takeover was simply precautionary and would be rescinded, pending the completion of an extensive government investigation into the circumstances related to the bombing.

The Tribal Council knew this government fact-finding exercise could take years to complete and would never lead to a satisfactory conclusion. They had their own suspicions as to who or what was responsible. First on their list - the oil, coal, and utility companies having major financial interests in utilizing and exploiting the reservation's natural resources. They were more likely responsible for the bombing than any conspiracy theory linked to an OPEC-funded terrorist organization. In addition, there was that ever present small pocket of militant racist groups not wanting any financial enterprise benefiting a Native American Nation or Indian Reservation to succeed. But, the most disturbing possibility was the one involving Native Americans themselves. Even with all the benefits that this building was going to offer to the Crow people, and to many Native Americans living on reservations throughout the United States, it may have been deliberately sabotaged by a politically motivated and unsympathetic group of Native Americans.

The most obvious suspects were the Government supporting "Urban Indians" spearheaded by members of George "Georgie" Ironhead's militant group from the South Dakota, Oglala Sioux, Pine Ridge Indian Reservation. The Council knew that members of Ironhead's squad had infiltrated the

Crow reservation, seduced Crow sympathizers with bribes and false promises, and circumvented the security protocols to be hired as members of the skyscraper's construction crew. They were certain that this was the manner by which the bombing attempt was implemented. However, it didn't matter to the Council whoever or whatever orchestrated the bombing. It was clearly understood that whatever the source, the prolonged investigation by the Feds into the failed destruction of this prestigious renewable energy powered monolith was sufficient to abort its progress and its positive impact on the future of the reservation's population.

— — —

To safely protect the site from future attacks, the National Guard, at the request of the BIA, were quickly summoned by the Governor to the reservation. The National Guard assumed jurisdiction over the reservation police, Federal Marshals and the FBI. The US Military, because of the still sensitive nature that surrounded the 1973 *Wounded Knee* incident on South Dakota's Pine Ridge Reservation, would not be joining the reservation's security forces.

The Guard's presence was not a favorable one under any circumstances. It set up a potential clash between them and the peaceful assembly of protesters, an unfortunate but not unfamiliar result whenever Native Americans decided to resist the unjust policies of the United States Government. Tensions were certain to escalate between the two opposing factions. Unless this impending tidal wave of opposing forces was defused soon, a confrontation at the site was inevitable, especially since the Guard were given direct orders, under Martial Law, to cordon off and restrict access to the building site, and eventually remove, with physical force if necessary, all protestors from the secured area.

Johnny Thunder Eagle was expected to arrive at the site in a few days, joining the group of concerned activists. His arrival meant not just another addition to the many angry and frustrated supporters of this threatened project. His status had been elevated. He was chosen in a hastily assembled Tribal Council meeting as the leader of this ad-hoc army of Crow residents, community supporters, environmentalists, construction workers, and project employees - a non-combatant army assembled here to support the world's greatest building project against the threat of termination.

Johnny would guide this army through a stonewall of stupidity and ignorance. He would lead these people to victory in a peaceful demonstration of unity and strength armed only with a secret weapon of Jim Bradshaw's design.

CHAPTER 30

THE COUNTERATTACK

NEW YORK CITY BEI HEADQUARTERS – THE SAME DAY

Jim made the long, lonely walk to the conference room, where forty-seven personally selected members of his staff and eleven members of the Crow Tribal Council were awaiting his arrival and their specific instructions to implement Bradshaw's four step plan identified as, *Operation Crow Freedom*. Of the plan's four critical steps, only the last step was the one that mattered. The first three steps were diversions, mere smoke screens to draw the attention away from the final solution. The plan came from intensive conversations with the Crow Tribal Council. It followed the pattern of a well-planned Native American ambush.

The lighting in the corridor was subdued. It was a dark journey for Jim. He knew thousands of people were depending on him to revive this building from its coma. He reached the Conference Room in a matter of moments, opened the door to the apprehensive and eager faces of the most talented and intelligent people in his organization. He assumed his position at the head of the conference table and immediately called the meeting to order.

"Good afternoon everyone. Before I begin, I'm certain you are all aware by now that my name and that of BEI have been revealed to the public through every media resource. It is an unfortunate consequence of the publicity that followed the bombing attempt, but it is the reality that we have to live with from now on."

"Our adversaries have attacked our skyscraper. Now, it is our turn to counterattack. You are all familiar with the details of our precise plan. Before we begin its implementation we must extensively review it - step by step. We cannot allow any errors in our individual assignments. Let's begin."

— — —

After two hours of extensive review, a weary Bradshaw began the summary exercise for the fifth and final time.

"What is the first step in *Operation Crow Freedom*?" he shouted.

In a knee jerk reflex response, everyone in the room spoke at once. Their responses were all the same - one word.

"Diversion!"

"Correct. And how do we achieve this initial diversion?"

This time Jim selected a person at random. He pointed and called her name.

"Janice, do you want to answer this one?"

"Yes, Mr. Bradshaw. In step one, we must prejudice any negative allegations against this project, in our favor, by immediately organizing and using the now interested media to favorably publicize this project to the general public via TV, radio and the newspapers."

"What else, Janice?"

"Assemble activist groups and set up a public relations campaign from coast to coast across the United States. Use these groups to initiate a ground swell of immense proportions and size to organize people to fight for our cause."

"Very good. Does everyone agree and understand this concept? As you know, it is already underway. We have many sympathizers at the site, in protest."

"It is essential that we earn the support from the general public to effectively transfer their positive interest to our sympathetic and influential Representatives and Senators in Congress. We could desperately use the President's support too, but we know we are not going to get it. President Ford has offered no public statements referencing the bombing of our skyscraper. The President is obviously isolating himself from either supporting or opposing the situation. He is not accessible to our organization, but we are lucky that Nixon's still not in office. All right, let's move forward. What is step number two? Joe, do you want to field this one?"

Joe eagerly stood up and emphatically gestured to everyone in the room, especially the lawyers.

"We will obtain a court ordered injunction prohibiting government interference in the construction of our skyscraper-"

"That's right," Jim interrupted. "At the very moment we are speaking in this room, the race is on. The BIA has already filed its legal documents against the project's continuation. Their actions are typically loaded with BIA incompetency. They are shortsighted, without any substance and they have grossly underestimated our ability to organize an effective counterattack. Our New York legal staff has worked quickly to file our necessary legal documents to counter the forthcoming BIA actions that intend to halt this project. This information is continually flowing between our New York offices and on-site legal staff in Montana."

— — —

It was frustrating for those associated with the project to be witnessing this Government conspiracy. After all, Jim knew if the bombing had been assessed under less biased circumstances, it would have been classified as a felonious malicious act of private property destruction, initiated on reservation trust land leased by him from the Crow Indian Nation with Department of the Interior approval. Legally, under these circumstances the reservation's law enforcement authorities would have the legal jurisdiction to investigate the crime. The BIA had no legal authority to intervene unless invited to do so by the Tribal Council Government, but it was imposing its will and asserting its authority because it could and because it simply wanted to destroy a project in which it did not approve or benefit.

The BIA's interference was obviously a premeditated and carefully calculated action. It was fueled by the possibility of it financially benefiting immeasurably from the final result. A victory over this skyscraper would greatly solidify its position as the preeminent authoritative force governing the Crow reservation and all Native American Nations.

— — —

The discussion continued.

"If we are successful in legally blocking any further Government actions against this project, do we need to go to steps three and four? Does anyone want to answer that question voluntarily?"

An overwhelming "Yes" chorus resounded in the room.

"And why is that?"

Again the group replied in unison, "Congress!"

"That's correct, Congress. Let us review the possible results of step two again. If we legally block BIA litigation against us on the reservation, it would not guarantee us a permanent solution. A step two victory does not guarantee that we can move forward without any further Government interference. As we know, Congress has the plenary power to impose any law or rule on the reservation if they so desire. They could vote to halt the project in a heartbeat if they felt there was a justifiable reason, political or otherwise to do so. If they did this there isn't anything we could do to reverse their decision unless we successfully carry out smoke screen number three - strict adherence to and forced legal implementation of the Fort Laramie Treaty of 1851."

"In a few days the Department of the Interior, the FBI and CIA, will attempt to convince Congress that there is overwhelming evidence in support of their claim that the bombing is a bona fide National Security threat. If they succeed in doing that, Congress most assuredly would vote against the continuation of our project, pending the never ending completion of their so-called investigation, effectively killing our skyscraper."

"Some of you here have been given a most crucial assignment of personally contacting all of my influential political allies in Washington. When you contact them, make them aware that we are prepared to use any means at our disposal, regardless of the cost, method, or consequences, to keep this project moving forward. We desperately need their favorable vote and their influence in convincing opposing members of Congress to vote in our favor."

It was obvious to Jim that no threat existed. A National Security threat could not be instituted on territory that, by treaty at least, was not technically part of the United States.

"Our legal staff is exploring the ultimate key to successfully initiate this step," he said. "The Crow Nation within its reservation boundaries is supposedly recognized by the United States as a, "sovereign government" an independent entity from the United States Government as defined and ratified in the 1851 Fort Laramie Treaty articles of confederation."

"According to the original tenets of the treaty, the Federal Government cannot, without the approval of Congress, impose its will or laws upon an established reservation government. However noble its original intentions, this treaty has an unfortunate history of many broken promises, lies and convenient Government interpretations. Reservation *sovereignty,* is no more than an impressive concept shamelessly promoted by the United States Government and never an absolute reality for any Native American Nation."

"We are well aware of this tenuous legal framework, but our legal staff is confident that our contacts at the Department of the Interior, will enforce the original intent of the treaty, and lobby Congress not to disrupt the building's construction, but as you know, this is not the final step. Are we clear on the first three steps?"

The audience expectantly nodded in agreement.

"Now, let's proceed to step four, our final goal."

"Bob, you're our international law expert, explain our proposed *Mount Everest* concept again to our group."

"Be happy to Jim. Here it is. Using the Fort Laramie treaty in step number three is not intended to influence Congress to vote in our favor or to vote at all. Its purpose is to keep them occupied in debate, while keeping the project alive and allowing our free access to the site. Our true intention is to establish the Crow Nation internationally, as an independent nation, a nation separate from the Government of the United States. In other words, the treaty's original intent would be followed to the letter of the law. We are intending to petition the United Nations for recognition of the Crow Nation as an independent nation. We will need to go international with this quest and seek the support and power from the countries of the world through the United Nations. This recognition would have to involve a majority of the world's most influential governments."

"We are sending a group of our best people, with members of the Crow Tribal Council Government, to meet secretly, with prominent United Nations' member representatives, to plead our case without United States representation. Believe me, we have an excellent case for Crow Nation independence. Wish us luck, we're going to need a miracle to pull this one off, but I am fully confident that we will do it, as I'm sure everyone in this room is too. Jim? You want to take it from here?"

Jim nodded his approval.

"Thanks, Bob. That is our plan. We do not have much time, but our actions carried out during the first three steps, will effectively mask our eventual goal. I am depending on everyone here in this room not to fail. We will win our battle. Our building will not be defeated."

Jim's enthusiasm was infectious as the room exploded with applause and shouts of victory. There were even some token "war hoops" from the Crow delegation. A few non-Indians present tried to mimic the sound, mostly with embarrassing comical failure.

The meeting was officially over.

The attendees picked up their assignments, packed them in their briefcases exited the conference room to scatter themselves hastily to their assigned destinations. It was now up to every one of them to succeed.

— — —

Jim understood before the project began there would be many bumps in its road to success. He was prepared for this bump, but not at the cost of the deaths of Neil and fourteen innocent people. It was never meant to happen this way but he had his arsenal of power loaded to keep it from ever happening again.

In spite of the Fort Laramie Treaty's tainted history in recognizing the Crow Nation's legal rights, Jim was confident that his day in the world's court, with his army of loyalists and United Nations support, would overwhelm the unprepared Federal bureaucracy, and that he would be able to remove any future Federal and State Government interference from the reservation and the project forever.

Although each specific assignment was critical to the success of *Operation Crow Freedom*, Jim knew his most important asset at the moment was Johnny Thunder Eagle. His process to regain control of the project site again could not succeed without Johnny's influential presence.

— — —

After the meeting Jim placed an important telephone call to Johnny.

"…Yes Johnny, I know the Government's terrorist attack premise is bullshit, but you're more than aware they have the power to impose their will upon your people and this project, right or wrong. They build their towers of power with lies and deceit to achieve their preconceived result, but don't worry, I have a plan to counter this abusive power."

"And what is that plan?" Johnny asked.

"I can't go into it over the phone. I will meet with you personally to discuss it. I am flying to Billings day after tomorrow. Meet me at the hospital around two, in Tony's room. I've made additional arrangements to assure our safety, just in case."

"Okay. I will see you then. Is there anything else you need from me?"

"No. Just ask the Great Spirit to be with us for Tony's sake, and for the sake of this project."

"Do not worry. The Great Spirit is always with us on the side of truth. Have a safe journey."

"Thanks, but the real journey is just beginning. See you soon. Good-bye Johnny."

As Jim hung up the phone, his mind started wandering in a million different directions. There was so much to do. Now, more than ever, he needed to trust the people in his organization to follow through with their assigned tasks quickly, honestly and effectively. One glitch or missed assignment from the plan's precise scheme could result in total failure. Even though Jim was overwhelmed by all this chaos and uncertainty, he still found time to fly to Billings and visit Tony at the hospital.

— — —

As scheduled, in two days, Jim met with Johnny. While sitting and praying at Tony's bedside, Jim explained "The Plan" in detail to Johnny. Although Johnny considered Jim's strategy ambitious and creative, he was not overly confident of it ever succeeding. After all, it relied solely on the United Nations' ad-hoc court of third world nations to circumvent the power and influence of the United States, form an alliance with other powerful and hopefully sympathetic world powers, and establish a majority to vote in favor of truth and justice for the Crow Nation. If Johnny understood anything about the history of Native American justice in America, he knew that anytime the Indian did battle with the United States Government, they would always lose. It was always the end result – no permanent victories - only endless humiliating long-term defeats. Johnny expressed these thoughts out loud to Jim. Jim replied to Johnny's doubts.

"Not this time," he said. "Not this time. This time it would be different. This time, the system would work not only for the Crow Nation, but also for all Native Americans. I give you my word. Justice would finally come home and fully compensate the American Indian."

CHAPTER 31

THE HISTORY REVERSED

THREE DAYS LATER

As Johnny Thunder Eagle left the hospital riding slowly in his Jeep to the building site and closer to the army of protesters, his thoughts focused on the deaths of his ancestors, fourteen innocents, Neil Hagman and the near death of Tony. It consumed him with a passionate rage never before experienced. He was never a combative person, never considered himself having much in common with a traditional Crow warrior, but today, the souls of his ancestors were infusing his body with the combative desire to fight to the death against the injustices that were being served from the palette that was colored with the wrongful deaths of Native Americans throughout America's history.

He recalled the tragic history of Native Americans, a history he studied at the University of Montana; as recorded in books, newspapers, pamphlets, articles and those remembered from Spotted Owl's stories. From these precious resources, Johnny acquired fragments of his people's history, their life, their loves, their culture, and the injustices that surrounded their heritage as a "red" man trying to survive in a biased "white" man's world. He constantly researched the complex history of how the Native American Nations of North America, had been interpreted by the newly established United States government and the people represented by this government, as a race of ignorant uncivilized savages, easily manipulated into domination, subjugation, religious enlightenment, and cultural reconstruction, so as not to impede the successful growth of this new Christian nation of selective "freedom" and technological superiority.

In his studies, he discovered a theory that surmised, that a war promoted by a superior nation, an unprovoked war against a weaker foe, one that cannot be lost, maintains the required continuity and power that aids in stabilizing an evolving society. He believed the United States, for whatever reason, used Native Americans as their "paper tiger" to strengthen their nation until this enemy was conquered, mercifully defeated, too weak and too few to fight back, rendered almost extinct, and forced to live within the restricted confines of sub-standard reservations. He understood why artificially imposed boundaries robbed a person of their freedom – why the inner spirit of Native Americans were so recklessly stolen from them by restricting them to these unnatural boundaries.

― ― ―

Johnny read a recently published book, which chronicled the carefully orchestrated elimination of the "American Indian" and their culture, during the last half of the nineteenth century. The conclusion of this book described the assassination of Sitting Bull, at the Standing Rock Reservation, and the appalling slaughter of innocent Native Americans by the United States 7th Cavalry at Wounded Knee Creek in South Dakota.

Johnny recalled the facts surrounding these events:

It was in 1890, December, on a day similar to today, that these two highly significant events in the history of a select group of North America's Great Plains Indians were sadly witnessed by the Great Spirit.

The first occurred on the 15th, when Sitting Bull, the great Hunkpapa Sioux chief, the strategic force behind the defeat of the 7th Cavalry, at "The Battle of Little Bighorn," while being arrested for his potentially hostile leadership in support of the United States Government's banned "Ghost Dance" movement., was shot and killed by Federally employed Sioux Indian police at the Standing Rock agency during his transfer from the South Dakota Sioux reservation to a military prison.

Two weeks later, on the 29th, four days after the Christian holiday of Christmas, over three hundred men, women and children of the Minneconjou Lakota, led by the their chief Big Foot, also allegedly supporting the Government banned "Ghost Dance", were slaughtered in South Dakota's Pine Ridge Reservation, at Wounded Knee Creek, by the same 7th US Cavalry, in what many historians consider the last significant "battle" in American Indian history. The United States Government promoted this slaughter as a great military victory for the 7th Cavalry, and awarded Congressional Medals of Honor to 20 of the 7th's "brave" solders.

Was this massacre by the 7th Cavalry simply a premeditated payback for the fourteen-year legacy of their Little Bighorn defeat, or simply the racist reflex action of tired frightened solders?

Johnny and history would never know the truth.

And just last year, the village of Wounded Knee was reborn as a place of Native American dissent and protest. On February 27, 1973, thousands of Native Americans representing over seventy-five Indian Nations, mostly from the Lakota Nation, led by the Oglala Sioux and organized by Thomas Wren, leader of American Indian Movement, AIM, joined forces to occupy Wounded Knee in an armed takeover representing a nationwide protest against three hundred seventy-one broken Government treaties, BIA corruption, and the tribal government's violent aggression against outspoken critics of its self-serving reservation policies.

For seventy-one days, this occupation, reported as "The Siege at Wounded Knee," was alive. When it ended on May 8, the Government, in their usual solution to an Indian uprising celebrated another victory of power by arresting almost twelve hundred protesters and killing two. The protesters' demands and investigation requests were given meaningless lip service with the establishment of special Government committees, but nothing of any value to the Native American

Nations resulted from the 1973 Wounded Knee takeover.

Ironically, Johnny thought, the US Government disconnected all electrical service to Wounded Knee during the occupation, something that would not be possible on the Crow reservation with this new building of self-generated electric power.

The Sitting Bull and both Wounded Knee incidents, because of their unjust, unprovoked, and racist nature, had personally troubled Johnny in ways he could never reconcile in his heart. The unnecessary deaths of hundreds of Native Americans, that should have never occurred, much like the deaths resulting from the skyscraper's bombing, always were part of Native American history.

— — —

The cold wind raced through Johnny's shortened braided hair, as he continued his ride in his topless Jeep. He did not feel the cold, as he guided the Jeep along the rutted road toward his destination. His speed continued to increase, his mind locked into a continuing historical catalog of information that was his birthright. His memories targeted many incidents similar to today's events.

This building was the reason he was here. He could now understand his purpose and his mother's words to him. He could finally find the power to nurture his people and help them raise up from the ashes of cultural genocide and create a new culture, a new life, and a new reason for living.

This building was their Messiah. The building was their answer to the "Ghost Dance." Their time had arrived to be born again. Jim Bradshaw was the prophet, leading them to the Promised Land, and Tony, thankfully alive and recovering, was the chosen one bringing forth the message from the Great Spirit.

This building would employ thousands of Native Americans and exhibit all the natural tendencies of a giant medicine tipi and tribal Crow village under one enormous structure of concrete, glass and steel. It was a building that would give his people more life fulfilling benefits than any ineffective BIA administered program.

This building would not allow itself to be stopped by racial prejudice, corrupt politicians, self-serving lobbyists of big business, or misguided Urban Indians. Somehow, there will be found a way to make the truth become known. Johnny's people, the Crow, and all the American Indian Nations knew the truth was something they valued beyond any lies the white man could manufacture. The truth was the only permitted path to the Great Spirit and everlasting life for all who choose to successfully travel it.

— — —

Reaching the building site, Johnny stopped his Jeep and symbolically applied war paint to his body and face. He prayed to the Great Spirit to assure Jim's plan would peacefully and effectively defeat his enemy.

The US Government and the BIA, puppets of the big oil, coal and utility companies were the evil forces to be conquered. There could be no victory, no satisfaction for the people, unless an unjust enemy, an enemy who threatened their existence, was defeated.

The Great Spirit's wisdom understood that Johnny's enemy represented the weak, for there is none so weak as those with power who use it to subjugate the powerless, pass judgment on the defenseless, and add fuel to their already dying existence.

On the eve of this country's 200th anniversary; the anniversary of America's original colonies' winning its freedom from England; and the beginning of an emerging democracy known as the United States which throughout its short history systematically and deliberately removed from Native Americans their freedom to live their lives as they were accustomed to living; history was reversing its path.

CHAPTER 32

THE AWAKENING

As Tony's eyes opened, they were forced to immediately shut from the sudden burst of sunlight that was thrust upon their unprepared pupils. After several blinks, they adjusted to their release from the darkness of unconsciousness and became aware of the reality that was offered to them. They began their natural process of focusing on everything in their vision path, while feeding the brain with the information necessary to understand the nature of their surroundings. The haze and confusion of Tony's newly awakened state, slowly started to evolve into the reality of his existence.

He found himself in a hospital bed. He noticed a cast on his left arm and leg. Intravenous tubes with needles were penetrating his body; it seemed from almost everywhere. An oxygen mask covered most of his face. There were monitoring devices of unknown functional purpose, directly over his head. They were all blinking, whirring and recording while sitting stoically on a stainless steel shelf. He could see them and hear their subtle tones clearly. He felt the desire to panic, but he could not. He had a drug influenced emotional barrier flowing through his body; forcing him to remain calm. The drugs inhibited his natural instincts to try to escape from this prison of pain. He did logically comprehend something for which he was eternally grateful. He was alive. He could see. He could hear. He could breathe.

He peeked under the covers to examine his body. He couldn't deduce much, other than he was in a blue hospital gown and his chest was wrapped in bandages. Then, he noticed an unusual situation. His penis, for some unknown reason was erect, and from its tip was a plastic tube carrying the familiar yellow fluid to a plastic bag. It was not a pleasant or comfortable observation.

...I'm pretty messed up...what the hell happened to me?...

Tony had no idea what his physical condition was, or how long he was lying in this bed. He knew he was in a hospital. He had no memory of how or why he had arrived here. He did remember an explosion and falling or flying, but he could not remember what was real or what was a dream. Reality and illusion blended in his confused mind, forming a new dimension of conscious meaning.

He noticed the walls of his hospital room were painted green. His reality had a color too. It was the color of another world, another dimension of time and space. He had indeed reached the Rod Serling world of the, *Twilight Zone*. He was just waiting for a cruel plot twist to thrust him into the Grand Canyon of time to be lost forever - never to remember - never to understand. Why did this happen to him? Did anything happen to Lisa or Johnny Thunder Eagle? Were they still alive? Were they even real? At this moment, he didn't know. He felt alone. He felt as if he was the only survivor in a sea of death. He needed answers or this *Twilight Zone* reality was going to drive him insane.

The sun continued to shine on his face. He drifted back to his safe world of dreams. After an hour of this serenity, he was again awakened from his deep sleep, only this time by a voice from a long distance away.

"Mr. Rullo. Anthony Rullo. Hello. Are you awake? Can you hear me? Anthony, can you hear me?"

Tony answered in a voice muffled by the imposition of his oxygen mask. "Yes...yes...stop shouting. Hurts my head. I can hear and see you fine. Who the hell are you?"

"I'm Doctor Foster. Doctor Larry Foster. Call me Doc or Larry, it doesn't make any difference to me. Welcome back Anthony. It is good to see you back with us today. Here - let me remove your oxygen mask. Don't think you need this anymore. If you experience any problems breathing, let me know and I'll put it back on."

Doctor Foster gently removed the mask, placing it on the end table next to the bed. He was your typical doctor in the traditional white coat – stethoscope hanging like a costume prop around his neck, a left breast pocket protector filled with a pencil, several pens, and a small flashlight. Thin latex gloves were hanging from one of his coat pockets. His hair was black - relatively long for a doctor, but it nicely framed his well-trimmed beard. He was average, incredibly average – in the middle of everything – height, age, weight, and skin tone. He looked concerned and professional, as he peered over his frameless glasses - glasses needed to reinforce his vision that had declined from the countless words, diagrams, pictures and research, he endured through years of medical school and internship . His voice was pleasant and reassuring. Tony liked his voice.

"There. How does that feel? Are you okay?" the doctor said.

"It's fine. I can breathe fine," Tony said.

"Good. Let me turn off the oxygen and we're good to go –"

"How long have I been here?"

"You've been here, semi-conscious, for about one week, Mr. Rullo. How are you feeling? Do have any pain or discomfort?"

"I can't feel much of anything, with all this shit running through my body. What the hell happened to me? Am I okay?"

"You're fine. You're healing nicely. You survived a fall induced from a building explosion. It was on the fifth floor of the reservation building. You were there. You either jumped or were thrown from the building. We don't know. You were lucky - very lucky that Mr. Thunder Eagle found you in time, otherwise, you probably would have bled to death. What do you remember? Is there anything that you can tell me?"

"I don't remember much. I remember the explosion. I remember being surrounded by an explosion. That's it. That's all I remember. Where was I when Johnny found me?"

"Mr. Thunder Eagle found you in a dumpster. He said the trash - *embraced your fall.* That's what he said."

"Johnny would say something like that. I owe him so much. Now, I owe him my life. He's a great friend. Hell, he's my best friend. So dumpster trash cushioned my fall and helped save my life, huh? I am lucky. What about Harry? What about anyone else? Was anyone else hurt besides me? What about the building? How is the building? Is it still standing? Tell me it's not destroyed. Don't tell me it's a pile of rubble, Doc. Don't tell me that."

"That's a lot of questions, Mr. Rullo. I'll try to answer them as best as I can. First of all…it was reported the building suffered heavy damage on the fifth floor - millions of dollars worth. As for the human element, most of the people occupying floor five during the explosion were injured, some were killed, but we don't need to discuss the details of that now.

What we do need to do is concentrate on helping you fully recover from your injuries. The prognosis for your full recovery is excellent. Your age and physical condition are definitely in your favor. You will require strict bed restriction for about two more weeks to allow your bruised back and pelvis to heal. You're injuries were numerous, but individually, none of them were life threatening. Anything else you need to know?"

"No. That's enough for now. I'm sure I'll have more questions as my head clears. My name's *Tony*. Call me *Tony. Mr. Rullo,* makes me feel like I'm fifty."

"Okay…good…Tony. Now I'm going to examine you, look at how your sutures are doing and take some vitals. Your chart looks very good. You're healing nicely… making excellent progress. If all goes according to plan, we hope to have you out of this hospital in less than three weeks…after that… you'll require a few months of rehab."

"It will have to be faster than that. I have a building to finish."

"We can't rush the healing process so don't worry about getting out of here sooner or working again on your building. Your building and body are on hold for a while. Besides, from what I understand, the building's construction has been temporarily halted by the Federal Government for National Security reasons. It's a big deal. It's been on the national news. The government is investigating the possibility of the bombing being part of an intricate terrorist conspiracy, but that's all talk for now. It's quite a theory. But don't worry about it. It will be there when you get well. You and that futuristic skyscraper both need time to heal before you can move forward again-"

"Excuse me, Doc. Did I understand you correctly? Thought I heard you say that my skyscraper project was being shut down. Is that true?"

A concerned look came over Doctor Foster's face, as he realized he had revealed more information about the skyscraper's condition than was appropriate to his patient's mental health and well being. He couldn't take it back, so he compromised his response.

"I'm sorry, Tony. I spoke prematurely. To be accurate, I really don't know if the project's construction is stopped. I just assumed it was."

"Well doc, let me make it plain and simple...shutting down this project is not an option. Only the owner – Mr. Mogul – and the Crow Nation have that authority. No one else – especially the Federal Government! It can't happen, even though I know there are people who want this project to die. Are you aware of that? I can't let that happen and from what I know of Mr. Mogul, he'll never let it happen." Suddenly, Tony remembered Neil's death. "You know a very close friend of mine, my boss, was killed because of this building - most likely murdered! It's difficult to understand why there are people in this world crazy enough to want to destroy this beautiful building and the dedicated people responsible for building it."

Tony's unexpected ranting, caused him to become lightheaded and dizzy. For a moment, he felt as if he would pass out. Doctor Foster, noticed Tony's sudden change in color and became concerned. He reached for the oxygen.

"Tony, are you okay? Please calm down. You can't allow yourself to become upset. You're in no condition to excite yourself this way. It's not helping you to worry about these things right now. There's nothing you can do about any of this from your hospital bed. So you need to relax and clear your mind of these distractions. You'll never get out of here in three weeks if you don't. Okay? I don't know anything more about this building. I didn't know it had so many enemies. I'm sorry. I shouldn't have upset you by saying anything."

"That's okay, Doc. It's just that it's all so new to me. It is upsetting me...I'll try to relax. It's not difficult with these drugs you have flowing through my body."

"Well...that's what they're for. Now, please allow me do my job and have a look at you."

Doctor Foster performed his routine check of Tony's damaged body. Other than the cast on Tony's left leg and arm, he was heavily bandaged from his chest down to his waist. The only way he could remove his bodily wastes was in bed, through a catheter or in a bed pan, with help - an embarrassment, that at times seemed more painful than his injuries. The doctor recorded the results of his examination, then discussed with Tony, in detail, the nature and extent of the injuries. Tony was relieved to know that he was expected to fully recover. Injuries to his body were a virgin experience. He had never been seriously injured in his short life, and was afraid. Doctor Foster was a great help in eliminating Tony's fears.

Most of these fears, however, were buried beneath his anger. He was angry about the bombing resulting in so many unnecessary deaths of hardworking innocent people. Moreover, he felt an uncontrollable rage towards those people who were responsible for these deaths. He wanted to rise out of his bed, from his imprisonment of plaster and gauze and stitches. He wanted to get even. He wanted justice. He wanted the truth to win over the forceful power of lies. It was this rage of energy that would give him the strength to rise above his injuries. Lying in bed, he mentally prepared himself for his three weeks of confinement. He would will his body to heal faster than nature would allow.

--- --- ---

Mr. Mogul's identity, the master builder behind the Crow Nation skyscraper, was eagerly revealed to the world as "James Jeffery Bradshaw" – the majority stock holder and CEO of

Bradshaw Enterprises International." During Tony's recovery, he too was formally introduced to this mystery man.

During his hospital visits, Jim Bradshaw described to Tony in great detail the story of his cancer, his recovery, his visions, and the Great Spirit's role in the skyscraper's conception and purpose. Tony now understood why he was chosen and how his unique talents destined him to be part of this purpose. Jim's revelations obsessed Tony to such an extent that he abandoned his desire to seek revenge with those who attempted to destroy the skyscraper and replaced it with the overwhelming desire to rebuild it. With the final piece of the puzzle revealed, Jim, Johnny, and Tony bonded into a brotherhood that was always meant to be part of their future.

But it was not supposed to happen this way. This wasn't the plan. Jim Bradshaw's identity was to be revealed following the triumphant completion of the skyscraper at a party honoring all those involved in its creation, most notably, Neil Hagman. Deaths, bombings or conspiracies were not part of this plan. The skyscraper represented the portal to a hopeful future. That was the way it was meant to be. According to Jim, these turbulent events were inevitable. He knew what was to happen, but he was hoping that what he knew was just one possibility from a selection of hundreds, just a distorted cloaked message from the Great Spirit. It wasn't.

CHAPTER 33

THE WAR

In the cold winter months, late in 1875, the previous year's discovery of gold in South Dakota's Black Hills, set off a chain of events that would know no equal in adversely affecting the history and lives of the Native Americans indigenous to America's Northern Plains.

The relentless and unrestricted assault of opportunistic gold miners into the Black Hills, would inevitably lead to hostile confrontations between them and the Native Americans settled there. The US Government did little to keep the miners from trespassing on these sanctioned tribal lands, where by treaty, were given to the Sioux Nation, "for as long as the grass grows and the rivers flow." Instead, they focused on protecting the selfish interests of the gold miners and the profit seeking white settlers, railroad barons, and support industries, that followed them into the Black Hills to reap the potentially enor-

mous financial benefits spawned from mining the "white man's yellow rocks."

In their disguised attempt to avoid an escalation of a bloody war between the two factions, the Grant Administration initiated a series of heavy-handed "compensation, protection and enforcement" manipulation tactics in dealing with the Lakota Tribes living and hunting on this gold rich land. One aspect of these tactics carried President Grant's offer to purchase the Black Hills territory from the Lakota in an effort to entice them to immediately leave and peacefully return to their government assigned reservations.

The Lakota refused Grant's offer and would not sell their land and relocate in order to appease the interests of the "gold rush" insanity. Why should they? It was their land by treaty. Their people were happy and comfortably settled in for the winter. They were peaceful until the gold miners invaded their land. The Black Hills were their ancestral tribal lands that could never be purchased or sold. On these lands the Lakota were in harmony with the Great Spirit, which meant the hunting would always be good and the food plentiful. The Black Hills were their sacred land, their 'axis mundi', and the place where the friendly spirits dwelled. It was their heart. It held their soul

Their answer to the bureaucrats from Washington, was simple and direct, they would not sell their land but would allow all those who wanted, to temporarily return to their reservations, but not before the spring thaw, when food would be available and travel easy. If anyone should leave, they replied, it should be the whites, not them. President Grant immediately deemed this response not acceptable. It was interpreted as open defiance against the United States Government's offer and suggested a potentially confrontational outcome

This defiance, the Government concluded, would inevitably lead to war. To avoid this war, Congress drafted hastily prepared legislation, signed into law by President Grant. This legislation ordered the Lakota tribes to relocate, by January 31, 1876, from their lucrative sacred hunting camps, to their food-starved reservations. Failure to obey this order would result in enforcement by the United States Army. The Lakota would not yield to this threat. They would not comply with this unrealistically and unfairly imposed order that was in direct violation of the "1851- Fort Laramie Treaty".

As a result, the Government's War Department was ordered to recognize these defiant Black Hills' Indian camps as hostile, and to use any means necessary to force them back to their reservations. The War Department would carry out this decision by using the full strength of the United States 7th Cavalry, led by General Phillip Sheridan. These misguided impudent actions to 'pro-

tect' both the Indians and gold miners from adversarial confrontations, would eventually lead to the "Battle of Little Big Horn," the greatest recorded US Army defeat by an opposing Native American force in United States' history.

Responding to their direct orders to immediately return all "hostiles" to their reservations, a frustrated and bored advance column of the 7th Cavalry, looking for any excuse to justify their existence and purpose on the Great Plains, attacked what they had assumed was the village of the rebellious Crazy Horse, an Ogala Sioux Chief, and respected leader of the Ogala Nation. Led by Colonel Joseph Reynolds, the 7th decided to prove their worth or worthlessness on March 17, 1876, by attacking without warning or reason, this peaceful encampment of Cheyenne and Sioux men, women and children. The Colonel decided the village was an easy target, an easy "victory", and an easy reward for his troops. The Colonel was mistaken.

Feeling secure and taking no precautions to guard against this unjustified attack, the village was surprised and defenseless when the dust of the approaching horse soldiers rose from the ridges east of the Little Bighorn River

Bravely and with fierce determination, the fleeing Cheyenne and Sioux managed to reach safety in the hills, saving their women and children and escaping heavy casualties.

THE WAR

The Ogala men then regrouped, out-flanked and counterattacked Reynolds' forces, forcing the army to retreat. The battle was won, but not without adverse consequences. The village was lost, burned to the ground by the soldiers. To further enhance their hollow victory the soldiers captured all the village's horses, leaving the post-battle village survivors to reach their next place of refuge on foot. Reynolds' unprovoked attack eventually paved the road to furious retaliation three months later by a dedicated army of thousands of Sioux, Cheyenne, and Arapaho warriors, united for the common purpose of defending their land, their freedom and their culture against the endlessly advancing self-righteous and arrogant army of white intruders.

After a few months of relentless, but futile confrontations, the end to it all would begin on June 17, at Montana's Rosebud River, when thousands of these warriors, led by Crazy Horse, stopped the onslaught of thirteen hundred troops commanded by General George Crook and forced their withdrawal to a base camp in the south. General Crook's army was accompanied and supported by over three hundred Crow and Shoshone scouts and warriors.

From the Rosebud, Crazy Horse's forces crossed to the valley of the Little Bighorn River, known to the Indians as the "Greasy Grass" and joined their village. Crazy Horse, would rest and decide what his next action would be against the onslaught of this determined white man's army

What soon followed, was the most infamous battle in the history of the Plains Indian wars, one that would come to represent the marquee event of anything remotely resembling Native American history as taught in America's schools. It took place near a three-mile long Native American village of ten thousand Lakota, Yanktonais, Santees, Northern Arapahos, and Northern Cheyennes, encamped along the Little Bighorn River in Montana. This village was located within the boundaries, on what would become the present day Crow Reservation.

On this fateful day, June 25, 1876, the aforementioned Native American army, went into battle. This army of warriors was determined, strong and large. Their opponent was overconfident, weak, and few. The battle was decisive and brief. In less than an hour, this Native American army killed every one of the over two hundred solders comprising General George Armstrong Custer's, 7th US Cavalry regiment.

The eastern newspapers of the day, sensationalized this battle on the eve of America's Centennial, as "Custer's Last Stand." Some described it as an unprovoked disgraceful "massacre", by Godless Indian savages. This biased reporting provided the fuel for inciting revenge from an outraged public, who demanded immediate retribution. As a result, in the months that followed, on direct orders from the "Great White Father" in Washington, thousands of Native Americans who resided on the wide-open plains of the Dakotas and Montana, were systematically hunted down by the 7ʰCavalry, killed at the slightest hint of resistance in their non-reservation villages, or taken prisoner, and forcefully returned to their assigned reservations or prison camps, all in retaliation for their actions against General Custer, the American people, and the United States of America. The reign of freedom for the Native Americans living on the Northern Plains was over

— — —

Nearly one hundred years later, this history of events was repeating itself, only with a different outcome.

On February 25, 1975, on a two-hundred acre building site near the Little Bighorn River within the Crow Reservation in Montana, not far from where Johnny Thunder Eagle was born, another soon to be well-known and documented confrontation would take place between an assortment of protesters from every race and nationality the United States had to offer, and the soldiers of the United States' National Guard.

Nearly two hundred solders of the Guard, led by Colonel George Armstrong Custer III, after almost three months of mindlessly guarding an idle site and a damaged building against the passive assault of sympathetic peaceful protesters, were forced to stand down on this day and leave the reservation in less than an hour. The thousands of Crow, Lakota, Cheyenne, and Arapaho Native Americans and their multi-racial supporters, were united on this day for the common purpose of defending their future, their freedom, their culture, and their building against the endlessly advancing arrogant United States Government. This time, the Crow were not fighting against their Native American brothers. They were leading the fight, standing by their side.

The Nation's newspapers humorously described this confrontation on the eve of America's Bi-Centennial, as "Custer's Last Stand" - a well planned peaceful surprise attack on the government, a "ground breaking innovation" by Native Americans. This positive reporting provided the fuel for the insatiable consumption of sympathetic Americans. A suddenly aware public now wanted swift and just retribution against the BIA for their attacks against the Crow Nation and this scared building. As a result, in the months that followed, thousands of Native Americans from across the United States would willfully volunteer their time and services in completion of this building. There was no interference and little mention of the incident from the "Great White Father" in Washington.

— — —

Unlike the events of June 25, 1876, the beginning of this fateful day began at the site, as it had for the past three months, with the National Guard guarding the building without incident or stated purpose, while being encircled by thousands of protestors, most of them Native Americans. During this time, sympathetic Native American brothers and sisters, traveled from reservations located in close proximately to the site, such as the Sioux from South Dakota, and the Northern Cheyenne and Black Feet from Montana, to gather in peaceful protest while defying the government imposed roadblocks that attempted to restrict their access to the site. In addition, hundreds more were infiltrating, arriving every day, from states as far away as California, New York and Florida.

They traveled by airplane, train, motor home, truck, car, jeep and horse. Some adventurous travelers even arrived on foot. An encampment of Indians by the thousands bordered the Rosebud and Little Bighorn Rivers. The BIA, Department of the Interior and Congress were unsure on how to handle the situation. This was greater than any protest they could ever have imagined or prepared for. The Indians were equipped with film and video tape cameras. Everyday events were being recorded and sent to any accepting news media in the United States and the world. They were fighting their enemy with its own technology, without guns, without physical violence. Only the power of truth would be needed to conquer the hypocrisy of the force that tried to suppress and subdue it.

— — —

For almost three months through Christmas and the New Year, the protest was passive and non productive. It had become old news, stale, almost a non-event. The media had lost interest in it, as it did during the 1973, siege at Wounded Knee. It was a stalemate, with neither side giving in to the other. The BIA was content to continue along this path, since as long as the skyscraper's construction was stopped, the intention of their disruptive plan was being served.

Today, however, all that would end. The protestors were prepared to offer something special to the world today, thanks to the efforts of the dedicated people successfully carrying out Jim Bradshaw's well conceived plan. It had been purposely leaked to the BIA that today there would be an organized demonstration by the protestors, possibly resulting in a violent confrontation. Tensions were running high within the ranks of the National Guard. They were told to expect anything from the protestors and if provoked, were prepared to fire their weapons.

The National Guard stood at the ready, their bayonets fixed and did nothing, mesmerized by this invisible force that was empowering them to stand down. They were hopelessly outnumbered, overwhelmed and were eventually forced to succumb to the peaceful power of the protesters. They had prepared for a battle that was not to be. Instead, their attention was concentrated on the faces of the crowd surrounding them. The faces with their many eyes directed the National Guard solders to look east, and witness from that direction what was about to happen next.

When the Guard's attention was fully focused, the planned event started to unfold. On cue, the thousands of protesters started to part, opening a long wide eastern path stretching to the horizon. The path, bordered by the broad shoulders of proud determined people, was created to allow a special team of men and women to ride on horseback, two by two, toward the National Guard's defensive formation. A thunderous sound was heard, as dozens of mounted horses were seen coming out of their self-inflicted dust cloud. Leading this new age Cavalry, determined and regal on his mount, was Johnny Thunder Eagle, flying the United Nations' flag of peace. At his right hand side was Stoney Creek Smith, holding another flag, the flag of the new Crow Nation.

Johnny rode toward Colonel Custer, with United Nations, and Tribal Council representatives behind his lead. He stopped in front of the Colonel, and while mounted on Swiftwind, read the international United Nations' proclamation that empowered the Crow Reservation as an independent sovereign nation, an impoverished third world nation, whose economic security was being unjustifiably compromised, threatened, and controlled by a nation of much greater power, economic wealth and military force - the United States.

Furthermore, the United States was being put on notice by the UN for the possibility of being charged with the systematic genocide of the American Indian, as defined in the United Nations' General Assembly resolution in 1946.

For the record and for the benefit of the news media present at the site, his people and the protesting crowd, Johnny read the UN's definition of genocide to the Colonel.

> *"...Genocide is the denial of existence to entire human groups, as homicide is the denial of the right to live of individual human beings; such denial of the right of existence shocks the conscience of humankind, results in great losses to humanity in the form of cultural and other contributions represented by these groups, and is contrary to moral law and*

> *to the spirit and aims of the United Nations. Many instances of such crimes of genocide are a matter of international concern. The General Assembly, therefore affirms, that genocide is a crime under international law, which the civilized world condemns, and for the commission of which principals and accomplices - whether private individuals, public officials or statesman, and whether the crime is committed on religious, racial, political or any other grounds - are punishable...*

"In addition," Johnny said, "the United States has clearly violated the rules and definitions relating to overt acts of genocide committed on all Native Americans, relating specifically today to the Crow Nation, according to 'Article 2,' as adopted during the 1948, Genocide Convention of the United Nations. These definitions in part stated:

> *...genocide means any of the following acts committed with intent to destroy, in whole or part, a national, ethnical, racial, or religious groups, such as: killing members of the group; causing serious bodily or mental harm to members of the group; deliberately inflicting on the group conditions of life calculated to bring about its physical destruction in whole or in part; imposing measures intended to prevent births within the group; and forcibly transferring children of the group to another group..."*

After Johnny was finished reading the UN resolution, he dismounted, approached the Colonel, and handed him copies of the official UN documents that legally recognized as of this date, and under international law, the existence of the independent Crow Nation.

"Colonel," Johnny said. "You are hereby ordered, under international law, as defined by the United Nations, to peacefully leave this building site and the borders of the Crow Nation immediately. Failure to obey this request will result in you being forcefully removed from the area in question by United Nations' forces. The Crow Nation respectfully asks that any confrontation be avoided at all costs, and you and your group of soldiers leave now without further incident. You shall leave our land, our Nation, and do not return, unless you are requested to do so by our Nation. President Ford is being notified as we speak. We require your decision now, Colonel."

The Colonel accepted the documents, remained silent as he looked them over with a pained and quizzical expression clearly etched into his face. The Colonel knew he soon would be receiving direct orders instructing him on how to deal with this matter. He decided not to wait. He was not about to become a convenient scapegoat for the Government bureaucrats and become a historical footnote, following in the footsteps of his great-grandfather. This matter could potentially become an embarrassing international incident. He did not want to be part of it. He did not want to be here. Three months away from his family and home was enough. He was tired of all this confrontational bullshit with Native Americans. It needed to end now and he was the person to make it happen. He would most likely face a Court Martial, but he was going to make his own decision despite that possibility. It was in the hands of the President and Congress now.

He read again the official United Nations proclamation handed to him by Johnny. He shook his head in approval. He addressed his troops and ordered them to assemble in their transports and leave the building site and the reservation in an orderly controlled fashion, avoiding a potential confrontation. The National Guard quietly and quickly left. The Crow Nation had won this battle.

— — —

Just hours before the Colonel was given this history making proclamation, the majority of votes required from the United Nations assembly, amid overwhelming protests from the United States and its "financially aided" allies, were cast in favor of recognizing the Crow Nation as an independent country. The United States would vehemently appeal this ridiculous anti-American decision.

The final step in Jim's plan had worked. BEI's appointed team was successful in convincing the United Nation's preliminary review board to tentatively approve the Crow Reservation petition for recognition as an independent Nation and for protection against an invading foreign government, such as the United States. This Government, that prided itself on the freedom and human rights for all of its citizens, was now being forced to honor what it had failed to honor for Native Americans for hundreds of years.

It was an original and effective plan, and for some unexplained reason, against all odds, it worked. The United States' government had always controlled the indigenous Indian Nations using the most obvious insidious hypocritical scam in history, promising them freedom from government interference, and the right to govern themselves independently using numerous "restructured" treaties, then violating these treaties, when it was in the United States' interest, culturally, economically or politically, to do so. The vested interests of railroads, oil, coal, lumber, and mining, were all more important to the United States, than the lives, welfare, culture, and freedoms of Native Americans.

The United States Government for the first time in Native American history could not conquer this nation without incurring the consequences from the protecting countries of the world. It was now time for the United States to atone for its sinful atrocities of the past against the original citizens of North America; time to accept the fact that this Christian based country had violated the very tenets of Christianity in its systematic and deceptive elimination of the rightful non-Christian owners of this country.

How long would this new Nation exist without crumbling to the adversity offered from the United States Government? No one could be sure, but it did not matter. For now, this newly established United Nations country, simply known as, "The Crow Nation," would be allowed the opportunity to evolve into an independent Nation, free to succeed or fail on its own ability to govern and sustain itself, while attempting to conquer its many United States' imposed obstacles.

CHAPTER 34

THE REHABILITATION

MARCH 1975

It was typical morning for Tony at the cabin, only it was Monday – the beginning of a new hopeful week. He had just finished an invigorating two-mile run and was sitting down to a healthy post-hospital breakfast of orange juice, herbal tea, scrambled eggs, and a bowl of shredded wheat with sliced banana, soymilk and honey.

It was twelve-weeks since the accident. Tony's healing bordered on miraculous, well ahead of schedule, and his rehabilitation was almost complete, thanks to Johnny and Stoney. They had helped his recovery with every natural remedy at their disposal. In fact, Tony believed, they had invented some new ones just for him. They took him on spiritual journeys within himself, willing his mind to naturally heal his body. It all worked. He was walking without a cane or a limp. His left arm was without pain and at full strength and flexibility. His back and pelvis felt fine. His body had responded. He was in the greatest shape of his life from spiritual meditation, a healthier diet, miles of running and rigorous workouts. He looked good and felt great. His body was healthy. His mind was refreshed. His spirit was strong. It was time for him to get back to work.

He had understood in the days before the explosion that he needed to maintain a healthier lifestyle. Now, with his body's mandate to heal itself in the most efficient beneficial way, he was forced to take the necessary steps. In addition to a regular exercise routine, he had given up coffee as his everyday morning drink of choice, and substituted herbal teas. He began taking daily doses of natural vitamins and supplements. He greatly reduced his consumption of alcoholic beverages. Most importantly, his health was enhanced and stimulated by the beginning of a delicate and discrete relationship with Lisa. She had been by his side throughout his ordeal, from recovery through rehabilitation. She was why he recovered as quickly and completely as he did. He could not have been this successful or felt so determined to heal his body and renew his spirit without her.

If all that was not enough, the history making emergence of the Crow Nation as an independent country, and the subsequent rebirth of the skyscraper further accelerated Tony's capacity to heal. The excitement of working on the building again - in an emerging Nation - had Tony sprinting through his days with anticipation. Life was good. He was happy. He felt free. It was about time.

During his weeks of rehabilitation, Tony and Lisa would take long walks in the forested areas that surrounded the cabin. They would talk only when they felt the need, but more often than not, they would just walk silently, holding hands, enjoying their private intimate moments together. Their walks among the simple intoxicating sounds of nature helped Tony to enhance his life's energy and follow the voice in his heart.

No matter where he was in the forest, Tony always felt he was being watched by the bear - the same bear that made its way into his yard and stared at him through the bathroom window. He never saw the bear after that day, but he knew it was around, watching him, hidden among the trees. Johnny told Tony he believed this was a special bear sent from the Great Spirit, waiting to give Tony its special message.

While shoveling large spoonfuls of shredded wheat into his mouth, Tony thought about his return to the project. In two days, he would travel to New York City. Jim Bradshaw, had scheduled a major project meeting to outline the critical steps needed to assure the building's successful rebirth. Lisa would be there. Johnny Thunder Eagle would not. Tony's thoughts were detoured by the ringing of the telephone. Tony removed his face from his bowl of cereal and answered. It was Lisa.

CHAPTER 35

THE OFFER

In the months following Neil's death, Lisa traveled often between her residences in Baltimore and Billings. The constant motion of traveling kept her occupied and distracted from feeling the pain. During her Baltimore visits, she occasionally traveled to Philadelphia, to be with her family, but mostly, she remained alone, embraced in her Baltimore apartment, emotionally isolated from the events that led to Neil's death and almost took Tony's life.

When in Billings, she dedicated herself and concentrated her energy working on the skyscraper in Neil's memory and in being with Tony, helping him heal. After the tragedies, they needed each other. Even though they both knew the love they felt for one another was real, they never mentioned it, or discussed the possibly of it ever evolving into something more than it was. For now, they were content to maintain a close and well-guarded friendship. Only the unknown future knew whether they would ever be allowed to reciprocate their feelings in an open loving relationship.

Because of the circumstances involving Neil's death, Lisa could not allow herself to nurture an emotional relationship with Tony, but now, after five months of mourning, she was beginning to feel more comfortable with the idea

— — —

On this Monday morning, Lisa was in Billings, thinking about all the circumstances that defined her life. Sitting in her apartment, she realized her memories of Neil were having less of an impact on her ability to move forward. She was feeling released from their grief induced bondage. It was time to allow Tony to become a more permanent part of her life. She decided her mourning period was over. *It was okay now*, she thought. *It was okay.* She adored Tony as a person. She loved their walks in the woods. She loved being around him. He was sensitive, warm, and loving. He always treated her with respect and affection. She knew that he loved her and would do anything for her. More importantly, she felt the same about him. What more could she ask?

It was an awkward moment for her. She was not sure how to do this. Reacting to these feelings, she put together a possible plan, one that would help ease Tony into her life. She made the necessary phone calls. She knew she needed to make all the arrangements herself, because her decision to follow through would have to be on her own terms, in the most cautious deliberate way possible. Tony had to agree to this, or it could not work. She was eager to let him know as soon as possible. Lisa picked up the receiver three times before she could finally dial his number. She started to make the call she was keeping herself from making all these months after Neil's death. Nervously dialing the number, she awaited the answer.

"Hello," Tony said.

"Hi, Tony. It's Lisa. Is this a good time?"

"Lisa? Hi. Anytime's a good time to talk to you. How are you?"

Tony was always happy to hear from her. He had adjusted to the idea of Lisa and him being just friends, best friends with an emotional history, best friends who happened to be in love.

"I'm fine...and you?" Lisa evasively replied, postponing the eventual reason for her call.

"I'm hanging in there. Just finished a run. Body's feeling good. Thanks to you and your help. What's up?"

"I've decided it's time to see you now."

Tony smiled. He always had time to see Lisa. "That's no problem. I'm here. I'm not going anywhere. You know the way and you certainly don't need an invitation. Do you want me to make something for breakfast? I think I have some edible food here somewhere. Do you like shredded wheat or eggs? I have some eggs. I could make you a cheese omelet."

Lisa's response was abrupt, ignoring Tony's feeble attempt at humor. "No Tony, I mean I want to *see* you. I want us to start seeing each other. I want us to start something real. I have been thinking about it a lot lately and I think it's time. I realize this decision is sudden, out of nowhere...and we haven't mutually discussed it, but what is there to discuss anyway? We know this is what we both want. I want to be with you as soon as possible. Understand? However, I don't want us to begin here – not here, not in Billings. It has to be away from here. Is that okay?"

Tony had to sit down from the impact of Lisa's words. He answered her weakly trying to control his sudden apprehension. He was shaking.

"I'm sorry. What was that? Could you run that by me again? I don't think I heard you correctly. You want us to begin an open relationship? You sure about what you're proposing here, Lisa?"

"Yes. Very. Well, what do you think Tony? Is this something that you want?"

"Are you serious? *What do I think*? I think you already know my answer to that question. My question to you is - *what do you want*? This is a big step for you – for us - huge. I just want you to be absolutely certain about what you're proposing. We've been down this road before and, I recall, it was a pretty bumpy ride. I don't want either of us to make a mistake and get hurt doing this. I never expected this coming from you now. To be honest with you, it frightens me –"

"You're surprised...?"

"Oh...just a little...never thought it would be you initiating this proposal."

"Surprise again...I did it! It was little ol' me."

"Yeah, I know. Listen Lisa, do me a really big favor here - be sure. Just be sure. Okay? That's all I ask. You know how I feel about this."

"I'm sure. Believe me. I'm sure. I want this to happen more than anything."

"Okay. All right. I believe you. Now reassure me. Let me know what you're thinking, what you're planning – the whole thing. Start with the 'when' and 'where' – especially the 'when'."

Lisa laughed. "Oh Tony, I'm so sorry," she said. "Are you okay? You sound a little shaken up. I'm sorry I had to do it like this. It wasn't very smooth or subtle - was it? But what the hell, when it's time, it's time. You know me. I say what's on my mind - no pretense. Sometimes, it's not the best way to do it. I know we both want this. You've been very patient - waiting for me to make a decision as to 'if'. Well, this is the 'if' and here's my 'when' and 'where'. There aren't many details. It's pretty simple. My plan is this - we get together in Baltimore, where we first met. I want to see you in Baltimore the day after tomorrow on our way to New York City before Jim's big meeting. I have some things to pick up in our Baltimore office before I head off to New York. We'll have almost a full day and night together. It will be a good beginning. Does that sound okay? Can you rearrange your schedule?"

"Are you kidding? Of course it's okay. Seeing you anywhere, anytime, is a good plan for me. You have no idea how much this means to me. I have a question and I don't mean to sound impatient, but I am a little confused. Why Baltimore, and not here? Why the distance? Why wait?"

"Calm down buddy. Calm down. You know this is a difficult decision for me. There's a lot of emotional baggage for me to sort through and the circumstances we have to overcome are not the most favorable. Tony, if I'm ready to take our relationship to the next level, I just feel more comfortable doing it this way. I want to spend the night with you. I want to make love. I just can't do it here in Billings. There are too many awful memories here. I need us to start fresh, someplace without the negative memories, without the guilt."

"Sorry Lisa. It's okay. I understand. It's a great plan. It works for me. I should've realized your reasons without asking. It should've been obvious. I just got caught up in the excitement of the moment. Let me take a breath and think this through..." Tony paused and became more assertive in his next response. "...Do you want me to make the arrangements in Baltimore? Hotel? Car? Anything? My flight is booked. I have a direct flight to New York. I'll need to reschedule an overnight stop in Baltimore. Other than that, everything else should be okay."

"No. You don't have to do anything. I've made all the arrangements. I needed to take control, or I would have talked myself out of it. That wouldn't have been fair to either of us. That's why I have already reserved a room for us at the *BWI*

Prestige Inn, in my name. I also have a rental car waiting for you at the airport. I have an early flight from Billings, the day before the meeting, so I'll be there, impatiently waiting, when you arrive."

"Okay, Lisa…you're quite the organizer. You've got everything under control. All I have to do is show up. I feel like a child waiting for Santa to bring me my special toy."

"It's my pleasure, Tony. I'm happy to be your special gift from Santa. Now…all you need to do is get plenty of rest. You're gonna need it," Lisa playfully said.

— — —

Tony and Lisa continued to talk for hours, getting into the details of their intertwined fate driven lives, the magical skyscraper and their future potential as a couple. Never once, did they discuss the details of Neil's death or the bombing. Never once, did they discuss their love for each other. They knew better not to destroy the naïve magic of the moment. After saying "good night," they both began to feel the apprehension beginning to build. The "I love yous" were cautiously withheld from either side, awaiting their formal presentation at just the right moment, when all the waiting and hoping would at last be memories of what was to be. They would remain apart and alone, until they could at last share their intimate moments together in Baltimore.

Lisa knew she made the right decision. She loved Tony and it was time for her to put the death of Neil behind her and start this new chapter in her life.

CHAPTER 36

THE DREAM

The night before her early morning flight to Baltimore, with everything meticulously in order for the trip, Lisa thankfully prepared herself for a good night's sleep. Impatiently waiting for the past two days to enter this moment, the moment that would lead to her defining relationship with Tony - drained her of all energy. She was exhausted. She fell asleep as soon as she closed her eyes and her head was resting comfortably on her down pillow. As her consciousness entered into a deep sleep, what followed was a dream that would alter forever all her well-intentioned plans.

Her dream began to filter its disturbing message into the recesses of her subconscious mind.

> *Lisa found herself standing naked and alone at the building site facing the skyscraper's glorious main entrance. It was a cool misty morning. The sun was shining - glistening the mist on Lisa's naked body and washing her with its warm golden rays. The entire skyscraper was glowing, embraced by a halo of sunlight.*
>
> *Her attention was diverted by a muffled roaring sound. She turned toward the sound and saw*

its source. Coming toward her she witnessed an emerging force of nature. Strong prairie winds were developing and blowing from the north. It was the beginning of a powerful wind storm - churning, blowing, and carrying anything in its embrace that was not secured to Mother Earth. It was increasing its intensity until it would become not like any natural wind at all. It would become a pure energy cloud on which one could travel through time and imagination, and it was coming for Lisa. She would not be allowed any chance to avoid its purpose as she was about to be swept up by its uncompromising power and carried away as its only passenger. She accepted her destiny, closed her eyes, and stood perfectly still, frozen to the ground. She waited. She began to feel the wind against her body. Her hair was blown straight back in a horizontal stream as if trying desperately to escape from what was to come next. She held up her arms letting the wind's passion consume her.

"I am ready," she said. "Take me."

Lisa's wish was granted, as the mass of kinetic energy spiraling toward her, reached her, engulfed her in its path, lifting her lightly beyond her own senses. She felt herself being carried into an endless sky, spinning and spinning, as if on a giant merry-go-round. The feeling was exhilarating and overwhelming. She began to laugh uncontrollably, feeling like a reticent spoiled child, a child that never wanted this ride to end. She spread her arms as if they were wings, and started to fly. She was carried forward in ecstasy and could see in the distance, toward an infinite boundary, a bright light. She continued her journey towards it. She saw an unclear shape far into the light. As she got closer to the light, its image became clearer. She knew when she reached the light she would see what it was and her journey would end, but she wanted it not to end, not to end. Then as suddenly as that thought entered her mind - it ended. Her ride ended. She fell gently to the ground.

She looked up from her defining moment and at this ride's end, at the light's beginning, she saw the image clearly. It was Neil calling her to come into the light, beyond her ended journey to a new place of being. She saw the place. It was beautiful. It was without equal on Earth and beyond her limited imagination. Lisa smiled. She eagerly began the short walk toward Neil. He gestured again for her to come to him. She walked faster and faster until she was running. Faster and faster she ran, straining with every stride but finding her efforts not rewarded. She realized that Neil was not coming closer to her, but moving further away. She soon discovered why.

She looked down and realized the earth was opening beneath her creating an ever expanding black hole. She was trapped and being unmercifully sucked into this infinite abyss. She watched helplessly, as Neil's image continued to get further and further away, smaller and smaller, until she could see him no more. She continued to fall deeper and deeper into the void. It was dark and cold and lifeless. She screamed but she made no sound. She knew death was waiting for her at the end of her fall.

Just before impact and the inevitable end, Lisa thankfully woke from her dream. She lifted her shaking, sweat-soaked, body from her bed and walked to the kitchen to get a cold drink of water. Looking at her ghostly reflection in the kitchen's window, she knew what was expected of her. Her future was dependent on her ability to endure the emotional pain that would be felt from the consequences of her actions. She needed to free her mind, her body and her soul forever. Only then, would she be allowed to travel to that special place that was waiting for her somewhere in time. Only then, could she be free, free to be loved unconditionally. The dream had told her what to do. This was the only way she could do it. She gathered her special paper, pen and gold ink; sat down at her desk, and began to write a letter.

CHAPTER 37

THE CURSE

The flight to Baltimore was turbulent, but mildly uneventful. There was however, one potentially troublesome problem. It was over one hour behind schedule. Tony looked at his watch. It was 1:35 PM. The scheduled arrival time was 12:15. Because of the delay, Tony was worried about Lisa. She was waiting at the hotel. She had taken an earlier flight. He imagined her becoming anxious, waiting for his arrival, not knowing where he was or if he was okay. His apprehension prompted a need to call her as soon as he departed the aircraft.

He felt the plane descend rapidly on its approach to its assigned runway at the *Baltimore-Washington International Airport, BWI*. A defining bump was felt as its wheels touched the runway. The roar of the reversing engines emphasized it had safely landed and was taxiing the runway to a complete stop adjacent to its designated terminal. Tony quickly released his seatbelt and began his exit from his window seat at the rear of the aircraft. As he rose from his seat he noticed an impenetrable wall of passengers with their carry-on luggage stacked in an endless single file between him and the only way out. The tedious exiting process had begun. The passengers appeared to be departing in slow motion. The stewardesses were saying goodbye to each passenger and the handshakes and pleasantries seemed to take forever. Tony felt purposely trapped, convinced passengers and crew were involved in a conspiracy to delay him from his intended goal.

Finally reaching the exit, after what seemed like an eternity, he used his less than desirable New Jersey etiquette on these unprepared Maryland travelers, to rudely push through the crowd, parting them like Moses parting the Red Sea. Patience was not one of his strongest virtues.

As he broke free from the crowd, he began running through the concourse searching for the nearest public telephone. He needed to call Lisa as soon as possible to let her know of his situation. She would understand the reasons for his unfortunate late arrival. It was typical. Lisa was the one who was always on time. Tony was the one always late. Besides, since Lisa had arranged to take an earlier flight from Billings via Minneapolis-St. Paul and his flight went through Chicago, he was expected to arrive later. *O'Hare International* was always so unpredictable. He knew she would use her early arrival time to get comfortable, rearrange the hotel room furniture, and have a great room service dinner waiting for them. Being with her again was all he could think about.

He searched through the *Yellow Pages* for the *BWI Prestige Inn* telephone number. A dime was deposited and he dialed the hotel. After several rings, the hotel clerk answered in an obligatory friendly tone, introducing himself as Brian. Tony made his inquiries. The answers he received on the other end were not what he expected. There wasn't any record of a, "Lisa Hagman," checking in and there were no messages from her for Tony at the front desk, but he was told there was an item delivered to the room, a room that had been prepaid by Lisa, using her *BEI* credit card. This was not part of the plan.

"Do you still wish to keep your reservation for this room, Mr. Rullo?" the clerk asked.

Tony hesitated for a few moments and a meekly toned, "Yes," was all he could gather the energy to say.

"That will be fine. When can we expect you to arrive?"

"I'll be there in less than an hour."

"Thank You, Mr. Rullo. Your room will be ready for you when you arrive. Thank you again for choosing the *BWI Prestige Inn*."

"You're welcome. By the way, do you have any idea what was delivered to my room?"

"I'm sorry, I really don't know. That item was delivered before my shift. Is there anything else I can help you with at this time?"

"No. Thanks. Thanks for your help. Good bye."

"Good bye, Mr. Rullo."

Tony hung up the phone forcefully in anger. Waves of anxiety and doubt were making their presence felt. It was happening to him again.

He tried to remain calm and centered. Nevertheless, he walked in a daze through the airport to the baggage claim area. His suitcase made two passes on the luggage carousel, before he had the presence of mind to pick it up. The rental car was quietly procured with hardly a word spoken between him and the rental agent.

— — —

As Tony began the drive to the hotel located less than ten miles from the airport, he desperately needed an emotional distraction. His fingers fumbled with the keys on the radio trying to find a station that would keep him from thinking of the inevitable. He found an AM talk radio station. Its participants were discussing the political climate of the new Gerald Ford

Administration. This was as unemotional and distracting as it could get.

He needed that, since uncontrollable emotional reactions consumed Tony at the most inopportune moments. Only now, he couldn't allow any irrational feelings to disrupt his confidence in Lisa. His history of emotional traumas, surrounding a seemingly endless series of failed relationships, was a consistent theme in his young life, but finally, he thought, this history was now irrelevant. In this emerging relationship with Lisa, it was a certainty for success. With Lisa, it would work. Because of this undeniable confidence Tony knew there would be a logical explanation for her not being at the hotel.

The radio talk show host changed subjects and was now discussing the previous year's Watergate hearings, the impeachment action against Nixon, and his subsequent resignation. Somehow, Tony thought, at this moment, Nixon was better off than he was.

― ― ―

In the past, Tony would casually share details of his previous relationships with family and friends. His endless stories with the unhappy endings were told to anyone who would listen. He always manipulated his sad stories into humorous adventures, always laughing on the outside but never having any emotional closure on the inside.

Even though he tried to maintain a happy facade, the listeners eventually knew that Tony was hurting. They cared and were sympathetic, offering endless suggestions on how he could develop lasting relationships. Tony listened to his friends' advice and tried to use it to his advantage, but every time all attempts would eventually fail. He firmly believed a pre-ordained destiny, for some unknown reason, was denying him access to a sustainable loving relationship.

He understood this was not a rational or provable theory. A more realistic reason for his failures, he believed, was due to some subtle action that he did or didn't do that resulted in these women losing any attraction they may have initially felt for him. Whatever the reasons, he hoped this time, with Lisa; destiny would finally allow him the opportunity to succeed.

He tried desperately to distract himself from thinking about his past, but his thoughts hopelessly focused on one failed relationship, that until now was the hardest for him to forget.

This unfortunate meeting happened several years ago while attending a weeklong "Designing with Nature" architectural conference in Los Angeles. At an environmental seminar on the conference's first day, Tony unintentionally sat next to Linda, a pretty 5'-6," green-eyed blond from Florida. Their mutual attraction was immediate. For the rest of the week they were constantly together, sharing their life experiences and making love anytime and anywhere they could. They were happy.

Eventually, their special week had to end. Tony needed to return home to his job in Baltimore, Linda to hers in Fort Lauderdale. Their limousine ride to the airport was full of laughter and optimism, but when they arrived, the laughter suddenly started to fade and was replaced with the sad uncompromising reality of separation. At the airport they tightly held each other's hands as they walked through the airport to their gates and flights home. Arriving at their departure crossroads, they reluctantly released their grasps and separated with a passionate kiss that said "good-bye," but also suggested the hope of a promising future together.

Tony left Linda with this hope in his heart. During the next three months after his return to Baltimore, he and Linda exchanged phone calls and letters constantly, trying to renew those magic emotions of their one incredible week together. Soon after, everything began to unravel for Tony, as fate began to weave its destructive web of failure.

On the day before Tony's scheduled flight to Fort Lauderdale, for his much-anticipated reunion with Linda, he received a phone call from her, a phone call that was so typical of all the last minute cancellations he had received throughout his adult life. Linda informed Tony she had to immediately return to her hometown of Miami because her mother was, without previous symptoms, diagnosed with a brain tumor. It was inoperable. Her mother's life expectancy was estimated to be less than three months. For Linda and Tony, it was to be a sad defining moment for them both. While tending to her mother, Linda rekindled a relationship with Frank, a former high school sweetheart.

Although Tony and Linda had long discussions on the telephone about their relationship, her mother's health, and the prospect of seeing each other soon, it was obvious that Linda had lost her focus and was becoming distant. Her evasive manner was an indication to Tony that something else was happening. That something else was her renewed involvement with Frank.

In less than two months Linda's mother died, the phone calls ended and Tony was forgotten. She wrote him a detailed letter explaining her situation with "Frank" and how sorry she was that it happened this way. Tony wasn't invited to the funeral, and he never saw or spoke to Linda again. This was a familiar pattern that continually repeated itself throughout Tony's adult life.

When he was active in pursuing a relationship, fate always dealt him a losing hand. Emerging relationships were ended by weather related catastrophes, sudden illnesses, traumatic emotional events, missed telephone calls, the return of an old boyfriend, and in Linda's case an imaginative combination of all these events. Anything that could happen to sabotage a relationship, a positive relationship that Tony wanted to advance, would happen. For some reason, some unknown force, at any cost, would not allow him to succeed.

— — —

Tony arrived at the hotel, parked the car in a prime spot close to the entrance, remained in the car listening to the last moments of commentary from David Brinkley and apprehensively began his walk to the hotel's entrance. Sensing disappointment, he left his suitcase in the car.

He entered the lobby, confirmed his room reservation, was given the room key, and despite all of his mind boosting confidence games, he knew it was all a waste of time. It was happening to him again. This love, this Lisa, who he trusted with his soul, was going to crush his heart. Even after they talked about the difficulties of the relationship and working through the inherited emotional hardships, there were doubts in his mind that Lisa would honor their agreement that if either of them ever decided to not follow through with pursuing their relationship, it would be discussed face-to-face, never with a letter, never with a phone call. They vowed always to remain friends who shared a common love bond. It was their solemn promise to each other.

As Tony opened the hotel room door, he felt the energy of rejection consume him. He knew Lisa was not coming. He was hoping against hope that these negative feelings were only a result of his trust and confidence being damaged from previous failed relationships - that this time these negative feelings could not be trusted.

He surveyed the room searching for a clue, a sign, anything that would prove him wrong. His eyes focused on something small and white and pretty leaning against a lamp – *the delivery*.

Tony saw an envelope on the end table next to the queen-sized bed. He walked over to face the inevitable. His hand was shaking as he picked it up. On it was written, "Mr. Tony Rullo, Room 320." Lisa was not here; instead there was this envelope. Inside it there was a letter. He reached inside. He stopped. He didn't need to read it. He knew what it said. Lisa was not coming. She had left him, as all the others before her. He wanted to rip out his heart and remove the source of any feelings from his body. What was he expected to do? He loved this woman beyond all that his senses could manage. He knew it was a tainted romance, but he always believed they could work through the inherent obstacles and make it work.

His curiosity and anger overtook his better judgment. He decided he had to read the letter. It was not a prudent choice. As his hand removed it from its paper enclosure, he felt himself become lightheaded and dizzy. He began to fall. He released the letter unread and watched it float back onto the dresser. He reached out to the dresser to break his fall. It didn't help. His legs buckled from under him and he collapsed to the floor in a heap of despair. He couldn't move. He couldn't cry. He couldn't make a sound. He could only lie on the floor and sleep.

A few minutes later, Tony awoke to face the truth. He called room service and ordered a hot tea and apple pie. It was all he could manage to eat. He looked toward the dresser. The letter was still there. He walked over, picked it up and held it tightly, almost crushing it as he prepared himself for the truth. He noticed the envelope. It was handmade from ivory parchment paper. On its surface was a half-inch wide stylized floral gold ink border. His name was also inked in gold with a calligraphy script font. Somehow, through the emotional turmoil that was this letter, Lisa's artistic nature would not be suppressed. It seemed insensitive that such a cruel message could be housed in such a beautiful package. What was he supposed to think? Was this woman incapable of understanding the emotional depth that consumed him in this relationship? Maybe the letter could clear up some of his doubts.

He unfolded it and read the words handwritten in gold ink.

> *Tony,*
> *I'm sorry. I can't meet with you today. In fact, I can't allow myself to see you for quite a while. Things have happened that I can not explain. Suddenly, I am not so sure about us.*
>
> *I want you to know that I love you more than you can imagine. It is something that is tearing me up inside and I do not know how to deal with all the emotions that keep me from accepting us as something to build upon.*
>
> *We started out wrong. It was something over which I should have had more control, but I didn't and I can't let go of the guilt. It has more to do with Neil's death then anything. I could never have ended my relationship with Neil as long as he was alive, but I know now that I can not seem to do it after his death either. Fate as usual has provided us a cruel twist. Since Neil died, I had to live with the grief of his death and the promise of our love. The problem is, I still love Neil and can never honestly resolve the emotions between you and me because of his death.*
>
> *A few days ago Tony, I honestly felt I was ready, but something happened to*

convince me that I was wrong. Trust me, I just can't do this now.

So today I must leave you to sort through all of these contradictions, all the remorse, and all the grief that will come along for the ride. I must be alone and away from you, my life and this horrible project. No building is worth someone dying over. First it was Neil, and then, almost you. I am going away until the building is completed. I need to clear my head of all this turmoil. After that, I'll be in touch. Do not try to find me, or contact me. I could not take seeing you until I am ready. I will not allow myself to hurt you again.

I need you to promise me that you will perform at your best and successfully complete the building as only you can. You owe it to yourself. You owe it to the world. Promise me.

I will miss you. I love you. I will see you again soon. I promise you.

*Forever yours,
Lisa*

That was it? That was the explanation? Not exactly the clarity Tony hoped would ease his emotional pain. He dropped the note to the floor and left the room. The door closed and locked behind him. He left the key and all his memories of Lisa behind that door. His tea and apple pie were delivered to a room filled only with loss, grief, and a good-bye letter that once lived in a pretty envelope.

Tony, drove to the airport and returned the rental car. He visited an airport bar an hour before the departure of his rescheduled flight to New York City. He abandoned his self-imposed prohibition on drinking.

"Screw it," he said. *"I'm tired of all this bullshit. Tired of being a nice guy. I'm going to drink this pain away. I deserve it. Screw it."*

He thankfully managed to board the plane feeling slightly buzzed, resolved to the firm commitment of never wanting to feel the pain caused by a "broken heart" again. The building was all he wanted to concentrate on now and soon all that happened to him this day would become a distant fuzzy memory. She's gone, he thought, and he would need to understand how to react to it as he had reacted to all the others. This one though, hurt the most and went the deepest into his soul.

The airplane reached a cruising altitude of twenty-five thousand feet. All that resembled civilization below was a random pattern of tiny flickering lights of unknown origin. To Tony they were only small insignificant points of time in a space that guided his memories into the paths of lost loves and detoured emotions.

He reached into his pocket and pulled out his father's gold pocket watch to check the time. Wrapped around it today was his mother's favorite heart shaped pendant necklace. It was to be Tony's gift to Lisa signifying his undying love, as it was to his mother from his father. It never found its recipient, and now it never will. He unwrapped the necklace from the watch and put it safely back in his pocket.

The bottom line phrase, *"...time after time he would try to connect, and time after time the connection would fail...,"* would enter his thoughts now in an endless uncontrollable loop programmed to disrupt whatever sanity he had left.

He needed to contact Johnny Thunder Eagle. He needed to experience another drug-induced Vision Quest. He needed to be released from this bondage of love and pain. He needed to be released from any emotions that would try to consume him and disrupt the creative forces in his life. The start of this journey, Tony's quest for emotional freedom, could not begin soon enough.

— — —

Housekeeping cleaned Tony's hotel room the next morning and placed Lisa's letter in a large plastic garbage bag that was filled with the discarded contents of many hotel rooms. The bag was placed with the rest of the hotel's evening trash, in the company of hundreds of bags filled with other hotel guests' left behind memories and waste.

CHAPTER 38

THE PROMOTION

Tony checked in at the New York *Verona* shortly before midnight. He fell asleep on the generic hotel room bed fully clothed without so much as disturbing the ersatz decorator bedspread. He awoke in the morning in a haze of confusion and doubt. He showered, shaved, ate a forgettable room service breakfast, and went for a walk among the masses. His western route over many short city blocks eventually took him to a meandering pathway bordering the Hudson River. He found a bench and sat down, his saddened face buried in his hands.

Between these hands, memories of Lisa were making their presence known, fading in and out of Tony's troubled mind as quickly as the river's flow. The distant sounds of the City comforted him in a symphony of noise that played to its own unique rhythm, its self-absorbed rhapsody, constantly changing, constantly adding to its mystery. Tony was listening to the city's music, trying desperately to recover from Lisa's unexplainable disappearance. He knew there was only one solution that would have the power to exorcize this pain from his heart – the completion of the world's greatest skyscraper. It would require all of his energy and focus. He looked up to the sky, toward the sun and knew he would dedicate every waking moment that was given to him on this Earth to achieving this goal. No more searching for the perfect person to love. No more *Lisas,* and the quest for someone to share his life. The decision had been made for him. Perhaps his failures at love were only meant to lead him to his predetermined path toward the truth. His choice was made for him. He was abruptly propelled onto his true path and nothing short of death or illness was going to keep him from achieving his destined goal.

Tony looked across the river to New Jersey, and Hoboken, his home. It was hard to imagine that this little impoverished city was the influence behind his creative instincts. He was grateful for all his life experiences, good and bad, that living in this city, a city in the shadow of Manhattan's skyscrapers, had given him in his short life on this Earth.

He was also grateful to have the New York City skyline available to him every day enabling him to channel the direction of his creativity. The City was not without its faults, however. It was a flawed source from which Tony developed a conflicted love-hate relationship. He loved and hated its overwhelming excess with equal passions. He loved its energy. He hated its insane pace. He loved its unlimited potential for almost everything that was ingrained in its existence. He hated how it suppressed this potential with passive ignorance. He loved having its resources readily available. He hated how most of these great resources were selfishly controlled by greedy power driven people. The City was organized chaos. Its chaos was a heavy blanket imprisoning its infinite opportunities for creativity. The Montana skyscraper was going to remove this blanket of chaos and all that was decaying in this exciting city, and replace it with its power to endlessly renew creativity and temper chaos into a seamless transition of natural order in harmony with the passions of nature.

THE PROMOTION

— — —

Tony arrived at the BEI office building via cab and took the elevator to the seventh floor. The "Resurrection Meeting", was being held in a small auditorium that could comfortably accommodate the over one hundred essential management representatives actively involved in the skyscraper project.

Jim Bradshaw promptly began the meeting at 2:00 PM.

"Gentlemen and ladies, thank you all for being with me today," he said. "As you are aware, our project, our magnificent skyscraper has been saved and with its renewal is born a new Nation. The ugly conspiracy of greed and power to kill our skyscraper has been defeated in a classic battle between good and evil, truth and deceit. Unfortunately throughout the history of man, that is the way it has always been - humankind's never ending war with itself. Instead of embracing each other, with love, as brothers and sisters, many people in powerful positions devise ways to forcefully manipulate their perceived adversaries for the sole purpose of contributing to their individual selfish interests and increasing their stockpile of material gains. I hope, that for this building, and us, this foolishness ends now."

"In order to guarantee that we remain one step ahead of those who may still wish to defeat our noble goal, I must ask an important question. Is there anyone in this room who is not willing to sacrifice their life for this project? If there is, now is the time to quit. There will be no questions asked - no reasons need to be given. The fact that you no longer desire to sacrifice yourself for this project is all that matters. We cannot allow anyone to work on this project who is not willing to give it a one hundred percent effort – all day, every day. If you think the pace and work was exhausting before our skyscraper was damaged, it will be even more intense now. So, if anyone wishes to leave – now is the time."

Jim waited and watched his audience. Not one person left the room. Jim was surprised, grateful and relieved. Wiping the tears from his eyes and trying to maintain and project a calm cool exterior, he said,

"Thank you. Thank you all," he said. "All right, now… are we ready to resurrect our building? Are we ready to thrust upon this world the gateway to their future? Are we ready to boot those greedy oil bastards back to their blackened oil fields?"

A resounding chorus of 'yes we are" followed, along with a standing ovation. Jim ignored the disruption.

"All right people. It all begins now. In a few days we will begin our skyscraper's reconstruction. Despite the damage caused by the building's premeditated bombing and the interference provided by our own government - among others – we are ready. Our construction budget is sound. Our workforce is intact. Our materials suppliers are waiting and their products are available for immediate delivery. We will resurrect our savior of concrete and steel. We will not fail. We have the sun's energy and the world's approval on our side." More applause followed.

"Good. Thank you. One more announcement," Jim said. "For the remaining duration of this project, I am appointing Charles Wilson, my Vice President for Operations, as permanent Project Manager, and Anthony 'Tony' Rullo, the talented young architect, the primary designer of this magnificent building, to the position of Executive Architect, both positions were represented by the late beloved Neil Hagman, before his untimely death. Everyone knows Charlie. He needs no introduction. But most of you here have never been formally introduced to Tony. So let me take this opportunity to introduce Mr. Anthony Rullo! Please give Tony a warm welcome for his wonderful well-deserved promotion. Congratulations

Tony! Come on up here so everyone can get to know you. Tony?"

The audience responded with a standing ovation and shouts of "Congratulations Tony," filled the room.

Tony was sitting passively in the audience observing the people, feeling their energy, listening to what Jim had to say, absorbing the profound impact of Jim's speech, when the words of the promotion slapped him on the side of the head with the subtlety of a train wreck…*what did he just say – a promotion…this isn't good…I almost quit because of Lisa and now this… I'm not ready for this…*Tony had no choice. He could not refuse. He stood up and made his way to the podium…*I think I'm going to be sick…*

Tony reached the podium and shook Jim's hand, mostly to keep himself from falling over from shock. Jim followed the handshake with a brief hug. He noticed the troubled, less than joyful look on Tony's face. He leaned over and whispered, "Hey…Tony…How are you?…Are you okay? I didn't mean to inform you of your promotion in this way. I didn't have the time to meet with you before this meeting. Besides, I thought you would've known by now. I let Lisa know a few days ago. I told her to playfully drop you a hint before the meeting. I know this is a lot to ask of you after your recovery time away from the project, but I have the utmost confidence in your ability. Don't look so troubled. Trust my decision. Trust yourself. By the way, where is Lisa?"

Tony whispered. "I have no idea Jim. She never mentioned anything about this to me – not one hint. I'm okay. Thank you. Thank you for believing in me. Let's do this. People are waiting..."

"Okay. You have the floor," Jim whispered.

They released their embrace and Tony turned to face the audience.

"Thank you. Thank you Jim. I am honored to be given this opportunity. It has been very difficult for all of us during the past few months. I only hope I will perform as well as Neil did in this position. I will dedicate myself to working to the best of my ability in Neil's memory."

Tony then said something somewhat unusual. "Neil…we all miss you and wish you well. I welcome from you any natural or supernatural assistance that you can offer me in this new position and in assuring Lisa's happiness."

The audience was stunned, not knowing how to respond to Tony's unusual statement. Then slowly, one tentative clap at a time, they broke into applause. An embarrassed Tony stood alone with his head bowed not knowing what else to say. Waiting for the applause to subside, Jim approached Tony clapping and nodding his approval, and gently put his arm around him.

"Okay…okay…yeah…well thank you Tony," he said. "I know we all share your feelings regarding Neil and Lisa. Neil is greatly missed, and will forever be in our hearts and minds. Now it is time for us to move forward as soon and as enthusiastically as possible to complete our great building! All of you in this room are asked to use all your talent, all your ability, and all of your inner spirit to carry through with this building of truth, to assure its successful completion. Immediately at the conclusion of this meeting, your assignments will be distributed. After that you will break up into your assigned work groups and begin our seamless march into the future. Good fortune to you all."

After a brief one-on-one post meeting conference with Jim, Tony exited the auditorium in haste - leaving New York City with the same feelings and purpose he had following his mother's death. Only this time he had a place to go and a person to see – Montana and the wisdom of Johnny Thunder Eagle.

CHAPTER 39

THE CONVERSATION

THE NEXT DAY

Tony's promotion should have instilled in him a tremendous sense of pride. It should have provided him with a positive source of personal fulfillment. It should have given him everything he could have wanted in his profession, proving his arrogant college professors wrong. In fact, it didn't award him any of these things. To Tony, the promotion was something only available to him by default, as was Lisa, both the result of Neil's death. He did not feel he deserved it. It was a tainted hollow victory. Neil's death and the pain Tony was still feeling from Lisa's departure were blocking his ability to experience any emotions other than disappointment. It wasn't an accomplishment. It was a punishment.

— — —

After Tony arrived back home, he immediately called Johnny.

"Hello Tony. Welcome home. How was the meeting?" Johnny said.

"Fantastic as usual. Jim was pure Jim – full of optimism and endless energy. Do you believe it? He promoted me to Neil's vacant position. It was a surprise. I hope he didn't make a serious mistake," Tony said.

"I heard the news. Congratulations. Do not worry. You will be a great leader. The Great Spirit is always with you."

"Thank you Johnny. I am looking forward to the challenge. Listen, I didn't call you to discuss work or my promotion. I called for a very personal reason. I need to see you. I need to talk to you."

"What is it Tony?"

"I can't discuss it over the phone. It's too involved – too much personal detail. It would be better for me to discuss it with you personally. Is that okay with you?"

Johnny sensed the urgency in Tony's voice and knew he required his counsel as soon as possible.

"Yes it is. Would you like to join me and my family tonight for dinner? We can talk after," Johnny said.

"Yes. I can make it tonight. Thanks Johnny. Thanks a lot. What time?"

"See you at six."

"Okay. I'll see you then. Bye."

"Good-bye Tony."

An evening at Johnny's home was exactly what Tony needed. He welcomed a hot meal surrounded by the warmth and comfort of Johnny's loving family. In his troubled state of mind, Tony needed them now more than ever. He had no one else to turn to. Other than his aunt and uncle, it was the only close family he had.

Tony had few words to say during dinner. He was waiting for the right time after the meal to discuss Lisa's disappearance. After the table was cleared and the dishes washed, Johnny and Tony retired to the Living Room.

"Sit down Tony," Johnny said. "Let us talk. You have said little tonight."

"I know. I didn't feel much like talking til after dinner. I didn't want to subject your wife to listening to my pathetic problem. Thank her for dinner. It was delicious. Don't let my half empty plate have her think any differently. I just wasn't very hungry."

"I will let her know. Now, tell me what is troubling you this evening."

"Well, here it is, direct and to the point. Lisa dumped me Johnny - two days ago. We were supposed to spend the night at the *BWI Prestige*. She never showed. Left me high and dry except for a handwritten letter left in our room. It contained an explanation that didn't make any sense to me. I'm having trouble understanding why she abandoned me. I need help." Tony tried to manage a feeble smile but couldn't hold back the tears.

Johnny was confused. "I am not clear on this Tony. I need to know everything about Lisa and you. Tell me how this came to be," Johnny said.

Tony told Johnny the details – the phone call initiating the meeting, the hotel, the letter, the disappearance – and everything else before and in between. Johnny listened intently and when Tony finished, offered his response.

"Tony, allow me to respond with these thoughts. My people, the Crow, throughout history. have shared a spiritual bond with a common purpose. The white man's world has influenced us to stray from this purpose. What we once believed was a Crow man and woman's love for each other is built on a foundation of mutual respect, sexual fulfillment and spiritual growth, all for the betterment of self, family, the clan and the tribe."

"Our personal 'love' for each other is filtered through the Great Spirit in unity with the love and respect for all things living. When the Crow man takes a wife, we take her in love, in honor, in respect, but not necessarily for life. Once the ceremony is performed to join us in marriage, we remain together as long as we are able to stay together in peace and harmony. Not all marriages should be permanent. Sometimes a marriage does not endure through time. If either partner feels that the marriage is not one of a lifetime, the man or the woman are allowed to dissolve the marriage without question. That is the way it was for my people."

"Unfortunately, you are not Crow. You are a white Christian man born Italian. From what I know of the stereotypical Italian male, is that he has a tendency to favor a romantic pursuit of women."

"So? What does that have to do with what happened with Lisa?"

"Tony, try to understand something that my people have understood since we came to be. Love can affect your behavior like a very strong drug. It can result in an illogical euphoria between two people who have fallen under its deceptive spell. It convinces them that everything about their relationship is perfect and that they can co-exist in this way forever while living in our imperfect world. As the flawed human reality that surrounds them begins to fall into focus, their perfect relationship will gradually dissolve into one filled with doubts and uncertainty. Their eyes begin to see broken pieces of their partner that each never saw before. The person they once felt so assuredly positive about, now becomes a definitive negative. The person that once was tolerable in all their personal faults, becomes intolerable. The person they once craved obsessively, they cannot stand to be around. The reality of their partner becomes distorted. To counter their unhappiness, they may begin to do things to each other that are irrational, hurtful, and in some cases violent. The most violent human acts are commonly inflicted on those we once loved."

"Presently, you desire in life a permanent fix for your feelings associated with Lisa's love, which is an impossibility. With Lisa, you have attempted to perceive the perfect woman, one who was capable of fulfilling all of your emotional needs. This goal can never be achieved - not in this world. This hopeless quest can never endure. It will fail and when it does you set yourself up for an endless series of emotional disappointments and distractions. That is where you are now. You have allowed yourself to react negatively to this failure with Lisa. This means you have allowed yourself to fail. You need to redirect your emotional energy in a positive direction. You must dedicate your life's love to your true purpose in life. Everything becomes clearer in your mind when you are truthful within yourself..."

Tony absorbed Johnny's response as a sponge to water. He was impressed by the depth of Johnny's response. He was somewhat unsure on how he could apply this information to his unique emotional experience with Lisa. It didn't matter. He would know in time.

... Johnny always seems to have the right answers... Tony thought.

Johnny continued. "...my advice to you is not to pursue any future relationships for awhile. It will only distract you from attaining your true destiny. Use the power that is driving you to fulfill your need to love and be loved, to fuel your passion for life and your passion to contribute something great for the greater good of humankind. Do not seek the love of one person to fulfill your need to be loved. Be honest and true to your beliefs. Do this and love will be returned to you over and over again. Do this. Free yourself from the bondage that has consumed you all your life. Would you be willing to trade the love of all humanity for the love of a single woman? Think about it. What is your life worth to you? That is all you need to ask. Be truthful in your answer and you will be at peace. I am finished with my advice. Take with you whatever you may find helpful..."

"Thank you. I will use your advice to get my head on straight," Tony said. "You are a great friend. I am honored to have you in my life."

Tony stood up and offered Johnny a hug, signifying his thanks and love for this man. The two men embraced, acknowledging the deep affection and spiritual bond between them. Tony's emotions took control and he began to cry.

"God, Johnny, I know I need to let her go. I know I need to redirect my personal energy to the skyscraper's success. I'll try to follow your advice, but it hurts so much," Tony said. "I miss her so much. It's tearing me up inside. My life shouldn't be about this. It is a waste of my talent. It is smothering me. How long before this pain leaves my heart?" Tony said.

"I do not know my little brother. I do not know. Just remember my words and seek the truth. Trust in your ability to seek the truth. Can you do that?"

Tony wiped his tears, took a deep cleansing breath, and sat down.

"Yes. I will try, but I need your help. I've been thinking of a way to release myself from this negative energy."

"And what would that be?" Johnny asked.

"I need a favor from you – a big favor. I need another Vision Quest. That's my solution. Can you do that for me? Can you do that for me soon?"

Johnny smiled. "Yes. I have already made arrangements. It was predicted you would request a Vision Quest, but reasons were never revealed," he said. "So if you agree, tomorrow at noon, not sunrise Tony, - that should make you happy – we will journey, as before, to the sacred grounds. You are welcome to spend the night here with us. We have prepared for you a room with a warm bed, a hot bath, and some clean clothes. Is that okay with you?"

"Of course it is," Tony said. "I was going to ask if I could stay here tonight. It's a long ride back to the cabin. Thank you for inviting me. You always know what to do. I feel better already."

"That's good. Before I forget…you need to know something very important about tomorrow."

"What's that?"

"Tomorrow is a special day, not only for you, but for the Crow Nation. You will not only experience a Vision Quest, but coincidently, it has been predicted by Stoney that the Great Spirit will be giving our people, your Crow brothers and sisters, a special sign, a spectacular vision in the sky after sunset, around the twenty-first hour of the day, that will signify the rebirth of our Crow Nation. I know we will both be eager to witness tomorrow's grand event."

"That sounds like a perfect ending to a perfect day." Tony said.

The two men continued to talk for hours until it was time to sleep and renew their bodies for tomorrow's long journey. As Tony was entering his bedroom, Johnny said, "Tony - one final word. What happened with Lisa was unfortunate, but trust me, you will fully recover. Concentrate on redirecting your love energy forward and not letting it consume your true destiny in life. If you are able to do this, you will be rewarded in your quest. Good night, my brother. Sleep well and in peace. I will see you in the morning."

"Thank you for your wisdom tonight Johnny. Peace my brother. Good night," Tony said.

CHAPTER 40

THE REBIRTH

Tony slept well through the night, unlike his past two sleepless nights after Lisa's disappearance. Following a relaxing breakfast and a hearty lunch, he and Johnny traveled the two hours in Johnny's Jeep, to the sacred grounds for Tony's Vision Quest and the evening's anticipated message from the Great Spirit. Unlike their previous visit, this time they were not alone. Thousands of Crow brothers and sisters were camped at the site waiting for the evening's prophetic experience.

Johnny and Tony selected an isolated area away from the many. They pitched a tent and started a fire. After dinner a conversation developed involving Tony's first Vision Quest.

"…Tony, by now, I believe you are aware of the message offered to you from your previous Vision Quest," Johnny said.

"I do Johnny. After my accident, lying in my hospital bed day after day, night after night, it was all I could think about - trees falling – trying to escape – the eagle - being saved – all of it, over and over. It eventually became clear. My Quest offered me clues about my future - the building's explosion - my escape from death. I wish I could have been able to understand what the symbolism meant before that fateful day, but then, we can't alter the future, can we?"

"No. We cannot. There is more to it Tony, than just the building's explosion and your survival."

"What's that?"

"What may not be as obvious to you from your Vision Quest, was the Great Spirit's commitment to protecting you from death then, now, and for the rest of your life. That was included in its message. You are protected. Do you understand this?"

Tony filtered Johnny's words through his mind before answering. "Not really. Explain it to me."

"I am sorry. I am not permitted to know any more than I have told you. I do know you and I will understand its full meaning in time. I do know that much. Now, let us put this behind us and discuss your awaiting spiritual journey."

"Okay Johnny. I'm ready. What happens now?"

"Tony, today's Vision Quest will not carry a message involving your future, as your first did. It will present to you another path, another message, one so profound as to not only enlighten you on your journey through life, but also enable you to relate to humanity's journey after death. That is what I know."

"How do you know? Aren't Vision Quests unique to each individual? How can you possibly know what mine will offer me?"

"Some Vision Quest messages are not unique to every person. On special days, and this is a special day, the Great Spirit offers to a chosen person a universal message. It was given to me three years ago and now I am told, it will be given to you on this day. It is time for you to share in this knowledge. Tony, we come from different worlds, but we are connected together through a common spirit. We are brothers in more ways than you can imagine. We all share the same life force and destiny. After death we will be united as one. This will be clearer after your Vision Quest. Stoney has directed me on my Vision Quests and has guided me in serving yours."

"Really? Thanks for *clearing* that up for me, but I'm still feeling a bit unsettled. Will any of what I experience in my quest relieve me from the pain of Lisa? After all, that's what I want," Tony said.

"This Vision Quest will provide no information on understanding your present or any future involvement with Lisa. You will need to find the answers to that question in your own way. I am sorry. You will eventually understand why this is so in time. Now, it is time for your journey…and don't worry about being anxious, the drugs will relax you. Are you ready?"

"I am. I'm ready. Set me free," Tony said.

Johnny prepared the solution for Tony and wrapped him in a buffalo robe. Tony sat on a heavy wool blanket over a thick bedding of straw to insulate him from the frigid ground. He patiently sat and waited for the drugs to take effect. It was not long before Tony felt himself loose consciousness and awaken in the otherworld.

> *When his eyes opened, Tony found himself lying on the ground, in a forest - aware he was living in a dream from which he could not escape. He stood up and looked around. He noticed a well-worn dirt path carving its way through the trees. It was beckoning to him, encouraging him to travel it, assuring him it would lead him safely and permanently to his home. He succumbed to its suggestion and began to walk along the path. He was convinced his home would be waiting for him a short distance ahead. He knew it was just over*

a distant hill past the largest trees. As he walked closer to the hill, cresting it to begin his downhill journey, he noticed that behind one of the many trees was a bear standing erect – his bear – the bear that was stalking him at his cabin, but larger – much larger – over twelve feet tall. Tony looked at it and smiled. "Hello to you Mr. Bear. At last we meet," he said.

The bear looked at him and appeared not to be offering a friendly greeting. No - this bear was angry. The bear let out a deafening growl, then ran toward him with undeniable fury and passion in its eyes. Tony could not move as he watched the bear come closer and closer to him. He could not escape its purpose.

The bear picked Tony up as if he were a lifeless rag doll. Its claws tore into Tony's flesh and its powerful jaws began methodically stripping away the meat from Tony's bones. Blood flowed violently from Tony's body from every conceivable wound. It formed an ever-expanding puddle on the ground. Bones became exposed where the eaten and ravished flesh was consumed. It would only be a matter of seconds before no flesh would cover his bones, no blood would flow through his veins, and no life would be left in his body.

Tony found himself witnessing the horror of his devastation, the horror of his own death spiritually from a distance apart from his body. He was able to see his other-self being destroyed by this bear. The mystifying part of this horrifying experience, was he felt no pain. His physical body lost its ability to feel anything, not pain - not emotion -not life. Tony continued to watch the flesh from his body disappear piece by piece into the bear's mouth. His body would soon be reduced to a skeleton of lifeless unconnected bones, but *somehow he sensed his death would not be defined by any traditional concepts. His body was not fully dead. Instead, he was struggling between a life-and-death existence, still in a fragile state of conscious being.*

Tony observed the bear, even in its crazed state, never attempted to consume his heart or brain. Instead, Tony's heart had been ripped from his body, thrown still beating to the ground into a blood pool. The heart remained there waiting for its rebirth. Tony's brain was removed from his skull intact and thrust into the air. It was still thinking, seeing, processing as it remained in the air, floating apart from its shattered scull, waiting for its vision. Tony's other body was lifeless, but Tony could observe all that was happening to it within his freed mind and outside his consumed body. This perception was an experience that was somewhere between a dream and an undefined otherworld existence.

The bear finally finished its feast, its appetite satisfied. There was nothing more to eat. It looked down at the bones, at the scull, sniffing them, poking them, while ignoring the beating heart and floating brain as if neither existed. The bear's attention was served. It recoiled backwards rolling on its back growling, snarling, pawing aimlessly at the air, and roaring in fear as it watched Tony's bones, scull, brain and heart unite and transform into a white cloud of pure energy. This cloud focused on the bear, instantly surrounding and consuming it within its boundaries of light. Tony's remains were gone. The bear was gone. Tony and the bear were now part of another existence, united as one.

This new experience was being introduced to Tony without definition and he was becoming increasingly confused as to understanding its meaning. He could feel the connection between his soul and that of the bear's in this cloud of energy, sharing this experience for a brief moment before their joined souls began their destiny to unite with the souls of all things existing in the ultimate fulfillment of life's infinite journey within the Great Spirit. He could feel his connection with everything living growing stronger and stronger, but was only allowed a glimpse, a preview of the things that would be offered to him in the next life.

Tony knew, because this was only his subconscious reality; he would never be allowed to reach death's ultimate goal. This experience for him would not continue beyond the limits of his induced vision. He prepared himself for the inevitable. He knew this experience was going to end. He did not have time to dwell on his connection to everything living, before this envelope of coexistence exploded into a cloud of fine black dust, throwing Tony from its shelter, onto the ground.

As the dust settled around his eyes, he felt a new emotional energy not like he ever had felt before. Now, was not only a moment in time, but also the eternity of what would be his life after death. The Now of this moment would be with him forever. If only, he could understand its power. If only, he could understand its truth. If only, he could understand in its capacity to unite humankind into a common goal, the goal of humanity to find its true purpose within itself.

Tony picked himself up from the rubble and proceeded to walk toward eternity, but this new path was dark and his pace was weak. So, like all who journeyed before him on this path, he found the journey endless, exhausting, and impossible to complete, but he continued. The bear was with him, at his side, protecting him on his journey to forever.

Tony's vision faded into the nothingness of a cold black existence, as his conscious reality cautiously awakened from its deep sleep. As Tony's eyes opened blurry and tear filled, Johnny was there to embrace and comfort him, keeping him warm – keeping him safe. His Vision Quest was over. The day had become night.

Johnny held Tony, while gently shaking him.

"Tony. Tony. How are you feeling? Are you okay? Do you know where you are? Do you remember the vision – its message?" Johnny asked.

Groggy from his experience, Tony answered. "...Hi Johnny. Is that you? I guess I'm back – huh? God, my head hurts. What was your question? Yes. Yes, I think I remember everything. It was very enlightening – totally frightened the crap out of me. I'm still shaking. I wasn't too excited about watching myself being eaten alive. I'm happy I magically managed to survive that ordeal. Yes, that was quite an experience. Don't want to go through that again. I don't think I can stand up. My head feels light. Is it still attached to my neck? I'm shivering. I'm so cold. I think I'm going to be sick. Why am I so cold? How long was I out?"

"Almost two hours. Here...take another robe and drink this tea. It will help settle your stomach, warm you and help you recover. I know your journey has been exhausting and frightening, more frightening than you could imagine. You may not sleep peacefully tonight. Don't worry about it. Tomorrow , the experience will have settled peacefully into your life and prepare you for your future. Your weakness will pass in a few minutes. Just relax, sit and rest. Do not try to stand until you feel your strength return," Johnny said.

"Thanks," Tony said, drinking the tea and feeling his emotions become infused with a new source of sensitivity.

"This experience will be with you forever. Remember it. It is a rare honored gift," Johnny said. "Not all are fortunate enough to have been witness to its power or to its message. What do you remember?"

"I don't really know. My head is still fuzzy, but if I would venture a guess, I would say the Great Spirit has attempted to convey to me a universal message relating to the spiritual connection between all things living. It is quite a concept, one I will embrace throughout my life," Tony said.

"Honor it," Johnny said.

"I will. I will for the rest of my life. I just need to sit here for a little while and think. The tea is working its magic." Tony said.

"Good. That's good. While you are contemplating what you have just experienced and working on getting your strength back, I now must give you another message, a message from this world, a message from Stoney."

"What is it?" Tony asked.

Johnny looked up into the sky and answered. "Tony, you will fly away from life, as I did, when I flew into life at my birth."

"Okay? Thank you for that obscure message. Now, what the hell does it mean?"

"Not now. In time, in time, you will know the answer, but not now. Now, it is time to watch the sky. Now, it is time to be enlightened and inspired. The Great Spirit's message is about to begin." Johnny said.

"Okay, but your vague message is something that will be continually troubling me," Tony replied.

THE REBIRTH

"Do not allow it. Do not spend any time thinking about what I have told you my brother. You will know all things in time. You will understand…"

"Okay Johnny. Okay. As usual I trust you…"

Tony sat next to Johnny and looked up into the sky for any signs of the predicted message from the Great Spirit. Within moments, Tony was given his answer.

Johnny and Tony, along with thousands, watched the night sky begin to glow with a faint blue and white light. This light was spoken of in Crow legend as signaling a radical shift in the fabric of the universe. Tonight, this shift would define future events on the planet Earth.

All witnessing this event hypnotically gazed into the star filled sky, as it began to erupt into a kinetic light show of many colors and many moods. It began with a shower of shooting stars by the thousands, streaming across the glowing blue and white sky. Then the sky erupted into a kaleidoscope of colors impossible to define and impossible to absorb by the limited senses afforded humanity. The dancing sky literally overwhelmed everyone witnessing it, giving to all an individualized charge of internal electricity. The changing shapes, colors and motion seemed endless. The light's intensity increased dramatically until it was blinding. The Great Spirit's spectacular light show maintained its magnificent display for only five minutes, but its power was without limit, and its message would impact the Crow Nation for eternity. It was an event sent somewhere from within the infinite expanse of the universe. All that were exposed to its mystery would be filled with a common spirituality and purpose, to assure the birth of a new Crow Nation.

PART 3: RESURRECTION

CHAPTER 41

THE NEW BEGINNING

Tony's eyes opened abruptly. It was five in the morning. His restless sleep was interrupted by the impossible-to-ignore ringing from his father's antiquated, "Big Ben," alarm clock. Just as Johnny warned, the previous night's experiences had left him confused as he lay awake throughout the night wondering what it all meant. What did his Vision Quest mean? What was the meaning of Stoney's message? Was the promise of a new world and the rebirth of the Crow Nation a certainty? What was awaiting him beyond this day?

On this morning of new beginnings, none of these questions needed answers. Today, the only questions that needed answers were those that charted the best way to resurrect a broken building – ones that would enable the Crow Nation Skyscraper to grow skyward again. Today, it was Tony's job to help answer these questions. Today, he would begin this quest simply by transporting his body from his cabin, to his truck and driving in the darkness through the cool spring air to the building's site.

Tony woke today accepting his new position with a renewed dedication. His energy was restored and his focus was centered on the project's success. His Vision Quest had indirectly provided him a needed relief from Lisa's negative influence. It had given to him a way to pursue his greater purpose in life.

Tony gathered up the essentials required for his comeback day. Before leaving his cabin, he thanked it for its hospitality and comfort during his recovery. As he shut the door behind him, he paused on the porch, surveying the surrounding area with his flashlight. He was looking for his bear. There was no sign of it. He was disappointed. After yesterday's Vision Quest, he expected it to be there. It had to be there. After all, it was his Vision Quest partner – his life-and-death companion. He wanted to begin his new day in the rebirth of a dead building with his bear walking symbolically at his side.

Disappointed, Tony entered and started his truck. As he was turning it to leave, its headlights reflected off a pair of glowing fiery red eyes contained in a large dark silhouette. It was a bear, *his bear,* fully visible, looking at him through the headlight's glare from the edge of the forest. The bear had been playing with Tony, playing peek-a-boo. It was always there watching him. Tony stopped the truck and looked at the bear for a moment, wondering if he should approach it. Tony was not given a chance to decide as the bear looked directly at Tony, stood erect, growled a greeting, turned away and disappeared into its shelter of trees.

Tony thought…*Well, Mr. Bear… thank you for visiting me on this wonderful morning… maybe we will formally introduce ourselves later…if not in this world, most certainly in the next…*Now satisfied and happy, he continued on his journey to the site. His trip was quiet, dark and filled with nervous anticipation.

--- —

Entering the construction site through the upgraded security checkpoints, Tony was greeted by many coworkers who remembered him from the building's previous life. They shouted his name and waved. Tony drove past the happy faces waving back to the people he so greatly admired. He reached an open field, the site's designated parking area, where hundreds of vehicles were already parked. He rode past row after occupied row until he found the next available space. He carefully placed his truck next to a gold and white 1968 Chevrolet Impala hardtop. It had a bumper sticker on it that read - *Official Crow Nation Skyscraper Rescue Vehicle – 1975!* He laughed appreciatively at the message, grabbed his backpack for his first full workday in almost four months and started his walk to the building. On his walk from his truck he noticed dozens of cars with the same message stuck securely to their bumpers.

...*I want one of those...!*

He shined his flashlight along the ground, illuminating his walk among the crowd toward the building's imposing silhouette. It seemed like forever since he was last here. He noticed that security personnel in motorcycles and jeeps were patrolling the building's active perimeter now defined by a new ten-foot high chain-link fence.

Seeing the building after such a long time and anticipating the erupting activity that would soon engulf it, instilled in Tony the same exhilaration he felt when his father took him to Yankee Stadium on opening day in 1964. However, here, instead of sixty thousand delirious baseball fans eager for another New York Yankee World's Series championship, there were hundreds of workers poised and ready to begin work again on this championship building.

Tony shook many hands along the crushed stone path leading to the skyscraper. He was escorted with other prominent project team leaders to the front of the crowd. Reaching the path's end, he stood directly behind a symbolic twenty-foot long, red, white, and blue steel chain strung tautly across the fence's dedicated employee entrance. Here, he waited patiently with the others for the official rebirth of one of the potentially greatest humanitarian construction projects in the world to begin.

— — —

Fifty feet inside the fence, facing the chained entrance, was a large flatbed truck. Standing on the empty flatbed, holding a "bullhorn," was Charles Wilson, illuminated by the many headlights aimed at him from the on-site company vehicles. He raised the bullhorn to his mouth and bellowed to the anxious masses.

"Welcome, ladies and gentleman, to the new beginning of our great building!" Charles said. "As we begin its construction on this momentous day, Mr. Bradshaw, wishes to thank each and every one of you for contributing your time and talent to assure its successful completion."

The crowd roared its approval.

"In a few minutes, you will hear the sound of a very loud horn, signaling the beginning of our never-ending day. From that moment on, this site will become a non-stop beehive of activity. The site will never sleep. It will never stop working until this building is completed."

"To assist you in maintaining our twenty-four-hour, seven day a week endeavor, a full service 'always open' cafeteria has been added to our construction site. You can't miss it. It is housed in a large dedicated green tent and has seating for hundreds. Beginning today, no one will need to 'brown-bag' their meals to the site. The cafeteria will be available for breakfast, lunch, dinner, and midnight or early-morning snacks. It will be operated, managed and staffed by the reservation's Crow men, women and children who will prepare traditional Crow meals, along with other cultural recipes. All cafeteria food is free, thanks to the generous stockpiles of food and beverages that will be donated by BEI throughout the project's duration. Although, voluntary financial donations are encouraged."

Another ovation was heard from the crowd.

"Okay. Are...we...ready? It is almost time. Take a deep breath and prepare yourselves as the Crow Nation Skyscraper welcomes you to take your place inside its heart! Watch for the sun's rise. It will signal its rebirth. Congratulations and good fortune to you all! Thank you, everyone!"

A thunderous roar came from the crowd. The site vibrated from its unbridled energy. Then as a faint glow on the eastern horizon appeared, the crowd became silent with anticipation. Their sun was beginning its rise. Their endless day was about to begin. Minute after minute passed – still silence. The sky became brighter. The crowd's patience became shorter. Then - a bright burst of sunlight appeared – a narrow sliver of the yellow fireball made its appearance and with it came a loud shrieking burst of noise from "the horn," ripping like a knife through the serene dark countryside. Immediately responding to this signal, the power to the site was turned on. Lights illuminated the area as abruptly as turning a switch on in a dark room. The red, white, and blue chain was detached from its supports and fell forcefully to the ground. Cheers filled the air as hundreds of black and white, helium-filled balloons were released into the early dawn sky. A wave of enthusiastic workers stampeded through the narrow entrance unto the building's site to begin work. After their landmark victory over this building's difficult struggle against its enemies, they could not begin to re-build this tower of truth soon enough.

Tony filtered through the masses on his way to the BEI construction trailer, the home of his initial project meeting. He stopped along the way to admire a flag flying proudly from a fifty-foot aluminum flagpole, adjacent to the cafeteria. It was the newly created flag representing the "Crow Nation." The flag was something the Crow Nation could be proud to defend and honor with the rest of the world. The flag's design was true to the beliefs of the Native American Nation it represented. Its colors of white, green, blue, red, yellow, and black were all represented in its design depicting a giant white eagle flying toward the sun with the Earth in its talons. The flag symbolized a renewed hope for a promising future. Each color had a symbolic meaning.

Pure white – the eagle - signified birth, the beginning of Life. Life's journey used Mother Earth's comforting green and blue. Life's sacrifices were represented by red, the color of blood. Yellow – the sun – was the color of hope. Finally, life's end was woven into its background using the unknown black of death.

A duplicate flag would be flown from the building's highest constructed elevation. This "flag of progress," as it was eventually named, would continuously be moved upward, until it reached its final resting place - the building's apex.

Sadly, flanking the Crow Nation flag, were fifteen additional flags. Fourteen were designed with a single gold star over a black background. These flags honored those who died in the bombing. One was a white flag with a single gold star, centered and rising ten feet above the rest. This flag honored Neil. These flags would fly as long as the building remained alive. Tony looked at the flags and felt a conflicting sense of pride and sorrow. Was money that important? Was power that ruthless? He would never understand the motives of the people responsible for these senseless and needless deaths.

What Tony did understand was that he was alive, on a personal journey of historical significance. Not only was he witnessing this historic event as it was unfolding, he was selected to be part of its message. Tony's renewed journey on this historic path would begin simply with an early morning project meeting involving a specially chosen team of thirteen architects and technicians. Their initial assignment - to evaluate the architectural and solar cell damage on all floors affected by the bombing.

Tony's team would be working in conjunction with the electrical engineering assessment team led by Peter Simmons, the project's new senior electrical engineer. Pete had replaced Martin Smith, the project's original senior electrical engineer, who was killed in the explosion. Both teams were to meet at the trailer before their walk to the building's fifth floor where they would inspect the damage, inventory it, define it, and then categorize it. They would perform this similar exercise for each affected floor on their list and assemble the information into a comprehensive report. Their report would be combined and analyzed with others from various technical disciplines, to determine the most efficient and best course of action to bring this building back to its pre-explosion condition.

The mechanical and structural experts would also be working on these floors inspecting their specific areas and piecing their parts of the broken building together. The building would be busy today, as all of its caretakers and creative experts would be playing detective, working together to enable the building to grow tall again.

The rebuilding process would be a difficult one. The explosion destroyed the project's continuity, replacing it with a new path of uncertainty, dependent on many for an accurate assessment of the skyscraper's condition. Assessing the correct order for assembling the pieces to this puzzle, and then prioritizing the rebuilding process within the framework of its newly established construction hierarchy would potentially add six months to a year to the building's already complex construction schedule.

— — —

At the trailer, handshakes and greetings were exchanged. Tony was excited to see these familiar smiling faces again.

"Good morning, Tony," Pete said. "Pleasure to finally meet you after all these months away from the job. You look well. How are you?"

"I'm doing fine Pete. Pleasure to meet you too. Too bad we couldn't have met under more favorable circumstances. It's so tragic about what happened to Martin and the others. There's not a day that goes by that I don't think about them," Tony said.

"I know," Pete said. "We lost many talented people that awful day. Martin was such a gifted engineer and a terrific person to work for...and Harry...well...it's a shame...just a crying shame...well...let's not dwell on this...we need to move on..."

After Pete's comments there was an understated agreement from everyone to not discuss the details of that horrible day. Instead they buried themselves in their work, committed to restore this building to its ultimate potential in honor of the fourteen people who died in the explosion.

The work would begin on the building's fifth floor. There, the team would inspect the damage and record the extent of materials to be replaced and repairs to be made. For Tony, it was the first time in nearly four months that he would be inside the building visiting the fifth floor – the site of his nearly being blown apart into a hundred pieces of mini-flesh. On that day, he was impressed by how quickly the building was climbing skyward, its structural frame reaching fifty floors of concrete and steel, a level that remained unchanged for four stagnant months. He had prepared himself many times for this fateful day and the potential trauma awaiting this reunion, but all his preparation could not guarantee how he would react when he physically returned to the scene of his near death experience.

The team made its way to the elevator that would carry them to the fifth floor. It bothered Tony that he was using the same elevator shaft where Neil tragically plummeted to his death. He didn't feel safe. He kept his feelings to himself – a mistake - for as the doors of the elevator opened, those awful memories that Tony wanted to bury slowly started to surface.

He apprehensively scanned the floor for anything or anyone suspicious. There was nothing. Except for his fellow travelers, the floor was empty - unlike the day of the explosion when hundreds were here working, laughing and living. Then the unavoidable happened. Tony's mind started to unravel into another reality, as he imagined seeing a group of co-workers across the floor whistling and waving at him. He saw Harry and Martin. He was convinced he saw Neil.

Tony left the group and began to walk slowly toward these ghostly images. He attempted to close the gap between him and the visions. Suddenly, as before, he saw a blinding flash of light, followed by what he imagined was an explosion. He became lightheaded and dizzy. He felt his body shake as everything faded to black. He fainted, fell to his knees, and eventually landed unconscious, face down on the concrete floor.

The men rushed over to Tony and stood over him with great concern – not sure of just what happened or what to do. They helped him sit up. Pete slapped him gently on the cheek, trying to shock Tony back to consciousness.

"Tony! Tony!" Peter said. "Tony, are you okay? Come on. Come back to us. What happened? Are you okay?"

Tony's eyes opened, as he shook his head trying to clear the cobwebs from his confused mind.

"Are you okay?" Pete asked again.

"Yeah. Yeah," Tony said. "I'm okay. What the hell happened?"

"I don't know. One moment you were upright and the next you were on the floor. I guess you fainted. You smashed your nose. It's bleeding," Pete said.

"I know. It hurts like hell. How does it look?"

"It looks fine. You look beautiful. Here - we got you some water. Somebody wet some paper towels, so we can make Tony's nose pretty again."

"Thanks Pete. Sorry, guys. I didn't expect this, but I should've known something like this might happen. The doctor warned me this might happen. My brain was playing with me. I saw things from that day. I saw people – people who died. I saw the explosion and then I blacked out. Well…hopefully that's over. I feel better now – except for my nose."

"You sure you're okay?" a concerned Pete asked.

"Absolutely. I'm okay – embarrassed – but okay. I'll work through the pain. Don't worry about me. We can't let this get in the way of our work here today. I'll be fine. Let's get to work so I can forget this ever happened."

"We'll work only if you're feeling up to it. That's what's important. No one here thinks any less of you. You've been through a lot. We all know that. Take your time. Make sure."

Tony stood up, brushed himself off, drank some water handed to him in a paper cup, put a wet paper towel to his nose, and looked over the floor again. This time, there were no ghosts to distract him. *Thank God*…he thought.

"I'm sure Pete. I'm sure. Let's get started. Look at this floor. It's a mess, just like me," Tony said. "We certainly have a lot of work ahead of us. It's like trying to put a jigsaw puzzle together, only you don't have all the pieces or the box with the picture on it. It won't be easy."

"I know - so let's get to it. Where do you want to start?" Pete asked.

"Let's start with the exterior walls and the solar cells," Tony said. "After that, my team will inspect the interior finishes, and your team Pete, can finish up on the miscellaneous electrical. When we're done on this floor we'll move up to the sixth and seventh. Then, if time permits, we'll travel to the ground floor and work our way up floor by floor to the fifth again. Okay, let's get going. This is going to be a busy long day."

"I know, but I'm looking forward to it. Can't wait to get this building back on track," Pete said.

"Me too," Tony said, while walking toward the building's exterior perimeter holding a paper towel against his bleeding nose.

— — —

After many hours of exhaustive inspection, the men sat down and compared notes. They assembled their findings and prepared to deliver the whole package to the secretarial staff tonight for typing, copying, and final assembly for tomorrow morning's review.

It was six o'clock. Time to end work for the day.

"That should do it for today, men. We'll finish up tomorrow," Tony said.

"Okay Tony. You know, I still can't believe this building's been sitting here in this condition for almost four months," Pete said.

"I know. There's so much to do. Clean up alone, should take weeks. It will probably be a full month before we can begin construction on the damaged floors," Tony said.

"I try not to think that far ahead Tony. *One day at a time* - that's my motto. It's all we can do. Right?"

"Works for me."

"Tony, are you driving back to Billings tonight or staying here for the night?"

"I'm sleeping here in the construction trailer. As long as I can get a hot shower in the morning, I should be fine. I brought a change of clothes."

"I admire your dedication," Pete laughed.

"It's not so much that. Didn't sleep too well last night. I'm just too tired to make the long drive back to my cabin – but tomorrow after work, it's Billings, for a little 'R&R,' and then back to the cabin."

"Okay. Great working with you today Tony. You did a great job – everyone did. See you tomorrow. Good night."

"Night, Pete. Great working with you too. Okay, everybody! Listen up!" Tony shouted to his crew. "I want to thank all of you for a very productive first day back on the job. Now, please go home and get some needed rest. We have to do all this again tomorrow at eight. See you then!" .

Peter escorted everyone to the elevators emptying the floor of all of its occupants, save one. Tony remained behind for a few minutes to tie up a few loose ends. When he was finished, he gathered up his stuff, headed toward the elevator, and noticed a familiar form walking towards him.

"Johnny! Is that you?" Tony shouted.

"Of course, my brother. Welcome back to our great building. I had to stop by to say hello and see if you are okay after last night's adventure. How was your night? Did you sleep well?"

"Are you kidding? I was a mess. I'm still recovering from last night. But I think you knew that. Good to see you, Johnny," Tony said. The two men embraced.

"Finished for the day?" Johnny said.

"Yup. It was an exhausting day. I was just heading down. Got time to hang out with me in our new cafeteria for awhile?"

"Yes, I do. I have time. Tony, your nose - what happened to your nose?"

"The short story is, I fainted. I fell to the floor, and my nose 'broke' my fall. The long story – well…I'll tell you that over a hot cup of tea. After that, we can talk about anything else - my vision quest…your emerging Nation…the building…but absolutely no Lisa talk…"

Lisa was becoming a quiet distant memory to Tony, thanks to the distracting energy of the exhausting workday and the emotional trauma of yesterday's experiences. He was thankful for that. Johnny had saved him again. "…God Johnny - there's just too much to talk about after what happened last night. My head's spinning. Where do we start?"

"It does not matter. All events are related in some way. We will just let the choices flow from their own paths."

"Somehow, I had a feeling you would say something like that. Let's go. I've had enough of this building for one day."

The two friends entered the new elevator that had replaced the one damaged in Neil's accident. As the doors closed behind them, Tony heard someone say – *welcome back, Tony…I missed you…the building missed you…*

"Did you hear that?" Tony asked Johnny.

"What, Tony?"

"Nothing…forget it. Thought I heard something."

The elevator continued its descent without further discussion from its occupants. Its steel doors opened at the lobby level. Johnny and Tony safely exited the enclosure and the lobby, bidding a fond farewell to the resurrected skyscraper. The Great Spirit was pleased.

CHAPTER 42

THE PROGRESS CONTINUES

THREE MONTHS LATER

Sitting alone, isolated – growing out of the ground, as a tree in a forest of one – was a noble symbol of power, without companionship – waiting for others like itself, to aid in its quest to evolve into a force of many. The building looked down on the people who had come to give it life and spoke to them.

People…Listen to me…I am the Adam of buildings. There is not yet an Eve. There will be, if you succeed in allowing me to live, to breathe – if I live, there will be an Eve, with many of our children to follow.

Help me people. Help me grow strong through my frame of concrete and steel, so my heart will soon beat, so my pulse will soon quicken, so my eyes will soon see, so my ears will soon hear, so the wind will flow through me as blood through your veins, so I will live, so I will breathe, so I will be free to help make you free.

I invite you inside me to work, to live, to heal, to express your desires and ideals, to force humanity onto a different path toward its ultimate fulfillment in life - to die in harmony with a common purpose. Fulfill your inner desires and you will fulfill your destiny. As long as you seek the truth, you will prosper. No one will ever lose. Humanity will always benefit.

Help me to convey the truth upon society. Help me to eliminate the myths and misconceptions that take people from the truth and lead them toward unfulfilled lives. Help me eliminate these myths by building upon my foundation of truth. Help me grow tall. Help me grow strong. Do not stop in your efforts to put another floor on me until I reach my goal. Help me reach my goal...

The people heard the building's message.

As bees to a hive, the workers gathered, assembled, and worshipped their icon of power that guided their rise to the top. The building was moving forward with a momentum that had a life of its own. Nothing could stand in its way. Without pretense, without ego, the building was driven toward a common goal – completion with a purpose, in fact and in function. It was like nothing before it and would be like nothing after it. It was the first, and others that would follow would possibly be better, possibly be more innovative, but they would never be the first.

— — —

The complex nature of the building's design necessitated constant revision of the Construction Documents. Talented draftspeople staffed the drafting tables in the non-stop production of the graphic information required to illustrate the never-ending construction details for the building's intricate design. The synchronization of all design, technical, and construction disciplines, was routine and essential to maintaining a flawless and uninterrupted workflow. To achieve this goal, engineers, architects, construction managers, and drafts people worked two twelve-hour shifts per day, ensuring a constant vigilance over the building's progress and making themselves readily available for any design questions or construction changes that required an immediate answer or solution. Quality was the rule. Nothing less than perfection was accepted by this elite staff of professionals. Because of their hard work and dedication, the skyscraper was able to adhere to its accelerated construction schedule.

The building's renewed construction was well ahead of its pre-explosion schedule. The structural steel framing was being erected at a frenetic pace - over two floors per week. Following the frame skyward was the building's skin, enclosing the steel in a curtain wall of solar beauty that knew no equal on Earth. The photovoltaic arrays absorbed the sun's energy, transcending their purpose brightly and happily in their place above the windows, spandrels, and steel mullions framing the concrete and granite facade.

The materials needed to construct, furnish, and adorn this building to its magnificent conclusion seemed endless. Its components came from many diverse and distant sources – the cement for the concrete was supplied from a BEI subsidiary factory in Washington State, and the structural steel was fabricated from a BEI owned foundry in Pittsburgh. Since solar technology was not readily available in the United States, photovoltaics came exclusively from Jim's company, *Sunflex,* of West Germany. The wind turbines were manufactured by several small independent European companies. To save valuable time, many essential building components shipped from distant foreign locations were transported overnight, via airfreight. Wood for interior finishes, framing and formwork, stone, sand, and gravel were indigenous materials acquired directly from resources located in Montana.

Deliveries were precisely scheduled. Delays were not tolerated. To insure this fail-safe operation, dozens of "back up" suppliers were on stand-by, available to respond immediately in the unlikely event the primary supplier was not able to deliver its product on time or in the quantities needed. Because of these costly time saving measures, construction costs were rising. The building's original estimated cost for construction would soon be exceeded. This inevitable outcome did not concern Jim Bradshaw. In the unlikely event that additional construction funds were needed, BEI would simply procure as many loans as necessary to keep the project moving forward.

— — —

Meanwhile, Johnny Thunder Eagle's involvement in the building's construction was significantly reduced. His new responsibilities with governing the Crow Nation were occupying his days now. He was consumed with the political growing pains that were inevitable in the evolution of an emerging Nation. His work focused exclusively on structuring a government that would embrace all the history, beliefs, and traditions of the Crow and marry it to the political realities of the modern, technological, religiously ambiguous world that surrounded this tiny Nation. Because of the events that led to this Nation's emergence, it was important to develop it without pretense or personal ambition. Keeping this new form of government solvent, peaceful, untainted, honest, and in harmony with Mother Earth, was a task that required all the wisdom and power that he could capture from the Great Spirit, *the maker of all things*. Johnny was confident in BEI's ability to carry it along on the true path, and of course it had Tony's spirit to infuse it with the energy of success. The building's future was in capable hands.

CHAPTER 43

THE MONTANA CHRISTMAS

It is Christmas Eve. Snowflakes, tiny medicine wheels of life, are dancing down through the night air from their skyward home, landing gently in assigned random patterns on the frozen dark ground. Their countless total is insignificant, only enough to blanket their domain with a depth that would be defined, by Montana standards, as a "dusting." Two vehicles, a jeep and a pick-up truck, are piercing their way through the snowflakes, traveling along a hard packed gravel driveway bordered by hundreds of miniature white Christmas lights. The lights' reflection off the snow covered surface helped to guide the drivers to the main entrance of a large house adorned with an extravagant display of holiday decoration. This house, located on a three hundred acre ranch nestled miles beyond the city limits of Billings, is the newly acquired Montana home of Jim Bradshaw.

As the vehicles pulled into the expansive driveway, a large front door opened and the host welcomed his guests.

"Merry Christmas! Johnny…Tony…Welcome to my home. Come on in. God, it's cold out here!"

"Hey Jim," they echoed. "We're here! Merry Christmas!"

"Thanks," Jim said. "Looks like we're going to have a fine white Christmas this year. Don't you just love Christmas in Montana? It's so refreshingly different from that experienced in Houston or New York. It has a surreal spiritual quality to it...mystical and magical. Don't ya think?"

"You bet," Tony said. Johnny just nodded in agreement.

Jim Bradshaw loved the concept of Christmas and its giving tradition, but ever since college he stopped believing and practicing its Christian principles as the primary reason to celebrate it. It was an honest choice. He decided to recognize Christmas for its infectious spirit and potential to promote goodwill in this world, not in its celebration of the controversial birth of Jesus Christ. He accepted the ridiculous notion of Santa Claus, toys, flying reindeer and how these absurd images were taken into the hearts of millions, at least for this time of year, as an accepted distorted truth. He kept this holiday in his heart as the season of peace and love - the time to give and experience happy times with those you loved – a time to say good-bye to the old year and welcome in the new.

─── ── ──

As Tony and Johnny entered the house, they found themselves in the vast open space of the "great room." The room was lavishly appointed with every conceivable Christmas decoration, except for any promoting a religious theme. Traditional holiday songs filled the multi-speakered room from a reel-to-reel tape deck housed in an armoire. Over four hours of uninterrupted Christmas music, including everything from Bing Crosby's classic, *White Christmas,* to the novelty of the Chipmunks', *Christmas Song,* would be played this evening. In the room were three Christmas trees, all about ten feet in height. Johnny's attention was drawn to one tree in particular because of its unique ornaments.

"Jim, what is this?" Johnny said. "Is this…what I think it is…Santa Claus riding a buffalo? Where did you find this? Here is another - an American Indian dressed as Santa with a bag of something. It cannot be toys. You did not know? Santa does not visit the reservation. These ornaments are very interesting. I am certainly impressed by the abundance of bad taste. Amazing. This entire tree is decorated using Native American themed Christmas ornaments. You meant to do this Jim?"

"I did," Jim said. "Had this one tree trimmed only with Native American ornaments, just for my adopted Crow family. I was hoping they would enjoy it and appreciate the ironic humor from it. Didn't intend to offend anyone. Guess we'll find out later tonight if I've succeeded. Besides, there are only a few tacky ones. There are many others on the tree that are quite beautiful and tasteful. Purchased most of them in Billings. There were a few stores that offered a wide selection of these special ornaments."

"I bet there were…probably for my confused reservation brothers and sisters. Jim, Christmas on the reservation is traditionally not the happiest time for the Crow people. There are many ambiguities and disappointments for my people associated with this holiday. Hopefully, our new Nation will change all that in the future. However, despite that digression, I will give you the credit you deserve. Your dead holiday trees are exceptionally festive – except for those few questionable ornaments on the *Indian Tree*. It is a honest celebration. I am not offended," Johnny said.

"Thank you Johnny. I am relieved to hear you say that," Jim said. "Okay, now that we're done critiquing my beautiful Christmas trees, let's sit down and relax. I didn't invite you both here early, before the party begins, so we could talk about my holiday decorations. We only have an hour or so before the rest of the party volunteers, and guests start filtering in. Before they arrive, I want to bounce around a few thoughts about our beloved skyscraper. Let's kick back with some hot-spiced cider…made it myself."

Jim prepared the hot cider and handed the filled china cups to the two men, stirring the contents of each with its own cinnamon stick. The sweet cinnamon aroma complemented the smell of pine that filled the room.

"Before I forget, I want to congratulate both of you. Let's raise our glasses. Tony, congratulations on admirably serving in Neil's tragically vacated position. You're doing a fantastic job. I know because of your close relationship with Neil, this was a very difficult position for you to accept. I am very proud of you for overcoming the obvious emotional obstacles. And Johnny - my goodness …Johnny…you have really proved yourself as a great leader in establishing your new Nation. It's been a great year for us in so many ways. Next year, after the skyscraper's triumphant completion, it will be an even better one. Thank you both so much. Drink up!"

Tony and Johnny graciously accepted Jim's compliments, with little pretense.

— — —

The three men then settled into a large overstuffed brown leather sofa, facing a healthy fire safely contained within the hearth of one of this home's three fireplaces. They propped their feet onto a rectangular coffee table cut to shape from a single block of solid dark gray Montana granite. The table had a dual purpose. It served its intended function as a coffee table, but through its physical nature, became a heat sink, absorbing and storing the heat from the fireplace into its mass – keeping both feet and body warm. Sitting comfortably, trapped in the sofa's embrace, listening to the music, staring into the fire, relaxing, they said nothing – fearful the peace and serenity they were feeling together at this moment would disappear if even a hint of disruptive outside influences were permitted to attend.

The flames from the fireplace were radiating a special glow upon the three men. Within these flames there resided a special message. Before the evening's end, they would capture the meaning of this message, and find themselves unified in the religious significance of this holy day, not through its traditional Judeo-Christian teachings, but through a purely universal message that would transcend all religious boundaries and restrictions.

In his trance-like state, Tony felt the need to first break the silence.

"God, it feels great just sitting here and doing absolutely nothing. Most relaxed I've felt in a very long time. Too bad a party will soon disrupt this peace."

Tony looked around the rancher's mansion and imagined being in a Colorado ski lodge. The interior was spacious - open and rustic - with one area's function flowing seamlessly into the next. On the entry level, bearing walls were few as columns supported most of the second floor and connecting walkways above. Tony was impressed by its architectural harmony and simplicity.

"This is a beautiful house, Jim," Tony said. "You have gone to great lengths decorating it for this holiday season. The lights outside bordering the drive to your front door, the giant wreaths, that beautifully lit live forty-foot tree outside, and the three Christmas trees inside this great room. It's an impressive display. It almost makes me forget Rockefeller Center …almost. Why haven't we been invited to this grand house before tonight? Keeping it a secret?"

"No… not at all," Jim said. "Hasn't been time. Hardly spend any time here myself. I've only owned this house for a few months. You'll be out here more often next year. I promise. By the way, Tony, I haven't seen your cabin yet."

"No problem. I'll have you over for some rabbit stew. Just let me know when. I was only kidding about not being invited. I know the project's insane pace has put a severe crimp on our social interactions. There's work and then there's more work. Not much time for anything else – but you know that."

Tony digressed.

"You know, since the death of my mother and father, the Christmas holidays have always felt empty and lonely, but not this year," Tony said. "This year, you have managed to make this one of my best Christmases' in a long time. The only problem, for me that is, in keeping it from being perfect is the loss of Neil and Lisa's unexplained disappearance. I wish they both were with us tonight, but what the hell; I'm very lucky to have both of you in my life. Happy we can spend this time together before the guests arrive. Good idea, Jim, and oh, before the festivities allows me to forget – thanks. Thank you for everything."

"You're welcome, Tony. The feeling is mutual," Jim said.

"Amen to that, my brother," Tony said. "So what's on your mind tonight, Jim? What do you want to share with us?"

Jim took a deep breath and replied. "A lot. A lot. In the midst of all the activity this past year, I've managed to find some down time to think extensively about my life, this building and the new Crow Nation. What happened to me makes perfect sense. Always did. Thanks to Stoney, Johnny, and help from the Great Spirit, I feel that my renewed life and tainted wealth are serving humanity in the manner in which they were intended. Thanks Johnny, for saving my life and helping me to understand. Thanks, for this second chance to make things right."

"You do not have to thank me, Jim," Johnny said. "We are all on this mission together. It is not difficult to feel good about your life when the Great Spirit guides you along the right path. You were on the wrong path in your life. Stoney and I were only the messengers from the Great Spirit asked to help you find your way back to your true home. Your life has been blessed by the Great Spirit and will benefit many. Through the creation of the Crow Nation and the skyscraper, you have enabled the Crow to become a proud people once again, determined in our quest to create the finest, freest, most spiritually connected country in the world." The men shook hands and embraced. Tony watched with the deepest respect and admiration.

"You know I am fortunate the Great Spirit has afforded me this renewed gift of life and with it, the opportunity to serve humanity. That is the greatest gift anyone could ever want. It is a gift that will require my lifetime to repay. I will always be happily in its debt," Jim said.

"There is no debt to be paid, only a promise to follow the true path," Johnny said.

"I will do that. I will do that until my last dying breath," Jim said.

"You're life will be rewarded a thousand fold. Our spirits will be rewarded after death," Johnny said.

"No one could ask for anything more. Okay. Now, it's time to celebrate Christmas. You remember how it goes - Santa Claus, toys and candy canes. Let's not forget that. I didn't ask you both to come here to discuss death and my good fortune. No, what I want to know…is *this*. After all we have been through, I am curious to know how you both feel about the effect this building will have on the world's future. Do you think we are setting the bar too high? Are you still buying into our utopian idea that this building will be the foundation from which a better future for humankind can be launched?"

"You know I do Jim. I know we all do – the Crow Nation does," Johnny answered.

"But why Johnny? We know what I've been promoting since the beginning. I want to know what you think," Jim said.

"My thoughts are not presented as my personal opinion. They are offered as the common goal among us all in harmony with the Great Spirit," Johnny said. "When you believe in this goal, it's easy to understand the purpose of this building. This building, in conception, construction, and completion, delivers a message from the Great Spirit. Its message asks humankind to utilize Mother Earth and the Sun as the sustainer of all life. By doing this, man's spirit will be raised to a level that will allow it to live life fully without judgment, without hate, without envy. This pure spirit will eventually flow, connecting everyone in a single unified soul. This unified soul will provide all the spiritual knowledge needed to enable all of humankind to fully understand the power behind the secrets of creation. That power is the Great Spirit. This building, our people and our Nation, will carry this message to the rest of the world and into eternity."

"Johnny, you are a gifted and well-chosen leader for your Nation. I only hope we are able to achieve a fraction of what you have described. Tony, what do you think? We've been ignoring you. After all, it is your design. You're the creator of this magnificent building. Enlighten me," Jim said.

Tony's eyes widened.

"*Enlighten you?* How am I expected to do that?" Tony said.

"Try," Jim urged.

"Okay boss. I'll try," Tony said. "Let's see…first of all, I agree with Johnny. It's difficult not to, since he seems to always have the right answers. But to add to his magic message, I'll say this…I feel that this building is about a promise, the promise to unify our world through the power of the sun. Of course this promise goes deeper and broader than that, but that is the heart of it – the beginning. We will begin this journey by attempting to provide architecture in its most perfect form. Through this building's architecture, we will allow opportunities for people to become the architects of their lives and their lives will become the architects of their souls, unified in a single purpose, as ants in an ant colony - everyone performing their life's work for the benefit of the community, which will personally fulfill their lives in so many other ways. Our building is the anthill. Within it, buried deep within its tunnels, we will build our future together, firmly attached to a star – our sun."

"There is one more thing that I have observed that is an absolute. It's that our continual progress in technology – progress in comfort – has assured humankind of no progress in enforcing or increasing its spirituality or strengthening its soul. Technology and spirituality have an obligation to exist together in harmony. So far, our technological accomplishments are far ahead of our spiritual ones. This building will help bring the two into a more meaningful balance – a true coexistence. We will deliver this promise by influencing the environment in a positive way. We will be giving humankind a vessel floating in the ocean of time. We will pull its oars in unison toward a predetermined life-fulfilling goal. That's about it. How'd I do?"

"Very well," Jim said.

"Really? I don't know," Tony said. "Sometimes I just open my mouth and these strange words come out. I'm not sure they make any sense."

"Tony, you have spoken clearly. We understand your message," Johnny said.

"I agree," Jim said.

"I suppose our building is the symbolic representation of a messiah. I think we can all agree to that. Jim...it's your turn. You started this philosophy session, so you'd better have something great to share with us. What deep dark secrets are you ready to reveal?" Tony asked.

"You really want to know? I don't know if you're ready for this," Jim said. "You both know my past life. I was an Atheist, but I have been converted to something else, that is for me still undefined. Now, as you know, I believe in a higher power over life, who in honor of the Crow, I give the name the *Great Spirit* or *Great Maker*."

"This is what I believe...I do not conceive of the Great Spirit as a single entity, a master over life, but as life being the master over the Great Spirit. Without life, there is no Great Spirit. Without humanity, there is no need for the Great Spirit. Without our intellect, there is no knowledge of the Great Spirit. The Great Spirit is the vessel holding life's universe. The Great Spirit is every minute part of its creation. This is the message we should carry with us this Christmas, through the New Year and into forever."

"I also wish that humanity universally abolish dogma-driven religion throughout the world. Part of the problem is the inherent contradictions between the philosophies and beliefs of the different religions existing on this planet. If there is a devil, then religion is its perfect tool to turn man against man."

"Organized religion also removes our capacity to be independent in understanding life as it is meant to be understood, through nature, using the instincts of our natural spirituality. Religion subjugates humanity into soulless mindless robots whose interpretations of life's purpose are based not on their capacity to think unencumbered thoughts, but to rely on faith alone to follow blindly a rigid set of rules and laws that are meant to define their lives. In reality they do just the opposite. Rigid dogma inhibits the natural growth of life as it is meant to be lived by humanity. To enlighten the spiritual aspects of our lives is not possible with the burden of organized standardized religions."

"We need to expand our spirituality beyond our limited senses. The passage of time has made man no wiser in his search for his reason for being. Only by believing in the concept of a unified soul, by believing in yourself as part of being a God to everyone as well as yourself, and everyone as being a God to you, can we achieve our true goal in life, understanding who we are, what we are, and what we will become after death. It will enable individuals to believe in themselves fully, before allowing themselves to embrace with their fellow human beings or accept any belief in a Supreme Being. That's it. I'm finished."

"*Amen and Praise the Lord*, Jim," Tony said sarcastically. "There's not too much more to say…"

"Agreed!" Jim responded. "I'm happy to get *that* out of my system. Now that that's over, and there appears to be no lightning bolts flying down from the heavens, it is time to release our over burdened minds and overworked bodies from these philosophical ramblings. It's time to return to the real purpose of this evening. It's time to ask both of you what you wish for on this season of hope, peace and love? What do you want for Christmas? Tell Santa."

"I wish for one selfish thing..." Johnny said. "...the success of the new Crow Nation and our building of truth."

"I'll second that. What about you Tony? What do you want?" Jim asked.

"I'll go along with Johnny, but I also wish that wherever Lisa is and whatever she is doing now, she is healthy and happy," he said.

"She is Tony. Do not worry. She is," Johnny said. As soon as the words left Johnny's mouth, he knew he had made a mistake.

A surprised Tony said, "What? What are you saying? Do you know something about Lisa? If you do, you'd better tell me now. None of this - *you'll know in time* - bullshit. Tell me."

"All I know is that uncertainty is something that we can be absolutely sure of in our life."

"That's a very profound statement of the obvious. What the hell does that have to do with what I just asked you? You didn't answer my question."

"I am sorry Tony, but there are some questions that are better left unanswered. To have knowledge of what you will not understand is not something that will benefit you now. Wait until the experience captures you. Then and only then will you understand and be at peace," Johnny said.

"What the hell...? You know...just once Johnny; I'd like to get inside that head of yours. I don't have a clue to understanding what you just said. Does it have anything to do with your other mysterious statement about my, *'flying away from life as you flew into life at birth'*," Tony said.

"Yes it does. Let us just be at peace and leave it at that. All your questions will be answered in time."

"Really? That's what you always say. You're not going to tell me what you know about Lisa, are you? That's just not right. You know what this means to me!"

"You will understand Tony – trust me. Let us put this in the past for now. I am sorry I have upset you. Forgive me. I should not have said anything concerning Lisa's fate. I am sorry. Are you okay?"

"Give me a little time. You know I can never be upset with you for very long. Just do me are really big favor in the future, if you don't want to upset me, then keep any information about Lisa that you are not willing to share to yourself. Okay?" Tony said.

"I will Tony. It will not happen again," Johnny said.

Jim was sitting, listening, and reflecting. This, he felt, was an enlightened moment for him – listening to the Tony and Johnny exchange. He wondered, as Tony did, about Johnny's response about Lisa. What could Johnny possibly know? For Tony's benefit, he didn't ask any questions. *Just let it go – for now...,* he thought. He interrupted the verbal exchange.

"Gentlemen. We are being much too serious," Jim said. "We should be celebrating. After all, this *is* a party. Let's keep the memory of Neil and Lisa in our hearts and begin our celebration of life, this pagan holiday season, the emerging new year, and our building's success!" Jim then pulled out a treasure buried deep within the recesses of a very large ice bucket conveniently placed next to the sofa. It was his official symbol of celebration. He held the cold bottled treasure enthusiastically above his head.

"In keeping with that spirit I am holding a chilled bottle of the world's finest champagne, Dom Perignon, 1959. It cost me over five hundred dollars...way overpriced. I only purchased it because it's supposed to be the best. I do that sometimes – buy something that's supposed to be valuable. It's a nasty habit of the rich. I do not care for champagne anyway…never did."

"Did you know that champagne was invented, 'accidentally,' in the 17th century by a Benedictine monk, by the name of – are you ready for this – Dom Pierre Perignon. Ol' Dom was making a special white wine for the French aristocrats using red grapes from the Champagne region of France. One big problem though, these special red grapes only matured late in the year. After picking, pressing and processing there wasn't enough time for these grapes to completely ferment before winter set in. This caused the grapes to undergo a two-step fermentation process - one in the late fall and again in the early spring - resulting in the development of tiny carbon dioxide bubbles. Experts considered these bubbles a major flaw in wine making. Bubbles were signs of an inferior wine. Dom tried and tried to rid the wine of these nasty bubbles – sadly in vain. Searching, apparently for divine inspiration to solve his problem, he received an idea that would turn his misfortune into good fortune. Somehow, Dom managed to convince the rich and powerful, this flaw was not a flaw at all, but a unique and rare quality. It worked. The pompous aristocracy accepted this new wine into their world. A new taste for sparkling white wine was born. The rest is history. Dom created a product of worth from one of conceived worthlessness. I love it."

"My father made a lot of his money by exploiting this concept. Diamonds, gold, paintings, antiques, all valued by what their worth is perceived to be, not what practical value they actually possess. Valuable only because people want them to be in order to give meaning to their economic criteria and over-inflated egos. Exploitation of this concept has made many people very wealthy."

"Back to champagne. Personally, I never liked its taste or its annoying bubbles. Most people don't, but will never admit it. To me, it is merely a symbolic celebration beverage of dubious worth. As a child, I was subject to the constant barrage of champagne and caviar during my parents' parties. It caused me to become immune to their implied unique qualities. Now, as an adult, their qualities are not worth any more to me than a common hamburger. Champagne and caviar - what a waste of good money. Anyway, I digress. Let's celebrate with it, despite my prejudices. I will pour us each a glass and since I know we won't be drinking one drop of this alcoholic liquid, we will use its purpose to toast to our continued health and success in this new bicentennial year. We will complete our toast by throwing our full glasses of champagne into the fire, followed by the half empty parent bottle. Agreed?"

"Sounds like a great idea," Tony said. "Smashing glass objects onto hard surfaces through open fires is much more fun than *actually* drinking their contents. It certainly will get Lisa off my mind."

Johnny just shook his head and said, "You whites are very strange humans. I sacrifice my elite status as a Native American Crow, by just associating with you both."

"Yes we know. We both appreciate the personal sacrifices you're making. I know you're only tolerating Tony and me because the Great Spirit ordered you to." Jim said.

"That is not true." Johnny jokingly said. "I only hang out with you Jim, for your money, and as for Tony, it's because he's Italian and has the secrets to making genuine New Jersey pizza, which I love."

"That is good pizza," Jim said. "Was that a little Crow humor I heard? Didn't think you had it in you. You could start a reservation Comedy Club with that material. But seriously, Tony – Johnny, I love both of you as if you were my brothers, which for all intents you are. You are my family. We have all experienced a lifetime of emotional trauma, both good and especially bad, in the last two years. Tony – you almost lost your life. That is the ultimate sacrifice. Thank the Great Spirit you survived. You enabled us all to survive. Let's celebrate to that - our survival! Merry Christmas and may we all live a fulfilled prosperous life in the new year. Happy New Year! Fare Well!"

Jim removed the champagne from the ice bucket, popped the cork from the bottle, and poured the champagne into three Tiffany, lead-crystal, champagne glasses. Each man lifted his glass joining the other two, in a triangle of celebration – arms outstretched to full extension, glass surfaces barely touching one another in a delicate salute to life.

No words were spoken. No toast was offered. Instead, there was an understood message and a bond between the three men that transcended any need for verbal communication. Their thoughts became one. Their emotions were connected. At this precise moment in their lives, everything in their hearts was about love. Everything in their souls was about peace. Everything in their minds was about truth.

They all believed in one thing, the natural unity of humanity through belief in the Great Spirit. It was time for everyone to work together to build this unified belief. It was time for everyone to start building the framework to enable their souls to come together in an endless parade of harmony. It was time for everyone's soul to be one with the universe. This was their toast.

Glasses were held aloft until the men felt compelled to simultaneously lower each glass from its lofty status, and with one continuous motion thrust them, with all the force that they could manage, into the leaping flames. Their efforts were well rewarded, by an explosion of glass and flaming wine that signified a visually meaningful celebration, overshadowing anything that could have been felt by drinking the cool bubble filled grape beverage.

Jim then lifted the half empty bottle of the five hundred dollar liquid and, as promised, threw it with a determined passion into the fire, hitting the hot brick hearth wall in a fittingly abrupt ending to the artificially valued treasure. The toast was complete.

The men were feeling good. They were ready for the new year, a new life, and all the positive success that they could squeeze into it. For now, their optimism was without limits.

They sat by the fire and smiled at their good fortune and promising future.

"Merry Christmas, my friends." A suddenly nostalgic Jim reaffirmed. "Merry Christmas."

"Merry Christmas, Jim." Johnny and Tony replied. The words were said and the greeting was conveyed. Although these three men confirmed that they did not believe in the traditional Christian values of Christmas, they allowed themselves to embrace its spiritual energy and found themselves feeling genuinely at peace. The magic of this moment engulfed them in a wave of holiday spirit. Maybe there was something to this Christmas story after all.

Their moment of total euphoria was shattered by the sound of the doorbell. Their uninterrupted peaceful holiday vigilance was over. The guests had arrived. The party was about to begin.

CHAPTER 44

THE MONEY GRABBERS

It is March 21, 1976, the first day of spring – the vernal equinox. America's bicentennial year was in full bloom.

Nearly three months ago, Jim Bradshaw's New York City, New Year's Eve celebration was memorable – an extravagant event shared with friends, employees, and most notably his parents. It was not just another one of his typically meaningless parties with a handful of acquaintances and discarded girlfriends. This year, it carried with it a special meaning. This was the year that his dream would finally come to be. This year, his building would become the world's building and the welcomed home to thousands of Crow Nation citizens. It would be his lifeline; fulfilling a life long search for someplace he could call his true home. He would be living in this concrete and steel sanctuary until its walls would capture and release his last living breath.

It was a little over a year since the building's resurrection. In that time it had risen to its goal of two thousand feet with over one hundred floors fully enclosed and functional. In another nine months, the remaining floors would be completed and the skyscraper would be ready for occupancy.

Jim excitedly filtered these thoughts, as he gazed upon the varied architecture of New York City. The spectacular midtown view from his glass enclosed fiftieth floor office was what every New York corporate executive's inflated ego considered the pinnacle of success. From up here, in his fortress of power, built from the addictions and cravings of the little people below, delusional feelings of immortality often consumed him. On more days than he could remember, he would aimlessly stare out from these glass walls with a confident smirk, Scotch and cigarette in hand, thinking how effortless it was for him to amass such enormous wealth. However, the events affecting him over the last few years changed all that. His immortal delusions quickly faded into the reality of his fragile mortality. Cancer and an impending death can do that. His miraculous recovery was his chance for redemption, a chance to replace his endless obsession in pursuing power and profit at any cost with new worthwhile endeavors, ones that focused on a healthier lifestyle, personal responsibility and human compassion. The skyscraper could not be built fast enough to provide the means to actively pursue all the good he could offer humanity in his lifetime. His anticipation to begin this new life was as fresh and exciting as a child awaiting the arrival of Santa on Christmas morning.

There was a new problem however, one that was threatening to block the successful attainment of this goal – money. BEI's accountants had underestimated the impact of the skyscraper's escalating costs. Jim's obsession to keep the project a well-guarded secret and finance it without having to acquire multiple loans from risky private sources or politically influenced financial institutions had become a liability. Real world economics were infiltrating his dreams like an infecting virus. His costly legal battles with the United States Government over his rights to construct this building on reservation land, his substantial monetary contributions to influential Third World representatives of the United Nations, and the increasing construction costs related to the building's intricate solar design technology, were rapidly draining BEI's allocated construction funds. The building's bottom line was fast approaching the color red. He was losing money every day the skyscraper remained under construction. His new businesses were also beginning to feel the squeeze. The profits from his real estate, cement, steel, and solar energy companies were no match for the millions he was able to generate daily from the endless consumption of liquor, cigarettes and gasoline – no match at all. He understood the reasons these industries were so seductive, why he was drawn into their web of self-promotion, and why their addictive paths to unharnessed profits were almost impossible to resist.

Jim was pondering the problematic financial future of BEI and the Crow Nation skyscraper, while casually reviewing his mail for the day. It was something he did daily at precisely 8:00 AM and 2:00 PM. Since the building's construction began, he was only in the office about three days a week, Tuesday through Thursday. His secretarial staff would filter out the obvious junk mail, bills and trivial correspondence from the daily pile, so what arrived at his desk was only mail important enough to require his personal attention. Still, the mail would pile up to ridiculous proportions.

This morning, one particular piece of mail, because of the envelope's poorly printed Government letterhead and weathered appearance, captured his attention. It was a registered letter that required his signature. The return address read, "Internal Revenue Service, New York City." Under his address was printed "Personal and Confidential to be opened by Addressee Only." Jim could sign it and return it to his secretary for processing or satisfy his curiosity and open it. He decided to open it

"What the hell could this be?" Jim muttered.

Jim had not seen one of these for a while. BEI's accounting and legal departments handled all corporate tax matters. Typically, he would review and sign the appropriate forms after BEI's financial experts processed them.

He did not have a good feeling about this. The IRS was one government organization that he usually didn't have a problem dealing with on his own terms. He had developed a very good working relationship with the local agents. What could this be about ...*another ploy by the Federal Government to stand in the way of my building's completion...?* Unfortunately, for Jim and the building, it was exactly that.

He held the one-page letter in his hand and read. Below the letterhead and address, the letter briefly stated:

```
James J. Bradshaw:
   Please be informed that the New
York City, Regional Office, of the
United   States   Internal   Revenue
Service, is implementing an audit of
Bradshaw Enterprises International's
(BEI) tax returns, for the years 1973
through 1975.
   A preliminary meeting has been
scheduled to discuss the audit review
process. The date for this meeting
has been tentatively set for April 10,
1976, at 10:00 AM, in Room 1107, of
our New York City, IRS Headquarters,
located at 110-West 44th Street.
   We will be contacting you on March
25, to confirm the date of the pro-
posed audit and provide additional
details regarding the information re-
quired for our review at that time.
```

                    Sincerely,

                    Richard Jones
                    Richard Jones, IRS Revenue Agent

The letter's meaning, in simple terms, was that the IRS had found sufficient reason or suspicion to schedule an audit of BEI's corporate tax returns. Jim found no need for concern. As far as he knew, BEI had done nothing improper or illegal. Jim personally verified that BEI's tax returns were honest and accurate. It wouldn't be difficult to prove this to the IRS. Audits were, at worst, inconvenient exercises in wasting valuable time. What Jim did not foresee, however, was that this scheduled IRS audit was only the first step in an elaborate Government scheme to discredit BEI. This IRS audit however, had the potential to develop into a major disruption affecting the success of his prized skyscraper.

"This is such bullshit," Jim said.

As he disgustedly threw the letter on a neat stack of previously opened mail, he was startled by unfamiliar sounds coming directly from outside his office. He could hear men talking, and his secretary nervously responding. *What the hell was going on out there?* He got up from behind his desk and began to walk toward the office door. Before he could reach it, the door was forcibly opened by a large man with a black vest that had "FBI" in bright yellow block letters silk-screened on its front and back. The FBI man was armed, wore a matching baseball cap with the same "FBI" initials, and smelled of cigarette smoke. Jim moved aside, allowing the large man to enter, and casually watched six more agents follow their leader into the room. The large man stopped and faced Jim.

"James Jeffrey Bradshaw?" the large man said.

"Yes," Jim answered.

"I have a court ordered Search Warrant giving us legal authority to search these premises for specific BEI business records, documents, and transactions. Do you understand the nature of this action as I have described it to you, sir?" The large man said.

"Yes sir. I am familiar with the intent of a Search Warrant. What I don't understand is the heavy-handed tactics and why this search is necessary. May I ask your name?" Jim replied.

"Yes sir, Mr. Bradshaw. I am Special Agent Frank Conroy, the team leader for this operation. I am sorry for the abruptness of our entry, but this is standard FBI and IRS procedure when ordered to conduct a legal search. Presently, we have twelve additional IRS agents dispersed throughout your organization. Some BEI employees and people from your legal and accounting staff will be ordered to stay on the premises for interviews and to assist us in our search in locating and securing pertinent information. Unneeded staff are being ordered to immediately vacate the premises. Your approval of our actions has no relevance on how we will proceed," Agent Conroy said with an implied authority.

"That's fairly obvious. May I inquire as to the nature and subject of this search, Agent Conroy?" Jim said.

"All I can tell you sir, is that this search is for the stated purpose of obtaining information from BEI documenting alleged illegal international business activities -"

"Such as - ?"

"Such as violations of international trade laws, bribery and tax evasion, in the years 1973 through 1975."

"Really? Should I be worried Agent Conroy?"

"I can't not say sir, but these are indictable offenses. You may be subject to arrest and imprisonment based on the accumulated evidence."

"Am I under arrest?" Jim asked.

"No, not at the moment, but consider yourself under an informal house arrest until our work here is concluded," Agent Conroy answered. "You must remain accessible at all times and on the premises during our work here."

"Okay. What else do you need from me now."

"Nothing at the moment, but we will need to interview you and some of your staff later today. After completing these interviews, you and your staff may be allowed to leave. Also, at the conclusion of our search, IRS Agents will require you to inspect and sign off on everything removed from these premises. They will provide you with an inventory list of these documents."

"Thank you, Agent Conroy, I appreciate your help. I believe I understand the procedure. I'll have my lawyers review the warrant and advise me accordingly. I have no problem remaining here and readily available. In the meantime, is there any way you can provide additional details on these alleged illegal activities?" Jim asked.

"I am sorry Mr. Bradshaw, that is all I know and permitted to tell you. Read the Search Warrant. You will be contacted by the IRS and the State Department later today with additional information. After we're done in here, we need you to escort us around BEI and witness our acquiring any pertinent documents from your files. I cannot emphasize enough that we require your full cooperation during our time here. Is that understood?" Jim noticed the agents were not subtle in their investigation of his personal office records. It gave thought to vultures descending on a dead decaying body.

"Yes it is, Agent Conroy. Yes it is. If you need anything - coffee, donuts, water, anything - just ask. Restrooms are down the hall to the right. Good luck gentlemen and good hunting. Where do you want me to wait?"

"Just a moment Mr. Bradshaw. I'll have one of my men escort you to the holding area," Agent Conroy said.

Jim was personally escorted by an FBI agent to a designated holding area apart from his staff. He was to remain here, until told otherwise. He was seated at an unoccupied desk not far from his office. He read the Search Warrant and the contents of the affidavit. The charges were many. Justification and evidence validating the charges were vague. The obvious purpose of this witch-hunt was to freeze BEI's assets, and create a defeated powerless shell of the once powerful corporation. It was an exercise in absolute power having unlimited authority over all who dared oppose it. Its sole purpose was to continue a repressed political agenda that favored the ongoing actions and monetary gains of select special interest groups. Jim thought as he left his office to the talents of the goon squad…*what a bunch of hard-nosed assholes…this is obviously another unjustified attack by the Government against BEI in an attempt to divert it from its rightful purpose…why wasn't I warned of this assault?…my well-placed snitches failed me…why?…* Jim thought.

— — —

During the day, Jim tried to remain calm and detached, but deep within himself, he was a man in turmoil. He needed to find out what was happening…and soon. He had to uncover who or what was setting him up for a fall. He had his secretary arrange an immediate meeting with his board of directors, corporate lawyers, and chief accountants. Before this meeting could take place, however, Jim received a phone call from his legal staff informing him the IRS and the State Department, were in the process of initiating legal proceedings against *Bradshaw Enterprises International,* for its violation of numerous United States' international trade laws, bribery of OPEC officials and members of the United Nations' Security

Council, and failure to record and pay taxes on its international assets from BEI's tobacco and alcohol sales. What made some of these allegations even more incredible was that the majority of them allegedly occurred just before BEI divested all of its financial interests in petroleum, tobacco, and alcohol products.

This well of Government conspiracy went much deeper than Jim could ever have imagined. He knew what this meant to the skyscraper's chances for completion. Presently, the building's construction was being financed from a dedicated Crow Nation account. It was replenished monthly. If Jim could not keep this account solvent, the existing funds would soon be exhausted, and construction would stop, as it did after the bombing. Only this time, there was nothing he could do in a timely manner to resurrect it. Since the Crow Nation was now recognized as a sovereign international Nation, the State Department and IRS, during their investigations, would prohibit all future BEI international business transactions, thereby terminating any further BEI financial involvement in the building's construction.

This elaborate plan to charge BEI, with illegal international business activities, bribery, and tax evasion, and to provide appropriate evidence to back up these charges, using the authority of the IRS and State Department, was a brilliant plan. Since, it was not as politically obvious or publicly dramatic as the Government's previous attempt to forcefully take over the Crow Reservation building site, it was kept from becoming a media event. The plan was carefully wrapped in a tight blanket of deceit, making it nearly impossible to trace its roots and attack its source.

Jim felt helpless. He was not prepared for this. He was exposed and subject, at this moment, to this rape upon the fabric of his creation. He was fighting against a powerful corruptive force, a force being used for its own self-serving perpetuation. It was a classic use of unbridled power acting without conscience or integrity to achieve its self-serving agenda.

During the day, all relevant original documents from the past three years were obtained by the FBI and IRS. Copies were made and given to Jim. The government search today uncovered evidence in company files that up to one week ago, never existed. As these files were gathered, BEI's accountants and lawyers reviewed them and assured the investigation team that they had never seen these documents before. The IRS was not convinced.

CHAPTER 45

THE LETTER

The Montana plains were quiet with anticipation – only the emerging Chinook winds could be heard as they blew across the barren landscape. Its swirling gusts would seek out three men - Jim Bradshaw, Tony Rullo, and Johnny Thunder Eagle - washing across them with a warm caress, soothing the crisis that was thrust into their world this day.

The gentle wind found an open window in Jim's Billings' office. It found him working alone, contemplating the events that had shaped his past and the ones that would now define his future. Jim felt the warm breeze flow across his brow. He flashed back to his redeeming moment in New York City, almost three years ago, when it all began. He remembered the moment on that hot summer day when he also felt a calming breeze caress his brow. That moment was magical. This moment was anything but that. This moment was heavy with the winds of failure.

Over two months had passed, since the rape of BEI, by the unknown selfish powers working within bowels of the United States Government. Jim analyzed the situation over and over again. It was becoming tedious – unbearably tedious.

His intellectual energy was failing him and with it his natural problem solving instincts. Up until now, solutions to problems had come easily to him, almost without effort. His superior intelligence, unlimited resources and dynamic ingenuity, had always managed to lead him to personally and financially rewarding opportunities. Now, unable to think objectively or creatively, he understood what it was like to be unsuccessful in achieving a positive workable solution to what Jim considered a simple problem.

--- --- ---

Jim knew there was potential for strong opposition against his attempt to create something revolutionary; something that was capable of radically altering the way humanity approached its built environment, and in the process, improve the quality of life of an oppressed race. Despite the overwhelming humanitarian benefits he was trying to achieve – the self-serving influences of government and industry were intent on seeing this building fail. Its failure would assure that their assault on the unknowing population could continue unhindered. The building's innovative design was a major threat to their stranglehold on controlling future alternative-energy choices in the United States. He knew this without question because he once was a willing contributor to that dynamic conspiracy.

If it were not for his cancer detour, he would still be stockpiling his wealth from the same obscene profits, gained from the inexhaustible consumption of alcoholic beverages, gasoline, and tobacco products. He would have remained a happy and successful billionaire indirectly killing and serving a less than desirable lifestyle to millions of people every day. Now this project, the antithesis of his previous successes, was being destroyed by a mindless industry controlling bureaucratic machine, consuming him in a way he found himself unable to defend. Again his actions, this time ironically for noble hu-

THE LETTER

manitarian purposes, were adversely affecting thousands of people a day.

He had run out of solutions within himself. He was tired of trying to do all of this alone. So, on this unassuming Sunday morning, he decided to seek help from others by writing a passionate letter to a select group of people; special people he had personally chosen for their unique qualities – qualities embracing integrity, intelligence, and loyalty. When he compiled the list, he found it added up to twenty-nine - twenty-nine - a prime number that represented his entire world of trust. Was it too big or too small? Could he trust that many people to succeed? Could he succeed with any less? He just did not know. He simply wrote down the names as fast as his mind could manufacture them, filter them, classify them, transferring his thoughts onto paper, with the dark blue ink precisely flowing from his ebony crafted fountain pen. When the last name was written and the ink dried – there it was - twenty-nine. It was a number that he would live or die with. He had no choice. He had run out of options and the energy to care.

Jim began his letter.

To my most trusted colleagues, employees and friends:

As you already know, BEI and our building of truth are in the embrace of a serious crisis. We have been charged with violating numerous Federal international trade laws, violations so well conceived by the powers behind their conception, that they will play out in the media and in the misguided minds of the general public as unforgivable and demanding the harshest of penalties.

These charges are without substance or validity. Nevertheless, the United States Government has prohibited the use of BEI funds for our skyscraper's construction during the course of their investigation and inevitable legal proceedings. Without BEI funding, the building is in danger of not being completed. So now in the light of this sober reality I am asking you to find a solution to this crisis. I am asking you to formulate workable alternatives to remedy our existing situation.

Before you begin on this quest, I will ask you an important question. Who are the underlying forces initiating this dilemma? In other words, who is _our_ enemy?

The answer to this question is the key to our success. For in order to win any war, in order to defeat any enemy, we must first define it — understand its weaknesses, its strengths, its motivations, its ambitions, and its passions. After we define it, we will understand how to defeat it, in our specific instance, not with physical force, but with all the forces of wisdom we can summon from the recesses of our minds and souls.

The enemy that is causing us disharmony and disruption today has many faces and fights us from many directions. It is the oily face of the petroleum industry. It is the black face of the coal mining conglomerates. It is the hidden faces of special interest serving politicians. It is the prejudiced face of racism

We cannot win our war, if we attempt to do battle with every one of our enemies, whoever they may be, at one time. To win, we must concentrate on the one enemy that is the conduit for all the rest. The primary enemy is the unrelenting beast coming from within the United States Government, specifically channeled through select representatives controlling the State Department and the Internal Revenue Service. This beast has challenged the financial resources of BEI and has restricted its means to generate income for our building of truth.

There is no doubt that when a paragon of truth and steadfast determination that is our skyscraper and the Crow Nation, threatens this beast's existence by offering to provide a benevolent service with absolutely no motivation for monetary retribution or political gain, then that entity, that threat, must be destroyed at all costs.

This beast has attacked us. It has attacked our dreams. It is trying to take control of our future. It is trying to take away our means to attain our dreams.

Knowing this, how do we defend ourselves? How do we drive this beast away? It is an easy solution. We can stop this beast by understanding the one absolute weakness that can destroy it..

It cannot survive in a sea of truth

The one certainty that is carried in my heart and in my soul- is this beast can never win. It can never win simply because we have the free path to the truth and are guided by the Great Spirit in our mission. This is what we must accomplish in the next three days - to conquer, cage and tame this beast with the power of truth

If we never deviate from this path, it can never win control of our dreams. It can never defeat us in our quest to build the greatest building in the world. It can never retard the growth of the newly born Crow Nation and Native American Nations throughout the United States. It can never alter our future. It can never deter our positive impact on the world.

Today, we can all conquer the beast by unifying our thoughts, visions, and intellects into a harmonious workable solution. Brothers and Sisters, let us become one in our thoughts, spirit and actions to defeat this enemy.

One final thought to ponder as you embark on your restless journey into battle. Remember, until everlasting harmony of humankind is reached — there can be no true happiness. There can be no true peace in the world. There can be no true family of humankind. Our true enemy is whatever force disrupts the harmony in our lives - the harmony that is every man and woman's birthright

I thank all of you in advance for your successful efforts. I am looking forward to seeing all of you at Wednesday's meeting.

Fare well.

Go in peace and love.
Your loving brother,
James Jeffery Bradshaw

That was it. He was finished. He had asked his twenty-nine to collectively develop the ultimate solution to overcoming the government's fortress of deception.

Jim intentionally omitted two deserving people from his honored list of "twenty-nine" - Johnny and Tony. Johnny was not included because he had previously informed Jim, at Stoney's request, that he should be actively involved in a special Tribal Council spiritual ceremony scheduled to be performed on the morning of the BEI *Resurrection Meeting*. This ceremony's purpose was to assure that the Great Spirit's blessing for success was bestowed upon the *Resurrection Meeting*.

Tony's omission however, was for a completely different and personal reason. It was Jim's decision to assign to Tony an individual assignment, one that was crucial to the skyscraper's success, but was, under the circumstances, highly unusual and almost impossible to obtain in the limited time that Jim allowed for its completion.

CHAPTER 46

THE FATAL DECISION

TWO DAYS LATER

The workday was winding down. Tony was packing up for the evening and was planning to eat dinner at *Kelsey's,* and then hit the road back to his cabin. His departure was interrupted by an unexpected visitor.

"Hey, Tony. Still working hard, I see."

"Hi Jim. This is a pleasant surprise. Yes, I'm still working. Our building may be in a coma, but there are always endless details to work on for its pending revival. Perfection never gets a day off. I think you told me that. Now, what do I owe the honor of this unexpected visit from one of my favorite and powerful people?"

"Powerful is something I'm not feeling at the moment, for obvious reasons. Anyway - I stopped by to talk to you about our big meeting tomorrow - our *Resurrection Meeting.*"

"Okay? Just what would that be? You know I can't wait to hear what your *twenty-nine apostles* have to report. Looking forward to it."

"Well...after what I'm going to suggest to you, you may want to reconsider your reaction. I'm giving you the option of not attending."

"Why's that? Why wouldn't I want to attend?"

"Tony, I've been thinking a lot about this. It's a little crazy, but hear me out. You know that you and Johnny were intentionally left off my list of twenty-nine."

"Of course. Never gave it a second thought. I knew you had your reasons."

"Well, just to be clear, my reasons had nothing to do with your ability to assist the group in arriving at a workable solution to our *little* problem. It's just that I needed both of you available to contribute in a different way. I needed something else..."

"What would that be?" Tony said.

"Both of you are very important to this building's success in so many ways. So, on the day of our meeting, Johnny, as you know, will be involved in a special ceremony with the Tribal Council asking for the Great Spirit's blessing...and... I'm asking you to not attend our *Resurrection Meeting* but instead work at the office to develop innovative alternatives - among other things - that will reduce some of the building's construction costs and effectively streamline construction. I know we've talked about this all before, but I want your input independent of anything presented at the meeting. I have all the prelim reports from our experts here for you to review. I have a hunch that whatever we come up with at the meeting will directly benefit from your contributions. I have confidence in you. You know that. What do you think? Will you do this for me?"

It didn't make sense to Jim, isolating Tony, alone, without help, but for some illogical reason he felt compelled to do it. Besides, he did not realistically expect any miracles from

Tony. He was only hoping Tony's imagination may streamline some of the building's critical design features without sacrificing their quality or overall performance. Jim was confident that the *Resurrection Meeting* would provide a positive result assuring the building's completion, without the exclusive financial resources of BEI. With Tony's additional input, Jim wanted to provide every opportunity for the building to succeed.

"What do I think?" Tony said. "I think that it is quite an unrealistic proposal, one that carries with it a heavy amount of responsibility...and ability...and there isn't much time for me to review that box full of reports. This assignment seems counter productive, more a punishment than an opportunity. Are you sure about this, Jim?"

"I'm sorry you feel that way. Believe me, it is not a punishment. I wouldn't be asking you to do this if I didn't think it was worth it. I'm positive about this assignment and that you'll do well carrying it through. We – the building – needs its creator's help."

"Okay. I respect your decision. I'll do my best. Don't expect any miracles."

"Just do the best you can. That's all I ask."

"That's about all I can do under the circumstances," Tony reluctantly said.

"Good. Thanks," Jim paused and contemplated his relationship with Tony. "You know Tony, we've been at this for over two years. The building would have been completed by now except for the premeditated roadblocks that have intentionally detoured it...but I know we will win this battle and we will win this war. I know we will. I just want you to know it's been an honor working with you. You are an incredibly gifted and talented person. When this is over, we'll take some time off together and have fun. Does that sound like something you would like to do?"

"Sure. Sounds like a great idea."

"We'll find you a new Lisa and maybe one for me, too. It's time for me to settle down and start a family. It's time for you to relax and chase women."

"Aren't we getting a little ahead of ourselves here, Jim? Let's get this building done – then, we can start planning the rest of our lives. Okay?"

"Yeah you're right, but it's always good to think ahead. You know we *are* permitted to have normal lives after this skyscraper is finished – if that's possible. We're going to have great productive lives and build many more like this one. You'll have your hands full."

"All right, if you insist. It all sounds good."

"Thought you'd agree with me. Anyway, it's time for you to quit work for the day and go home. Hungry?"

"Very."

"Okay. Let's get something to eat - my treat."

"Thanks. Jim, tell me honestly. Do you think our skyscraper can be saved?"

"Absolutely. I have no doubt."

"I wish I were as confident as you."

"Don't worry. My twenty-nine will come through for me, just like you will in your assignment."

"I'll try. Okay. Let's go. I have a lot of work to do. Don't forget to shut the lights on your way out. This building doesn't provide its own power - not yet. Remember, you're paying the electric bills."

"Don't I know it…"

CHAPTER 47

THE CEREMONY

MAY 16, 1976

At sunrise in the Crow Agency, Town Hall building, the mood at the Tribal Council meeting was solemn, but optimistic. Judgment Day had arrived for the Crow Nation. It was time for its resurrection – and the beginning of its new history. Stoney Creek Smith, Johnny Thunder Eagle, and members of the Council were preparing to perform a unique ceremony, one not historically linked to any previously performed. This ceremony was promised to destroy the forces of evil that were blocking the Crow Nation's gateway to a promising future. It was given to Stoney Creek Smith in a vision. It was uncharted territory...*territory that had to be carefully traveled*...Stoney told his people.

Stoney was chosen to conduct the ceremony. He addressed the Council.

"...Our building, our Crow Nation skyscraper, the cornerstone of our new Nation, is in trouble," he told them. "There are misguided powers forcefully keeping Jim Bradshaw's company from fulfilling our skyscraper's chosen destiny, making it impossible for him to continue financing its construction. It is our mission to conquer these misguided powers with the power of the Great Spirit through the truth, conviction, and will of the Crow people."

"Jim Bradshaw, our friend and brother, will be at the site later today, seeking ways to continue our building's construction and promote the future prosperity of our Nation. Jim will use the means to achieve this end from the physical world beyond our Nation's boundaries. He has no choice. That is his reality. That is his strength. That is his mission. His wealth was the means used to establish our freedom. His commitment to the Great Spirit, was the means by which he achieved the truth."

"Today, it is our mission to go beyond the physical world and seek help from the spiritual world, from the Great Spirit. Our ceremony will seek out the Great Spirit's benevolent power. We will redirect this power to those willing to share it, away from those willing to abuse or destroy it."

"This is the only true way. Until everyone is able to share their power for the good of all - only then can true harmony be achieved and evil defeated. This is our goal - harmony among all people - the ultimate fulfillment of life's purpose. Let us begin this quest by asking the Great Spirit to guide us to this goal using the power dormant within the sleeping Crow Nation Skyscraper."

"History has taught us how evil becomes an overwhelming force against us. It methodically increases its power always at the expense of others, stealing it outside its boundaries from those it can control using lies, deceit and fear. It continuously steals from its targets. Unless the targeted can resist and are capable of renewing their power easily and seamlessly, they will eventually become weaker, helpless victims, dependent on their adversary for renewal under the most devious unfortunate of circumstances. Our skyscraper has become a helpless victim, a target of evil. Our ceremony today will help remove this abusive power from our new home and replace it with the benevolent power of the Great Spirit. This ceremony will bless our skyscraper of truth with the power to continue to grow strong and tall - unencumbered by the forces of evil and empowered by the power of all things good. That is the purpose and nature of this ceremony. We have all agreed to its method. Let us begin."

The Council was silent. They were confident. Stoney assured that. They would allow their faith in the Great Spirit to guide them along its true path. They knew the path of truth could only be traveled one-way; without failure or deception.

The ceremony began with the thirty-seven men and women of the Council, the newly established governing body of the Crow Nation, consuming a prepared drink that opened their minds to a spiritual connection focused solely on ensuring the building's successful rebirth and renewal. They then sat down on the buffalo robe covered floor, forming a circle and holding hands. All sources of light were extinguished and infiltrating paths sealed. The room was pitch black. The Council was now devoid of external sight, divorced from the visual influences of their physical surroundings. Their sight was now turned inward so they could clearly see the path set before them, each person locked inside their own reality – locked in a personal eternity – the infinite black hole of the ever present. They were seeing as one. Their senses and mental awareness heightened, as they physically transferred to one another their personal spiritual energy and path to the truth. Their thoughts became intertwined creating a unification of purpose. They remained transformed, silent and still in this darkness for one hour.

At hour's end, they released their hold and stood up. They embraced in the darkness. Candles were immediately lit to subtly illuminate the room as their eyes focused on a previously fabricated earth cone that was placed in the center of their circle. This cone was created from the soil obtained from the building's site. It's base was nine feet in diameter, symmetrically peaking to a height of six feet. One foot below the cone's apex, inserted at a sixty-degree angle, one hundred twenty-degrees apart, two-thirds into the cone, were three six-foot rods, one of wood, one of glass and one of silver. The three rods symbolized Earth's physical resources - each used in its unique way for beneficial and destructive purposes. The wood rod represented those renewable materials given naturally to humanity without alteration; the glass rod was a symbol of those things created by man from the combination of natural resources, and the silver shined from those tainted artificially induced riches gathered from within the Earth's bowels for selfish and vain interests.

The Tribal Council's ceremony was focused on the unification of the complex and the simple, the conflicted and the peaceful, the helpful and the destructive into one harmonious entity. From this union, the power of harmony would unite humanity into a force with a single purpose – to seek the truth and to live in peace. A life of confusion would be transformed into one of certainty. It would become an unforced journey filled with unlimited vision and enlightenment. Expectations would constantly be fulfilled and disappointment would never exist to detour anyone from the achieving their life's true destiny.

The three rods were linked together, one-third below their exposed ends, with a rawhide tie, unifying them, symbolizing the sharing of their individual powers. A candle made from a mixture of wax and buffalo dung was lit and placed carefully on the cone's tip. A dusting of powdered buffalo dung blended with a very small portion of phosphorus was lightly sprinkled over the candle causing a shower of sparks and a pungent aroma with the resulting smoke of harmony to fill the room with a forceful gentleness covering every reachable surface in a bath of elegant indifference. The smoke's unprejudiced journey in seeking and embracing everything in its finite path, symbolized the free and honest union of all things given to humanity by the Great Spirit. It was showing the way to finding the truth.

At the ceremony's conclusion, Stoney, Johnny, and the Council prayed and patiently awaited the outcome of the anticipated BEI meeting at the site. They knew their spiritual energy was contained in the infinite smoke of harmony, being carried by the winds of change to the building - reviving its heart and renewing its soul.

CHAPTER 48

THE MEETING

Time, that phenomenon that constantly moves forward and never retreats, has evolved into another scientifically defined twenty-four hour day. Humanity, in its attempt to harness and control time, has assigned to it quantitative values that increase incrementally to define its passing through a normal day. These values are relevant to where one happens to be on Earth during a specific moment. As long as the Earth never ceases to exist, never stops rotating, never stops revolving around the sun; our seconds, minutes, hours, and days will always be rigidly defined, always on a consistent, never-ending parade that leads into a never-ending future. That future instantaneously becomes the present, then the past, then the present again, as this cycle repeats on its way to forever.

To capture every moment, we precisely record time with an incomprehensible assortment of man-made timepieces. There is one of these timepieces - a clock - on the wall of a large conference room. The moment is now. Two of the twelve black numbers assigned to its simple round white face are being singled out by the clock's "hands," one long and one shorter. By accepted convention they indicate one o'clock in the afternoon, Mountain Daylight Savings Time, the time assigned to BEI's *Resurrection Meeting*. The clock has spoken. It was time for this meeting to begin.

― ― ―

On a sign taped to a door is printed in large block letters; "Main Lobby - Conference Room One – BEI Resurrection Meeting – 1:00." Conference Room 1 was located within the skyscraper's partially completed first floor sky lobby. It was designed by Tony to function as a small auditorium, with tiered stadium seating for one hundred and fifty people. Today, however, an additional ninety-four invited guests were violating that capacity. Every dark red velour covered seat was occupied. The overflow crowd found various ways to accommodate their numbers by standing along the walls and sitting in the aisles in an accepted intimacy – an obvious but ignored safety violation.

In addition to this confined elite group of attendees, standing outside the room's walls were hundreds more of the uninvited, all eagerly awaiting the word and immediately available to contribute anything they could, to assist in the building's resurrection.

The infamous *twenty-nine* had filed in together occupying the first two rows, many carrying boxes containing copies of their just completed, three hundred page report. They had stayed awake for days to accomplish what Jim and the project required – a workable plan. They had performed just as Jim believed they could. Their plan was simple – so obvious that it could not be seen until this crisis forced the smoke of harmony to clear their obstructed eyes.

― ― ―

As soon as the room was filled with its eager participants, its doors were closed and locked behind them. The room became a sanctuary. It held tightly the spiritual energy of all who were embraced inside it.

Bradshaw approached the podium. Silence greeted him as he prepared to address the crowd. The room's lights were dimmed. A single spotlight focused on Jim.

"It is my pleasure, my brothers and sisters, to welcome you to our *Resurrection Meeting*. Thank you for being here today. Many of you are employees of *Bradshaw Enterprises International*, with titles describing your chosen professions, titles such as – accountants, lawyers, managers, administrators, architects and engineers, to name a few. These titles individually categorize you in an accepted segregation. Within the employ of BEI, you are generously paid for performing specific tasks related to your fields of expertise. That is not relevant today. Today, everyone in this room is equal. Today, your titles and professions have no value. Today, only your individual contributions to our cause have relevance. Our success cannot be assured unless we are united as one, empowered in an unencumbered and successful journey toward our skyscraper's completion."

"Allow me to briefly summarize the circumstances that forced us to schedule this meeting. Our lobbyist controlled United States Government has allowed the State Department to kidnap our building using the insidious fabricated accusation that BEI violated numerous international trade laws, bribed OPEC and failed to pay its required income taxes from 1973 to 1975. The result of these accusations is that BEI is now under investigation and is considered a National security liability. It is not permitted to engage in business dealings with international clients during the Government's investigation of and subsequent legal proceedings against BEI. As you all are aware, the newly created Crow Nation is now officially recognized as an independent country within the United States and therefore is an international territory."

"Ironically, our role in creating this new country has given the State Department the backhanded legal authority to block our building's future. Make no mistake about it; the State Department's goal is to hold our building hostage for years in a series of court proceedings and appeals, perhaps a lifetime's worth, until these charges are resolved or our resources to defend ourselves are depleted."

"This brings us to our present situation. Our previously allocated construction funds will be exhausted in a few weeks. After that, it will not be possible for BEI to provide any additional money to continue construction of this building. We needed a way to reverse this reality. So three days ago I challenged twenty-nine of my most trusted colleagues and friends to devise a plan to resurrect our skyscraper – a plan to bring it back from the dead. They have responded to this challenge. I am holding in my hand their response – a report that houses a plan to save this project and assure a living future for our skyscraper of truth and the Crow Nation."

"Since this report was completed only hours ago, I have not had an opportunity to review it, nor will I at this time. I have faith that whatever is offered between its covers will provide the means to a brilliant solution. So, in order to validate my faith, I will ask Charles Wilson, one of the authors of this critical document, to do the honor of summarizing it for me and the others who were not afforded the opportunity to contribute to its worthwhile content. Charles, if you please."

Jim stepped down from the small stage. Wilson took Jim's place shaking his hand as they passed. Charles addressed the crowd.

"Thank you, Jim. Thank you everyone."

"When Jim sent a letter to twenty-nine of us requesting our help in rescuing our building from it present crisis, we were both surprised and honored to be asked to perform such a critical assignment. Jim presented us with a difficult challenge. As usual, he did not make it an easy task. We had three short days to develop a workable plan, analyze it, and assemble it into a viable report. Some way, through blind faith and dumb luck, we managed to succeed. Jim knew we would, but my wife or my bed have not seen me for three days and nights. I'll worry about seeing her and getting some sleep tomorrow – that is if Jim does not have any more surprise assignments waiting for me."

A brief moment of laughter filled the emotionally charged room.

"After receiving *the letter,* we wasted little time. In less than two hours, we assembled to brainstorm the assigned task. After discussing our options, we suddenly realized the United States Government and their corporate lobbyist allies, did BEI a favor. They forced us to develop a new methodology and an improved financing strategy for our building. It was obvious to the group that for this project to move forward, BEI, would need to surrender its direct financial involvement in it and transfer total responsibility for the building's construction to the Crow Nation. That is our unanimous recommendation."

You could hear the air leave the room as soon as this bold statement left Charlie's lips.

…What?…what did he just say?…

"Settle down everyone…settle down…I will explain… there's more pieces to this puzzle. If requested by the Crow Nation – BEI will volunteer its professional consultation services and assist in the construction of this building. This action will effectively circumvent the State Department's sanctions against BEI's direct financial involvement in this great building, but still keep BEI indirectly involved in its creation."

"Furthermore, BEI, will make available as many of its resources as possible in assisting in the development of the Crow Nation. We will help provide the means for it to generate a self-sufficient economy and evolve into a financially viable Nation. The Nation, with our help, will pursue the acquisition of loans and foreign aid from the global market to help finance its future. A word of caution - any potential financial assistance offered from large corporations within the United States, will be carefully screened for conflicting interests and harmful agendas."

"We will begin the Crow Nation's road to economic security by inviting all the building's contributing solar cell and wind turbine energy companies to the Nation to manufacture, distribute and sell their products directly for the building's construction and for the world's future expanding renewable energy market. We will also invite many exciting new alternative energy industries to the Nation, such as those devoted to hydrogen, steam and electric powered automobile production. The Nation will accept only those industries that are environmentally responsible – ones that abide by the laws of Mother Earth – creating in their operations - no pollution or toxic chemical by-products. We will expand the Nation's agricultural production and enter the international marketplace. We will develop additional recreational opportunities within the Nation, including theme parks – that is correct – solar powered theme parks, to attract tourist dollars. We will invite people to visit and learn from our building. It will become a major educational and tourist attraction. Of course, we will charge admission, except for students and approved benevolent non-profit organizations."

"These are only the highlights of what is contained in our report. You'll find additional details and information as you read its entire three hundred and twenty-six pages. We welcome any suggestions and comments that will improve its purpose and enhance its development. By following the recommendations as outlined in the report, we will complete a great building that will represent the cornerstone, the symbol of freedom from the tyranny of the powers that constrain development of renewable energy and the Crow Nation. We will never detour from this quest."

"This summarizes the report. In a few moments, we will pass out copies to those who were not part of its creation. Please read it carefully and deliberately. We invite all comments that assist in its improvement and assure its implementation. Before we do anything, however, it is up to Jim to bestow upon it his blessing. Jim?"

The room slowly erupted into one filled with silent optimism, a unique expression tuned to the emotions of the people. These emotions captured the room as Jim once more took center stage...

— — —

...In the many days Jim spent in a sweat lodge with Stoney, he could feel his body and soul being transformed within him. His cancer was not only being forcefully removed from his body, but he could feel it being replaced by something else. He did not know what it could be, but it was a renewal of whatever he was or was to become. His journey was being mapped out before him in his many illuminating visions. This moment was one of them. His spirit – his energy that he fully devoted to this worthwhile cause – this skyscraper - was being redirected to something else. He was allowed to personally own this special gift for only a limited time. It was never his to keep. He was required to pass it on to the next worthy proponent of this grand prize. It was the only way to keep ahead of evil, divert its attention, and sap its energy until it died and disappeared into its other world, just as his cancer did. Evil was the cancer in this building's body. A renewed spirit of all that represented good was removing it...

— — —

Jim loved "Plan 29's" purpose and originality. He became weak with gratitude and was humble and modest in his response.

"Of course. Of course I enthusiastically approve the report. How could I not? It's brilliant, a wonderfully obvious, realistic and workable plan. I'm excited about its endless possibilities. Now, for the rest of you who did not participate in its preparation, it is time for you to contribute. Read it, critique it, and present your written comments to Charlie, before leaving this room. After all the comments are reviewed and assimilated as part of the report's fine tuning, then it will be revised accordingly. After the final is prepared it will require an enormous amount of effort on everyone's part to achieve its proposed goals. Be prepared for the endless hours of hard work that are to follow."

"On a personal note, regarding my unbridled control of this glorious project - the undesirable circumstances that resulted in this meeting and the subsequent report as a result - have enabled me to realize how self-absorbed I was throughout the skyscraper's history. Maybe I am the primary reason we are in the crisis we are in today and the reason fifteen have tragically died in support of our cause."

"It appears I have been unintentionally arrogant in my implementation of this great project. I have been trying to achieve this endeavor on my own terms, in my own way, seeing myself as a crusader pursuing a noble cause. Fortunately, my 'twenty-nine' made me realize that I cannot and was not meant to do this alone. It was egotistical and naïve of me to think this. Our Government's endless resources, coupled with self-serving big business influences, have proved what a vulnerable target I was. The "29 Report" enabled me to realize that I was given the opportunity by the Great Spirit to be the initial conduit for this project, but not its final solution."

"This obviously was the Great Spirit's intentions for me all along. I was its stepping-stone to a much greater plan. I understand that now. I am willing and at peace to pass the baton to the next standard bearer of this great creation. It is time for BEI to move forward. Beginning tomorrow, I am assigning the infamous *twenty-nine* to meet with the Tribal Council Government to describe in detail the implementation strategy for this great plan. We will ask them to help lead us on this new path to their future - the path to unification, harmony, and prosperity. Sorry, Charlie. Your wife will at least have you for tonight."

"My friends, it has been an enlightening personal journey for me – one that I will never forget and always hold true in my heart as long as I live. Thank you for showing me the way to victory. I wish you the best and together we will finish this monument to humanity. I am sincerely proud of each and every one of you today. I want you to know that," Jim said to the crowd. "Would Charlie and his twenty-eight disciples please stand so we can all show our appreciation for their efforts."

The embarrassed twenty-nine stood up to loud indefinable raucous sounds of appreciation.

"Thank you, Charlie. If we are true in our beliefs, we cannot fail. Remember, the Great Spirit is with us. Let us go forth and be one with nature and one with humanity to succeed in this once in a lifetime achievement. Thank you and fare well."

With that statement, the meeting was over and the attendees, including Jim, began the difficult task of reviewing and commenting on the three-hundred page document.

After several hours of hard work, the participants were finished with their formal critique. Red lined reports were collected by the "29" for final revision preparation. The exhausted left the conference room to join with the hundreds patiently waiting outside. The lobby became the scene of a grand party. The people partied until late in the evening, forced to finally go home for a sound night's sleep and a renewal of their body and spirit. With tomorrow would come a brand new day of hope. The Crow Nation would control the building's future and the destructive resources within the United States Government was powerless to stop it. The building's success would be assured along with the emerging power of the new Crow Nation.

Jim left the party and walked to the construction trailer to call Tony with the good news. Tony was not answering. He must have left the office for the evening or had decided to ignore all calls until his work was finished. That was typical Tony behavior. He tried the cabin – no answer. Jim felt that something wasn't right. Probably indigestion from too many party snacks. He would try calling Tony again later.

CHAPTER 49

THE DECISION

Earlier in the day, Tony walked the site, pondering the building's future. His sad eyes surveyed the building as it stood lonely and wanting. The building stood silent, offering no easy answers.

Later in the day, just prior to the start of the "Resurrection Meeting," Tony left the site and drove to the Billings' office. Except for a small janitorial crew, the building was empty. Most of the staff were at the site, poised and ready to implement the plan spawned from today's meeting – not Tony. He was following through on Jim's insane request – alone - to develop a comprehensive list of alternatives that could significantly reduce the skyscraper's estimated construction cost for completion. What could Tony's cost-cutting recommendations possibly contribute that the *twenty-nine* wouldn't have already proposed or worse, rejected – probably not a thing. That's why this assignment didn't make sense. It was a waste of time, an unrealistic, thankless assignment. Despite this sobering reality, Tony was determined to put his doubts behind him and trust Jim's judgment. He would give it his best effort. He owed that much and more to Jim.

The one positive aspect about this task was that Tony preferred working alone, just as he did when initially designing the building. Alone, he reasoned, he was able to concentrate fully on extracting any solutions he unknowingly had hidden in the deepest recesses of his mind. He did not work well with others when idealistic principles or unencumbered imagination were the prime movers. In fact, he was convinced his creative juices required isolation or else they would become contaminated with the extraneous noise of other people's thoughts. He sincerely believed this.

— — —

Tony switched on the lights in the dark and empty design studio. He fondly looked over the unstaffed drafting tables and seemingly endless stacked rolls of drawings. During the last two plus years, this was Tony's second home. The best and most important work of his life was produced between these walls. He could feel his hard work and dedication radiate from the drawings that captured and held the secrets to the design of the century.

This studio would now shift gears and serve as his inspiration for creating practical alternatives to streamline the skyscraper's proposed design. He `needed to create a method to complete this building within the boundaries of limited funding, resources, and time without compromising its integrity or purpose – an idealistic premise that he knew was next to impossible to achieve.

Tony began his review of the numerous architectural and engineering reports, including his own, defining the building's status. He reviewed these reports for hours. He listed and summarized their individual cost estimates, which in total provided the money required to complete the building as designed from its existing damaged condition. This bottom line total would be used to estimate the dollars saved from his proposed budget reducing recommendations.

He then prepared his summary report. In it, were hundreds of alternative suggestions for reducing the skyscraper's construction costs, among them his proposal to use recycled materials for the building's exterior finish. By using select recycled and indigenous clay materials found on the reservation, a hybrid masonry product could be produced and fired in on-site fabricated kilns. The remaining unfinished floors not presently encapsulated by the specified granite exterior wall system could easily be finished using modular site-fabricated masonry panels.

Another was the obvious compromises in the application of the building's interior finishes. Work in this area could be delayed and initially left incomplete until additional funding became available.

Finally, he reluctantly prepared a comprehensive outline of the many non-essential elements within the building's design that could be deleted, modified, or postponed. Items such as the sky and botanical roof gardens, grass roofs, exterior observation decks, geo-thermal heating and cooling, tele-communications satellite dishes, the 100th floor Native American Museum, the final floor observatory with its radio telescope and giant white eagle statue with its apex laser - enhancements essential to the building's spirit and environmental harmony - were offered as a sacrifice to help assure the skyscraper's future. He hated to casually recommend that any of these features not be part of its original construction, but he did. He didn't know what else to do. It broke his heart.

Even with the implementation of every design alternative listed in his report, Tony understood they had little effect in significantly reducing the building's overall construction budget. To achieve that end, Tony would need to provide recommendations that would severely compromise the building's self-sustaining function and quality. This was something he would never propose and one that Jim would never accept. The intricate technical complexities of the building's original solar panel and wind turbine powered design, provided little potential for manipulation. Its design was related more to a finely crafted precision instrument than to a present day conventionally constructed building. Components could not be removed or changed without affecting their critical inter-relationships in maintaining the building's self sustained power generating systems and integrated harmony.

This reality was evident from the information presented in the mechanical, electrical, and structural reports. These reports confirmed that the components required from each engineering discipline were essential to providing the building's intended self-sustaining function. Unfortunately, they consumed over sixty-five percent of the total construction budget. Tony had a few ideas to possibly reduce a small fraction of their costs, but could not suggest anything definitive without first reviewing all possible options with each engineering project team. That effort could take weeks to complete. Jim will be disappointed in the delay, but he had to know this. He had to expect the complex level of information included in these reports would take more than one day to analyze and report.

On a positive note, the materials' reports revealed that over ninety percent of the wind turbines and photovoltaic cells were purchased in advance and warehoused on-site for future installation. This foresight effectively assured availability of these essential components, but unfortunately not the required costs of skilled labor for installation.

Tony added up the money saved from his recommendations and others offered in a few reports. It wasn't nearly enough. It was obvious that what was needed more than any innovative or cut throat construction altering manipulations, was the possibility that BEI could somehow procure additional funding from independent resources. At the very least this would enable the building to be constructed as close to its original design as the additional funds would allow. Tony could provide as many design alternatives as he could, but they would not make a significant difference in assuring the skyscraper's success. Independent Crow Nation funding and ownership, which would effectively remove BEI from the project's direct control, was the only realistic solution. Tony had unknowingly arrived at a premise similar to that offered in the "29 Report." He included this observation in his final summary.

Tony was finished. His work was done. He had exhausted the potential of his limited resources. In his depressed state of mind he concluded it was a pathetic inept attempt. He had tried his best, but it wasn't close to being good enough. He could not offer any miracle solutions that would guarantee the skyscraper's completion within the severe Government imposed monetary restrictions. He felt worthless. He had failed - just as he failed Lisa, Neil, Jim, and his parents. Most importantly, he had failed himself.

Tony carefully documented the results of his research in a well-organized handwritten report. He made a dozen copies and delivered them to Jim's office placing them on his desk with a note that simply and deceptively said;

> Jim,
> This is the best I could do today. I am disappointed in my effort. I am going for a drive now to clear my head. I won't be going home. Don't try to reach me. I will meet with you tomorrow at 6:00PM to discuss

> this matter in greater detail. Hope the "R"
> meeting was a success. I tried. I failed. I'm
> sorry. TR

— — —

Tony walked back from Jim's office and sat dejectedly at his desk. He began to reflect on who he was, what he was, and how limited he had found himself to be. His intelligence was always something he questioned. For all the books he had read, for all the knowledge he attempted to acquire, he found himself with severe limitations in how he was able to process this information. He was by no means a genius or a person of above average intelligence. All he had was a stubborn perseverance to muddle through and work harder than anyone else to achieve the same results that a more gifted person could achieve using less time and less effort. He regarded himself as someone with only a "blue collar intellect" competing in a world with those of higher intellectual ability. His professors in college recognized his limitations. They saw him as a burden, a person who was below their standardized intellectual expectations. They could not recognize his obscure talent or foster a desire to develop any of his unique abilities.

Throughout his life, it was difficult for him to retain sufficient information to build an acceptable recall knowledge database. Highly intelligent people were able to do that. He did not come close. His memory was not photographic – but more like undeveloped film. His memory needed constant replenishment. If the information were not written down or sketched so he could see it, or built so he could touch it, he had a tendency to misplace it in his mind. It was part of who he was. He was a dreamer. He had to compensate for this limitation. He understood that much about himself.

What he could offer the world was his idealism, integrity, and dedication to the specific technologies and potential of solar powered architecture. It was his passion. He had few other talents to build on. Even with this one attribute, he still needed to constantly review and refresh this knowledge. He had to process the information over and over again, with the hope that his final conclusions utilized all the facts available and were valid.

With the help of many talented people he accomplished something life fulfilling - the skyscraper's design. It was one of those once in a lifetime achievements that somehow he had managed to successfully capture. It was a success, but to achieve it, he had to continually fight through his intellectual limitations and inherited emotional needs. His success was constantly reinforced by the positive contributions from Neil, Lisa, Johnny, and Jim. These people were the driving forces fueling his creative energy. Their friendship, encouragement, and love, had kept him afloat.

Now, he was beginning to drown, as one by one these resources were taken from him. He still had Jim and Johnny's support and love, but for some purely irrational reason – focused on some purely irrational emotional need – they were not enough. He still required that unique one on one emotional exchange from Lisa. Without it, he was empty. With it - he was fulfilled – complete. He could process. He could think. His ability to retain and pursue knowledge was dependent on his ability to obtain and nurture unconditional love. That was the essence of who he was. Since he possessed only limited skills necessary to achieve this elusive goal, he was continually denied satisfaction, and his path to an intellectually fulfilling life, was a continuing struggle. He existed in a continuous loop of unfulfilled achievements – in life – in love – in knowledge.

— — —

On this eventful day, there was a meeting, one that found a solution guaranteeing the skyscraper's climb to the future - its results revealed to hundreds, not Tony. Tonight, Tony would remain hopelessly isolated within his own world, falsely defeated, and ignorant of anything happening outside his self-imposed exile that gave meaning to his existence. Within this isolation he assumed he was loosing the greatest building in the world and with it his partnership with destiny to make a positive contribution to his life and humanity.

This latest obstacle in the skyscraper's journey was draining the creative energy from the shell of who he was. Neil's death, the bombing, his near death, Lisa's disappearance and now this crisis, had him staring directly down the barrel of life's loaded gun, watching it ready to explode in his face with a life ending violence.

It had been a long exhausting day. It was late. Tony rested his head on his cradle of arms and fell asleep. In his sleep, he saw a bright flash of light, followed by images of – the bear, the great white eagle, Jim, Johnny, Lisa, Neil, his mother and father. Many voices, many images, many messages randomly floated through his mind enticing him on his confused path to his final destination.

Tony's personal thoughts dominated.

> *...those first sketches in my hands were supposed to hold a small piece of hope for the future...they didn't...I was supposed to find the truth within my own heart and soul... I didn't...my life was supposed to be about love of all humankind...it wasn't...Instead...I found deceptive evil in those people who control the resources and who use these resources to increase their power at the ex-*

pense of the masses...deliberately ignoring the simple beauties of life and embracing that of worthless conquest...staying blind to life's profound messages present in nature... uninterested in climbing up the ladder of creation...remaining ignorant of their destiny to reach a common goal with humanity as to life's purpose...the skyscraper was to be our ant hill...unifying its followers in a single purpose as ants working together in an ant colony - performing their life's work for the benefit of the community...by building our colony together we were to unify the world through the power of the sun...humankind's progress in technology – progress in comfort – has assured it no progress in understanding its inherent spirituality and the strengthening of its soul...humankind's technological accomplishments have tragically out paced its spiritual growth...this skyscraper was to bring the two into a balance – establishing a meaningful coexistence...with the promise to influence the environment in a positive humane way...giving humankind the vessel to allow them to begin pulling on the oars at the same time and in the same direction...

Jim's enlightened philosophies floated into his thoughts.

...infuse the people of this Earth with truth and purpose and their lives will be rewarded with an abundance of good fortune...

> *from this skyscraper we will promote everything good and beneficial to humanity...*

Neil's early words haunted Tony.

> *...Tony you are special...special...accept it...fate has smiled on you....you are rebellious...in a positive creative way...you see the hypocrisies, the lies, the deceit and want to eliminate these negative elements from the world...everyone, including you and me, is born for that one event in their life that is their legacy and their birthright to fulfill... this building is an extension of humanity without the guilt of displacing nature or the reprisal of being dependent on environmentally unfriendly resources for its existence...*

How Tony arrived at where he was today was a combination of many things – many people – all favorable, but Lisa was the primary reason for his optimism. His parents filled the void before her. This building provided the energy and optimism after she disappeared – until now. In his thoughts at this moment, he was emotionally empty inside. He had nothing. He had no one.

Lisa's ambiguous words of love resonated in his heart. He was alone...

> *...I know you Tony...I can feel your pain... you are harboring doubts about yourself... you want to quit life...don't do it...no building is worth someone dying over...I want to see you...I want us to start seeing each oth-*

> *er...I want us to start something real...I want to be with you forever...I want you to know that I love you more than you can imagine... but I don't know how to deal with it...I can't accept us as something to build upon...I must leave you to sort through all of these contradictions, all the remorse and all the grief that will come along for the ride...promise me... complete the building...you owe it to yourself...you owe it to the world...I will see you again soon...we will live for that moment... Tony...*
>
> *...I love you...*

His spiritual journeys with Johnny were to be the keys to his future. They were intended to render him immune to his emotional nightmares and save him from falling into a sea of self-destruction, always giving him a needed spiritual energy, telling him what paths to follow. They were enlightening, fulfilling and disturbing; but reinforced and provided him access to his spiritual freedom. Unfortunately, his relentless tendency to produce a wall of emotional baggage within himself blocked his access to this freedom. He needed to purge himself of that barrier – somehow – someway – and soon as Johnny's messages abounded.

> *...use the power that is driving you to fulfill your need to love and be loved, to fuel your passion for life and your passion to contribute something great for the greater good of humankind... do not seek the love of one person to satisfy your life's need to be fulfilled...be honest and true to your beliefs...*

you have the power to free humanity from the bondage of paying for their right to live...do this and love will be returned to you many times...free yourself from the bondage that has consumed you all your life...would you be willing to trade the love of all humanity for the love of a single woman...the Great Spirit will guide you along the right path to your true home...through the building...and the creation of the Crow Nation...you will enable a proud Nation to create the finest, freest, most spiritually connected country in the world...this building, in conception, construction and completion delivers a message...its message asks humankind to utilize the sun as the sustainer of all life...man's spirit will be elevated to a level that will allow it to promote life without judgment, without hate, without envy...this pure spirit will eventually flow, connecting everyone in a single unified soul...this unified soul will provide all of the spiritual knowledge required to enable all of humanity to fully understand the power behind the secrets of creation...that power will be given a name...the Great Spirit....this building, our people and our Nation will carry a message to the rest of the world and into eternity...we come from different worlds but we are connected together in spirit...we are truly brothers...we share the same life force and destiny...after death we will all be united forever as one...

Tony's Vision Quests consumed his thoughts beyond anything else.

> *...trust in the Great Spirit's guardian eagle to watch over you...protecting you whenever you are in danger...ensuring your future when you witness your death spiritually apart from your body...as you struggle between a life and death existence in a fragile state of conscious being...as your heart awaits its rebirth...within an undefined other world existence...transforming into a white cloud of pure energy...another existence, everything united as one...allowing you to feel the connection between your soul and the bear's...as your joined souls begin their destiny to unite with the souls of all things living in the ultimate fulfillment of life's infinite journey within the Great Spirit...as your connection with everything living grows stronger and stronger...as this connection within this envelope of coexistence explodes into a cloud of fine black dust exposing the eternity of what would be renewed life after death...a moment forever...believe in its power...believe in its truth...believe in its ability to unite humankind into a common goal...to find its true purpose within itself...you walk towards eternity on a new dark path it will feel endless, exhausting, and impossible to complete, but continue...the bear will follow you at your side, protecting you on your jour-*

ney to forever...when you reach forever you will feel yourself fall and float and then...

Tony's eyes opened and his head bolted upright. He was infused with a powerful message and a powerful feeling of purpose.

...I know what I must do...I know what I must do now...

It was obvious. There was nothing more for him to do here. Tony realized his life had come full circle. He was taken back to the time when he sat by Baltimore's Inner Harbor contemplating his life – this life - his future – this future.

This time it was not the uncertainty of his future that was the problem. This time it was the uncertainty of a building's future that caused Tony doubts about his reason for living. Why live when your only future is a life with a defeated purpose? Was the building's possible resurrection sufficient reason to hope for a life with purpose – or was it just another illusion – a false purpose - pursued as part of life's never-ending ambiguous reasons for living?

Tony didn't fully understand what was happening to him tonight. He was feeling and thinking things he knew did not make sense. Never-the-less, in spite of his confusion, he believed he had been given a direction from the Great Spirit and was determined to follow it to its intended conclusion.

He was given his answer today. It was time for him to abandon this project and embrace his future, not the building's. It was a selfish decision, but for him, an honest one. He had nothing left to offer. It was time for him to end this senseless and meaningless existence. It was time.

Tony listened to his phone ring for the third time within the last five minutes. He ignored it. Somebody was persistent. The phone had been ringing constantly since six. It most likely was someone from the project, possibly Jim, to check on his progress. In any case, he had no desire to answer. He had nothing he wanted to discuss with Jim or anyone else tonight. Instead, he immediately left the office and drove directly to the park.

— — —

Jim hung up the phone. He had been calling Tony at least once every hour since the meeting ended. This was his third and final attempt in the past five minutes in trying to contact Tony at the office. As in all of his previous attempts, there was no answer. He was trying to give Tony the good news about the *Resurrection Meeting's* "29 Plan." It would just be what Tony needed to make him smile and relieve him from the burden he must be feeling from trying to complete Jim's torturous assignment.

...*Where was Tony?*...Jim thought.

Something was wrong. Jim decided to look for him. His first response was to drive to the office. He would also ask someone to check *Kelsey's* and Tony's cabin. Jim's departure was delayed by a phone call. It was Johnny.

"Hello Jim. Congratulations, on your victory today," Johnny said.

"Thank you Johnny. Please extend my appreciation and personal thanks to the Council for all the spiritual energy generated from the ceremony. We could not have succeeded without this power from the Great Spirit. I know it assured our success. Listen, I don't want to cut you short here, but I was just heading out the door to look for Tony. There may be a problem."

"What do you mean, Jim?"

"I can't find him. I've been trying to contact him all night. He should be at the office. I called him there, but there's no answer. Has he contacted you? Do you have any idea where he is?"

"No. I have not been in contact with Tony today, but I am not surprised that he is not available. Jim…I have received some unsettling news tonight from Stoney about him. I was hoping it was not to be."

"What is it. What do you know?"

"What I was told about Tony is, at the moment, he is troubled," Johnny said. "He cannot win the battle between his heart and mind. Unfortunately, he does not know of our victory today. I was told he will unselfishly try to save the building by sacrificing himself. He will be seeking this path. We must allow him to take that path. His destiny can not be changed."

"I don't understand. What are you saying, that Tony is going to take his own life? How could Stoney know that? How can you be so matter-of-fact about it? If it's true, we have to stop him. Tell me Johnny, what else do you know? Do you know when this will happen? Do you know where?" Jim asked.

"No, I do not. That is all I have been told. Do not worry, we both will understand in time. There was a reason you left him off your list of twenty-nine and assigned him the difficult task of saving the building alone. It was your destiny to do that. It was his destiny to accept."

"That doesn't speak well for my motives. That is a very disturbing scenario. It's not a very rewarding future for Tony, after all he's accomplished for me, the Crow Nation, and our skyscraper. I don't know why I gave him that assignment in the first place. He should have been at the meeting with the rest of us. Why did I do that? I feel responsible in some way for anything harmful he may do to himself."

"It is not your place to pass judgment on yourself. It is not your fault. All I know is; Tony has been granted a future that allows him to follow his rightful path. The Great Spirit will protect him now. Go to sleep. Do not worry about Tony.

His fate is not in your hands. Everything will be bathed in a clearer light tomorrow. Trust me. Our future is also promised. Good night, Jim."

"Johnny…wait…don't hang up. We need to find Tony and talk to him – tell him the good news - talk him out of any crazy thoughts. We can't let him do harm to himself. We can't allow it. For Christ's sake, we're talking about a life here - Tony's life. He's our brother!"

"There is nothing we can do for him now. His future is written."

"I can't accept that."

"You accepted it for yourself, now you must accept it for Tony."

"It was different for me. You know that. My life was saved, not ended. I could never forgive myself unless I tried to stop him. I can't talk about this anymore. It's wasting valuable time and it's making me ill. I have to go now. I have to find Tony. Please, come with me. Help me find him."

"I cannot. It will not change what will be."

"I'm sorry, Johnny. You're not making any sense. I must do something - anything. I'm on my way to the office to look for him. You can meet me there if you change your mind. Hope to see you there."

"I will not be meeting you at the office tonight. Good night, Jim. May the Great Spirit guide you and keep you safe."

Jim hung up the phone in disgust. He could not accept Stoney's message and Johnny's brutal decision to let Tony die. He had to find Tony. He had to alter destiny.

CHAPTER 50

THE JOURNEY ENDS

MAY 17, 1976

The signs read, "Park Closes at 11 PM – Violators Will Be Prosecuted." It was midnight, but it was of no concern to Tony. It was, as he wanted. The park was empty. There was no one around to bother or arrest him. He needed to be here tonight, away from the lonely isolated confines of his cabin. He was restless and wanted to be surrounded by the sleeping faceless people and energy of the city. This park was the perfect place for him to wait until the events of tomorrow consumed him.

It was here, during lunch breaks away from the office, that he liked to sit and dream. It was his private place. It was here he would think of Lisa, about his love for her, and their possible life together, about Neil and Johnny, and the unbelievable opportunity Jim had given to him. These relationships were special to him, a seamless flow of love and friendship, never again to be experienced in his lifetime.

Neil's death and Lisa's departure had shaken him more than he ever thought they would. His devotion to the project had provided him little isolation from the shock and no easing of the burden in his heart. He had loved Lisa beyond his own senses. Their potential life together defined his existence and purpose. He always imagined he was intended to take care of her after Neil's death. She wasn't supposed to leave him. It made it difficult for him to restructure a life that was promised for them, only for himself. He needed to take control of his life now. Nothing else mattered to him today.

He was afraid and lost in this park trying to find a temporary peace. Here in this postage stamp sized green haven was his shoulder to cry on. His head was buried deep in his hands. The teardrops rolled upon his cheeks. The salty droplets licked at his lips. He cried until he couldn't cry anymore. He said his prayers to his mother and father for perhaps the last time and then he slept until the sun's early morning rays and awakening sounds of the city tapped him gently from his dreams. This new day was to promise him a new life. It finally was his turn to live.

He made a final stop at *Kelsey's*, making sure there was no one there from the office to detour him and keep him from his mission. He ate a hearty breakfast of eggs, pancakes and bacon, abandoning his usual health conscience breakfast. When he finished, he had a special Italian cold-cut sub and thermos of coffee prepared "to go." He was ready for his long day's journey into an endless night.

— — —

Tony entered his truck and began his final ride to the almost deserted building site. He arrived in a hurry, parked the F-100 in a remote location hidden behind a large boulder, about a half-mile from the site's fenced perimeter. He began his clandestine walk. He approached the building through a seldom used unguarded gated entrance in the security fence. He unlocked the gate using his magnetic pass key - a key only available to a select few of the project's elite. He reached the building and entered one of its emergency fire exit stairwells using the same key, avoided detection from the predicable scanning paths of the security cameras and started his climb up the countless stairs that would take him to the empty building's designated observatory floor – the building's last barren unfinished floor. In what would seem like forever, his legs burning from the climb and his lungs breathing heavily from climbing almost two thousand feet, he reached his destination. As he walked from the stair tower, he stopped for a moment to ponder the realities of his creation. It was partly his self-inspired design and now he was at the top of this mountain of concrete and steel, now standing unfinished, and through no fault of its own, in danger of not fulfilling its promise to the Crow Nation and the world.

It was to be the tallest building in the world – reaching an incredible two thousand feet. At this height, the weather varied considerably from that experienced at ground level. Temperatures could be as much as twenty degrees cooler. Winds were constant, sometimes gusting up to fifty miles per hour. It was this source of energy the wind turbines would use to propel their blades in the countless revolutions required to supply sustainable power to this great building.

Tony imagined the turbines capturing the wind and could almost hear their whining singing sound as their blades revolved, knowing that they, in conjunction with the solar cells, would generate all the power necessary to sustain this building's life. It was to be a beautiful accomplishment for humanity, the benchmark for future buildings. Without this harmony, humanity would die. In harmony with nature, humanity would prosper and live.

At this moment in time, all the technological innovation promised for this skyscraper was no longer relevant. As far as Tony was concerned, it was all an elaborate lie. This building would never be finished. Its dream would never be fulfilled. Tony's role in this skyscraper's dubious future was over. It had no future. His unfulfilled luck with love was now complete. He had loved this building and now it was lost - just like Lisa - just like all the rest of the things that were so important to him.

— — —

Looking up through the observatory's open steel framing he could see the flag of the Crow Nation flying proudly from the skyscraper's apex. He was honored to be part of this historic achievement. He picked an isolated covered spot on the floor and sat down. Here, he waited for hours - slowly and methodically eating his lunch, savoring every bite of his favorite sandwich with small sips of his creamed and sugar sweetened coffee, watching the sun, ever so slowly, ever so deliberately, descend into the western sky. As he watched this golden life force arch its path along the bright blue horizon, Tony knew Jim would eventually be looking for him after realizing he was not honoring his 6:00 PM meeting. It would only be a matter of hours before Jim decided to search the building, but it didn't matter now. Tony would never allow himself to be found. Jim would eventually be too late in his attempt. Dusk would arrive before Jim, and with it the time for Tony to begin his journey.

Tony found a prominent column in the center of the floor, and attached with tape a paper on which was written a poem of his creation. It was his parting gift to the world and a testimony to his inability to adapt to this relentless obsession he had for Lisa. The poem was hand printed on bright yellow paper in large black type. It would eventually be read offering its message to anyone fortunate to discover it.

Tony's poem:

UPON LOVE'S DESTINY

by Tony Rullo

It started with a look.
And upon your gaze I did stare,
Until my presence became one with yours.
An eternity passed before us in an instant,
And we knew we had been here before.
Awaiting the question, but not knowing the nature of the answer,
We held out our hands for an answer.
Touching, we felt our senses thunder
So never used but only for times like these.
Embracing, floating.
We fell into a dance of wonderment and desire.
Holding, desperately holding and holding each other tighter.
Only to hopelessly feel our grasps slip until we tumbled to the ground apart,
Separated forever.
Only our hearts remaining as one.

— — —

Tony removed the gold pocket watch from his pocket, opened its cover, read the hands positioned over the numbers on its faded white face and said, "It's time..." He walked to the building's perimeter to the south facing observation deck entrance. He released the safety gate guarding the unfinished area. He walked across its floor and climbed the railing onto the ledge wrapping around the deck's cantilevered floor. On this ledge, high above the Earth below he felt safe. Tony

THE JOURNEY ENDS

gazed down at the unfinished landscaped areas and roads below. There was a rain cloud beneath him. The setting sun was glowing below him. Its golden rays touched his eyes, filling him with unlimited power and forced him to smile. He felt as if the building was smiling also. It was telling him, it would honor his life after his death. He noticed some birds below and above them soared an eagle that claimed the sky as its own. What was it doing here? The eagle appeared to glow with an intensity that matched the sun's. Like the eagle, Tony would own the sky soon. He was ready.

He needed to purge himself of the hypocrisy and inhumanity of this world. He needed to live, as the building would, free, alive and honest. He thought of Lisa, her love for him and how he had failed her in his promises after she left

He heard Johnny's words echo inside his head, as he looked up into the sky and understood their meaning:

"...*Tony, you will fly away from life as I did when I flew into life at my birth...*"

He heard the words from his first Vision Quest, spoke to him by the great white eagle as he launched himself from the ledge:

"...*Let yourself be free. Let yourself fall. Do not be afraid. You will not die. You will live forever...*"

He understood the words now as he floated in the air. The thick air held him in suspension for a moment and then he descended. This life was soon to end, but another was soon to begin. He closed his eyes, never to feel the impact. It was finally over.

A vaporless mist surrounded Tony's body. He could not see it. He could feel it embracing him. He did not understand the why of its existence, only it knew its truth. He felt the Great Spirit enter him and Lisa's spirit consume him. Tony could feel the love of all those who went before him. Every being's spirit embraced him. He smiled. He was forgiven. He was loved. He was free. In this "death," he finally had reached the top of life's skyscraper.

— — —

Moments later, Jim Bradshaw, and two security guards walked from the north stair tower and entered the skyscraper's threshold floor. They searched the area for Tony, finding only an empty paper bag, a sandwich wrapper, used napkins, and a thermos placed neatly behind a column. One of the guards noticed the yellow paper taped to the column.

"Mr. Bradshaw. Look at this, sir," the guard said. "It appears to be a note from Tony."

"What's that Tom?" Jim responded.

"From what I can see, it appears to be something written by Mr. Rullo."

Jim walked over to the guard and removed the paper from the column.

"Dam!" Jim said. "It's a poem – his poem - and from what it says, it doesn't sound very optimistic. It's about him and Lisa. I know it. He can't get her out of his heart. It's sad. We all tried to help him get over her. We may be too late to help him now. I think we may have lost Tony, Tom. Maybe this floor was his final stop...*please don't let Johnny be right about this*...Okay, let's not think the worst. Let's search the rest of the floor and then we'll work our way down floor by floor. After that, we'll start all over again. Tom, find more people and begin searching from the bottom up. Maybe we'll get lucky. Maybe we'll find him. Let's hope the Great Spirit wants us to. I'll never forgive myself if we don't...*dam you Johnny*..."

— — —

THE JOURNEY ENDS

Matching this moment in time, surrounded by the new Crow Nation, Johnny Thunder Eagle was riding Swiftwind toward one of Montana's beautiful sunsets. He stopped for a moment and felt Tony's spirit enter him. He knew Tony had found the truth. Johnny smiled, said a prayer in his native tongue, and continued his ride. The circle of life is so simple he thought. Why is humanity always trying to complicate its purpose?

He wondered how humanity could continually take the horizontal path in life when all it leads to is death without reason. Until man understands that life is a circle that continually leads into itself in its harmony, will there be life after death and in this death there will be reason.

The sun continued to set as Johnny rode into the evolving darkness. He stopped his ride, dismounted near a stream bordering a light timber forest and set up his camp. *This is a good place to sleep, he thought, a good place to sleep...* The stars high above his head began to fill the sky in all their infinite beauty...*It is a good place to sleep...* He took his journal from his saddlebag and with his pen he began the story – the story of a skyscraper – a legend that would change the destiny of humanity and his people's future forever.

CHAPTER 51

THE END

SOMEWHERE IN TIME - IN ANOTHER DIMENSION

The Great Spirit's messenger, its great white eagle, was circling high above the Crow Nation skyscraper. On its back was a man, smiling and well. He had finally become one with the Great Spirit. The eagle departed the Montana sky flying into the setting sun toward its new destination. The man held fast and felt the speed of the eagle's travel through distance and time embrace him. In a thought's moment he knew the destination he was to travel, and within that same moment he had arrived.

— — —

Somewhere in a place beyond time and imagination, another SUN was also setting on a beautiful day. Lisa looked into the SUNSET and said her daily message to someone she missed very much.

"Good night Tony. I will always love you. Rest well, be at peace, and always remain who you are. You will understand as I did this meaning. I know I will see you again in time."

THE END

As Lisa was about to leave, she turned and looked again into the setting SUN, and paused stoically as she saw something in the distance rising out of the SUN's waning glow. It grew larger and larger as it approached her. She could see its silhouette. She knew it was that of an eagle – a white eagle of great size – the Great Spirit's messenger. She could also see that on its back was a man.

She stood paralyzed with excitement, as it came closer to her, descending ever so gently. The eagle landed softly, just a few yards from her feet. It tucked its wings into its sides, let out a gentle scream, while looking into Lisa's eyes with a calming hypnotic stare freeing her from any fears.

She saw the man and began to understand.

The man slid off the eagle's back. As soon as the man's feet touched the ground, the eagle, in a flash of blinding light, disappeared into another dimension.

The man walked toward Lisa, held out his hand grasping hers, holding it, *as if to never let it go*, and spoke;

"Hello, Lisa."

"Hello, Tony. Welcome home. We've been waiting for you," she said.

The gold necklace appearing around Lisa's neck reflected the last glimmers of SUNLIGHT from its heart shaped pendant.

EPILOGUE

What is it about humanity that consistently detours itself from its natural purpose?

Tony's disappearance remained a mystery, except to Stoney and Johnny who kept it a closely guarded secret, only sharing its secrets with Jim. It was summarily concluded that Tony took his own life, although his body was never found. His "death" was felt as an unwarranted tragic loss by all who knew him. It opened up a tidal wave of controversy and investigation. Investigation into his disappearance paved the path to the truth, truth led to purpose, from purpose spawned inspiration, inspiration stirred the pot, generated the food for consumption and everyone became hungry with an unquenchable appetite to have this building completed. People from everywhere unselfishly volunteered their labor. The sympathetic rich throughout the world, donated millions to the Crow Nation for the skyscraper's completion. No corporation, special interest influence, or government bureaucracy had the means to stop its creation. The outpouring of love and commitment overwhelmed any power that attempted to stand in its way.

President Carter dismissed all charges against BEI and assigned the newly created Department of Energy's - *Solar Energy Research Institute*, to assist in the completion of this building in any way possible – but only within the strict requirements established by the Crow Nation. Jim Bradshaw and BEI were free to contribute again.

The skyscraper confronted every obstacle thrown its way and conquered them all. It could not achieve the proposed July 4, 1976, completion date, but that was not important. All of its hopes for fulfilling a new future for the Crow Nation, Native Americans, and their brethren were realized. It was without Tony, Lisa, and Neil, but Uncle Dominic and Aunt Carmen were there to represent Tony in spirit, arriving in Tony's little red 850, parking it next to a red 1972 *Pontiac Firebird*. Lisa's and Neil's families were there representing their namesakes. So on this symbolic July 7, 1977 day, Jim Bradshaw dedicated the building to the departed's memory, hard work, and love. The building was finally ready to allow its worthy anointed children to enter its womb.

The building's official first day was christened with the beacon of life, energized from the heart of the white eagle statue mounted at its summit. Its laser light reached toward the stars, seeking the beginning of creation and the ever hopeful purpose of humanity.

The light carried with it a message back from the stars.

*"...The mysteries of life are many.
The answers are there, if only we just take the time to listen..."*

On the building's cornerstone was carved another message:

A LIFE THAT IS IN COMPLETE HARMONY WITH NATURE, HAS COMPASSION FOR ALL THINGS LIVING AND ALLOWS THE FULFILLMENT OF YOUR LIFE'S TRUE

DESTINY, REMOVES ALL DARKNESS FROM THE RECESSES OF YOUR SOUL AND REPLACES IT WITH AN ETERNAL LIGHT.

HUMANITY SHALL LIVE TO BALANCE ITS EXISTENCE WITH THE EARTH, AND FROM THIS WILL LEARN TO LIVE WITHIN ITS WOMB AND BE CONNECTED TO LIFE FOR ETERNITY."

**STONEY CREEK SMITH,
NATIVE AMERICAN
APSAALOOKE**

As this day of celebration was slowly coming to an end and the sun gradually disappeared over the horizon, finished with its miracles for the day, a magnificent living skyscraper existing within the embrace of the new Crow Nation simply said, "Thank You."

— — —

After the triumphant completion of this legendary skyscraper, as predicted, dozens of independently owned self-sustained solar powered residences, commercial buildings, skyscrapers and wind farms were built on America's Native American Reservations. Some of these reservations petitioned for independence from the United States, and many were approved, chartered, and recognized as independent nations by the United Nations and the world. Jim Bradshaw's vision as given to him by the Great Spirit was now part of a new world order.

This path to the Earth's future, could not be denied. This building, and all that would follow in its honor, would save lives, give humanity new reasons for living, and a defined purpose after death.

The Great Spirit's prophecy had come to pass.

By implementing the proposals defined in the "29-Plan," the Crow Nation and its people continued to grow stronger and prosper. Their future was assured. Although the path to this future was paved with the lives of many, their lives could never be extinguished. They all would remain alive as long as this building was alive, and this building would be alive for a long long time.

After all, memories and legends live forever.

TONY'S INNER HARBOR LETTER

July 15, 1973
To whoever reads this,

The fast approaching light of darkness enveloped my being and lifted me upon the plain of non-existence, hurtling me at tremendous speed into the abyss that is time. I can not understand the circumstances surrounding the events that are strung together in an endless stream of time, never ending until death - my death - causes this being to cease being me.

The energy that surrounds me and is flowing inside me tells me more - there's more, but not how to free myself of these chains - these boundaries that prevent me from being more, and as I think, as I listen, as I wonder, I am becoming less of me - waiting for the answer - dying slowly waiting for the answer. Can I stop me from dying slowly waiting for the answer?

I wonder about acquiring absolute knowledge, but how? I am limited by my limited knowledge to go beyond its inherent and cruel limits. But my limited knowledge keeps me from the truth and truth is the key to knowing whatever I am. I am frustrated knowing that I can be more and this vehicle that is me is full of too many contradictions and ambiguities to allow me to see beyond my own limitations. Are these limitations, my limitations, or just life's clever diversion to limit me from going beyond what we perceive as limited?

So I struggle. I cry. I feel rejected. Without unlimited knowledge, my comfort cannot be. That is my crutch. That is my limitation. I am lost inside of me and cannot find a way out or in. My mind lies trapped inside my body. I am alone among many who think they are not alone because they are among many. I can not see. I can not hear. I can not utilize the full capacity of my brain beyond the limited capacities of my knowledge. I am hoping for a miracle to lift me beyond what I perceive myself to be and into another plain of unlimited knowledge.

How can I succeed beyond what is me?

Tony Rullo

INFLUENTIAL REFERENCES

- Brown, Dee: *Bury My Heart at Wounded Knee – An Indian History of the American West.* New York, NY: Thirtieth Edition, Henry Holt and Company, 2001.
- Crow, Joseph Medicine: *From the Heart of Crow Country.* Lincoln, NE: University of Nebraska Press, 2000.
- Deloria Jr., Vine: *Behind the Trail of Broken Promises – An American Declaration of Independence.* Austin, TX: University of Texas Press, 2000.
- Dupree, Judith: *Skyscrapers.* New York, NY: Black Dog and Leventhal, 1996.
- Ewing, Rex A.: *Power with Nature.* Masonville, CO: PixyJack Press, 2003.
- Hirschfelder, Arlene: *Native Americans.* New York, NY: Barnes and Noble, 2006.
- Hoxie, Frederick E.: *Parading Through History-The Making of the Crow Nation in America, 1805-1935.* New York, NY: Cambridge University Press, 1995.
- Lowie, Robert H.: *The Crow Indians.* Lincoln, NE: University of Nebraska Press, 1983.
- Pevar, Stephen L.: *The Rights of Indians and Tribes.* Carbondale, IL: Third Edition, Southern Illinois University Press, 2002.

- Scheer, Hermann: *The Solar Economy – Renewable Energy for a Sustainable Global Future*. Sterling, VA: Earthscan Publications Ltd, 2002.
- Tauranac, John: *The Empire State Building-The Making of a Landmark*. New York, NY: St. Martin's Press, 1995.
- Terranova, Antonina: *Skyscrapers*. New York, NY: Barnes and Noble, 2003.

CPSIA information can be obtained at www.ICGtesting.com
230310LV00009B/2/P